JESS WALTER

LAND
OF THE
BLIND

CORONET BOOKS
Hodder & Stoughton

ISBN 0 340 81993 6

Typeset in Plantin Light by
Palimpsest Book Production Limited,
Polmont, Stirlingshire
Printed and bound in Great Britain by
Clays Ltd, St Ives plc

Hodder and Stoughton
A division of Hodder Headline
338 Euston Road
London NW1 3BH

To Bruce, Kristie, and Ralph,
and in memory of Carol

ACKNOWLEDGEMENTS

Thanks to Anne Walter, Dan Butterworth, Jim Lynch, Cal Morgan, Lina Perl, Wayne Brookes, and Judith Regan for various acts of criticism, enthusiasm, and patience, and to Tony and Suzanne Bamonte, whose book, *Spokane's Legendary Davenport Hotel,* was a valuable resource.

In the land of the blind the one-eyed man is king.
– Erasmus, *Adagia*

I

IT IS CUSTOMARY WITH THIS SORT OF THING TO START WITH A BODY

I | HE SITS ALONE

He sits alone in the interview room, his unshaven face in his hands, a guy about her age and not exactly bad looking, for a loon anyway. He's familiar and yet she can't place him. It is the kind of familiarity that grates like an unwelcome song. She gives him names: Dave. Steve. Rocco. It is none of these. The Loon wears dirty blue jeans and a long-sleeved black shirt with the top two buttons open. He is tall and square shouldered, and even though his clothes are a mess, they fit. They are not the clothes of a bum. He seems . . . if not successful, at least employable. His hair is dark and long and tousled and the only thing keeping him from being handsome is a missed haircut or two.

And the eye patch, of course. The patch is black and covers his left eye, its strap slicing through his long hair. And even the eye patch isn't so much a flaw as an alarming accessory, making him seem untrustworthy and roguish. A pirate, Caroline thinks.

Caroline Mabry is a police detective, although for the last several months she has not been a very good one. She has burned out on the job or lost her way or stopped believing in it, and while her colleagues were polite at first, there were no illusions once she was put on swing shift—*swig* shift it is called, the refuge of burnouts and

3

department drunks six months from retirement.

Certainly she's too young for swig shift, just thirty-seven, and yet here she is, stuck on a Friday night watching some lunatic sweat and shift and get his story as straight as his addled mind will allow. The Loon looks around the walls of Interview Two—her favorite, and even that is depressing, that she actually has a favorite interview room. It occurs to her that if she saw this pirate in a bar instead of sitting at a table in a police interview room, she would want to talk to him. Jesus. When did she begin looking at suspects and derelicts (*not bad looking; employable*) as potential romances?

The desk sergeant comes toward her with a clipboard.

"So that's him?" Caroline asks.

"That's your guy. Fuckin' nut. Want me to run him off?"

"Nah. It's probably nothing, but if we don't talk to him and it turns out there's something here—" She doesn't finish the thought.

"Want me to stick around? Or I could send someone back."

"Nah," she says, "I got nothing else to do. I'll listen to his UFO story and then I'll call the bin."

The desk sergeant is only too happy to take an order that requires no work from him. "Your call."

Caroline turns back toward the interview room. "He wouldn't give you a name?"

"Nope. And no ID."

"Run his prints?"

"Yeah. No record. No warrants. Nothing. Just a guy who wants to talk."

"Does he look familiar to you?"

"Sure. He looks like a pirate." The sergeant walks back toward his desk.

Caroline returns to the door of the interview room and watches the nervous guy chew his nails. That's what you get when you volunteer for swig shift—UFO abductions, ninja attacks, black helicopters, listening devices, ghosts, Bigfoot, transgender experiments, pirates, and worst of all, the perpetually, chronically, criminally lonesome: those loons flirting with the edge, tired and confused, and, above all, alone—snap-eyed, breathless people who claim to have information about a murder (usually Kennedy's or Princess Di's or Jimmy Hoffa's or Elvis's or Jesus') but who really just want to talk about when daylight savings time begins and why the Safeway moved and how the children never call and what channel *Wheel of Fortune* is on.

She watches this Loon, in his black shirt and eye patch, its strap nested in his bushy hair, and thinks there is something different about him, something she can't quite name. Of course, it could be nothing more than her fascination with the place he was arrested. The clipboard duly reports that This Particular Loon was picked up at 8:03 P.M. when patrol responded to a guy scaling the scaffolding of the old Davenport Hotel—the twelve-story Spanish Renaissance landmark that is the most famous building in Spokane, even though it has been sitting vacant the last fifteen years.

Like any native, Caroline has always known about the hotel, but she really became aware of it in college, when she was researching a paper on the writer Thomas Wolfe and found in his journals that he "arrived into Spokane in good time and to the Davenport Hotel and a bottle of Scotch and conversation," and left the next morning "west from Spokane through country being more barren all the time." The effect on Caroline of reading this entry was something like finding a picture of one's parents when they were young and good looking, and experiencing a shock and a sense of loss because they had once lived interesting lives. She was shocked to find that her hometown was considered—in the 1920s, at least—Seattle's jazzy sister, that Teddy Roosevelt and Charles Lindbergh and Ethel Barrymore had happily come by rail, that Calvin Coolidge and Douglas Fairbanks and Amelia Earhart and, yes, Thomas Wolfe, looked forward to a night at the Davenport as an outpost between the deep forest and the desert scablands.

By the time Caroline was an adult the Davenport Hotel, like Spokane, was long out of style, stripped of its silver service and gilded furnishings, its gardens and tropical birdcages, and remodeled in the plastic-and-shag fashion of fifties motels, the final indignity being the family swimming pool that replaced the rooftop tennis courts and putting greens. The hotel had closed in 1985, the same year Caroline read Wolfe's brief account in college. Five years later, she responded to her first call at the empty hotel—rousting some bums—and she couldn't believe that this dark, abandoned husk, its marble staircases covered with pigeon shit, was the same place Wolfe had once sought out.

For fifteen years, she watched attempts at renovating the Davenport come and go like an addict's promises— Caroline herself was a dues-paying member of the Friends of the Davenport. Then, finally, just after the turn of another century, the remodeling began in earnest, and Caroline caught power-washed glimpses of cornices and sills, lathe-and-plaster guts of old rooms slid through telescoped tunnels into street-level Dumpsters, replacement chandeliers and banisters carried in, the gunk scraped out of the swimming pool. Even a cynic like Caroline—no great fan of symbols—imagined that if the project were ever finished, it could signal nothing less than Spokane's long-awaited rebirth.

So maybe she finds some vague significance in the fact that the Loon was caught haunting the Davenport. He had apparently climbed a construction fence to some scaffolding and into an unlocked window. A bus driver saw the Loon crawl through the window and called the police, who found the disoriented man staring out a window on the twelfth floor, head in his hands. According to the report, he was crying.

From the notes and the desk sergeant's brief description, she can imagine what happened next: The patrol officers had the guy lie facedown on the floor. Distraught and unaccustomed to this sort of treatment, he didn't get down at first and they were rough with him: a knee in his back, firm grasp of his wrist. He didn't fight. The officers handcuffed him and determined two things—he didn't have a weapon, and he was an EDP, Emotionally Disturbed Person. They shone a flashlight in his one good eye, and the pupil did what a good pupil does: shrink. So he wasn't overdosing on drugs—more likely a mental patient skipping his meds. He had no identification and seemed unwilling or unable to give them his name. In response to questions, he simply shook his head.

The patrol officers became progressively friendlier with the Loon, offering to take him back to his group home or his parents' house or his drug treatment center or his pirate ship, to whatever institution he had escaped from. But to every question he responded by sitting quietly, as if he were not even in the same room.

The patrol officers were more perturbed than anything. They could lock the Loon up for breaking and entering, but he had stolen nothing from the old hotel and hadn't even cracked a window getting in. Assuming he had no warrants, they'd just as soon let him go back to raiding Dumpsters. One of the cops decided to level with him. Look here, Patch, he said, if you don't tell us what's going on, we're gonna have to charge you with breaking and entering, or trespassing. Or mayhem.

Murder, joked his partner.

This caught the Loon's attention. He made eye contact.

What we're trying to tell you is that you need to co-operate or you're going to jail, the patrol officer said.

Okay, said the Loon, his first word.

The cop asked who the guy was and what meds he skipped, what he was doing in the hotel and if they could take him home.

The Loon didn't acknowledge the questions. Instead, he took a deep breath and said: I'd like to confess.

The cop laughed. I don't think that's necessary, he said. We caught you in the building. You might be a foot or two past the confession point.

But the Loon had latched onto the idea and wouldn't let it go. Do I talk to you, or to a detective? To whom do I confess?

The patrol cop made eye contact with his partner. To whom? This over-educated crazy pirate motherfucker was going to make them create paper. All he had to do was tell them where he lived and he'd be home free. They could do this easy, but he was just obstinate enough to make them create a bunch of unnecessary paper.

Look, said the cop, I'm not sure what kind of detective you think is going to want to hear about you breaking into an empty building—

The Loon interrupted the cop. Homicide, he said.

2 | SHE LIKES SNOW

She likes snow. At least that's what Caroline has begun telling people who ask why she stays in Spokane instead of going west to Seattle or south to California. The very fact that people continue to ask why she stays in Spokane must mean *something,* although she doesn't know exactly what. Foolishly or vainly, or both, she had imagined that the question implied she had so much on the ball—that she was so tall and attractive and ambitious—that Spokane was too small and slow a city for someone of her talents. For years she talked about going to law school or trying to get a job with the FBI, but the timing never seemed right; she got caught up in being a police officer, in the romantic idea of it, and briefly in the romantic idea of her old, married patrol sergeant.

But now, at thirty-seven, the question of why she stays has taken on other meanings. Caroline has never married, and she feels the accelerated pace of female aging and worries that features that were once sharp have begun to look severe. She has noticed that older women have one of two kinds of necks: big, bullfrog jowls or tent poles under stretched skin. And while she still draws looks from men, she's not sure whether that proves something good about her or something bad about men. And each morning she stands in front of the mirror to see which neck she is growing. She's just finished her fifteenth and hardest year as a police officer, a year in which her mother passed away from cancer. Her two-year relationship with her bartender boyfriend died of less natural causes, and she found herself buried in a long and painful and personal case—the murders of several prostitutes. Now, the old question carries with it an unbearable weight— and an unspoken *still:* Why are you (still) in Spokane? Then, standing in line one morning at a coffee shop, she heard a couple of telemark skiers defend Spokane, and soon she was giving the answer she heard one of them give: I like the snow. And it says something about her life and her lack of friendships and meaningful relationships that no one has ever said, "But Caroline, you hate snow."

It's snowing now, light flakes coming in at an angle and temperature of thirty-three degrees, hitting the ground and dissolving right away. Standing in line for a coffee, Caroline watches the windblown flakes and thinks of their precariousness, the conspiracy of temperature and airspeed that created them, and their frailty, making it all the way to earth only to disappear. She pays for her tea and a black coffee for the Loon and walks across the small courtyard to the empty Public Safety Building. She checks her watch: 9:00 P.M. The Loon has been stewing twenty minutes. Her old married mentor, Alan Dupree, used to say that bad guys are meat: the tougher they are, the longer you cook 'em. This guy is soft, loose at the bone. Twenty minutes ought to be plenty of time for the Loon to give up whatever he's got to give.

She opens the door and steps inside, removes her jacket and sets it on the chair behind her. The good-looking

Loon looks up, reaches for his eye patch, and smooths it absentmindedly, the way a person might pat down a cowlick.

Well, she thinks, here we go. "I'm Caroline Mabry," she says. "Sergeant Burroughs said you want to talk to a detective."

Up close he is jittery, and his cheeks are hard and sunken beneath a week's growth of whiskers. But he doesn't stink like a derelict. His features are less sharp than she first thought, and he is more familiar. "Are you—?" he begins.

"A detective?" Caroline nods. "I am."

"Good," he says. "Okay. Right. Okay. Before we start, is it possible to . . . can we . . . is there any sort of *off-the-record*? I mean . . . can we set some ground rules?"

"Sure." Caroline smiles and lies with a practiced nonchalance that worries her. "We go off the record all the time."

"Okay." He closes his eye and nods. "Well, then . . . I want to confess."

"That's what I hear. And this has something to do with a homicide?" She makes a wager with herself. Robert Kennedy. No, John Lennon. No, wait. He's the Son of Sam.

The Loon nods. "Yes," he says. "A homicide."

"A recent case?"

"I don't want to talk specifically."

"Oh, sure," Caroline says. "Let's talk generally about homicide. Generally I'm against it. How about you, Mr.—"

He ignores her attempt to get his name. "Please. This is hard enough. I don't quite know how to start."

"Well," she says, "it is customary with this sort of thing to start with a body."

"No," he says. "I can't. It's not . . . it's not like that."

"No body?" Of course, she thinks. He's committed his crime on some astral plane. He's murdered someone's soul.

"No, I mean . . . it just . . . this isn't an unsolved case from the newspaper or something. It's nothing that you know about." And he adds, "Yet."

"Okay. You tell me. Where should we start?"

"I don't think you understand what I'm trying to do here," he says.

"I'm trying to understand, Mr.—"

He catches her gaze. His one eye goes back and forth between hers, as if trying to choose the friendlier of the two. "Are you religious, Caroline?"

She is surprised he has remembered her first name, but she lets it go and thinks about the question, the angle. If she says yes, she is religious, does the Loon experience a moment of epiphany and give up the whole thing? Or does he shy away, thinking she'll be judgmental? If she says no, does he close up because she is a heathen? Or does he feel liberated, able to talk freely? She decides to go with God.

"I have my faith," she says, and has to look away because that's an even bigger lie than the one about going off the record.

"I wish I did," says the Loon, and rubs his face.

Caroline leans across the table and puts her hands out, palms up, and thinks of the last car she bought and the salesman who struck this pose: What's it going to take for you to drive this car off the lot today? "There's something you want to get off your chest."

"Yes," the Loon says.

13

"You told the sergeant you wanted to confess."

"Yes."

"Then you need to tell me what you did. And who you did it to."

"Why?" he asks.

"Because that's what a confession is."

"I don't think so," he says, and cocks his head. "Isn't the confession separate from the thing being confessed? There's the crime, the action, which is crude and violent and without context. And then there is the confession of the crime, which is *all* context, *all* motivation and—" He looks at the ceiling. "I don't know. Cleansing. I mean, there must be millions of crimes every day. But a confession? A real confession? I'd guess those are pretty rare."

She stares at him, drawn in by his extravagant Loon logic and that nagging familiarity. Who is he? She mentally shaves him, trims the hair. Who does she know with an eye patch? "Look," she says, "you can't confess without naming a crime and a victim."

For the first time, he is engaged. "Of course you can," he says. "The victim is just a shadow, an expression of the idea of a specific crime. The crime is the real thing, the actual, the ideal, the light behind the shadow."

"Are we still talking about a confession?" Caroline asks.

"Yes," says the Loon. "A priest doesn't want to know whom you lusted after or what you stole; he wants to know whether you are sorry. God doesn't want names."

"Then maybe you should've turned yourself in to a priest," she says. "Maybe you should confess to God."

"I don't believe in God," he says. "I believe in the police."

This whole thing is getting away from her. They stare across the small table at each other and she thinks of college, of sitting up late at night after bottles of wine, in conversations just like this one, usually involving some horny sophomore poet or philosopher, just before he changed his major to business and got engaged to someone else. A couple of times, she found herself seduced by a young man's boozy rationalization of the shortness of life and the subjective nature of morality. She's always had three weaknesses when it comes to men: dark eyes, big pecs, faulty logic.

She considers the Loon and loses herself in his one dark eye, which seems to compensate for its missing partner by exuding twice the emotion. The eye floats in its socket like a deep blue Life Saver. "I'm just not sure what I can do with a confession that doesn't admit to a crime," she says quietly.

"I'm not asking you to do anything, Caroline. Just listen."

She checks her watch: 9:40 P.M. Maybe the desk sergeant is right. Cut this nut loose and she's home in an hour and twenty minutes watching TV. Still, this could keep her from filling the last of her shift with paperwork.

Apparently he sees her indecision. "Look," he says, "you probably get people admitting crimes all the time. But what are you getting, really? You know what the guy did or you wouldn't have brought him in. And he knows you know. He's not confessing. He weighs his options and tells you only as much as you already know, as much as he can get away with. You trick him into telling more, but you both know the rules. It's a formality . . . confirmation of what everyone already knows.

"But this thing"—he scratches at the table—"this thing I want to tell you . . . nobody knows about it. Nobody knows what I've done."

The quiet in the room is different from normal quiet between cop and suspect or even cop and loon, and Caroline shifts uncomfortably.

"Tell me this," he says. "When was the last genuine confession you heard? I don't mean excuses or plea bargains or justifications or extenuating circumstances or coerced testimony or the half-truths of confidential informants." His chin rests on the table and his arms are spread out. "When was the last time a man came in and opened himself up, unburdened his soul, when nothing was compelling him to do so? When was the last time someone gave you the truth?"

"I don't . . ." She feels flushed. "You want a confession without consequences?"

"If you mean prison, I know that's a possibility." He pulls back a bit, smiles sadly, and Caroline begins to think that maybe this Loon really did something, maybe there's more to this than delusions and skipped meds. "But this thing that happened," he says carefully, "was the result of a lifetime of harassment. Betrayals and pressures. It will never happen . . . it *could* never happen again. It was a radiator boiling over.

"Consequences?" He squeezes his eyes shut. "All I have left is consequences."

It is quiet for a moment. "Okay," Caroline says. "You want to . . . confess." She's used that word a hundred times and it never sounded like this. "You want to confess without incriminating yourself. And then what? Go home?"

He doesn't answer, just looks down.

"Well," she says, "that would certainly speed up the criminal justice system."

It is Friday night. There are no other detectives in these back offices. It is one of the idiocies of police work: the criminals work nights and weekends, while the detectives are home for the six o'clock news. The office behind her is dark. What harm can there be in indulging this Loon for an hour?

"Okay," she says. "I'll do it. I'll hear your . . . confession."

"Thank you." He looks around the room. "Okay."

They stare at each other for a few seconds more and he takes a series of deep breaths. Finally, he leans forward. "Do I start or—"

"There are a number of—"

"It's just, I've never . . . how do you go about this?"

"Well, usually we just talk. We can tape confessions. We can do it on video."

He looks uncomfortable with all of these options.

"Sometimes we have the suspect write out his version of events and sign it."

The Loon perks up. "Yeah," he says. "That's it. I'd like to write it. Yes. It should be written down. With context and meaning. That's the only way."

"I'll get you a pad and a pen," she says.

"And some more coffee?"

She grabs his cup and exits the interview room. She leaves the door unlocked; he's not under arrest. All around her, the Major Crimes office registers its indifference to the semantic games of Caroline and this crank. After all, she thinks, a confession is a confession is . . . Dark computer screens track her across the room, colleagues' family pictures watch from their perches on the soft cubicle walls. At her desk—no pictures—Caroline pulls a legal pad from the top drawer and grabs a pen. She walks out front and nods to the sergeant as she fills the Loon's cup with stale patrol coffee.

"So was I right?" The sergeant looks up from a snowboarding magazine. "He a fuckin' wack job?"

"A shithouse rat," she says.

"Yeah, I figured." He returns to his report. "You gonna cut him loose?"

"In a minute."

When she comes back the Loon looks uncertain, as if he's having second thoughts. She sets his coffee down and he takes it gratefully.

"Can I ask you something?" he says.

She waits.

"Have you ever been responsible for someone's death?"

She notes the timidity of the words. Not *Have you ever killed someone* but *Have you ever been responsible for someone's death*. "Yes," she answers, to both questions.

"What was it like? For you?"

"Better than for the dead guy," she says. But he doesn't respond to the joke and she remembers the feeling, the smell, the gun in her hand, the man no longer moving toward her, finished. "It was bad," she says, more quietly.

"Afterward, it was hard . . . personally?"

She doesn't answer.

"I just wonder if it's possible to live with something like that," he says.

18

No sleep, shallow breathing, hand vibrating, the flash when she closed her eyes. Caroline looks down.

"I've been having these dreams," he says, "where I did something wrong. Something terrible? But it's almost like I've done it in another world. Like no one around me knows. But when I wake up . . ." He swallows. "Do you ever have dreams like that?"

She thinks, Fuck you, but says simply, "No," and slides the legal pad to him.

The Loon picks up the pen and writes across the top of the page: *Confession*. His handwriting is precise and practiced. He considers his one word, then crosses it out and writes *Statement of Fact*. He exhales, as if that were it. Then he shakes his arms, cricks his neck, and looks around the room. "Could I be alone to do this? It won't take long."

"Okay." She stands to leave. *Statement of Fact*. This guy's a lawyer, she thinks.

"One more question, Caroline," he says as she's on her way out.

She turns back from the door. His hair has fallen over his eye patch and he looks like a kid all of a sudden. That's the thing about men, even crazy ones; after a while, they all turn into boys.

"Why'd you become a police officer?" he asks.

Caroline doesn't hesitate as she reaches for the door. "I like the snow."

Not every kind of madness is a calamity.
– Erasmus, *In Praise of Folly*

II

Statement of Fact

I | ELI BOYLE'S DANDRUFF

Eli Boyle's dandruff was more than enough indignity for one child. In fact, the word "dandruff" barely did it justice. He was like a snow globe turned upside down, drifting flakes on the Empire State Building or the St. Louis Arch or the Golden Gate. Our classmates made sudden noises—clapping their hands or dropping books—just to see Eli's head snap around and the snow dislodge and cascade from his head, drift onto his desk and settle on the floor of the classroom. When he sneezed, teachers would stop lecturing until the ash settled. It was hard to believe a human head could flake so much without losing actual mass, and the glacial till of Eli Boyle's scalp was discussed with some seriousness as a potential science project. Walking down the hall, the dead, flaking snow covered his shoulders like two lesser peaks beneath Boyle's Everest of a head. So, as I say, at least the way I remember it, Eli Boyle's dandruff would have been enough humiliation for one kid to bear, enough embarrassment to ruin his life the way lives are ruined in elementary school, before they actually begin.

But dandruff was only the first of Eli's afflictions. I will list them here, but please don't think me cruel, or blame me for piling these horrors upon him. I was not his Maker; Someone Else visited these burdens upon Eli Boyle, Someone Far Crueler Than I. Or just more indifferent. And don't think for a moment that I take anything but the most humble responsibility in relating these difficulties. When I am finished with this confession, this affidavit, this statement of fact, it will come as no surprise that Eli Boyle turned out to be a better man than I, and nothing would make me happier than to report now that the adolescent version of that good man started life with a clean slate, or at least a clean scalp. But I cannot. So I offer this accounting with no great joy, but with a fidelity to truth and a desire to re-create for those who care, for the record, I suppose, an Eli Boyle whole and pristine, just as he was then, all the more amazing when you consider the list of ruined parts that comprised him:

He had bad breath, like he'd eaten sour cream from a cat box. He wore braces on his teeth and his legs; had acne and a unique bacon-flavored body odor; picked his nose and ate what he mined; exhibited a zest for epic, untimely flatulence (the Social Studies Incident of 1976; the Great 1980 Pep Assembly Blowout . . .); wore black-framed, Coke-bottle glasses; had thin red hair, skid marks in his underwear, and allergies to pollen, cotton, peanuts, and soap. He had a limp, a lisp, a twitch, waxy ears, gently crossed eyes, and was—how to put this—afflicted by the random popping of inappropriate erections, boners as we would say then, as we *did* say then, through his gray, standard-issue PE shorts.

His overprotective mother dressed him like a janitor in Dickey overalls and flannel shirts at a time—the mid-

1970s—when everyone else wore designer jeans and varsity T's. He was the oldest kid I ever knew to wet his pants at school, to cry, to sit in the front of the school bus, to call out for his mommy. He rode a three-wheeled bike with a flag on the back because of "balance" problems; ate a special lunch with no milk or cheese or whole grains; and had grand mal seizures, blackouts, muscle spasms, and fits of gagging. He had to wear corrective shoes because of a deformed foot. He had scoliosis, skin lesions, and scabies, and the nurse was always hauling him off for impetigo or indigestion or impacted turds or any of the other nasty bugs that he carried around like his only friends. The fact that he lived in a trailer wasn't awful in itself, because the great, prematurely bearded quarterback Kenny Dale also lived in a trailer, but Eli Boyle lived alone with his mother in the worst park in the worst trailer, an old gray can with a dirt lawn and stained sheets for curtains.

He was what we called then "a B-Flat SpEd," which meant that while he was in special education, there was nothing really wrong with him. He was brighter than the other SpEds and was able to pull B's and C's in regular classes, with the occasional A, although he was a miserable failure in that rigid and unforgiving society that is really the only society. It occurs to me now that he may have been mildly autistic, but we didn't know that word and so we felt accurate then in calling him a spaz, a loop, a 'tard, a dork, a dweeb, a dick, a freak. It was said that even the other 'tards in special ed made fun of Eli.

So that's him, as complete and flawed and tragic and sad, as wonderful as I can remember him, as pure and imperfect, as unforgettable as anyone I've ever known. Eli Boyle. The man who saved my life.

And the man whose life I have taken.

2 | YOU MUST FORGIVE

You must forgive the formal informality of this tract or report or confession, this statement of fact. Even before this trouble I was told that I write like a disgraced lawyer (so is that irony or premonition?) and since my ambitions and insecurities pulled me toward a political career that anyone with a local newspaper would know flamed out brilliantly and prematurely—here I go offering the obvious as proof of the obvious—I have developed that unique, self-serving, solipsistic style of intellect that arises among attorneys, politicians, and strip-club dancers (I plead guilty to two of the three) and that is why I might now and then lapse into the kind of writing that we lawyers are trained to commit, using language to obscure and obfuscate rather than clarify and communicate.

So, when I say that it is Eli Boyle's life that I have taken, you may ask yourself, Is he simply being meta-phoric? Yes and no. But let me say, there is nothing metaphoric about this confession, nothing metaphoric in my hatred and rage and my thirst for revenge, nothing metaphoric about the person I set out to kill, the handgun I held in my hand, the blood that crept across the floor beneath my feet.

But that is all ending, and before I tell the ending I must tell the beginning:

Start by picturing my neighborhood in the mid-1970s: poor and uneducated and ignorant of even those facts, a strip of sorry homes three blocks wide and a mile long, a thin cut of plywood shacks, trailers, and single-story war-era baby boomer starters that kids at school called the "white ghetto," weeds and falling shingles and axle-rusted pickup trucks parked on gray yards next to vacant lots where kids smoked pot and cigarettes; a grocery store on the near end, the gravel pits of an excavation company on the far, a long street of houses pinched like an ant farm between the dirty plate glass of the Spokane River and our rutted, potholed road, after which my neighborhood was named:

Empire.

Life on Empire Road began at the bus stop. I have heard that our first conscious memories occur at four or maybe three, but my first sense of myself was in the socialization of later elementary school, fourth and fifth grade, and it was as a fifth grader, a short, insecure eleven-year-old, that I first remember seeing Eli Boyle.

He had decided to walk down the long row of dreary houses to our bus stop because the torture at his own stop had become unbearable. Once again, I ask you to imagine a neighborhood stretched like a rubber band until it is too long and too thin and strained in the center. Picture six bus stops along this strip of despair, mine second in line. My family was typical of the Empire neighborhood: poor and white, father a night custodian, mother what was called then a housewife. There were four of us kids. My sister Meg was five and in kindergarten, so Mom drove her to and from school. Shawna was four and didn't go to school yet.

So that left little brother Ben (two years younger than I) to trudge with me the long block to our bus stop. There, twenty-five kids gathered beneath a willow tree that wasn't so much weeping as oozing. Beneath this tree, a nest of kids aged six to sixteen quickly found places: the older you were, the deeper you went into the tree and the more adult your behavior. The willow tree sat in the front yard—although I hesitate to call that tangle of bunchgrass and clover a yard—of Will the Hippie, who wasn't a hippie and wasn't really named Will, but such was the intelligence that flowed around the bus stop because he used an American flag as a curtain on his broken living room window. Add the fact that he'd painted the word WILL on his garage and certain assumptions were made, assumptions which were deflated two years later when the man whose name was not Will sat on his roof with a Korean-made assault rifle and shot out the windows of about a dozen cars and houses in the neighborhood and murdered two dogs and six mailboxes before walking up to the county sheriff's car and surrendering to the two frightened deputies huddling on its floor.

Like me, Eli was a fifth grader the first time he made his way to our stop. I was in the process of leaving my brother and venturing deeper into the willow, not quite to where the oldest girls and boys were making out and doing research on the tensile strength of bra straps, but to the midpoint, where the sixth and seventh graders stood smoking cigarettes and the occasional joint. I had pilfered four of my dad's Pall Mall cigarettes, running my finger along the luxurious, cellophane-encased package and the lion crest. "Pall Mall." I said it over and over. It was so elegant. I wanted it to be my name. "Hello. My name is Paul. Paul Mall."

"Good God Friday, where are you going, Clark?" my brother Ben whispered, but I ignored him and kept moving, past the smaller kids and deeper into the branches. The bigger kids did not look up when I arrived at their denim circle in the midway point of the willow, shuffling in my bell-bottom corduroys, the one pair of "cool pants" I owned and the only pair I ever wore to school. They didn't acknowledge me when I reached in the pocket of my yellow polyester BMX polo shirt and they didn't flinch when I removed a single white cigarette, squinted my eyes, placed it between my lips, and pretended to pat my pockets like a man who's lost his wallet.

"Anyone got a light?" I asked. And then, finally, horribly, they noticed. Bushy heads turned and from that clutch of lanky, narrow-eyed trouble stepped Pete Decker of all people, who looks in my memory like a seventh-grade Clint Eastwood and who, it was rumored, had been kicked out of Golden Gloves boxing for cheating or biting or paralyzing a kid, depending on which version of the story you heard. Flame leapt from Pete's lighter and he narrowed his eyes and took me in, the cigarette dangling from my mouth. Below that, my Adam's apple bobbed with a nervous swallow.

"Good, huh?" he asked.

I nodded, inhaled, and coughed twice, my eyes smoking red. By now the sixth and seventh graders were watching, because they'd never seen Pete go out of his way to do anything to a smaller kid but take his money and knock him into the street. But Pete just stood there, watching me hack away on my first cigarette, eyes watering, nose burning.

"Smooth," he said.

I nodded, unable to speak, and had the sense that the crowd was moving in on us, surrounding us. Even Tanya Bentitz and Eric Mullay looked up. Usually they were entwined, bobbing for tonsils during the entire wait for the bus, rolling around in the furthest reaches of the tree, beyond our imaginations. I remember wishing (or perhaps I have constructed it now; you need only run your own elementary school memories to test the accuracy of mine) that I could step away too, that I could go back to being part of the circle instead of the meat inside it.

"What's your name?" Pete asked.

"Clark," I said.

"Been smoking long, Clark?" Pete asked.

"Couple years," I said. Which means I would have started at nine.

I once imagined tracking Pete Decker down. I thought about starting a smoking clinic in which Pete got smokers to quit by giving the same treatment he gave me that day. Quickly, without dwelling on my pain, because it's not my pain that matters, here's what happened:

Pete stepped up toward my face, his eyes slits. He formed his index finger and thumb into an OK sign, lifted them to my face, and performed a perfect example of what we used to call *flick-the-cherry*, knocking the burning ember from the end of the cigarette so that it was no longer lit. Before I knew it Pete had me in a headlock, had pulled me to the ground, yanked my arm up into my back, let go of the headlock, and with his other hand grabbed a handful of my hair. He beat my face into the gravel at the spot where the road blended into Will the Hippie's yard. I remember the sound of my nose hitting the ground. I remember opening my bleary eyes and seeing the tiny pieces of blood-spattered rock scatter before my face. And I remember that Pete dragged me—eyes clouded, nose clogged with blood— a few feet to where the burning cherry sat smoldering in the grass.

"Eat it," he said. I did, reached out with my tongue and enveloped the burning ash, pulled it into my mouth and swallowed.

"Cool," Pete said, and he let go of me. Of course it's easy to criticize Pete Decker's behavior at the bus stop that day. Easy to imagine him a bully or a criminal and assume that he has made nothing but trouble of his life since. But as someone who has done wrong, I have to tell you: I never smoked another cigarette after that day. Which just proves my point. There are a hundred ways to save someone's life. And, I suppose, just as many ways to take one.

But Pete Decker's impromptu smoking intervention is not the story I set out to tell and, in a way, it is simply prologue to the real story, which began that day as well. As I crawled, whimpered, and bled out of the long arms of the willow tree, the crowd turned away from me, rather than earn a beating for sympathizing. From the ground, I watched as even my brother Ben turned away, hiding the family resemblance. Every pair of shoes faced away from me except one, a pair of smudged black shoes with metal braces hooked to the soles and connected to straps at the calves. And when I looked up at the bent legs and scoliatic back, at the pinched, dandruffed shoulders that owned those shoes, I saw the only person in the crowd who measured me with anything but disdain. There, standing at my bus stop, a line of snot on his upper lip, grease in his hair, a look of sheer empathy and . . . fucking beatitude on his miserable face, was Eli Boyle.

3 | HIS PITIFUL PRESENCE

His pitiful presence that day was undoubtedly what kept Pete Decker from completing the remodeling project he'd begun on my face. Had I known the importance of what would happen at that bus stop that day with the appearance of Eli Boyle, I might have begun studying it myself, for it would turn out to be a near-perfect real-world expression of an experiment that microbiologists have long re-created in the lab. They know that viruses and pathogenic bacteria will adhere to damaged cells in the human body, that the real nasty bugs are attracted to those broken and bruised places that blood has trouble reaching, and that the body will sacrifice a foot, say, to save the rest, and that if you have an infection in your throat and sprain your ankle, the virus or bacteria or parasite will do its best to make the journey from your throat to your ankle.

Eli became my broken ankle. That day, still full from the meal of me, Pete Decker retreated to the back of the tree and, presumably, picked my bones from his teeth, but I have to think he also had his eye on the horrible newcomer. Because the very next day Pete was all over Eli Boyle, knocking his glasses off, snapping the buttons off the cuffs of his flannel shirt, and grabbing his underwear and yanking them out of his pants and giving him—and here I defer to each reader's age, socioeconomic class, and basic geographic orientation—a wedgie or a melvy or a crack-back or a slip-and-slide or a jam sandwich or a thong-along or a line-in-the-sand or a famous-anus.

Eli took his punishment in stride, picked up his glasses, quietly pocketed the snapped button for his mother to sew on later, and left his dirty underwear wedged up his cakehole until Pete Decker had moved on to terrorize elsewhere. After my own beating I had resumed my place at the street, with the terrified little kids, who stood with chattering teeth, clinging to their lunch money and repeating in their minds, Don't turn around, Don't turn around. In those early days I never ventured to help Eli Boyle—although, honestly, what could I have done?

Every day after that, Eli tried to arrive just as the bus did, hoping to limit his exposure to Pete. Our driver, Mr. Kellhorn, was notorious for his erratic timing, though, showing up at various times between 7:22 and 7:29, which might not sound like a big deal to adults, but for kids hoping to avoid having their underwear winched into their asses, it was a horror. The other bullies allowed Pete to have first—I apologize in advance for my word choice—crack at Boyle. Some days, when Pete missed school (we whispered about juvenile detention, or theorized that maybe he'd finally gone ahead and killed his parents), some lesser bully would make sure to spit on Eli or yank on his underwear or make him lick shoes.

For his part, Eli attempted the defense that every afflicted and hunted beast attempts, the defense of a sand dollar that settles into the ocean floor or a beaten dog that cowers beneath his forepaws, the worthless twin

35

defenses of shrinkage and anonymity. Eli stood with the little kids, his big, greasy, flaking head a foot above theirs, staring at the ground, sniffling with whatever airborne bug he was carrying that day, trying to look inconspicuous as the dandruff flaked down around his greasy head.

I stood only a few feet away, but Eli and I never spoke. In fact, none of the underclassmen at the bus stop ever spoke, staring instead at our shoes or looking down the road, praying to the God of afflicted children that we would see our bus—the color of sweet potatoes—rising over the hill behind us and making its way to our stop. My little brother Ben would whisper under his breath: "God's noggin, would you hurry?" He had recently become an inveterate taker-of-the-Lord's-name, and he'd taken to jotting down new ones when they popped into his head, eager to amaze and thrill us older kids with the range and poetry of this one sin. Even then, Ben planned to have this sin be his signature. "Christ on a bike, what is taking so long?"

The air went out of us when the bus arrived—two hydraulic sighs as a matter of fact, the first when the brakes set and the door opened and the second when all of the smaller kids finally exhaled and pressed for the door. These littlest got on first, sliding three to a bench seat in the second and third rows; then came Eli, spinning right around the pole into the seat behind the driver, the safest seat, obviously, but also the worst seat socially, because it marked him as a coward and a brownnose and a boy with no friends. After my failed attempt to smoke, I had become a sort of leader of the third, fourth, and fifth graders—king of the geeks—and so I settled into the fifth or sixth row, sharing a seat with only one other kid.

After we little kids had boarded the bus, the older kids emerged from the leafy curtains of the willow tree, Pete Decker and the other delinquents grinding their cigarettes into the gravel ashtray of Will the Hippie's front yard, blowing smoke down the rows of little kids, pushing their way to the back of the bus, Pete pulling his fist back and causing some poor kid to flinch, before he and the other seventh and eighth graders settled in the back three rows, all stretched out and reflecting a chilled boredom.

I suppose Eli had been at our bus stop two weeks before I actually made eye contact with him—the eye contact of death-row prisoners, part better-you-than-me, part but-for-the-grace-of-God, part empathy, part worry that his terrified face reflected my own. Obviously, I had noticed Eli Boyle before; he was a billboard for adolescent horror. But I had been so overwhelmed with my own self-loathing that I hadn't really contemplated his, which I saw must be both epic and lonesome. I stood in the aisle of the bus, in the first row, staring at Eli until it crossed my mind that I could sit next to him, that in my improved role as the kid who tried to smoke at the bus stop, I might effect some social change by sitting next to the least of us all, the spazziest, dorkiest, queerest, loosest nut on the tree. We would face the beatings together after that, the two of us, and we would slowly change the world.

Then again, maybe not. Behind me, my brother Ben was pushing me in the back, hurrying to be seated before Pete Decker emerged from the willow tree and climbed onto the bus. But even with Ben pushing me, I couldn't break eye contact with Eli. Once I'd taken hold it was like a live electrical wire, and I shook at the depths of his anguish. He seemed not only to suffer—what was life, after all, but suffering, and who knows that more than a kid—but also to understand his own position, to know that there was something more than crippling in his physical appearance, in his personal odor and his bad eyesight and his lack of coordination and the host of bugs and bends and sprains that comprised him. It was as if he knew the future offered no reprieve and yet he kept showing up anyway.

"Sweet cheese of Jesus, move it, Clark!" Ben groused behind me. "They're coming."

I found my seat and Ben slid in behind me, just ahead of Pete Decker, who walked with his elbows out, smacking the heads of every kid on the inside of the bench seats. A couple of those kids ducked and Pete balled up his fist or pushed out the knuckle of his middle finger, smacked the offending kids, and moved down the row.

Eli had turned to face the window again; he would stare out that window right behind the driver until we pulled up at school.

It is hard to fathom, I suppose, but the next bus stop— Eli's old stop—was even worse than ours. While we at least had the willow and the cover of Will the Hippie's house, this stop stood at a bare corner and so there was no cover at all; it was the difference between jungle and savanna. The dominant male at this stop was a twice-flunked eighth-grade goon named Matt Woodbridge, who had driven out all the little kids until it was just him and his crew: three slope-headed seventh graders, all of them smoking in broad daylight and daring anyone to say anything about it. The day Eli and I made eye contact, I thought about how Eli had arrived to take my beatings for me, how he'd looked down on me with such sympathy, and I was suddenly hit with the realization that Pete Decker and the button-popping, glasses-slapping, underwear-yanking routine of my bus stop was an improvement for Eli! I mean, hard as it is to believe . . . *he actually chose to come to our bus stop.*

Even today I have trouble fathoming it, trying to imagine the tortures that Matt Woodbridge had devised, persecutions horrible enough to make Eli walk three blocks to catch the bus with an animal like Pete Decker. I did a paper on torture in college and I can never forget the worst ones: the glass tube shoved into the penis and then broken while the tortured person is forced to drink glass after glass of water, the legs encased in a vise and put in a burlap sack and then pounded with hammers until the burlap is the only thing holding them together. Right after these horrors I place whatever Woodbridge did to drive Eli down to our bus stop. And so that day, on the bus, I looked up as Woodbridge passed and at that moment I hated him, and I must have betrayed something on my face because he stopped in the aisle and turned to face me, a look of disbelief on his pockmarked, wispy-mustached face.

"What?" he asked. "What, motherfucker?"

The bus erupted in a chorus of "Ooohs," and someone yelled from the back of the bus, "Kick his ass! Kick his fuckin' ass, Woodbridge!"

"Nothing," I said quickly, and dropped my eyes.

"You bet nothing," Woodbridge said. "Nothing and a fucking ass-kicking if you ever look at me again, motherfucker." And he continued sidling back toward the end of the bus, toward his seat in the back, the polar opposite of Boyle's seat. "Little shit."

I knew what we all knew about Woodbridge, that his brother Jesse had been an A student and a good athlete who had been killed in the eighth grade in some mysterious way (I'd heard, variously, that Matt shot him with their father's gun accidentally, that he got drunk and fell out of a pickup truck, and that he slashed his own wrists) and that Matt dealt with his brother's death and with his parents' grief by beating the shit out of every kid he saw, by flunking his classes, by riding his motorcycle across the flower beds of all the houses in the neighborhood, by stealing our bicycles, by selling pot to little kids, by shoplifting, fighting, fingering, smoking, dealing, shooting up, vandalizing, and generally being the worst form of life on the bus. I think that while he didn't know it, he was trying to live up to his dead brother, trying to remain a perpetual eighth grader like Jesse.

I stared straight ahead, hoping Woodbridge would ignore me, but of course he couldn't. "Who is that motherfucker?" he asked the back of the bus.

"That kid?" Pete Decker laughed. "That's the fuckin' Marlboro man." His gang erupted in laughter. Pete and Woodbridge had an interesting cold-war relationship; like nervous superpowers, both knew the only thing they couldn't afford was to lose a fight, and since each was the only one who had a chance of beating up the other, they existed in a kind of strained equilibrium. As long as there were pathetic little shits like me to terrorize, they had few dealings with each other, except maybe to bum a cigarette or fence some stolen property.

Now that I had crossed one of the superpowers, I tensed, waiting to be nuked.

"Nah, that's just Clark," Pete said then. "He's all right."

The air seemed to leave the bus just then, and a great light and warmth rose up inside of me. I don't recall, but the other underclassmen must have snuck glimpses at me then, glimpses of admiration and envy. To be pronounced "all right" by Pete Decker was more than just the commutation of my death sentence; it seemed almost a coronation. I had been plucked from the ranks of the pathetic and small, and given a place among the Pete Deckers and Matt Woodbridges of the world. Clark Mason? That motherfucker? Aw, he's all right.

The bus rumbled down Empire toward the last stop on our strip before it turned out of our neighborhood and came up for air on Trent—the busy industrial street that cut us off from the rest of the world. The whole world felt different. I remember staring at Boyle, wondering if he had heard the exchange, if he'd realized what had just happened, my sudden ascension out of his world. But he just sat with his thick glasses against the window, his index finger working his nose like a puppeteer on speed, Eli alone in the nightmarish world of his freakishness, his apartness, and, I suppose it's safe to say now, his seething ambitions. I see him in my mind now and I realize that all of these forces of his personality were concentrated then on the humble goal of sheer survival, the cold, flat wish that he be left alone, and he was being forged in a way by the challenge of his youth. What did he see out that window while he sat there, catatonic and seemingly impervious to the beatings and taunts and stares? I think now, looking back, that his fear may have amounted to less than I ever imagined, that he had actually figured out a way to shut down, to distance himself from his broken self.

Or maybe that's just what I want to believe, an idea that I cling to for my own peace of mind—that Eli had figured out a way to leave the awful physical world behind, to block out the bullies and assholes, to ignore the scorn, to somehow be on our bus and soar above it too, riding on the thinnest of daydreams.

4 | I SHOT SOMEONE

I shot someone in the face with a rubber band that I had stretched along the length of a ruler. I don't recall the victim or my motive (I acknowledge the irony, of course, this casual parallel to the trouble before us today), but my fifth-grade crime doesn't matter except to explain why I was alone in the school office on a late-fall day in 1975, sitting with my head in my hands, waiting for the principal to come back.

I sat in a chair across from the desk of our distracted principal, Joseph Bender, and I practiced looks of contrition and sorrow and prayed that I not slip and call him Joe Boner, the name by which we all knew him. I recall his office as a massive tomb, windowless and cold and the place I waited for my hack—a quick swat or two on the ass with a thick wooden paddle, the gold standard of school punishment circa 1975. Joe Boner was a tame hacker because he kept his emotions under control. There were other teachers—being an attorney with a working knowledge of libel, I won't name them—who could take out years of their own frustration by blistering the asses of children like me. I only saw Joe Boner go overboard once, when Dennis Gilstrap asked the lunch lady if he could kiss her "boobies" and Mr. Bender promptly pulled Dennis out of line, bent him over, and swatted him so furiously that his gum flew across the room and—I know this part of the story must sound apocryphal, but I saw it myself—stuck to the wall of the cafeteria, where it stayed for two weeks as a kind of monument to adult boundaries.

As I sat in the principal's office that day, I was understandably nervous, even though I didn't really fear a hack like the one that had de-gummed Dennis Gilstrap. More likely I would get a reasoned swat and be sent back to my classroom to study our poetic spelling list, which I repeated in my mind—distance, influence, affluence, confluence—as a way to keep from dwelling on the swat I was about to receive.

That's when I heard, outside Joe Boner's office, the principal talking to a woman, trying to calm her down. "No, I'm very sorry. It is unfortunate." I leaned toward the door, as if a few inches might help me hear better. "No, Mrs. Boyle," the principal said, "I assure you, it won't happen again."

When he opened the door I looked back and saw Eli Boyle's mother, wearing a kind of peasant's dress and a scarf over her head, an almost pretty woman in her early forties who looked that day, and every other day that I saw her, like a person who has lost something very important.

"Eli is a very special boy, Mr. Bender," she said. "He's sensitive."

"Yes," the principal was saying, "I know he is and I'm sorry he's had to go through this. We are taking care of it, Mrs. Boyle." And that's when Joe Boner saw me sitting at his desk. "Oh, Mr. Mason. That's right. Why don't you go back to your class? And no more rubber bands, okay?"

He tousled my hair and I sat there a moment longer than I needed to, amazed to be escaping my punishment. Once again, Eli had indirectly saved me. I nodded to Mrs. Boyle, hopped out of the chair, and hurried for the door, turning at the last to see Eli's mom settle into the chair, and to see Mr. Bender close the door behind me.

I suppose that meeting was the reason that, the very next morning, Joe Boner escorted Eli Boyle into my classroom. Eli had started the school year in the other fifth-grade class, taught by Mr. Gibbons, a cross-eyed alcoholic who had been at the high school until two years earlier, when he was asked to leave after some vague complaint by the parents of a girl who had been getting "extra credit" for "correcting papers" as Mr. Gibbons's "after-school aide." Now Eli was standing in the class of *my* teacher, the eternally cute Mrs. Chalmers-Wright-McKinley, who had been teaching at our elementary school for fifteen years and at least three divorces and who seemed incapable of forsaking any of her ex-husbands' last names. We gathered that there had been some problem in Mr. Gibbons's class involving Eli, but we had trouble getting details. Actually, that's not entirely true. We had no trouble getting details, but their context and order eluded us, and so we knew little beyond the glimpse of a meeting that I'd seen between Eli's mom and Joe Boner and the rush of playground intelligence:

Kevin Klapp, who was in Eli's old class, claimed that the trouble began when everyone went out for recess one day. Eli stayed glued to his chair and when Mr. Gibbons came over to see why, he found that Eli had shit his pants. According to Kevin, Mr. Gibbons then yelled at Eli and slapped him. Heather Lindeke said that what actually happened was that after the pants-shitting episode, Eli's mom came in and Mr. Gibbons called Eli "a retard," and Mrs. Boyle demanded that he be put in our class. No, said Marshall Dickens, what actually happened was that Eli only farted, and when everyone went out to recess, Mr. Gibbons yelled at Eli that he'd "prefer it if you did not shit your pants in my classroom anymore" and that was why Eli's mom pulled him out of that class. What did I believe? All of it, I suppose. I didn't put any of it past the people involved, that Eli might shit his pants, or that Mr. Gibbons might make him feel even worse than he did or even slap him, or that Mrs. Boyle might come to Eli's defense.

Whatever the reason, Eli limped into our classroom that day, staring at his corrective shoes, ready for new humiliations. He stood in front of the class, while behind him, Mr. Bender whispered to the teacher and gestured with his hands. Mrs. Chalmers-Wright-McKinley, her high hair spun like soft vanilla ice cream, frowned and shook her head and even covered her mouth as Joe Boner spoke quietly, relaying the actual story of Eli's banishment from Mr. Gibbons's class. But while she listened with obvious sympathy and perhaps even empathy, she made no move to ask Eli to sit down and he stood there like a courtroom exhibit while they whispered about him. Finally, we saw our teacher mouth the word "terrible" as the story reached its critical juncture. Just then Eli twitched, as he often did, in some leftover spasm or convulsion, the brackets on his leg braces clacking together, a late-autumn snowfall loosed from his head. Twenty-eight sets of eyes followed those dandruff flakes to the floor.

Mrs. Chalmers-Wright-McKinley thanked the principal

and walked him to the door. Then she put her arm around Eli, who was a foot shorter than she.

"Welcome to our class, Eli," she said. "Class, say hello to Eli."

We said hello. He never looked up. For all her good intentions, Mrs. Chalmers-Wright-McKinley was torturing Eli.

"Eli? You may sit wherever you want," said Mrs. Chalmers-Wright-McKinley. "Do you have any friends in this class?"

This seemed to me like classic adult stupidity. *Do you have any friends?* Why not just knock the boy down and let us stab him to death with compass needles? Eli looked up through his thick, black-framed glasses and one of his cockeyes went directly to me and—to my endless shame, I prayed that he not say my name—he looked back at the teacher and shook his head no. *Do you have any friends?* What kind of question is that? While Eli stared at the ground, our teacher moved a few kids and put Eli smack in the middle of the classroom.

Jeff Fletcher, who was now sitting behind Eli, plugged his nose and stuck his tongue out to indicate that Eli stunk, and when Mrs. Chalmers-Wright-McKinley turned her back Fletch pulled his desk back away from Eli's. The students on his right and left did the same thing, their desks screeching as they slid across the tile floor. Eli didn't look up, just stared at the notebook open on his desk, drawing pictures of tanks.

I have yet to mention Dana Brett. I suppose I haven't known how, in this ugly world that I am relating, to describe someone so wonderful. Cute? The girl was entirely composed of porcelain, tiny features on a round

47

face beneath black hair that curled up at her collar so that her face was perfectly framed. She wore ribbons in her hair. Ribbons! A redundant bit of packaging perhaps, but still. Ribbons! Miniskirts and vests. And suede boots that laced up the front. There is nothing so hypnotic as the romantic daydreams of the hopelessly presexual, and back then all of my daydreams involved young Dana Brett and unlacing those boots.

She sat in front of Eli and was the only one who didn't move her desk when Mrs. Chalmers-Wright-McKinley turned her back to address the class on Hopi Indians or adding fractions or whatever she was selling that day. She droned on as the desks moved away, until Eli was an island, or rather an isthmus, connected only by the honorable Dana Brett's desk. And when the teacher finally turned around and saw what had happened—the desks magnetically repelled from Eli—she became intent on making it worse. "All right. Move those desks back. Jeff Fletcher, why did you move your desk away from Eli's?"

Of all the cruelty exhibited that day, I still think that question—no matter its intent—was the pinnacle. In one question, she codified what we all knew, made it official and made a horrible mistake: she gave a lousy prick like Jeff Fletcher the opportunity to actually be funny.

"Well," said Fletch, looking around at us, gathering strength, "he smells like a bag full of turds."

In the laughter that followed, Eli never looked up from the tanks he was drawing.

5 | I SMOKED WEED

I smoked weed every day as a kid. Not so much during the time I'm relaying now—the fifth-grade hell that Eli and I shared like some awful creation myth—but from that summer on, pretty much nonstop until the tenth grade. Looking back, those fifth-grade days were the night before battle, the last days spent in complete sobriety. I'm not sure why I offer that bit of information now except to interrupt this harsh story with the reminder that these were different and difficult times—the mid-1970s, after all—when a preteen might be expected to smoke dope every day. It is probably the least endearing and most enduring habit of a whole generation of politicians, this desire to confess, and I can't help wondering if—in admitting fumbling around with a few joints, a smart Arkansas redneck could win two terms—I might not secure a white-trash landslide by acknowledging that I toked regularly at twelve and never had trouble inhaling, that, in fact, I carried the respectful nickname Old Iron Lung.

Still, as I said, I feel the need—perhaps the political necessity—to halt the narrative momentarily and take refuge in the time and place of all of this: the desperateness, the poverty, the harsh world in which I was raised. I would kill (once again, I acknowledge irony) to be able to report that I simply went to school and got good grades;

that I sat next to Eli Boyle on the bus and demanded that he be treated with respect; that I insisted that he, in fact, did *not* smell like turds (sadly, though, he did); that I did not crave more than anything the respect of my class-mates, this societal juice, this cultural cachet, this . . . *approval,* this immeasurable measure of popularity, not only from the suede-booted Dana Brett—love would be more defensible—but also and more importantly from the school toughs, the pubescent dictators, the dope-selling *jefes,* the Pee-Chee-carrying warlords of the Empire bus stops.

This is the only way I can think to explain what happened at the end of that school year. Throughout that year my lot was improving incrementally, Pete Decker's pronouncement that I was "all right" having thrown open the door to the middle of the willow tree, where the tough kids hung out, although I was still a year away from the furthest depths of the branches, where the mystical act of making out was occurring, glimpsed only as a clutch of arms and legs and sweaters and jackets and hair and the occasional flash of braces and skin.

I never tried to smoke at the bus stop again, but I continued to steal my father's cigarettes to give to Pete Decker, who honored my new status by not demanding such bribes, but rather *accepting them with prejudice,* a fine distinction that would serve him well in his later career of Mafia capo or generalissimo of some Latin American junta.

"Whatcha got for me, Marlboro man?" he would ask.

His gift to me was allowing it to seem as if I had a choice. I would pretend to be checking to see if I had cigarettes on me. "Oh, here you go." Then I'd stand there and nod with admiration at his stories of stealing bikes out from under little kids or shooting stray cats in garbage cans. And the midtree circle wasn't the only new access I acquired. I crept toward the back of the bus, too, abandoning the fifth and sixth graders I used to huddle with in the front until I ended up ten rows back, next to a sweet kid named Everson, a flutter-eyed seventh grader who spent every morning bent over in his seat, rolling joints and putting them into little Sucrets cough drop boxes. He hummed songs while he did it, Southern rock tunes that I didn't really recognize, but which were familiar enough. I guess he must've sold all the joints in that Sucrets box each day, because the next day he'd be at it again, rolling joints and humming. Everson was bone skinny and had long blond hair like a girl. He was nicer than the other seventh and eighth graders, though, and he seemed to get a pass from Decker and Woodbridge, I guess because he supplied them with dope.

"Where do you get the papers?" I asked.

"Stepdad's stash," he answered as quickly as possible so he could get back to his song and his job.

"How much does that stuff cost?"

"Ten a lid."

"How much is a lid?"

He looked right at me and just kept humming. "Nobody knows for sure. That's the cool thing."

It seemed okay with Pete that I sat with Everson and one day I even held out one of my dad's Pall Malls to give to my new friend. He looked at it and made a face. "I hope you don't smoke those," Everson said.

"What do you mean?"

"Cigarettes? Disgusting. Filthy habit." And he flipped his blond hair and went back to rolling joints.

I didn't ride the regular bus home in the afternoons. In the fall I played flag football, and in the winter basketball. Except for the great prematurely bearded quarterback Kenny Dale, I was the only guy from my neighborhood who played sports, and so the only people on the activities bus to Empire were me and Everson, who told the teachers he was staying after school for drama and the school paper, but who actually sold the last of his dope to the football team. The bus would cruise past the high school, then the junior high, then come pick up us elementary school kids, and I'd sit in the seat in front of Everson, who never hummed or had anything to say in the afternoons, since his joints were all rolled and sold. He just stared out the window, like Eli.

So I never had to see what Eli endured in the afternoon bus rides, only in the mornings. And in those mornings, while it may sound unlikely and defensive, I began to try to protect him from Pete Decker. Sometimes I saved my cigarettes until Eli arrived at the bus stop, hoping I could distract Pete. Other times I picked up a rock and threw it at a passing car, hoping I could interest Pete in some cruelty that didn't involve knocking Eli down or wedging his briefs in his shithole. But Pete was relentless; he continued to torment Eli, dropping burning cigarettes in his backpack, flicking his ears, and, at least once a week, giving him a wedgie. One day in the winter, Pete reached in Eli's pants to yank on his underwear and immediately withdrew his hand. "Oh, that's sick!" he yelled, and he hauled off and decked Eli, knocking his glasses off and dropping him to the ground. "He isn't wearing any underwear!" On the bus that day, I watched Eli's reflection in the window and I swear I saw him smile a little bit.

I think it was the underwear thing that upped the ante for Pete. He actually began walking up the block to meet Eli, taking the backpack off his shoulder and spreading all the books and papers as he walked back to the bus stop, Eli bent at that crooked waist in his flannel shirt, picking up his things and limping along toward the bus stop in his corrective shoes, pausing to push his glasses back up on his nose.

In the spring I turned out for baseball, but on the first day I forgot to wear a cup and a line drive short hopped me in the nutsack and I had to go to emergency, where the doctor told my mom I had a twisted testicle and would have to take the baseball season off, or at least until my right nut reacquired its flesh color. So I started wearing special underwear and riding the bus home right after school, where I got to see the second half of Eli Boyle's nightmare. Pete treated him the same way at 3:00 P.M. that he had at 7:20 in the morning, calling him names, making fun of his clothes, knocking him down. It was about that time, in the spring, that Pete Decker decided he was tired of beating Eli up and that someone else needed to beat up Eli. Me.

He talked about it for a couple of days, telling me things that Eli had allegedly said about me, that I was a fairy and a fruitcake and that I had humped my own grandma. I remember wondering, if I were a fairy, would I want to hump my grandma?

I managed to avoid fighting those first days, saying that Eli wasn't worth it, or I didn't want to get snot on my fists, stuff like that. But Pete kept bringing it up, saying that if I didn't fight Eli people would assume it was because I was his boyfriend. Still, I avoided it. And every day Pete would hover over me. "When are you gonna fight that punk? He's making you look stupid."

One morning, sitting next to Everson, I leaned over and asked what he would do.

"I don't fight," he said, without looking up from the joint in his lap.

"Why not?"

"No one expects me to."

"Why?"

He shrugged. "Against my nature."

"If I don't beat up Eli, then Pete's gonna kill me."

"Yeah," he said. "It works that way."

At recess, I sought out the lovely Dana Brett, who had impressed me with her courage and humanity when she didn't scoot her desk away from Eli's that day. I explained to her my dilemma, without looking up into her angelic face, her Nestlé's brown eyes. She listened patiently, while a few feet away the other girls in our class asked questions of romance to a Magic Eight Ball. She would always be unlike those other girls, more measured and rational.

"Are you afraid of him?" Dana asked when I'd explained my problem.

"Eli? Of course not."

"Well," she said, the long lashes flashing down once on those big, round eyes, "then you better fight. If you don't, they're gonna say you're a puss."

I think we are capable of fooling ourselves in a lot of different ways. People talk about what makes a child an adult, as if there is some physical or emotional or mental threshold we cross, but I tell you this, and if you are honest with yourself you will know it is true: the thing that makes us adult is our ability to delude ourselves. That's all. Children know what they are. Try telling a fat kid he looks good, or a child who is a bad athlete that he just needs to try harder. He knows better. But as adults, we start to believe the bullshit. We tell ourselves that cheating on our taxes isn't really stealing and that the job candidate with long legs is really a better fit for the company. We look at our lives and pretend that we aren't money hungry and consumed by status, that we have kept the morals and ethics of our college years, that we are healthy and not fat, distinguished and not old, that gray looks sophisticated in our hair, that it doesn't hurt her if she doesn't know, that it's not really lying if he doesn't find out, that we deserve a break now and then, that we had no choice, meant no harm, didn't know what would happen, would take it back if we could, that we are still liberal and open minded and easygoing and not afraid. We come up with rationalizations and justifications after the fact, and then we convince ourselves that these things are *true*. We pretend we are doing the best we can.

But every man dies the death of his own making.

Me? I took a step toward being an adult that day. I told myself that if I didn't beat Eli up, Pete Decker would pound us both. I told myself that I would go easy on Eli, that I'd pull my punches. I told myself that we would make eye contact and he would see that I didn't really mean this, that I could do this and not actually do it, that I wasn't beating him up, not like Pete Decker and Matt Woodbridge did, that I was different from them. *That I was different*. That is the biggest lie—that we are different than they are.

The brakes squealed on the bus and Pete was up behind me, rubbing my shoulders, extolling me, whispering random combinations of guttural words in my ear.

"Fuck up that fat dickbreath cockbite fuckball!"

"Kick that smelly fag dipshit's ass!"

We moved along the aisle. Below our feet, the floor of the bus was lined with a grooved rubber strip and my tennis shoes squeaked as I moved to the front of the bus. Pete hovered behind, inches from my ear: "Break his fuckin' four-eyed, pig-nosed face!"

Such trouble has a way of congealing the passengers of a school bus, and I felt their oozy, collective eyes on me as I moved down the aisle. I was about to beat up the most pitiful kid in twelve grades. I, the kid who offered cigarettes in fealty to Pete Decker, was about to join his ranks. In their eyes, how could I be any different?

Eli was the first off, of course, and he'd begun moving in his quick crooked shuffle, bent at the waist, trying to hide in his own clothes.

"Boyle!" Pete yelled from behind me. "Hey, Boyle!" I felt Pete gently take my book bag and set it on the ground. Eli just kept moving, and Pete dispatched his two goons to run after him and drag him back. I stood under the willow tree, my mouth dry. The bus pulled away and I watched it go, the faces pressed up against the back window, kids having flooded to Pete Decker's seat, hoping to see the first moments of our fight before the bus pulled away.

The goons dragged Eli back and pushed him toward me. Still he didn't look up.

"Are you gonna fight, or are you a fag?" Pete asked Eli.

56

He didn't answer. He stood in front of me, staring at his shoes. He shifted his weight and his leg braces clacked together.

Pete pushed Eli in the shoulder. "Come on, queer."

I raised my fists slowly and moved forward. He looked up then, and I realized I'd never seen Eli full-on like this, from the front. He was usually looking sideways or averting his gaze or covering his mouth or looking away before you could get a fix on his face. It was egg shaped— too much forehead and chin, all the features and pimples packed in between, the black glasses, the braces on his teeth, like some perfect rendering of the collective nightmares of adolescents.

Pete Decker stepped away and it was just Eli and I squared off in the gravel between the street and Will the Hippie's front yard. Our eyes met and I tried to let him see that I was sorry for what I had to do. He sighed.

And then he hit me. Twice. The first punch connected with my nose, the second clipped my ear. I kicked at him and caught him in the leg and he hit me again in the face, a hammer that buckled my knees and sent me sprawling, crying, onto the ground. From my side I looked up through teary eyes to see Eli running away, crying, his knee braces rattling, Pete Decker a few steps behind. Pete caught him and dragged him to the ground and by the time I got to my feet, he was pounding on Eli. I felt my nose. It was bleeding. Twenty yards up the road, so was Eli's. Pete just kept cocking his fist and letting Eli have it. Eli was crying for help, honking like a goose, trying to squirm away. Pete's goons were cheering the beating their boss was delivering. Finally Pete climbed off him, opened Eli's book bag and scattered everything, set his lunch pail on the ground and stomped it into scrap metal. Then he kicked Eli once in the side and came back toward me.

"That was a good fight," he said, slapping me on the back. "That fucker jumped you, man. He didn't fight fair at all." Pete was panting. There was sweat on his upper lip, making the hair below his nose look almost like a mustache. I looked at one of the goons, who seemed ready enough to accept Pete's description of the good fight and the idea that I had somehow been jumped, and I wondered if Pete's goons even processed their own thoughts. "You'd have killed him if he fought fair," Pete said. And he began walking toward his house, a goon on either side.

I looked up the street, to where Eli had already gathered his things. He was no longer crying, and he seemed oblivious to the damage he'd done to my face. He walked home, bent at the waist, as if nothing had happened.

At home my sisters were playing Barbies on the porch, and they stared at me wide eyed as I came up the sidewalk. Being all of five, Meg saw her job as explaining the world to Shawna, and so she bent over and whispered, "Clark got all beat up."

"By bad guys?" Shawna asked, and Meg nodded.

Ben had stayed home sick that day and he was on the couch, reading a Flash comic book. He looked at me as if I were covered in blood—which, of course, I was. "Hot Christ buns," he said, "what happened to you?"

That brought my mother from the kitchen, where she usually spent the afternoons sorting through the Avon cosmetics and sundries that she stockpiled in the house. She was supposed to sell these Avon products door-to-door in the neighborhood and at swanky Avon parties that she shamed friends and relatives into attending, but my mother didn't like to bother people, and so the Avon products had taken over our house and our basement was filled with boxes of foundation eyeliner and birdhouses and perfume (I got regular nighttime erections just thinking about the case of "Nights of Romance" perfume underneath my bed.) "Who did this to you? Was it that boy, Pete Decker?" She waved a pair of Avon candlesticks at me. "I'm going to march down there and talk to his mother."

"No," I said. "I just fell down."

But she wouldn't buy it, and finally I had to admit that it was in fact Eli Boyle who had done this to me.

Ben slapped his forehead. "Jesus meet the neighbors!"

Even Mom was changed by this bit of news. "Huh," she said. "The boy with the . . ." She gestured around her face as if we were talking about the Elephant Man.

"Yeah," I said, staring at the ground.

"Oh," she said, and looked down at the candlesticks in her hands. The idea of waving candlesticks at the mother of such a boy was less interesting and my mother just sort of shrugged and half turned back toward the kitchen, suddenly faced with a problem potentially worse than her son being beaten up by a bully: her son being beaten up by an Eli Boyle. "You . . . um . . . you should talk to your father about defending yourself, Clark," she said. "And you shouldn't get into fights."

Staring at my bloodied face, Ben shook his head. "I'll say."

6 | MUHAMMAD ELI DISAPPEARED

Muhammad Eli disappeared from the bus stop the very next day. I guess his mom began driving him to school, but however he got there he was in class when I arrived, sitting in his desk, open-pit nose mining. The nickname—Muhammad Eli—was Ben's idea and I have to say that I was happy that it didn't catch on. In fact, I was shocked that day to hear that I'd actually kicked Eli's ass. Even the people who'd witnessed my beating bought into Pete Decker's fiction and suddenly I understood the power of propaganda. At the bus stop guys clapped me on the back and told me they'd heard it was a great fight.

"That asshole's lucky he ran away," said one of Pete's thugs. "Clark was about to kick his ass."

"About to?" Pete asked. "My boy whipped his ass."

At recess, Dana Brett strode up to me in her suede boots and miniskirt and told me matter-of-factly that I was a bully. I didn't know what to say: cop to being a bully (which I wasn't), or admit that a spaz like Eli had actually beaten me up? At lunch I watched Eli work the edges of the playground, the way he always did, picking his way along the chain-link fence. I wanted to apologize. I really did. But how do you apologize to someone who has, in fact, beaten you up?

Eli wasn't on the bus that afternoon either. I sat staring out the window, the sun high and bright, washing the blue from the sky.

"Clark the Hammer," Pete Decker said. "Big Bad Clark Mason."

The next morning Eli still didn't show at our stop, and Pete and his gang took this as proof that—despite what they'd seen—I actually inflicted great damage upon my opponent. I slumped past Eli's empty seat behind the bus driver and sat near the back. When Woodbridge got on the bus he stopped at my seat, stuck out his lower lip, and nodded slowly, approvingly, as if checking out the latest model of bully.

"I heard you beat that fat, greasy-haired faggot's ass," he said. "Queer probably transferred to another school."

"Fuckin' retard fag queer," Pete muttered.

"Yeah," Woodbridge said. "Fuckin' fag."

At school, I looked for opportunities to make eye contact with Eli, a shrug that might communicate that we were both victims in this, that we had both come out with bloody noses, that no harm was done. But Eli had found his place beneath the rest of us, and he scurried around with his head bowed, staring at his black shoes.

I tried to catch sight of his mother driving him to and from school, but they left early for school and apparently left late for home. Spring was a blink, just a suggestion of time, all shadow and no cast; it was the first season that I remember going faster than I expected, and the first time I realized that time actually moved in a certain direction, toward something that wasn't just the piling up of days and weeks and school years, but a point that had its own weight. It was like the first time you realize, as a kid, that all the escalator steps aren't collected in the basement. That spring I saw myself in junior high and high school and beyond, and I saw the kids before me and after me as fellow travelers, and like any whiff of mortality it was powerful and frightening. I'd like to say that I found in this season of epiphany the time to offer a quiet apology to Eli, but to be honest the days were made up of Presidential Fitness Tests and Smear the Queer and the accidental grazing of Marcia Donnely's left boob, one of only two actual boobs in our class (Marcia Donnely's right being the other). And then, one day, it was the last week of school and we cut off the brown grocery sacks that had covered our textbooks, and we used knives from the cafeteria to clean the gum off the bottoms of our desks, and we prepared for the last days of fifth grade with the awareness that life was beginning.

Every summer I took over a newspaper route for an older guy in our neighborhood, and this time I promised to let my brother Ben help me out. We started the last week of school; I got up at four-thirty and pedaled around with him pointing out the houses that took the paper and then sliding it into the rusted metal tubes and snazzy-looking new plastic boxes. It was almost six when we came riding back down Empire Road toward our house. We pedaled through a couple of backyards and came out at the RiverVu Trailer Park—the only accurate word of that title being *Trailer*, since there was no *Vu* of the *River* and this was certainly no *Park*. I rode past the trailer of the great, prematurely bearded quarterback Kenny Dale, his cherry GTO in the driveway behind his parents' Mercury. I stood on my bicycle pedals and tried to look into his window, trying to imagine the things he must do to cheerleaders in that little trailer.

And then, out of the corner of my eye, I saw Eli emerge from the last trailer on the street and begin walking down the strip of houses. I circled around and watched from a block away as he shuffled in that familiar walk, the clattering of his leg braces the only noise competing with the birds in the neighborhood.

When I got home, my mom had made pancakes for my little sisters. I can still see Mom at the counter in the kitchen, short and slender in one of my dad's big gray sweatshirts, which covered her like a bulky dress, and a pair of fuzzy slippers, smelling like a catalog of Avon products, the smoke from her cigarette curling around the long hair piled atop her head. "Clark? I'm making the girls some pancakes."

"No time."

I ran past her, got my book bag and my Nerf football, and ran back into the kitchen, grabbing my brown sack lunch off the counter.

"What do you mean no time? There's always time for breakfast."

"Not today. I'm riding my bike to school."

Finally, she turned. It's funny. The small things I took for granted then torture me now in their simple perfection: a plate of pancakes, a hand on my shoulder, a look of deep concern. You have no idea when you're so eager to escape your own house, your own life, your own childhood, of the sad truth that no one will ever care for you like that again.

"You can't ride your bike, Clark. It's three miles."

"I can ride three miles."

63

My dad came out in pajama bottoms and no shirt, rubbing his head and patting his belly, inadvertently mastering the test of coordination that we used to dare one another. He kissed Mom on the top of the head and she handed him a plate of pancakes.

"You're not riding your bike to school on an empty stomach."

"I'll eat there."

I started for the door and she put her hands on her hips. "But school doesn't even start for an hour and a half."

"Gotta go," I said, and ran out the door, tossed the canvas newspaper bag on the porch, and climbed on the banana seat of my Schwinn Scrambler. Maybe I could apologize on the road. But Eli was nowhere on Empire and so I pedaled down the busier Trent, keeping my eyes open until finally I saw him, a hundred yards ahead of me, walking along the railroad tracks on the other side of Trent. He moved with that same inward shuffle that he used at school. He favored his bent left leg, but since the toes on his right leg pointed in a few degrees it was a kind of double limp, exaggerated by his leg braces. Something about his walk had always seemed familiar to me, and as I shadowed him down Trent I understood what it was: some old black-and-white movie I'd seen in which a gangster was shackled and cuffed and hobbled down death row while the other prisoners hissed and made catcalls. With his leg braces, his hippity-hoppity, stare-at-the-ground gait, that's what Eli Boyle appeared to be, a prisoner on his way to his maker.

I checked my watch. It was six-thirty in the morning. I had been assuming that Eli's mother drove him to and from school every day to keep him from being beaten up; in fact he had been walking all this time, leaving two hours early to avoid Pete Decker and Matt Woodbridge. But no, that wasn't quite right; he hadn't walked to school to avoid those two bullies. No, he hadn't started walking until the day he and I fought. My belligerence was his last straw.

I rode so slowly on the shoulder of the road that I could barely stay up, zigzagging my front wheel to keep my balance. Every few minutes a tractor trailer or molten-aluminum truck from the Kaiser plant would blow by and I would nearly lose my balance, but I kept at it, watching Eli on the tracks, across twenty feet of weeds and scrub grass. He never looked up. He arrived at school at a quarter after seven, a full hour before the bell would ring. I padlocked my bike and followed a safe distance behind, unaware that the school even opened this early. He walked past the janitors, who smoked cigarettes and carried rolls of toilet paper into the bathrooms. I followed him past the office, where the principal, Joe Boner, leaned against the secretary's desk, pleading with her about something. Past the glass trophy case with its pictures of former students who'd died in Vietnam and the award named for Woodbridge's brother. Finally, he turned into the gymnasium. I was stunned. Of all the places for Eli to kill an hour before school, I would never have guessed the gym, a veritable torture chamber for a kid like Boyle.

I caught up and peeked in the gym, but he was gone. There was an entrance to the boys' locker room at the end of the gym, but no way he'd have made it there before I got to the door. He'd simply disappeared. I wondered for a second if I'd made the whole thing up. Imagine. Eli Boyle walking two miles to school. Two miles back. With his gnarled legs and crooked feet? Imagine the fear he had of the bus stop, of the bullies of Empire. Imagine him going into the gym, of all places.

Then, in the gaps between the bleachers, I caught a glimpse of greasy hair, of overalls and flannel. I crept up behind the wood bleachers, which were pulled out so that only the bottom two rows were accessible. But it was enough that someone could slide underneath, and that's where Eli sat, on the floor beneath the bleachers, amid the gum and candy wrappers and smashed popcorn, slats of light coming in between the bleacher seats. He sat with his notebook open, writing something, or drawing, possibly the tanks and airplanes that he was always sketching.

His back was to me, and if he knew someone was watching he gave no indication, just sat curled up on himself, as if he could pull in more, disappear from the world. I opened my mouth to say something—*I'm sorry*—but nothing came out. I backed out of the gym and made my way down the hall. I peeked in the office, but the principal was now gone and the secretary was staring out the door, her head tilted, mouth wide open, like she wasn't seeing whatever was in front of her eyes, like she was imagining something entirely different.

My movement into her field of vision snapped her out of it, and she wiped at her eyes. "What are you doing here?" she asked.

"I go to school here," I said.

She straightened some things on her desk and swallowed. "I know. I mean . . . it's very early."

I opened my mouth to say something, but the principal's door opened and Mr. Bender popped his head out.

"Look, Peg, I'm sorry if I led you to believe that this was anything other than two people—"

She cleared her throat and nodded toward me, and Mr. Bender followed her gaze to me, standing flat-footed in the doorway.

"Oh, hello, Mason. What are you doing here?"

"I go to school here," I answered again.

"Right," he said.

He came out, his eyebrow up, like he was figuring a problem. "Okay then, well. I was just having a discussion with Mrs. Federick. And . . . if I led you to believe, Mrs. Federick, that"— and now he looked from me to her and back again—"that . . . uh, that the other bus driver I was telling you about would approve of me . . . you know, riding your bus . . . well, obviously, I've got a lot of time invested with that bus driver. As you do with your . . . bus driver. One ride on another bus doesn't . . ."

He seemed confused by his own words and he turned and went back into his office. Mrs. Federick stared at his door and I slipped away.

That day we cleaned out our desks and went outside for a huge game of tug-of-war with the other fifth-grade class. In a rare moment of kindness, Mrs. Chalmers-Wright-McKinley allowed Eli to skip the game, but his parole was cut short when she forced him to stand in the middle and be the judge of which team won. A ribbon was tied in the center of the rope and two lines were painted on the grass, about fifteen feet apart. We had to pull the ribbon over the line closest to us and Mr. Gibbons's class had to pull the ribbon over the line closest to them. In the middle stood Eli, staring at the ground.

"Go!" Mr. Gibbons said, and we pulled with everything we had, boys and girls alike. The rope snapped tight and then began moving toward their side, and something about the screams and the strain on that rope transformed Eli. He skipped to his right, holding up his right hand to indicate that Mr. Gibbons's class was winning. Fletcher and I were in the front; we led a charge back the other way and Eli sidestepped toward us, raising his left hand. Now the ribbon changed direction again and Eli, caught off guard, lost his balance but then regained it and began sliding away from us again. Staring at that ribbon, his eyes seemed engaged for the first time I could remember, and he smiled and made a funny noise that I realized was a kind of rusty laughter. I had to block Eli out to help my side stop the erosion, and the ribbon settled in the middle, and when I looked up, Eli had his arms straight out, indicating we were back at equilibrium. Behind me I felt something give, and then Fletcher lost his balance and kicked my legs out from under me, and the rope was pulled quickly the other way and from my back—as I was dragged across the grass—I saw Eli sliding sideways quickly, his right arm straight in the air, his glasses having fallen to the end of his nose, so intent was he on calling the progress of this match. The ribbon crossed their line, and he threw both his hands in the air to indicate that the match was over. Then he bent his knees and pointed both hands at Mr. Gibbons's class. They had won. He stood there for the longest time, both his hands pointed to his right, panting, a half-smile on his face. Then he straightened up, pushed his glasses up on his nose, and looked from one side to the other, shyly, as if asking, Did you see what I just did?

Everyone let go of the rope, the teachers blew their whistles, and we were escorted back to our classrooms to wait for the bus to take us home for the summer. No one said a thing to Eli; he simply curled up on himself again, slinking away before the moment could be taken from him.

7 | I'VE BEEN THINKING

I've been thinking about the purpose of a statement such as this. It is intended as a confession, obviously, something of a legal document (even scrawled on yellow pad, like some manic trial note). And yet this statement also has more than a whiff of memoir, of the commission of my death to paper. After all, who writes a memoir but the man whose life is over? The memoirist believes that he will live on in transcription, but in fact he is describing a life rather than living one, abandoning the visceral for the verbal. It is a kind of surrender.

I am finished. All the pretty detectives in the world can't change that. There is only one ending to a story like mine. And before I get on with that long and unforgettable summer of 1975, before I finish telling how Eli saved my life, and how I conspired to commit a murder twenty-five years later, I will reveal that ending—not just the ending of my own story, but the ending of all stories. It is this:

I died alone.

Now perhaps I should have confined myself to a strict legal document, *wherefore* and *in furtherance* and the like. But such a document could never begin to convey the depths of my misdeeds, nor of my contrition; there are facts here that simply do not adhere to the rigid structure of the Revised Legal Codes of Washington State.

Take the summer, for instance. What statute covers the feel of the sun that summer, its immediacy and grace, its heat on my browned forearms, on the tanned skin of my neck and shoulders? How can a lawyer explain the rush of pavement beneath my bicycle tires or the defiance of gravity committed by my tennis shoes? Perhaps you remember the length of your own July days, the endless possibilities that existed from the seat of a Schwinn, the swagger of boys moving down a suburban street with the streetlights beginning to hum and spark, the fearless poise of it all. The longing.

That summer, days lasted forever. Somewhere a scientist is proving that time is bent and yawned by the forces of childhood and summer, and the jury awaits his inevitable arrival in Stockholm open armed, individual jurists sobbing because this temporal genius has finally proven that our childhoods are longer than our adult lives, and that time is not a line, as they have been trying to deceive us into believing, but a slope, picking up speed and danger as it goes on.

For myself, in that long June of 1975 I rose early and patted my long, thick hair rather than comb it. I fought with my brother and sisters over the last bowl of Cocoa Puffs or Super Sugar Crisp or King Vitamin; no matter what kind of processed, sugared cereal we ate, my mother bought only *last bowls* of the stuff. We planted ourselves in front of the TV with zealous punctuality, and yet we never so much as smiled at the crap that played before us: Underdog and Dick Tracy and the Go Go Gophers and Mr. Peabody and Klondike Cat ("Savoir Faire has stolen my cheeses!"). The point of cartoons is not enjoyment. Check the face of any kid planted in front of the tube. It's not fun. It's a business. They don't like cartoons any more than we like work; it's what they do.

By ten each morning, I was on my bike. I'd ride down to Everson's house and we'd pretend to have karate fights or play touch football or just tool around on our bikes, acting like kids instead of the pot-smoking losers we were about to become. Some mornings I'd scrounge through the dryer for change, and Everson and I would race off to the store for baseball cards. I can still see the 1975 Topps baseball cards. They made them a shade smaller that year, for what reason I couldn't possibly say, with the team name shadowed on the top, the player framed just below that set against two-tone cardboard, his name in all caps, his position in a tiny baseball on the bottom right, unless he was an All-Star (the Dodgers had four that year: Messersmith, Garvey, Cey, and Wynn), in which case his position was written inside a star. I tore these tiny men from the package and marveled at the afros and sideburns and mustaches that peeked out from under their ball caps and wondered at the world that opened up to people with afros and sideburns and mustaches, at the vast number and range of boobs that they must be exposed to. I flipped the cards over and read through the stats as if they contained some secret—map of the human genome, key to the universe. To this day, my mind is full of the detritus printed in six-point type on the backs of those cards. I can't remember my bank account number or my sisters' birthdays, but I remember that Richie Zisk had exactly one hundred RBI's for the Pirates, that Pat Dobson won nineteen games for the Yankees, and that Ralph Garr hit a cool .353. I scraped and stole for the quarter that each package cost and never gave a thought to Everson, who must've had thousands of dollars from his school-year dope sales, but who bought exactly the same number of packs as me, peeling singles off a thick roll.

For the first half of that summer, stoic Everson never mentioned pot; nor did he ever have any, at least when I was around. He was just a kid, like me, but with longer hair and a shorter vocabulary, and even though he was going into eighth grade and I was going into sixth, that disparity disappeared that summer in a haze of tag and hotbox and bike races and baseball cards and mud pies and dandelion soup and ice cream trucks and corn on the cob on soggy plates . . . a life. A real life, ordered and meaningful and simple.

And then Pete Decker got out of juvenile detention.

I don't think I realized that the neighborhood was peaceful until it stopped being so. For the first month and a half of the summer, as long as we stayed in our turf and didn't venture into Matt Woodbridge's fiefdom four blocks down the street, we were safe, seemingly able to stay out until the sun was completely gone without fear of being beaten up. And then, on the day Pete got out of the clink, it all ended.

He'd been gone six whole weeks—a sentence deferred until summer so that he could finish the school year— for stealing car stereos. A whole pile of eight-track players had been found behind Pete's garage. Six weeks in juvenile hall wasn't likely to mellow Pete, a fact I realized when I finally saw him, on a Friday at the end of July, walking down the street, a cigarette dangling from his fingers—ambling, really, like he wasn't even going anywhere, like he was pacing a long hall.

That very weekend, summer ended. The weather stayed hot and school remained closed, but from then on the world didn't feel the same. Bikes were stolen and their parts were seen on other bikes; rocks were thrown through windows; garbage cans were spilled out on the street, and mailboxes were knocked from their posts. That weekend Everson and I stopped *playing,* and started just *hanging out.* Waiting. We knew that at any time Pete could come out of his house and take charge of things. Little kids like my siblings continued to play, of course, because that's all little kids can do (their ability to "hang out" still unformed) but it was with one eye on the street, in close proximity to their houses, riding their bikes in small circles in their driveways or on the strips in front of their houses, no longer venturing down the block. Bike traffic fell by two thirds. No one dared walk anywhere anymore, lest they be caught out on the street.

Still, Pete stayed to himself those first days, walking the mile strip of Empire as if he were the only one on it, cigarette in the left corner of his mouth, left eye squinted shut against the curling smoke. It felt as if he were taking the measure of the neighborhood, seeing if anything had changed, who needed to be put in his place, whose ass needed kicking.

We convinced ourselves that maybe things had changed, and gradually, the next week, we ventured out with our bikes and our baseball cards, but stayed close to our own yards. Then, one afternoon while I engaged in the exquisite task of sorting my baseball cards in the front yard, Pete was suddenly there, leaning against the fence next to my house. Everson was with him, looking as if he'd been kidnapped.

"Hey," Pete said in his preternaturally scratchy voice. "What the fuck are those?"

"Baseball cards."

Pete held out his hand and tipped his head back and I looked up at Everson, who shrugged. I stood and brought him the card I happened to have in my hand, an outfielder named George Hendrick of the Cleveland Indians. Pete held it in his hand, turned it over, and made a face like he'd eaten something sour. "What do you do with it?"

I shrugged. "You collect 'em."

"Why?"

I shrugged again. "For fun."

He looked down at the card. "So what, you look at the pictures and beat off? Are you queer, Clark? I mean, Clark's kind of a queer name, ain't it?"

"No." And I don't know what came over me, but I really believed I could explain myself to him. "See, you try to collect all the guys from every team and then you see who's better by the stats on the back. You can measure them against each other and they all start to make sense. That's the only way baseball makes sense, is if you understand how the numbers work against each other."

Everson closed his eyes. Pete turned the card over.

"See," I said, "George Hendrick hit nineteen homers. Reggie Jackson hit twenty-nine and had more RBI's, too. So he's better. In fact, he's the best." My voice lost any force behind it. "See?"

Pete stared at George Hendrick's card for a while and then he tossed it back at me. "We're gonna go party. You comin'?"

I looked at Everson, who was staring at the ground.

Pete stepped forward. "You ain't a puss, are you, Clark?"

"No," I said. "No, I'm ready to go." I left the baseball cards on the porch and we crossed the rabbit hills on our bikes and walked them through the weedy railroad fields until we reached the riverbank where Pete had stashed a six-pack of warm beer that he'd stolen from someone. The three of us passed those beers around and Everson brought out a joint and we drank and smoked and then Pete collected whatever money we had, to pay for the beer—which he'd stolen—and the joint, which he expected to be paid for even though Everson had provided it. These were, in order, my first beer and my first taste of marijuana, and if I felt anything other than a sore throat and nausea I don't remember it. Since that day I have seen people loosen up and become wild on the effects of alcohol and dope, but I don't remember any of us smiling or laughing that day, and I guess that's because Pete drank most of the beer and inhaled most of the pot.

The next day, he organized a kind of boxing tournament with gloves he had left over from his Golden Gloves days. He enticed a couple of little kids into the tournament as lightweights; they sent each other home bleeding and crying. Next were Everson and me, whom Pete called the middleweights. We swung wildly and connected each time with the other's ear, until our ears were red and sore, which is when Pete realized we were purposefully not hitting each other in the face. He stopped the fight and informed us that we were pusses and that if we didn't fight each other, we'd have to move up in weight class and "get your pussy ass fucked up by me." So we ventured out slowly, our gloved hands in front of us, jabbing each other in the nose or the chin or the brow. Then I caught Everson with a shot to the jaw and he got mad and nailed me in the nose, and the rest was just a mess of bleary eyes and blood in my mouth and swinging fists, until I remember looking down on Everson on the ground and Pete pulled me away, whooping and shouting that I had scored the upset.

That night we went with Pete to steal bicycles from the other end of the neighborhood. We rode the bikes over the rabbit hills, then put them in Pete's garage, where he stayed up all night, taking them apart and putting them back together with parts from other bikes, trying to make them unrecognizable, although when kids saw Pete riding their stolen bikes they never said anything anyway.

In the morning, Pete gave Everson and me each a stolen bike and had us sit a block apart, facing each other. He gave us each a crutch from when he'd broken his leg.

"Now ride at each other," he said.

"What?"

"You know, like them old guys used to do." Pete struggled for the word. "What's that called? You know, guys on horses, with them long spears?"

"Jousting?" Everson asked, and was immediately sorry.

We passed twice without touching, just holding our crutches out in front of us, but Pete was becoming impatient, and the third time Everson caught me in the shoulder with the rubber stopper on the bottom of his crutch. The impact spun me sideways and my front tire slammed into his back tire and we were both thrown onto our knees and elbows, instantly skinned, our bikes collapsed in a heap of spokes and gears.

"Motherfuck," Pete said reverentially. The next day we

shoplifted cigarettes and sunflower seeds and looked at dirty magazines. On and on the summer seemed destined to go, an ever-descending spiral. We drank bottles of sweet red wine that Pete liberated from a neighbor and took pills that Pete said were speed, although, again, the only thing I remember feeling was slightly sick and edgy. We broke into a garage and stole gasoline, which we proceeded to sniff until we were dizzy and sick. We used the rest of the gas to start fires, and burned things that Pete had stolen: purses and clothes and toys. We engaged in all of this behavior with no sense of fun or purpose— other than fighting off Pete Decker's boredom, but that was enough. We feared Pete's boredom far more than we feared being caught stealing or drunk.

"I'm bored," Pete said one day, after he'd been out of juvie for about two weeks. "Let's *do* something." We sat in the draw between the rabbit hills, in the thick weeds, smoking one of Everson's joints. He and I exchanged a worried glance, but Pete just stood up and wandered away and Everson and I sighed with relief.

The next morning, something felt different in my house. I wandered around the house, scratching my head, trying to put my finger on it. My parents didn't seem to notice it, nor did my sisters or my brother. They went about their business, Dad getting ready for work at the cement plant, pulling on his coveralls and packing his aluminum lunch pail, Mom folding clothes, my brother and sisters eating their cereal in front of the TV. Dad couldn't find his wallet and he stormed around a little bit, but finally he just headed off for work without it, kissing my mom and ruffling my hair, like I was still a little kid. Then it hit me. I ran back into my bedroom.

Something was different in my room. The top of my dresser was clean. *The top of my dresser where I kept my baseball cards.* I looked behind the dresser, knowing that four hundred baseball cards were not going to fall back there. I checked the drawers and under my bed, and asked Ben if he'd taken them. He looked up from his Count Chocula cereal, a spot of milk on his lower lip, and then shook his head and turned away from me to the TV.

Pete. Pete Decker had broken into my house and stolen my father's wallet and taken my baseball cards. He could have killed us or taken one of my little sisters away or . . . there was no telling the damage he could've caused, and there was nothing I could do. I went outside and threw a baseball against our front porch, grinding my teeth together.

"Hey, queer."

I turned to see Pete standing in the street, Everson at his side, looking sheepish. They were both dressed in several layers of clothing, heavy winter coats and hats, making them appear to be bloated. It was already almost eighty degrees, and yet they stood there under heaps of heavy clothing, as if they were preparing for the final assault on Everest. I even forgot my stolen baseball cards for a minute, venturing toward them. "What—"

Pete held out a handgun. "You comin'?"

I must've looked horrified, because Pete laughed—giggled, almost. "Change your shorts, junior. It's a BB gun." And to prove it he turned and shot my neighbor's German shepherd in the ass, sending it yelping around their yard. "Get dressed."

"Where'd you get the guns?" I asked.

"Found 'em," Pete said, and he smiled at me, a smile

as cruel as that particular arrangement of lips and teeth can be made to appear.

Mom looked in on me as I put on sweatshirts and extra pants and my heaviest coat. "What are you doing, Clark?"

"Nothing."

"But why are you dressing like that?"

I shot her a glare. "I'm not doing anything, Mom."

She stared as if she didn't know me. I went outside, and Pete and Everson began walking before I reached them, and together we headed down the street, bulked up in our winter clothes like the sons of some fat gunslinger. Pete tossed me the BB pistol he'd shown me; Everson was carrying one just like it, an air-powered gun that fired one BB at a time, in a slow arc that you could see from behind the gun. For his part, Pete had a more dangerous weapon, a rifle that shot pellets that gained speed by being pumped as many times as a bony pair of arms could pump.

Pete seemed giddy with the dangers that lay ahead as we walked across the rabbit hills and toward the river. "Fuckers ain't gonna know what hit 'em." He walked a few feet ahead of us and my fist kept tightening around the air pistol, watching his back, thinking about my baseball cards, about Pete roaming our house while we slept. I imagined the BB going into the back of his neck, then rolling him over and firing over and over into his face. Finally we reached the spot where Pete hid his stolen beer, marked with a two-by-four stuck in the ground, and Pete went into the woods and returned with three welding masks. He gave one to each of us and we put them on, lowering the green glass visors over our faces. We walked toward the river like valiant white trash, like knights of the end table, knights of the TV tray, knights of the white ghetto.

As we walked, Everson leaned in toward me and whispered, with dread, "We're fighting Woodbridge. And some of his friends." But I could only imagine killing Pete.

"Here's what we do," Pete said as we entered the rail yard above the river. "We pin 'em down in a gunfight, and while you guys keep 'em down, I'm gonna circle around and ambush the motherfuckers from behind. Got it?" He began pumping his rifle, bringing his arms together in a scissor motion until he strained against all the air pressure he'd built up in his gun. "You motherfuckin' got it?"

We nodded and kept walking. We heard them before we saw them. We had come down a hill onto the flats overlooking the river. They were in a stand of trees just on the other side of an old gravel pit at a bend in the river. Pete lowered his welding shield over his face. Then Everson lowered his. I tightened the strap on my forehead and lowered my shield. We ducked down. It was quiet: the only noises were the babbling river and my own breathing behind the dark-tinted welding mask.

We crept up on the stand of trees, Pete in the lead, Everson and I behind him. My hands were shaking and sweaty, the stand of trees suddenly empty.

"Crap," Pete said, and almost as soon as he said it I felt a shot, like a bee sting on my hip. The air was filled with the popping of air guns. They had outflanked our plan to outflank them.

"Get down!" Pete yelled, and we did, diving for cover in the stand of trees that Woodbridge and his army had just evacuated. I remember seeing Pete dive forward, roll, and shoot back over his shoulder, the pneumatic thuck of his pellet gun. I fired too, a higher, popping sound, blindly aiming into the brush just above the river, where the shot had come from.

Pete yelled and Everson and I looked over, frightened, but he wasn't hurt, just excited, pumping his gun and firing into the brush. "Come on, motherfuckers! Come on, Vietcong pussies!" Even through two shirts and a heavy coat my side hurt where I'd been shot, and I could feel a welt forming.

Everson and I pressed ourselves to the ground and fired over our heads as quickly as our single-shot BB pistols would allow us, pulling the trigger, then releasing the hammer and pushing it into place, firing again. Throwing the BBs would have been as effective. After a few minutes Pete slapped me on the shoulder, pointed with two fingers, ran his hand along his neck, gestured with his eyes, and ran away. Apparently our counterattack was beginning. I watched as he ran serpentine, bent at the waist until he disappeared into the brush along the river. We kept firing until we realized no one was shooting back. For a moment it was quiet.

Everson lay next to me, breathing as heavily as I must have been.

"Do we keep shooting, or what?" I asked.

He just shrugged. "It hurts," he said, and he lifted his sleeves to show me a purplish bruise on the inside of his forearm.

"Yeah," I said. We lay there on our stomachs, listening to the river.

Next to me, Everson fumbled in his coat pocket. I

figured he was going to produce a joint; Pete got mad at him now if he was ever without dope. Instead he pulled out my George Hendrick baseball card, which had been folded in half.

I just stared at him.

"Pete sold 'em to me."

"All of 'em?" I asked. I took the ruined card from him.

Everson nodded. "This morning. He came to my house and said I had to give him twenty bucks for all of 'em."

"Were they all like this?"

"Burned or crinkled up or folded like that. I'm sorry, man. He's an asshole."

From the brush along the river we heard a few pops and we tensed, then a voice from far off: "Where are you guys?" Everson and I both started. It sounded like Pete.

"Were we supposed to follow him?" I asked.

"I don't know," Everson said.

There were a few more pops from down near the river. "Come on, you pussies!"

My side ached where I'd been shot. I looked over my shoulder, wondering if we could just run home.

But Everson pulled his shield back down over his face, and I did the same. I swallowed and stood, and Everson and I began running toward the river, our footfalls sounding like air rifle shots. I spun my head from side to side trying to find Woodbridge and the seventh-grade goons he stood with at the bus stop, but there was no one.

"Come on, you pussies!" Pete yelled again. His voice was coming from a draw along the riverbank that Everson and I were approaching. I tried to picture Woodbridge and his guys down there in the draw, with Pete pinned down between them. I imagined Everson and me bursting into their camp—which looked in my mind like a machine gun nest from one of those black-and-white war movies my dad watched—and spraying Woodbridge's army with BB's. But in my mind it was Pete I would be shooting, firing over and over into his sinewy body, my baseball cards falling from his pockets.

When we reached the top of the draw, we could see what had happened. Pete was at the bottom of a short depression, pinned down by Woodbridge and his friends on the far end of the draw. From the lip of the draw, I could see Pete's back, as he pressed himself into the ground, and I could see Woodbridge's guys at the other end, their air guns now trained on Everson and me. There were three quick pops, like the first popcorn in an air popper, and on my left Everson yelled "Ow!" and fell. I watched him go down as something zipped past my head, but I kept running, my breath heavy behind the welding mask. Somehow none of the shots hit me, and I just kept running toward Pete, my air gun now trained on his back, my teeth clenched.

Woodbridge and his guys fired another volley, and I heard one of the shots ping off the welding shield. Finally I dipped into the depression where Pete was hiding, and they couldn't hit me anymore. I lifted the mask away from my face and stared down on Pete, who cowered there before me. I was amazed at how small he looked from this angle, realized for the first time, maybe, that Pete was just a kid like us, same skin and bones and lean muscle. I was five feet from him when he spun around suddenly, deep fear in his eyes, his pellet rifle pointed at my face.

It felt like someone hit me with a bottle or a baseball bat. My head snapped back and I dropped to the sand. I reached up to cover my face. Something warm and gooey mashed between my fingers. I wondered what could have been in the bottle that I'd been hit with. I tried to open my eyes, but there was a rush of pain and everything went a dark purple and that color was my pain for just a minute, so that I could see how badly this hurt and it was a pain that I could hear, too, a scream that came from deeper than my voice box, deeper than my lungs, and I was surprised to hear it sounded like my voice. I screamed until my air was all gone.

I could hear Pete's voice, too: "Oh fuck!"

I was rolling around on the ground, both hands covering my left eye. The world seemed to expand into this purple and then contract, all of the pain and blood and everything pulling back into the socket of my left eye.

I pried my right eye open and blearily looked up to see Pete running away, climbing the bank of the draw. He was pulling Everson with him.

"Wait," I said quietly, but they were gone.

There was no noise except the trickling river at my side. I began to cry. That brought more of the purplish pain, and I felt like throwing up. My hands were covered with blood now, and I pulled them away and the blood ran down my face and pooled in the sand. I put my hands back on my face, thinking maybe I could hold my eye in its socket. I lay there a few minutes, moaning and trying to figure out the sinewy things I felt against my fingers.

I stood and fell back into the sand, the pain seeking out new levels. I got back up and began walking. I made it a few steps and sat down in the sand again. I got to my knees and threw up. That's when I fell back in the sand, beaten. I couldn't do it. My first thought that wasn't pain was that they would name an award for me, as they had done with Woodbridge's dead brother. I hoped Ben would fare better without me than Woodbridge had without his older brother.

I lay back in the sand and cried, suddenly picturing my mother standing on our porch, wondering where I was. "Here I am!" I yelled, and the salty tears boiled in my mangled eye. Then I just started yelling and crying, scratching around in the sand, panicking, I guess. I don't know how long I yelled and cried but finally I felt a hand on my chest, patting me, reassuring me, and at first I thought it was my mom, but then I realized that Everson had come back. Of course he had.

"It's okay," Everson said.

I opened my right eye and stared into the black-rimmed glasses of Eli Boyle.

"It's okay," Eli said again. "I called for help." And he held my hand.

*The lady smiled; for the gallantries of a
one-eyed man are still gallantries.*
– Voltaire, *"The One-Eyed Porter"*

III

CRIMINALS ARE NOT EARLY RISERS

III

I | CAROLINE, GO HOME

"Caroline, go home." Her sergeant interrupts her midstream, although she wasn't getting any closer to explaining why she's let some loon waste the last five hours confessing, or how, at three o'clock Saturday morning, he's still at it, hunched over his second legal pad and his fourth cup of coffee, no end in sight.

"Just go home," her sergeant, Chris Spivey, says again from the other side of the phone. "Get your nut a bed somewhere. We'll roust him Monday morning and he can tell us all about how the aliens probed his ass." Spivey is the first sergeant she's worked for who is younger than she is; at first she found this merely disconcerting, but now he seems like any other boss, officious and rigid, and apparently none too thrilled about getting a phone call at three in the morning. "Caroline, I won't authorize overtime for this."

"I didn't call for overtime," she says. "But what if there's something here?"

"Lock him up. Commit him. Shoot him. I don't care. Just go home."

She sighs and looks back through the window at the Loon. He turns the legal pad over and begins writing on the back of the page, in a small and controlled cursive, the way she's seen delusional people write in the margins of phone books and on countertops. "Okay," she says into the phone.

"What's the matter with you, anyway?" he asks. "Where's your head these days?"

A fair question, that.

She's been checked out, barely functioning, coming to work and sitting at her desk, taking hours to fill out the simplest reports, forgetting phone numbers and names. It's no better at home, where she sits down on the couch and forgets to take off her coat, or sits at the kitchen table, or surfs the Internet until dawn, bidding on things she doesn't need in online auctions: parasols and turntable needles, laser printers and fishing lures. Two nights ago she played chess in a chat room. She hates chess.

Where's your head?

The last few months have felt like someone else's life: surprised at her own behavior, watching silently over her own shoulder, wondering when she started liking bourbon, why she doesn't shower on the weekends anymore, when she started playing chess. It's a symptom of depression, maybe, this feeling of detachment from oneself. Sometimes she retraces her steps, examines the last five months for the moment she began drifting—her mother's death, her boyfriend moving out, the retirement of her best friend and the man she quietly pined away for, her former sergeant, Alan Dupree.

But she came through all of those things. No, this started later, after Caroline interrupted a guy who was about to murder a young hooker—a whisper of a girl named Rae-Lynn Pierce. At some point it dawned on Caroline that in fifteen years as a police officer, this girl,

Rae-Lynn, was the only person she'd ever really *saved*. Maybe there were potential victims of criminals that she arrested, people whose lives were better off because of Caroline's actions, but those were abstractions, shadows. They were certainly not real people that she could point to and name. Rae-Lynn Pierce was real, and she was alive because of Caroline.

That's why, if she had to pick the moment when everything finally went to shit, when she lost focus and found herself dreaming of giving up, it would have to be the day three months ago when she heard that Rae-Lynn was dead, from an untreated case of hepatitis. Six weeks. That's how much time Caroline had given Rae-Lynn Pierce.

After that, Caroline began to lose interest. But it was more than a professional crisis; it was as if she had walked for fifteen years, only to find herself at the gorge of middle age, alone. She began to think of it as exactly that sort of transaction—fifteen years of her life for six weeks of an addict's fuck-ups. She fell asleep in meetings, stared out from her desk, let cases stagnate. Spivey moved her to nights, and her depression got worse, more isolated, darker.

And now this Loon, and she's being what . . . a psychiatrist? A confessor? Certainly not a cop. What did the Loon ask? Had she ever been responsible for someone's death? Maybe that's why she has let him sit in there for the last five hours, because she knows exactly how he feels, desperate to confess but uncertain what for.

She checks her watch. Ten minutes past three. She stalks across the office, unlocks the door to Interview Two, and steps inside.

"That's it," she says.

He looks up at her and smiles. "I'm finished, Caroline," he says, and she is deflated, as much by the smile and the way her name sounds as by the announcement she's been waiting for all night. His right eye is red, as if he's been crying again.

"Done?" She catches the whiff of letdown in her own voice.

The Loon flexes and unflexes the fingers on his right hand. "Well, not completely, no. But the preliminary part, the setup, you know—the key people. The hard part is done. The context and explanation." He pats the legal pad. "It's all here. All that's left is the details. The recent stuff."

Caroline doesn't quite know what to say. She sits across from him. "Look, I'm sorry, but I can't just sit here all weekend while you work through . . ." She flips the yellow pages of the legal pad. ". . . whatever you're working through here. I know this is important to you, but I'm not even supposed to be at work right now."

When he doesn't say anything, she keeps talking. "My sergeant said I've got to send you home. They won't even pay me for this. I'm supposed to be at home. Sleeping."

He just stares.

"See, this isn't how it works."

"I'm sorry, Caroline. I'll get right to it, now. I promise. Thirty minutes."

"No," she says. "You're going to just have to tell me what *all* this is about."

"I am," he says, and he pats the legal pad. "I am trying to tell you what *all* this is about." He pulls the patch away and rubs his left eye, but the movement is so fast she can't quite see what the patch is hiding. "It's in here. I'm coming clean."

"I think maybe you need a doctor."

"No," he says. "I'm not crazy. Please. You'll see. Just stay with me here a little bit longer. We've gone this far. Look, if you go home now, I might just drop the whole thing. I know I will. And no one will never know what happened."

He scratches his head and thick waves of hair fall forward, covering the strap to his eye patch for a moment, until he pulls his hand away and the hair falls back, more or less into place. "Please," he whispers. "Help me get this one thing right. I've made a mess of everything else, but this one thing . . . Please."

"I can't."

"Please."

"No."

"Please."

She looks around the room. "You have to give me something in return."

"Like what?"

"I don't know. A name."

"My name?"

"That'd be a start."

He thinks it over. "I can't. Not yet. You'll contact my friends and family and when this gets out . . ." He shakes his head.

"Then the victim. The person . . ." She thinks about the tentativeness of his phrasing earlier. "The person you . . . did this to."

He covers his mouth and lines form around his good eye.

"Look," Caroline says, "you should know that this is a complete violation of how I'm supposed to do my job." She's leery of admitting as much to him, but she keeps talking. "I'm trusting you here. I need to know this isn't bullshit."

"I'm afraid . . . it'll get away from me. I'm not ready. Not yet." He looks down at the legal pads in front of him. "Not until I'm done."

"I won't do anything with the name. I'll sit on it until you finish."

"You won't do anything?"

"No."

"I can trust you?"

"You can," she says without thinking about it.

He reaches out and takes her hand. His hand is big and warm and she lets her hand be enveloped; it's been a while. "Really?" he asks. "I can trust you?"

"Yes," she says, and it's true.

He lets go of her hand, sits back in his chair, and stares at her until she feels her own face drift away and he is staring at some point beyond her. "Pete," he says.

"Pete."

"Pete Decker. His name is Pete Decker. The man I . . . the man who . . ."

"Decker." She lets a moment pass, but he doesn't say any more. "Okay. Pete Decker. That wasn't so hard, was it?"

"No," he says. "It wasn't."

2 | THE TRUTH HURTS

The truth hurts only if you're comforted by lies. That's what Caroline has always believed. She doesn't spend much time deluding herself: believing there is a reason things happen, that Mr. Right will come along, that people will change. She wonders, Is this me—this unleavened cynicism—or is it the job? Could be the job. You have to be a realist to be a cop, otherwise, the shit you see . . . it blackens your heart.

After Rae-Lynn Pierce died, Caroline forgot that for a few days. She went around re-creating Rae-Lynn's last six weeks, hoping she'd find some meaning there. Maybe Rae-Lynn had saved some child's life. Or reconciled with her family. Six weeks. Forty-two days—six of them spent in drug rehab, before she walked away from that; the rest spent on the street, getting high and fucking strangers for money to get high. Her two-year-old daughter was taken away during those six weeks, and a few days later Rae-Lynn was arrested for soliciting. She spent the night in jail, and four days after that she was found dead, curled around a warm-water drainpipe in an alley behind a Thai restaurant.

No, it was better not to know. Otherwise you find your-self staring at people on the street, wondering when you might attend their deaths. She's tried to joke about it, slough it off, duck behind her old shield of cynicism, but she lacks the strength to hoist that defense, as if the weight of her old self is too much to bear.

Maybe that's why she's letting herself be drawn in now, because this Loon's case is still theoretical and clean, a totally hypothetical crime—the *idea* of homicide, the *idea* of confession, of contrition and punishment. Usually this job begins and ends with the corpse: its rigor and stench, hypostatic pools, smallness of an unanimated body. But with no body . . .

D-E-C-K-E-R, P-E-T-E. She types the letters into the computer to check against local and national crime databases. It occurred to her that the Loon might be lying as soon as he gave her the name, but she could also see that the name Pete Decker wasn't random, that it had meaning, and she could see the Loon was giving her *something,* and that's all she wanted, she sees now, some excuse to keep listening, to allow the Loon to keep writing. Or maybe to keep from going home. Maybe he could've given her any name and she would've left satisfied that she wasn't being taken in by this guy, that she wasn't being seduced by his line of confession and trust, by the misery in his right eye and the mystery of his left. She wonders for a moment if the Loon's name might not be Pete Decker, but she doesn't think so. He didn't say it that way, not the way you'd say your own name, but like a name that had been in your head for some time, one that you didn't say aloud very often. Like an incantation or a name chanted at a séance. Like someone you've killed.

On her computer screen, Peter Ralph Decker's Greatest Hits scroll down in front of her: petty theft; auto theft; battery; second robbery; a whole range of assaults—third, second, and first, employing everything from his fists to a roofer's nail gun; two DUI's, two possessions—one with intent to deliver; four probation violations; two noncompliance findings, and a couple of protection orders. And that's just as an adult. He has a nine-count juvenile record that she doesn't even bother with. By her count, he's spent fourteen of the last nineteen years in some kind of correctional facility.

She checks to see if Pete Decker is in the can even now. He's not. In fact, he's just finished his longest stretch—four years on the possession with intent to deliver. She reads the details. Stupid bastard had only been out of prison for two months when the cops stopped his car and found almost a half-kilo of coke in the backseat. Claimed he "found" the drugs outside his apartment. Hard to imagine how that story didn't fly.

Caroline writes down the address that Pete has on file with his probation officer. She finds herself hoping that Pete Decker *is* the victim in this case. A decent lawyer might manage a case for justifiable homicide or self-defense by doing nothing more than presenting Pete Decker's long record in court. There could even be scenarios in which her Loon was protecting himself, or maybe protecting other people, from the impending violence of this drug dealer Pete Decker.

She jots down Decker's last known and sends the report to the printer. At her desk she grabs another blank legal pad, and continues on to the interview room. She unlocks the door and sticks her head in. The Loon is still bent over the legal pad, mouthing words as he writes them. He looks up, already in midapology.

"I'm sorry, Caroline. I know this is taking too long, but I'm really . . ."

She tosses the new legal pad before he can finish the sentence.

He catches the pad and smiles. "Thanks," he says. "I'm getting close. Really."

"It's almost six," Caroline tells him. "I'm gonna go out for some breakfast. You want something?"

"Some more coffee would be great. Maybe a cinnamon roll." He rubs his mouth. "I . . . uh . . . I wanted to tell you . . ."

Caroline steps inside and waits.

He looks embarrassed. "That name I gave you?"

"Pete Decker?"

"Right. That's not it. That's not the person . . ."

"So who is he?"

"Nobody," the Loon says. He's lying. "I just wanted to give you a name. I need to get through this and then I'll tell you everything . . . I promise. You have to believe me."

"You want black coffee again?"

"Sure. Thank you."

"I'm going to have someone from patrol check in on you. And . . . I'm gonna need your belt and your shoes."

"My belt and my shoes?"

"I can't leave you in here with anything you might use . . ."

"Use for what?" She doesn't answer, and it takes a few seconds to register on his face. "You think I'm going to hang myself." He makes it sound like a decent idea.

She just holds out her hand. He removes his belt and shoes and slides them across the table. She looks at the shoes but sees no blood on them. When she looks up he is smiling and she sees it again, that nagging familiarity.

"Are you sure we haven't met?" she asks.

"I'm sure."

"You just . . . seem familiar."

"Trust me," he says. "I would remember meeting you."

She is embarrassed and slightly confused by how good this makes her feel.

"My name is Clark." He says it with great meaning, perhaps as amends for giving her a phony name for the victim earlier. She has been thinking of him as the Loon, as her Loon, for so long, she has to repeat the name to herself. Clark sticks out his hand and she shakes it. Although Clark isn't the name that seemed to be on the tip of her tongue, she sees right away that he's telling the truth and she decides she's been mistaking him for someone else, that he just has one of those faces.

"Nice to meet you, Clark."

"I wish it were under different circumstances," he says.

She thinks, not half as much as I do.

3 | PETE DECKER'S APARTMENT

Pete Decker's apartment is on the fourth floor of a seedy building that Caroline knows only because it's across the street from the coffee shop where she and some of the other detectives used to go in the mornings for tea. It is a squat, squalid building at the end of downtown, an old railroad hotel remodeled into flop apartments that house more than their share of criminals and addicts, people in the throes of recovery and teen pregnancy and AIDS, the chronically troubled and luckless. She parks in front of the building and opens the door, climbs the stairs three levels and finds herself in a dark, dank hallway, lit by a single bulb. There are six doors on the fourth floor, profanities scratched into the wood. She reads the graffiti and finds that Tina gives good head, that Joe B. is a motherfucker. None of the doors has a number or a letter. Caroline looks down at her notebook. Pete Decker lives in 4B. It could be any of the six. She checks her watch. Not quite 7:00 A.M. She doesn't have to worry about Pete—if he's even here—skipping out in the morning. As a group, criminals are not early risers.

She leaves the building, happy for the fresh air, crosses three lanes of theoretical traffic, and opens a door into the warm smell of her old coffee shop. She stopped coming in after the barrista—a young bundle of stomach muscles and dreadlocks everyone calls Goose—asked her out one morning.

She walks across the dark floor and smiles at two of the coffee shop regulars, a youngish father and his round, blond, agreeable son, who is torturing a cinnamon roll for information.

"Hey," says the father, who hasn't bothered to learn her name, as she hasn't bothered to learn his; the beauty of coffee shop culture is its sustained surface cordiality, like an office without that irritating work.

"Hey," she says back.

"Haven't seen you here in a while."

"No," she says, and continues to the counter. Luckily, Goose isn't working; the pierced girl behind the counter gives her a warm smile.

"Can I get a twenty-ounce chai tea?" Caroline asks.

"Certainly," the pierced girl says, and the snappiness of this exchange, this entire morning, makes her feel as if something has changed. This is what her life felt like before—normal exchanges with people one step removed from strangers: driving, walking, talking, sitting in a dark coffee shop and indulging in a cup of tea.

She picks out a day-old pastry, pays, and sits at the window, watching Pete Decker's apartment building. No one comes or goes, and she thinks maybe she's missed something—misread his record and the down-and-out address. Ah, but it's early for heavy drug traffic anyway. She's a little groggy, having stayed up all night while Clark the Loon worked on his opus. The tea warms her throat.

She watches the fourth-floor windows, but no lights come on. Just then a car, an old beat-up Honda Civic, pulls up to the curb in front of the building. Caroline grabs her tea and stands.

"See you," says the father as he wipes frosting from his boy's mouth.

"Okay," says Caroline, and she pulls on her gloves and leaves the coffee shop. She jogs across the street just as a young woman steps out of the car. From first glance Caroline sees that the woman is a meth addict, one of those forty-year-old twenty-year-olds that the drug produces, eyes red and deep-socketed, skin sallow and puckered.

The girl sees her coming and her fried nerves go off scattershot; her arm cocks and her lip twitches. "What? What?"

"You live here?" Caroline is friendly, firm, and holds out her badge. "In this building?"

"I didn't do nothing."

"I'm sure you didn't. It's okay. I need to talk to your neighbor."

"Who?"

"Pete."

The girl answers reflexively. "Don't know him."

"Sure you do," Caroline says. "Look, I just need to see if he's okay. Have you seen him in the last few days?"

"No," she says. "Something happen to Pete?"

"I don't know yet."

The girl thinks about it for a moment and relaxes. "I wouldn't mind if somebody finally killed that fucker. He steals everything."

"Will you show me his door? I won't tell him that you did."

The girl shrugs again. "If he ain't dead, I wouldn't

want to be the one to wake him up. He got a fuckin' temper, him."

"Oh, I'll be gentle," Caroline says. She follows the girl back up the stairs, into the fourth-floor landing. The girl points at a door and nods solemnly. Caroline nods back and hands the girl her tea, then waits for her to make her way quietly down the stairs.

When she hears the girl's door ease closed two floors below, Caroline smells around the door. It stinks, but she isn't sure if it's *that* stink. Caroline puts her ear to the door. Nothing. She knocks on the door to Pete Decker's apartment. She rests one hand on the nine-millimeter in her shoulder harness, and with the other reaches for the door-knob. She is surprised when the knob turns and the door opens, and she finds herself staring at an even younger girl, about sixteen, wearing nothing but a flannel shirt.

"Hi," the girl says cheerily.

"Don't answer the fuckin' door," says someone, presumably Pete, who is also presumably alive, in a tangle of blankets on a mattress on the floor. Caroline steps in, past the girl. The apartment consists of this one room, about twelve feet by twelve feet, nothing inside but the mattress and a new thirty-two-inch color television across from it. The walls are chipped and covered with shit and there are bags of chips and cookies all over. There are six people along the walls of the room, boys and girls, teenagers, and they all have the blank eyes and cat-box smell of heavy meth users.

She recognizes Pete from his mug shot. Alone on the mattress, he sits up, pissed off and bare chested. "What the fuck time is it?" Pete stands and he is naked, as skinny as the teenagers in the room—a bantam rooster, hard and small. Quarter-size bruises cover his body. "Don't answer the fuckin' door unless I tell you to!" Pete yells again, and he shoves the sixteen-year-old girl, who looks like an empty flannel shirt as she flies across the room.

Caroline steps toward him, inside the range of his fists. She grabs him by the throat just as he swings at her. She deflects most of the punch, and catches the rest in the neck; she is taller than he expected, and not as easy to move. This is a guy used to hitting down at his women. Caroline gathers herself, tightens her grip on his neck and swings her knee up into his balls. He grunts and slumps, and she pushes him back down on the mattress. He rolls over onto his side, moaning.

"You must be Pete," Caroline says, and shows her badge. She picks up Pete's jeans, feels in them for a weapon, and comes away with a long pocket-knife that she slides into her own pocket.

"Anybody in here eighteen?" she asks the owl-eyed teenagers. "Yeah, I didn't think so. You've all got twenty seconds to get your clothes and get out of here. And if I ever see any of you in here again, you're going to jail."

As Caroline continues to look for weapons, the teenagers scramble into their shirts and shoes, grab their bags of Doritos, and hurry out the door. Only the flannel girl is left. She pulls on a pair of pants and wipes her bloody lip with a white T-shirt. "Where do I go?"

"You his girlfriend?"

"Yeah."

"How old?"

The girl considers lying. "I'm sixteen," she says finally.

Caroline gives her two dollars. "Go to the coffee shop across the street and get yourself a cup of hot chocolate.

I'll be over in a minute." The girl leaves and Caroline turns back to Pete, who makes no move to cover himself or his sore testicles.

"Bitch."

I could shoot him, Caroline thinks, and she immediately thinks about investigating her own crime: the trail of witnesses, the barrista, the teenagers, the father with the blond son, the girl who showed Caroline the door; Caroline's handprint on Pete's neck, the police slug in his chest. Maybe she'd confess, ask for three legal pads and some coffee and sit down next to Clark the Loon, drawing a line between all the events in her life and this one crime.

"Pete," she says, "you should get some friends your own age."

"Fuck you."

"You're a lucky man, Pete. I'm not gonna arrest you today."

Finally he pulls the dirty blanket over himself. Caroline walks to the window and looks down on the street. She sees the young flannel girl cross the street, swing around a parking meter, and go into the coffee shop. Caroline turns back to Pete.

"I need some information about a guy named Clark. You know him?"

"No."

Pete Decker is used to having cops ask if he knows someone. "Come on. Think. Clark something. About my age. Mid to late thirties. Dark hair. Good looking. Little over six feet tall. Has an eye patch."

With that last bit of information, Pete Decker sits up in bed and smiles. "Clark? No way. How is he?"

"He's okay. So you do know him?"

"Sure, we was like . . . best friends when we were kids. You know, little kids. Rode bikes and shit. Before—" He doesn't say before what.

"You know his last name?" she asks.

"Clark? Oh, fuck. Sure. You know. Clark . . . uh . . . starts with an M. I used to know it. You know, when we were kids. So how is Clark, man? Still the same?"

Not knowing what he was like before, Caroline isn't sure how to answer.

"Man, I haven't seen Clark in . . . fuck, years."

"You don't keep in touch with him?"

"Clark? Nah, man." He looks around the one-room apartment. "Yeah, I don't keep in touch with too many people from the old neighborhood, you know."

"Clark have a beef with anyone, someone he might have wanted to hurt?"

"Clark? Nah," he says. "No, everybody liked Clark. He's funny. Smart as shit too. Get all A's and shit. I used to tell him, 'Clark, don't worry about your ol' buddy Pete. You go make something of yourself. Ol' Pete, he'll be fine.' You know why? I used to kind of protect him from bullies 'n' shit. We was tight."

Pete sits up in bed. "Yeah, Clark, he was the kind of guy you always knew would be okay. Played sports and banged all them cheerleaders, even with . . ." He raises his hand absentmindedly to his own left eye. ". . . You know, the accident and shit."

"Yeah, his eye. How'd that happen?"

"Oh." Pete looks around nervously, as if he's wondering about the statute of limitations. "Some kind of accident. You know. Kids."

"When did you see Clark last?"

"Huh." Pete thinks. It does not appear to be his strong suit. "Oh. Probably 1979. Yeah. Probably then."

Caroline nods. She's not sure whether to be upset that this has turned out to be nothing, or glad that Clark whose-last-name-starts-with-an-M the Loon told the truth when he said Pete Decker was nobody.

"Okay, Pete," she says, and she crouches in front of him. "In just the last ten minutes, you've committed six felonies. I'm gonna give you a break, but I need you to do some things for me. Four things. Can you do four things for me, Pete?"

"Sure." He sits up, all sunken cheeks and vacant eyes, and she knows he will do nothing, that twenty minutes after she leaves, the teenagers will be back and they will all be smoking crystal and watching Pete's stolen TV. "Anything," he says.

She pulls out her notebook and writes, *1. GIRL.* "That girl," she says. "The one you hit. Never see her again. You understand? Send her home to her parents."

"Yeah," he says.

2. TV, she writes. "This morning, you take this TV back where you stole it from."

"Okay," he says.

"Monday morning, you go to your probation officer and tell him that you're using again and you need to get into treatment." She writes, *3. Treatment.*

"Good," he says, "I've been thinking that I need some help to . . ."

She doesn't bother listening.

"And number four. You avoid me. Because if you don't do all four of these things—and we both know you won't—then I'm gonna shoot you in your fucking head. Do you understand?" She writes, *4. Me.*

"Yeah," he says.

Caroline rips the page from her notebook, tosses it on the bed, straightens up, and starts for the door.

"Hey." Pete has pulled the blanket up to his neck, suddenly modest. "Will you tell Clark I said hi?"

She's a little unsure what to make of this. "Sure," she says.

"And tell him that if I could, I would've voted for him last time."

And that, of course, is when it hits her. She stops cold at the door to Pete Decker's apartment and closes her eyes. She did vote for him.

4 | CLARK ANTHONY MASON

Clark Anthony Mason works over the third legal pad just as he did the first two, almost in a state of self-hypnosis. Caroline watches him with a new kind of fascination. Tony Mason. No shit. He chews the end of his pen and takes a sip of the coffee she gave him. She didn't say anything when she got back from Pete's, just handed him the coffee and went to write an intelligence report encouraging the drug detectives to go back and visit Pete Decker. She looks in the window of Interview Two. So that's Tony Mason. Now it's obvious: the solid good looks, the weird diction, the politician's bearing. Before, she couldn't see past the dirty clothes, the long hair, and especially the eye patch. She kept running the current version of the Loon through her memory (Who do I know with an eye patch?) rather than trying to picture him without it.

Caroline checks her watch. It's going on nine o'clock Saturday morning. He's been at this almost twelve hours. She walks back to her desk and flips through her Rolodex until she finds the number of a newspaper reporter she nearly dated before remembering that she hates newspaper reporters. She taps out the number and Evan O'Neal answers on the second ring.

"Evan. It's Caroline Mabry. I'm sorry to bother you at home."

"How you been, Caroline?" Evan covered cops back when she was on patrol, but now he's a government reporter.

"Good. I need to run a name past you: Tony Mason."

"The kid who ran against Nethercutt?" Kid. Only in politics does someone in his thirties qualify as a kid. But in truth he *had* seemed like a kid, standing at the opposite podium against the gray-haired four-term Republican, looking as though, if elected to the House of Representatives, he would act immediately to change the mascot and make Homecoming a formal dance.

"Yeah, that Tony Mason."

"No shit? You seeing him now, Caroline?"

Funny that a cop would call a reporter and the reporter would assume that it was about romance. She's not sure if that says something about her, or Evan, or Tony Mason. She looks up, through the small window of the interview room. "Yeah, as a matter of fact, I am seeing him," she says.

"You get fixed up?"

"Something like that."

Evan is quiet for a moment.

"What is it?" Caroline asks.

"It's just . . . I don't know . . . you can do better."

"Yeah," she says. "I'm starting to think that. What do you know about him?"

"Mason? Just that he got thirty-six percent and that was twice as much as anyone expected from such a lamb."

"Lamb?"

"Yeah." Evan shifts the phone. "Nethercutt owns the

seat, just like Foley did before him, so the Democrats have to pick their spots, only take a big run every six years or so. The rest of the time, they just throw lambs to slaughter—an old labor tough or a cute young lawyer like Tony Mason. Some political outsider who gets outspent five-to-one and goes home disillusioned and broke."

Caroline writes down the word "lawyer." She's beginning to recall details of the election now, and she wonders if her lax memory has to do with her job, or the funk she's been in, or if the loser in any election just naturally fades from memory that quickly—the Dukakis syndrome. "Wasn't he rich?"

"Mason? Yeah," Evan says. "Cashed out some tech stock and spent all his money trying to get elected. That's the only reason he even got thirty-six percent."

"Do you have a list of his donations?"

"I got his filings at the office. Sure."

"Fax it to me?"

"Monday?"

"Today?"

"It's Saturday, Caroline."

"I know. But you owe me." She gave Evan a tip once about a former police chief who drove around drunk at night, pulling over teenage girls and "frisking" them.

"Okay," Evan says. "But remind me to never go out with a cop."

"Why?"

"I'm just not sure I could pass the background check."

She ignores this. "So does he sometimes go by the name Clark?"

"That's his real name. Clark Anthony Mason. He didn't think the Maxwell House Dems would vote for someone

III

with two last names. And he thought Anthony sounded too professorial or blue blood or something. If you can imagine some kid from the Valley worrying about being too blue blood."

Evan laughs as he remembers. "Boy, that's classic lamb behavior, worrying about the menu while the restaurant burns down."

"What do you mean?" Caroline asked.

"It's just . . . here's this kid, doesn't look twenty-five years old, all stiff and square, grows up in the Valley and goes off to Seattle, comes home thinking they're just going to hand him a congressional seat. And . . . Jesus, that eye."

"Yeah, he wears an eye patch," she says. "I don't remember that from the election."

"No, he wore one of those glass eyes, didn't move at all. You got the feeling he sat in front of the mirror until he figured which angle the eye looked straight and not cockeyed. That was the only way he'd face people, straight on, without moving his eye. On his posters, he was always staring right at you. It was a little creepy, especially in the debates. Guy moved like a robot."

Caroline had just assumed he was stiff and liked that about him, that he didn't seem polished. But mostly she voted for him because he was for gun control and Nethercutt wasn't. Over time she'd become a one-issue voter. "I was trying to remember what exactly he ran on . . ."

"Oh, the usual economic development crap; he was gonna bring high-tech jobs here. 'Course, back then, you couldn't run for dogcatcher without promising you'd bring computer jobs to Spokane. I have to admit, your boy really sold it, though."

"So how did Nethercutt beat him?"

"Mostly by ignoring him. Let the PACs and the issue people run the negative shit: that he was a flaming liberal, that he burned flags and liked Internet porn. And of course there was the Seattle thing."

She vaguely remembers television ads that had knocked Mason for going to college and working in Seattle, ads that accused him of being in the pocket of liberal Seattle power brokers.

"Yeah, that provincial shit is the gold standard in Spokane," Evan says. "We don't trust anyone who *doesn't* live here and we assume anyone who *does* live here is stupid."

"You know what he's done since the election?" Caroline asks, and she thinks, I know what he's doing. He's sitting in my interview room, writing his memoirs.

"No idea."

"But he's not still involved in politics?" she asks.

"Mason? Nah. Lambs never run a second time. They go back to their insurance offices, or their teaching jobs at the community college." Evan clears his throat. "So, are you gonna keep going out with the guy?"

"I don't know," Caroline says. She looks up in the window again and sees that Clark is still writing, that his face is shot with hard memories, with misgiving and regret. She leans forward and watches closely. And watching him like this she knows there is a body somewhere. *Tell me, Clark. Who did you kill?*

Caroline sits back. "Yeah, you're probably right," she says to Evan on the phone. "I can do better."

. . . remember this plain distinction . . .
your conscience is not a law.
– Laurence Sterne, *Tristram Shandy*

IV

Statement of Fact

I | NOBODY EMERGES WHOLE

Nobody emerges whole from childhood. I know this. And I don't pretend to think that the shattering of my left eye that day on the south bank of the Spokane River was in some way unique or was an unfair burden, that it put my suffering on a par with the suffering of someone like Eli Boyle. Truth is, I have got along fine with one eye. I can't say that it was a help in my run for the Fifth District congressional seat, or that I would knowingly choose the patches and glass eyes and dark sunglasses that I have worn since childhood, or that I have gone more than a day without shifting my gaze to the floor in the presence of the binocular, ever conscious of the fact that I am incapable of that most basic human communication—looking deep and straight in someone's eyes.

But except for the external nature of my scars, I don't imagine myself different from any other adult, limping and scuffling and scurrying along with all manner of insecurities and fears and defects, the results of bad parentage and low self-esteem, of being unprepared and unprotected in a world that seems on its surface so inviting and safe. The world is not safe. I need only continue the story of Eli Boyle's life to prove that.

But I am afraid I won't be able to offer a full accounting

of Eli's indignities, for instance during our junior high years—the classroom-clearing farts, the daily capture and rolling of boogers between his fingers, the untold humiliations dreamed up by his classmates. There is simply not time.

So, Detective, in the event that I am unable to finish this statement, this story of Eli's life and death, which is also in some small way, I realize, the story of my own life and death (and the string of failures that connects them), then at least I can offer some proof of fidelity to you, to this arrangement you have made with me, to the comfort and understanding of your two eyes.

To you, Caroline, I offer this:

I did it.

I killed Eli Boyle.

If such a statement is all the court wants, then I am happy to no longer be an officer of that temple of disasters. And if such a confession is all that is required for deeper forgiveness, well . . . I don't look forward to the lines in heaven.

I took my friend's life, metaphorically and unintentionally when we were young, and then, two days ago, I ended it literally and with malice. And forever. And yet that is not the only crime I have to confess, and it is certainly not the most heinous, and if you think Eli Boyle is the only victim of my greed and anger, then you underestimate the heart's potential for darkness.

You told me this process usually begins with a body.

You may find Eli's at a house at the west end of Cliff Drive, not in the main house, empty and cold, with its Gatsby staircase and deco chandeliers, but in the small, dank apartment above the garage out back. He is lying on the floor, in a lake of his own blood. He is on his left side, with his left arm behind him and his right against his head, as if something important has just occurred to him. There is a long black hole in his head, from his jaw to his scalp. I put the hole there.

I will forever be haunted by the look on his face in the moments before the horrible event played itself out. I saw that look once before, a look of surrender, of disbelief, a look that asks how life can keep getting *worse*—a look I first saw on Eli Boyle's face twenty years ago, during a moment that now seems like the first step toward his death, the first blow.

We were in high school. (I skip the horror of junior high with the request that you pause a moment to calculate your own adolescent social pain, multiply it by a thousand, and figure that you are still well short of Eli Boyle's.)

We arrived the way every kid has ever arrived in high school, taller but no smarter than our elementary selves, swimming in self-consciousness, wishing at once to be universally loved and left alone. I had been fitted for my first glass eye, and hated the way it sat unmoving and creepy in its drooped socket, staring straight ahead while my other eye bounded like a puppy from corner to corner of my skull. I will share a few of my old nicknames, skipping over such obvious names as Cyclops and Patch and Cap'n Hook, names insulting only in their lack of imagination. My favorite—Dead Eye—worked on two levels, in that case to describe both my injury and my free-throw shooting accuracy in basketball. I appreciated Ol' One Ball for its suggestiveness, McGoo for its canny reference to the old goggle-eyed cartoon character, Eye-nstein for its nod to my high grade point average, Glass for its jazzy simplicity, Lefty for its ironic coolness, and Lighthouse for its clean imagery.

As I said, I smoked pot nearly every day in junior high school, but then quit suddenly before my sophomore year of high school. Two things happened that summer: My former friend and supplier Everson moved to Sacramento, and I woke up one morning six feet tall and 175 pounds. With the sudden physical change I decided, the way teenagers decide, that from that moment on I wasn't who I had been. I was now an athlete, in spite of the lung damage caused by three years of pot smoking and the even more daunting disadvantage that I couldn't see a thing out of the left side of my head.

Most coaches, it turns out, will make room for the early-developed on the offensive and defensive lines in football and on the bench in basketball, so I managed to make teams and even start a few games and figure in their outcomes. But I doubt that I distinguished myself in anyone's memory of those games—except once. That moment took place during my senior year, against our hated basketball rival in their packed, raucous gym, when the player ahead of me fouled out early in the fourth quarter and the coach sent me in to kill time, hoping that I would do nothing to ruin our chances.

I didn't. Instead I had my best game ever in those six minutes of that fourth quarter, pulling down a couple of rebounds, hitting a jump shot and two free throws, until we had managed to tie the score with about a minute left, at which point our team got a steal and we began to run up the court for a three-on-one fast break. I had duly filled the left wing and was sprinting toward our basket, looking to the point guard in the center of the court, playing out all sorts of athletic fantasies in my mind, when I strayed slightly out of bounds, bearing down on a cheerleader for the opposing team who was just then kicking up one leg on my vast blindside. There was a gasp and a clap of thunder. I hit her square, with the whole left side of my body. They found her three rows deep, unconscious and bleeding from her nose. The referees blew their whistles and met at center court to see if I could be whistled for a foul for killing a cheerleader. The game stopped, the fans threw programs and Coke cans, and the coach pulled me out for my own safety. We lost by six points. The poor cheerleader, I found out from the newspaper story, had a broken collarbone. And I never scored another point in basketball. That experience, with its long rise and sudden fall, as much as I can trace it, describes the arc of my high school life.

For Eli high school was by no means perfect but was at least bearable, a drastic improvement on the earlier grades. He spent four periods in regular classes and two periods a day in special ed, and he began to outgrow a few of his afflictions, leaving his leg braces and corrective shoes behind. As we got older most of the bullies and dickheads dropped out or were arrested or they spent their days so stoned that they couldn't muster much antagonism, even toward a shit magnet like Eli Boyle. We eventually caught Matt Woodbridge in eighth grade, and left him there when we moved on to ninth. For all I know he's still in eighth grade, forty years old, firing spitwads, looking up "fornication" in the library dictionary, and demanding to fight some kid at lunch. Pete Decker turned out to be too small and skinny to be an effective bully once the rest of us hit puberty. He and I never spoke about what he did to my eye. In fact, we rarely saw each other after that except for the few occasions I saw him walking in the neighborhood and found myself amazed at how small he'd become. He'd ask about some sport I was playing, or which girl I was going out with, and then we'd go our separate ways. He became less and less real to me, and I can't even say that I hated him. It was more like I stopped believing in him. I never had any sort of confrontation with Pete; none of the kids he terrorized ever came back to wreak Hollywood vengeance. Pete just stopped coming to school and eventually faded away, into the big willow tree, into the bad dreams of children.

With the slow extinction of our classic bullies, Eli's torture in high school came from a less dangerous but far more insidious place: the culture of boys and girls and make-out parties, of dances and football games, of going out and going steady and going all the way, of the complex system of bases—first and second and third—a world ruled by sex in which few of the inhabitants were actually having it, but all of us were always daydreaming and working toward it, hoping that something we did or said would lead us to a beanbag chair with a girl in it beneath a black light, fumbling around, hands down tight pants, desperately trying to figure out what to do with the stuff we found in there.

Eli, obviously, was not getting much *stuff*.

On his best days in tenth and eleventh grade, he was invisible—ignored or tolerated, safely in place at the bottom of this hierarchy. On his worst days he slipped on ice and his books flew across the lawn, or he sneezed and covered his desk in snot, or he wore a black coat that was two-toned by his abiding dandruff. He had been the target of our mockery for so long that by this time the whole thing was starting to feel like nostalgia, and even with his slow improvement a true Eli moment could still be counted on to elicit waves of laughter.

But not from me.

He had saved my life. So as quietly as I could—my own social status being constructed of such fragile material —I helped Eli. I picked up his books and offered him a Kleenex. I wiped the flakes from his coat. I sort of became his sponsor in those days, and if we both understood that a kid like Eli needed a sponsor to live among the athletes and clean complexioned, we were also careful to adhere to the rules of such a relationship and the rigid caste system that meant we didn't talk much at school.

Did I feel my own stock rising during this time? I can't say. I knew I was striving for that thing we called popularity, and I doubt there was a more aggressive and eager-to-please teenager than me. I sought out the best parties and most popular girls and joined and followed and dressed and hung out and made out as if my life depended on it, as if redemption lay in becoming homecoming king. I joined every club and ran for office in every club I joined. I've heard (secondhand, actually, from a mental-health professional by way of my angry ex-wife) that my desire to belong comes from a deep sense of personal fraud—the feeling that I don't fit in—a situation I fought by joining more groups that I didn't fit, thus increasing my feelings of fraud and pushing me to join more groups, causing more fraud, and on and on until I found myself president of both the French and Spanish clubs, without speaking a word of either.

In the same way, I dated dozens of girls, not really

because I liked them, but just to see if they actually would date me. I ascended a sort of social ladder, finding that if Anita Wallace would go out with me, then it was okay for Sheila Kerns and then Wendy Bellig, and as long as I didn't try to skip too many steps, it was only a matter of time before the Amanda Rankins of the world parted their pom-poms for me.

My tireless pandering and joining and self-promotion may have prepared me for my later political life, but it didn't allow much room for Eli or anyone else during high school. And yet the distance between us wasn't entirely my doing. We didn't have a single class together in high school until the beginning of our senior year, when we ended up, implausibly, in the same physical education class, during the last period of the day. It was an experiment in what was then called mainstreaming, working developmentally disabled and other special education students into "normal" classes with their "normal" peers in the slim hope they would someday pass for "normal." And so every day the loopy and infirm and blind and drooling made their way from what was euphemistically called the Resource Room to the gymnasium, because some administrator had decided their usual daily humiliation wasn't enough, and they would be well served to have footballs bounce off their faces, have golf clubs sail out of their hands, crack one another in the shins with floor hockey sticks, while the "normal" kids stood back and laughed.

I still see the terror on Eli's face that first day in class, the terror on all their faces, nine boys who'd been pushed aside and discounted and beaten up and ignored and loathed for as long as they could remember. There were fifty of us senior boys and nine of these special cases, each suffering from some manner of retardation or dwarfism or water on the brain or who knew what else—what afflictions and defects might have caused those lax mouths and blank stares. Eli existed as sort of a bridge between the two worlds. Most of his classes he took with us, but since he was in the Resource Room two periods a day, he was still, undeniably, one of them.

They dressed silently in a separate corner of the locker room, eyes on the floor. A few of my classmates lobbed insults, feeling them out, but it was halfhearted. We all emerged into the gym in the same gray sweat shorts and shirts, us joking and laughing, them staring at the ground. "Pencil! Pencil! No no no!" yelled the kid we called Repeat, who may have had a form of Tourette's before it was called that. "Go home go home go home! Please please!" he screamed as we lined up in front of the first-year PE teacher, a guy in his twenties named Mr. Leggett, who had one of those throbbing veins in his forehead and who looked on his new charges with deeper disdain than any of us felt.

"Gentlemen," he said, "looks like we're gonna have to play a lot of dodgeball."

And we did play dodgeball, or rather an even lower-skill variation called battle ball, in which two teams stood on either side of the gym, against the walls, and simply pelted each other with hard rubber balls. The rules were simple and barbaric: You threw a ball at the other team, and if you hit someone, that person was out of the game and his team had one less member. If you somehow caught a ball thrown at you, then one of the people on your team who had been put out earlier got to come back in. You threw balls at each other until one team was wiped out completely.

We had enough kids for six teams of ten. Mr. Leggett picked five "normal" kids to be captains, and then one of the special ed kids, a stuttering overweight mess of a boy named Hank. The captains picked their teams. Hank picked me first—"Cl-Cl-Cl-Clark." When Hank's second pick came around my friend Tommy Kane from the basketball team was still available and I pointed at Tommy, but Hank picked his own classmate, Louis the dwarf, instead. Then he picked Curty the blind kid, who may have been—my apologies to the other guys in the class—the worst battle ball player in the history of that cruel game. When his next pick came around, Hank took Repeat, and as we stood in the gym I did the math and realized that our team of ten was going to be me and the nine misfits. Eli was the last one taken, and he shuffled over to where our team was wheezing and muttering and smelling and he shrugged at me as if he were sorry that I had to be drawn into his nightmare.

My friends in the class doubled over in laughter to see me on the SpEd team. It could have been my friendship with Eli that got me on with the Special Eddies, or the fact that I was a class officer and therefore well known and approachable to everyone, but more likely it was the fact of my glass eye, which must have seemed familiar to them. I wonder, as a member of the football and basketball teams, as a guy who dated the occasional cheerleader and got A's, but also someone with a prosthetic eye, if I might not have seemed like something they could aspire to: one of *them* made good.

We divided the gym in half and the teams spread out and began drilling each other with these hard rubber balls. The first game my team lost in four minutes, all nine of my teammates thrown out on the first try, their palsied legs knocked out from under them, their thick glasses knocked off. I let a soft throw hit me in the foot and we were done. Mr. Leggett called us girls.

By the very next game I noticed something odd: even though we were getting killed, Eli loved this game. His face reddened as he concentrated, trying to dodge the balls—he rarely did—but while battle ball was a nightmare for most of the SpEds, it seemed to engage his imagination, like the tug-of-war game from elementary school, and the tanks he drew. It wasn't long before Eli was the best of the infirm and slow.

Even with Eli's improvement we played battle ball all week, and I doubt there was a more complete rout of a squad than ours in the history of war or physical education class. Pop, pop, pop. The balls would slap against the pale skin of the SpEds, and they would trudge over to the side to examine their welts. The real skill in the game wasn't hitting another player with a ball, but catching one of the other team's throws. No one on my team ever caught a ball to allow a teammate back into the game, and in the end there would always be ten grinning, bloodlusting high school kids against me. I'd jump and fall and sidestep until finally I was hit too.

Eli got progressively better, as good as his crooked legs and scoliotic back and twitchy arms would allow, and by week's end he and I stood side by side against the wall, while the rest of our team compared bruises on the sideline.

The worst and most realistic aspect of battle ball was that once your side began to lose, it was nearly impossible to come back. The other side would fling the balls, and if you didn't catch one, they'd bounce off the wall directly behind you and come back to their team, so you not only had fewer men, but your diminished ranks were without ammunition, and you spent the whole time dodging until you inevitably tried to catch a ball and were put out. That was the situation Eli and I faced. All ten balls were on the other side, where all ten of their players were still alive, shifting and stalking in their gray PE shorts and shirts. Their leader was the lanky pitcher on our baseball team, Erskine Davies, the Rommel of battle ball. He paced behind the lines of his team, staring at Eli and me, trying to figure how to get us out while inflicting the most pain and humiliation.

"Chili! Chili! Chili! Corn bread and carrots! Sunrise Jell-O!" yelled Repeat, who, when keyed up, would yell out that day's lunch menu.

And I don't know what it was, but something about standing next to Eli there, against the wall, facing down that firing squad of ten coordinated and binocular kids, led by the cannon-armed Erskine Davies, made me angry, made me want to win. Or at least not lose so badly. "We need to catch one," I said.

Eli looked over at me, a look of inspired and resolute determination on his face. Catching a single ball wouldn't win us the game, of course, but it would accomplish something we hadn't done in a week of battle ball: it would get one of our pathetic teammates back into the game. It would mean progress. And that was something.

The other team stood across from us, ten strong and preternaturally threatening, a cast photo from *Lord of the*

128

Flies. They smiled and exchanged knowing glances and then Erskine said, "Now!" and they delivered a full throttle, the throwing of all ten balls at once. I ducked, and Erskine's throw hit the wall behind my head like a gunshot. We sidestepped and dropped and rolled, and when the balls had finished careening off the wall and back to their side, Eli and I were still alive. Of course this pissed them off; for the next two minutes they fired indiscriminately, and we dodged every throw.

That's when Erskine whispered to one of his team-mates, and then they both smiled like dogs in a gravy parade. Erskine took the kid's ball, stepped forward, and gave us the old up-and-under.

The bastard lofted that ball in the air, as soft and as high as he could, barely over the line to our side. Before I could warn him against it, Eli left our wall and began running toward the gimme. I think of this moment in slow motion—Eli leaving the foxhole while I yelled out, "No-o-o-o!"—but such was Eli's lack of speed and co-ordination that I may be remembering in real time, the ball sailing up sweetly against the gymnasium lights, Eli clattering out slowly toward it, knees knocking, arms outstretched, black glasses looking straight up.

The other nine boys, of course, were cocked and loaded as Eli ran toward them, his eyes on the ball floating down from the ceiling.

"Eli, wait!" I yelled. But in battle a man's true nature emerges, and I unhappily admit that I did not leave my spot against the wall as my comrade ran bravely to his battle ball death. I suppose, in my defense, that there was nothing I could have done anyway. Eli was a goner as soon as he pulled away from the wall. Even the SpEds on the sideline could see what was going to happen. "Corn dog! Corn dog! Corn dog!" yelled Repeat. "Cottage cheese!"

Eli ran forward until he was only ten feet away from the firing squad, his eyes straight up on that ball in the air. Erskine Davies took a step forward, his back twisted and torqued, the rubber ball behind his head. The other boys followed. And the next thing I remember is a sound like popcorn. Nine hard rubber balls hit Eli in the space of a half second, knocking his legs out from under him, blowing his glasses off, pelting his arms and legs and nuts and lofting him straight into the air and onto his back, his broken glasses skidding to rest a few inches from my feet.

Eli lay on his back on the hard gym floor, eyes bleary, nose bleeding, but still concentrating on that first cruel ball—lofted up as nothing more than a trap, a lure, an insult to his intelligence and coordination falling to the ground beside him, and as an afterthought perhaps, or maybe with his last bit of strength, Eli reached out from his back with one hand and caught it, the ball settling in his hand like a bird in its nest. And while the rules were unclear on what this meant, to catch a ball after being so completely pummeled, we all stood there reverently and the gym—and maybe the whole world—went quiet for a second.

I am not overstating this. Imagine what it takes to turn a whole gymful of high school boys—however briefly—into human beings. This is what happened: the world changed. Nothing less.

And from his back, in this new world he had just then created, Eli Boyle pointed defiantly to the sideline, where Louis had already taken a tiny step onto the court.

"Louis," Eli said. "You're in."

2 | THE LEAST UNHAPPY

The least unhappy, I once read, are those who never attempt what is beyond men. I think this must be true—what else would a failed politician say?—but I also think such an idea assumes the same boundaries for all men.

This is not the case.

So it didn't matter that as soon as Eli stood up that day, another ball took his legs out from under him and he was put out of the game. It didn't matter that as soon as Louis ran into the game, Erskine Davies threw a ball that thwacked against his little shoulder and sent him sprawling. It didn't matter that as I stood against the wall, stupefied by what I'd seen, a hard rubber ball racked my 'nads and my team was officially, brutally, put out of yet another game of battle ball.

It didn't matter because we'd all seen something amazing, seen it with our own eyes, an act of such super-human coordination and concentration, it would have seemed unlikely in the hands of the great prematurely bearded quarterback Kenny Dale. From a hunkering SpEd like Eli Boyle? It was a fucking miracle.

For days the story was told all over school—by the SpEddies as a kind of fable, the story of what could be accomplished with hard work and faith, and by the rest of the kids as a rich and impossible tale, a Ripley's moment, the world's largest fungus, the beard of bees, the stream of water running up a pipe, the twenty-six-foot-long tapeworm, the man who fellates himself, the dog who flies a Cessna, the turnip with a map of the world on its surface. The mildly retarded kid driven into the air in a game of battle ball, hit by nine balls at once, who still managed to reach out with one hand and catch the tenth.

In spite of everything, children know a miracle when they see one.

And so, if for the SpEds Eli's athletic moment was magically inspiring, for the rest of us—worshipers of entertainment—it was supernaturally funny, so entertaining it became meaningful. Who knew the SpEds could be so much fun! People talked about transferring into the mainstream PE class in the hopes of seeing something similar—Curty the blind kid catching a football, Louis the dwarf dunking.

I think we forget sometimes the halting sameness of high school: each day is like the day before it, six periods of class break in all the same places, lunch at the same table, the same jokes and asides and greetings from all the same kids, the same clothes and songs and dances, and if school is truly preparation for life, it is mostly in this way, gearing us for the rigid schedule, the stifling patterns, the lack of variation that an adult strives for so that he can resent it the rest of his life. How much money do we pay for an education that will allow us to loop our necktie the same way each morning, to be given a regular parking spot to park our BMW every day, to buy a summer home so that even our vacations become routine? We are drilled in this unending sameness in high school, and only the insane and the inspired ever get past it.

But for a moment during my senior year, Eli Boyle introduced an entire high school of jeans-clad lemmings to the world of the insane and the inspired, to the idea of transcendence. And again, if you think I am overstating a fluke play in battle ball, ask yourself what get passed along as miracles these days—weeping statues, brief remissions from cancer, hazy pictures of Jesus on the stumps of trees. How little it takes for people to quit their jobs and move to compounds in Montana and New Mexico, to put on robes and eat macrobiotic foods. How badly do we want a miracle of our own? How much would we like to open the front door and, just once, find God standing there? Or vintage Angie Dickinson?

No, Eli's catch that day was a miracle, plain and simple, and it grew, as miracles are known to, in the days afterward, and with each telling. Eli was knocked unconscious. He had a concussion. He flew fifteen feet in the air and a shard from his broken glasses jutted from his forehead. He rolled twice and caught the ball in his fingertips and then rifled it at the other team. He single-handedly brought the 'tards back.

It wasn't long before Eli's simple break in the monotony sparked an even more compelling and dangerous concept, an idea that came from the only teenage desire even close to our desire for sex: our need to flout authority.

Open rebellion.

The Eli Movement started slowly but spread exponentially. It was based on a simple idea that had never occurred to the school administrators who decided to combine the Special Ed class with ours. The idea was simply this: what if the SpEds won?

Clearly, the administration had decreed that Special Ed kids be mainstreamed "for their own good," so that in the powerful currents of high school normalcy and conformity, their defects and debilitations might be diluted and they would rise to meet the lowest expectations and eventually blend in. It was as if the administration saw these kids as effluents that we could wash away downstream.

But what if it worked the other way? What if we learned from them? What if they—happily slobbering and babbling their way through life—had it dicked, and the rest of us, with our vain anxieties and ambitions, were the fools? What if we not only failed to raise the SpEds to our level of mediocrity and conformity but giddily fell to theirs?

This idea caught on the way everything catches on in high school, first as a goof—one kid allows a Special Ed guy to hit him in battle ball—and then as a kind of fashion. During one battle ball game, our opponents elbowed each other out of the way to try to get hit by a ball thrown by Curty the blind kid. After battle ball we played football and Hank, our captain, picked the same group of misfits and me, and while Mr. Leggett stewed and paced and yelled, our football team rolled to victories over the other teams, whose non-Special Ed members ran the wrong way and fell to the ground and faked spasms and fits and stumbles and crashed into one another as my teammates, Repeat or Curty or Louis or Hank, ran through their lines for touchdown after touchdown. It became an art form, a contest to see who could give up the most points to the SpEds.

My team won the football league and the floor hockey

league and we won the basketball championship, and Mr. Leggett fumed until I thought he'd explode. He made other kids captain and still the teams came out the same way, with the freaks and me on one team. He pulled noted athletes like my friend Tommy Kane aside and challenged their pride, but he underestimated the Eli Movement. Tommy, for instance, responded to Mr. Leggett's challenge by playing an entire game in his jock, with his shorts around his ankles. It was wonderful. The Special Ed kids were now the first ones dressed down for class and the last ones to leave, high-fiving and whooping and talking a kind of trash to their non-Special opponents. "Ha-ha-ha! Goulash goulash goulash!"

Everyone seemed to enjoy the new order except Eli, the one who'd inadvertently started it, but who knew it to be just another kind of joke. He stood off to the side, refusing to have any part of these new games and their condescending rules. Eli believed it was wrong to mess with the rules of games, any games. These were sacred to him. In fact, I don't know who liked this new world less, him or Mr. Leggett. I guess Eli would rather have a beating than this condescension. And Mr. Leggett simply wanted beatings.

Word of this extended prank spilled over the banks of our PE class and flooded the school, and for a brief month or two during the fall quarter of high school in 1981 Special Ed kids had an odd social cachet, a sort of mascot cool. Jocks and motorheads and stoners high-fived the SpEds as they walked down the hall (they low-fived Louis), signed Curty up for driver's ed, and relied on Repeat to tell them what we were having for lunch. Girls pretended to swoon when Hank, our captain, thundered down the hall. A few kids even overdid it and began wearing pocket protectors and black-framed glasses and hemming their pants three inches above their shoes.

For just that one moment Special Ed kids were cool. And they ate it up.

All but one. One Saturday afternoon in February, I was sitting in my room listening to the new Styx album when there was a knock on my door. I took off my headphones and found my mom standing at my bedroom door, looking confused. "There's someone at the door for you."

My brother Ben stood in the hallway. He shadowboxed me. "Good luck," he said. "And remember, stick and move. Use your jab."

I walked to the back door and opened it. There stood Eli Boyle, staring at his black shoes. It occurred to me that although he'd saved my life he'd never been to my house, and I hadn't mentioned him to my family since the day of our fight.

"Clark?" he said, and I realized too that he'd never called me by name.

"What is it, Eli?"

He looked up. Then he looked past me into my house, which I'd always thought of as small and modest—a one-story, three-bedroom war-era starter—but which must've seemed lavish compared with his mother's trailer. Eli pushed up his black-framed glasses and looked down at my shoes. "Do you think you could help me?"

3 | DANA BRETT'S RACK

Dana Brett's rack showed up one day that fall, out of the blue and at least three years late, as if it had been held up somewhere in shipping. By junior high school most of the girls who were going to have breasts had them, but Dana remained petite and girlish and generally uninterested in her own looks. So I lost track of her, as did all of the boys, until her rack just arrived one day our senior year, on picture day as a matter of fact, when Dana stepped out of her brother's car wearing a kind of tube top beneath an open button shirt and, well, I don't mean to sound disrespectful, but . . . Sweet Jesus.

That morning, like all mornings, I stood with some of the other football players in front of our low-slung open-corridor high school, hands in the pockets of our Levi's and our lettermen's coats, trying to effect nonchalance and having as much luck as a pack of ass-sniffing puppies. We joked around and made fun of one another, scoffed at the thin tires on Benny Fennel's Javelin, rolled our eyes at the hood scoop on Eric Oliver's GTO, and fantasized about Robert Muckin's Corvette. But mostly we watched—watched young girls get off the buses, watched older girls arrive in cars, watched the two young female teachers at our school arrive for work. Minds that couldn't retain a bit of Pythagoras or Plato or the periodic table easily held a full accounting of every pair of pants owned by every cute girl in school. "Amanda Rankin is wearing her double buckles," Tommy Kane said, and we all turned, riffling our mental catalogs. Ah yes. The double buckles.

So you can imagine the commotion when on that morning David Brett's passenger side door opened and out stepped two breasts that none of us had ever seen before, attached to his sister Dana.

"Holy shit," said Tommy Kane.

This was, of course, the same Dana Brett I had fallen in grade-school love with, whose boots I had fantasized taking off. Dana was cute in grade school, but physically she'd never moved beyond that. While we began looking for "hot" and "foxy" and "stacked" she remained "cute" through junior high, and by the time we got to high school she hid herself in baggy dresses and jumpers and she fell into that strata of students we simply called brains. Most of the girls who'd exhibited grade-school brains pretended not to have them by high school and skidded into second-skin jeans and T-shirts and feathered Farrah Fawcett hair. But Dana only grew smarter as those other girls' clothes got tighter. She devoured chemistry and psychology and advanced composition and became a valedictorian candidate, all the while staying in jumpers and baggy dresses, so that I never stopped thinking of her as a precocious fifth grader under all that fabric. And since there were so many other girls to date, the Stacy Bogans and Rhonda Parsons of the world, the Mandy Landinghams, girls who looked at us in long takes that seemed to promise some eventual business involving the removal of panties, I didn't think of Dana Brett, except as my old grade-school friend. I spoke with her in class, but in the halls and at games and dances and "events" we existed in different worlds.

Even now, I diminish her by comparing her to the empty pairs of jeans that we pursued, by talking about her sudden breasts as if she were no more than them, but I am only telling the story the way it happened, telling the moronic alongside the miraculous, the mistaken as well as the inevitable. We didn't know it, but Dana Brett was the class of our class then, both beautiful and genius; and yet, because we had no measure for female intelligence and reason, we missed it in the glare of ass-splitting jeans and two-scoop halter tops. We missed the dead-level power of her eyes, which could cut right through a high school boy, size him up, and dismiss him like just another problem. We missed Dana Brett, with her straight A's and her straight hair, her baggy, frumpy jumpers, her pretty, makeupless face, and the plain sketchbook she carried around as a journal, her thoughtful conversations and incisive questions, the sadness that she seemed to own. There are many things I must atone for in this confession, but none hurts more than admitting that I went so long without seeing what was in our midst.

But if Dana Brett was nothing to us before, she was certainly something that day in front of the school-picture day, the day something finally coaxed her from her jumper into a tight shirt and new jeans, the day we saw what had developed beneath those layers of clothing, the day we saw that Dana Brett was not a girl anymore.

"Hot damn," said Tommy Kane. "Who ordered the tit sandwich?"

As she got closer, the other boys fumbled greetings but most of them didn't even know her name and she looked past them, to me, and I admit—here and now—being too stupid to realize that this transformation might be for my benefit.

"Dana," I said simply.

She smiled and said, "Hi, Clark." We all watched her walk into the school.

There aren't many opportunities for change in high school. Your peers know you too well, your habits and tics and weaknesses and strengths, and any variation is called out, pointed out as fraud. There are only two days on which real change is allowed, when a kid can remake himself. The first day of school. And picture day.

That Monday morning was picture day, and so kids sported new haircuts and clothes, entirely concocted visions of themselves. My younger brother Ben, a sophomore, began his two-week smoking phase that very day, wearing a blue blazer and carrying our grandfather's pipe in the breast pocket. "You do realize," he said through gritted teeth, "that these pictures could resurface when we are adults. Nothing wrong with looking sophisticated, Clark old man." I still see his class picture from that year above our mantel, in that blazer, the pipe clenched in his teeth, like a tiny Noël Coward.

The same morning that Ben and Dana remade themselves, amid countless other new hairstyles and clothes, Eli got off his bus and made shallow eye contact with me. I nodded imperceptibly. He wore a pair of my old jeans, a tight, secondhand T-shirt that read THE HONORABLE MAYOR OF FUNKY TOWN, and a pair of my old tennis shoes. His hair was parted down the middle and dried for the first time ever with a blow dryer that we'd bought for him at the flea market in our neighborhood (when we fired it up and leveled it at his forehead, he looked like a comet, all that dead white skin tailing his head). His black-framed glasses had been traded—despite his mother's protests ("Henry Kissinger doesn't seem to think they're embarrassing!")—for the big, teardrop aviator lenses favored in sunglass form by navy pilots and the immensely cool California Highway Patrol. He wore an off-white jacket meant to lessen the impact of his dandruff, and about a quart of my father's English Leather, which had proved the amount necessary to mask his various odors. As a finishing touch, I put a rattail comb in his back pocket, tail up.

He didn't exactly look good, not yet, and he certainly didn't look very natural. On him my pants looked stumpy, with their cuffs rolled up, and my expensive Puma tennis shoes pointed in slightly toward each other on his pigeon toes. And while his hair looked better, it was still thin and red and covering a complexion like the surface of the moon. But there was something there, something small and significant, and I think it was this: in one weekend, with one change of clothes and glasses and a small bit of coaching, Eli had managed finally to turn the corner, from one of *them* to one of *us*.

But like everything Eli did, his timing couldn't have been worse. He chose to leave *them* when the Special Ed kids were on the verge of being cool, though that didn't matter to Eli, who could tell condescension from acceptance.

He descended the stairs from his bus and I nodded slightly, as nervous as he was. I moved my shoulders with his every step, mouthing to myself, *Good, good, good.* "Hey," he said, without making eye contact with any of us, as I'd coached, and a couple of my teammates nodded in spite of themselves. I said nothing.

He walked the way I'd coached, one hand in his pocket, head back a little, ambling—like the "Keep On Truckin' " guy, I advised—as if he had nowhere to be. Just as I'd instructed in my nonchalance lessons, he chewed gum as he walked and kept his eyes half shut, as if he might fall asleep at any time. Luckily he was well past us when he walked into the flagpole in front of the school.

If Dana Brett's newfound shelf had shocked the guys in the front of the school, they were totally unimpressed with Eli's attempt at cool. He walked past us to the school, and it was only Tommy Kane who twisted his face, looked back at Eli and then at me.

"Hey Mason," he said. "Is Boyle wearing your pants?"

In the split second after he spoke, I did the math, factored out where this would go if I confessed to spending my weekend helping Eli dress and walk and comb his hair.

"What?" I looked back at the door he'd just disappeared behind. "What the fuck you talking about, Kane?"

"Those star-back jeans. I got the same pair but yours have two stars. Boyle looked like he was wearing yours. You guys swapping clothes after PE now?"

The other guys turned. But I was ready for this. A one-eyed boy doesn't make it through school without knowing how to deflect mockery.

"You know what I think, Tommy," I said. "I think you're spending a little too much time staring at dudes' asses."

And like that, the crisis was no longer mine. The lettermen laughed—not at my relationship with Eli, but at Tommy's noticing it. Such were my political instincts, even then. But as a politician I knew that I risked making an enemy unless I finished the play and rescued Tommy from the trouble I had caused him, by diverting once more.

"You guys see Dana Brett's rack?" I asked.

Nine heads nodded and woofed and smiled and the morning continued like all mornings did then, only with a couple of small, subtle changes registered in the landscape: Dana Brett had announced her intention to be noticed, to be in play. And Eli Boyle had announced his intention—above all odds and against great obstacles—to fit in.

I was to have a role in both of these events, and of course in that awful moment when those intentions crashed together.

4 | I HAD SEX

I had sex for the first time that fall, if one could call
those ten or fifteen seconds of dizzying release sex, in
the back of a garaged Jeep Wagoneer, with a collection of
soft fleshy parts and irritating conversational tics whose
first name was Susan and whose last I will keep to myself
(there are legal considerations and, besides, this is my
confession, not hers). Despite my short duration and
ham-handed performance, it was a great relief to have
finally done it, since the other football players saw virginity
among our ranks as nothing less than a character flaw
and possibly a sign of homosexuality. Of course no one
knew I was a virgin, because before any of us actually
had sex we had all lied that we had, inventing girls from
other schools and friends of cousins and experienced
neighbor ladies. I see those studies reporting that 72
percent of high school boys have had sex and only 12
percent of high school girls and I think I know why: the
census takers' inability to track the huge population of
imaginary female sex partners.

But in Susan I had a real partner, and this changed
me in some way. Namely, I wanted more. I liked sex.
Liked everything about it. Hoped to get better at it. And
so I stayed with Susan for the rest of the school year,
even though I couldn't think of a thing we had in common,

except our mutual recognition that I needed practice having sex. And so we did, almost daily. We had so much sex in Susan's parents' Wagoneer that I couldn't bear to see her family driving around in it, her brothers and sisters belted into the backseat that we used like a gymnast's apparatus. I still can't see a Jeep Wagoneer on the freeway without becoming aroused, and more than once I have narrowly averted accidents after following a Wagoneer's path too far in my rearview mirror.

As I dated Susan that year I got marginally better at having sex in off-road family vehicles. The entire school, of course, knew that we were together, and knew the instant that we began "doing it." We groped in the hallways and she waited by my car after school and outside the locker room after games and we went to dances—Homecoming, Sadie Hawkins, Christmas, and Sweethearts—and groped outside the gym. We wrote notes and talked on the phone, and people combined our names into one: ClarknSue.

Looking back, I realize now that Dana Brett's rack arrived the very week I had sex with Susan. But at the time, I didn't connect those events, didn't realize that Dana would hear about it, and that she would dress that way not to impress the high school boys, but to impress *me,* to get me to notice her the way I'd noticed Susan.

And I did notice Dana, but I was so single-minded then—a mad scientist devoted to my work with tall, statuesque Susan, we were like a small Intercourse Research and Development firm—that it never occurred to me to go out with anyone else, especially my old grade-school friend, the eternally presexual, perpetually cute Dana.

For her part, I think Dana must have realized fairly

quickly that I wasn't interested, for she was back to wearing baggy jumpers and combing her hair straight. But the rack was out of the bag, and the other football players hounded her for a few weeks, asking her out and offering her rides home, before they eventually gave up. Tommy Kane was especially smitten with Dana, and he asked me about her constantly. I even tried to fix her up with him. But she wasn't interested. So the guys called her frigid and surmised that she was a lesbian, based solely on the evidence that she had laughed when Tommy asked her to climb into the backseat of his Ford Maverick.

"I hate dykes," Tommy said, and in our base stupidity we all agreed. What possible good was there in a woman who wouldn't have sex with us? I would love to say that I didn't participate in these Cro-Magnon conversations, in this emerging male idiocy, but this is, after all, a confession. We bragged about the things we did *to* our girl-friends, as if they had no part in it. We banged them and humped them and screwed them and nailed them, and if they did anything to us we still took credit ("I *got* a blow job last night"). As with everything I am confessing here, from my first snub of Eli at the bus stop to the events of . . . fifty-two hours ago, I offer no excuse except this: I was young and male and I was pretty sure I'd invented sex, just like I invented driving fast and making fun of people and eating french fries.

With all of this attention to sports and student government and, of course, my groundbreaking work in Susan's parents' Wagoneer, I didn't have much to do with Eli, except on those Sunday afternoons when he'd call to make sure the coast was clear and then come by the house so we could work on his appearance. He was plainly disappointed by our progress. He'd been dressing right for two months and nothing had changed. Even though they'd finally broken up our mainstreaming gym class ("They're making a mockery of physical education!" Mr. Leggett testified at the school board meeting), the SpEddies had retained a bit of their mascot cool.

But Eli lost even that measure of popularity. If anything, he was worse off. At least he had been the best of the worst. Now he was the worst of the best. If I were him, I might've choked on the irony.

One Sunday in the late part of winter, we sat on my front porch and watched my sisters skip rope on the sidewalk in front of us. It was probably February or March, one of those days that strobes between warm and cool, the sun flashing in and out of clouds.

"What am I doing wrong?"

"Nothing," I lied. "I don't even know what you mean."

"You know what I mean," he said. "Why isn't it working?"

I looked over at him. Eli was four inches shorter than me, about five feet eight, not too fat or too skinny, and while he still hadn't mastered the blow dryer, his hair didn't look awful anymore. His face was still too wide and his skin was still a problem, all pale and pimply, but it was getting better. Honestly, he didn't look that bad. The problem was deeper: context and history and a collection of problems that went to his core.

"Level with me," he said. "Be tougher on me."

"It's hard," I said. "People have thought of you one way for so long . . ."

"There are only a few months left in school," he said. "Please . . ."

I looked at him and saw those same eyes I'd seen on the bus in grade school, searching my face for something he'd missed, some rules that no one had told him. "I'm serious, Clark. I'll do whatever you say. Just please, help me."

"Well, there are other things besides clothes and hair," I said.

He pulled a pencil and pad from his pocket. "What?"

"Well, there are things that probably can't be helped."

"Tell me."

"I don't know."

"Yes, you do."

"Well, you're a senior and you still ride the bus."

"I don't have a car," he complained.

"I know," I said. "You asked what it was and I'm trying to tell you."

He wrote this on the small piece of paper and said, "Other kids ride the bus."

"Yeah," I admitted. "There are other things."

"Tell me."

"Well." I sighed and looked down the block. "There's . . . you have a bit of a lisp."

"What elth?"

"That's funny," I said.

"Come on. What else?"

"Well, your hands shake."

He wrote on his paper. "And?"

"You limp when you walk. And you twitch and make funny noises. You still pick your nose too much. And . . ."

"Slow down." He wrote on his paper. "Okay, what else?" he asked.

"That's it."

"What else?" he asked.

"You smell," said my sister, who had stopped skipping rope.

"Shawna!" I said, and she ran off.

Eli's chin slumped to his chest and he nodded, as if she'd confirmed what he suspected. The problem was that he and his mother didn't have a shower in their trailer, just a tub, and his mother would only let him take baths twice a week ("You'll wash the oils off your body and end up with dry skin. And I will not have that on my conscience").

So we started the second phase of the Eli reclamation the very next day. I began driving Eli to school an hour early. I used the extra hour to shoot baskets, and since it would have drawn unwelcome attention for Eli to arrive early simply to take a shower at school, he lifted weights for twenty minutes, then showered and dried his hair.

But perceptions don't break easily, and by senior year few people were likely to notice that he smelled better and that his arms and shoulders had begun to develop small buttes and gullies from the weight lifting. He was still Eli. And, in truth, any progress would have been too slow for Eli, who by April saw our impending graduation as the date of his death.

"It's not helping," he said as we sat in my backyard later that spring, throwing chestnuts over my back fence. "Everything is the same. It's never going to change."

"It's not the same," I said. "It's better."

"It's not," he said. "There's gotta be something we can do."

I felt so bad for him I began work immediately on the

final stage of the Eli Project. "Let me think about it," I said.

Eli went home and I called Susan and canceled our afternoon of Wagoneer tag. Then I got out the phone book and called Dana Brett at home.

"Clark," she said breathlessly. I had never called her before.

"Dana, are you going to the prom with anyone?"

There was a brief pause. "No," she said.

I drove over to talk to her. She lived in a part of town that had been built on old apple orchards—a nice neighborhood of older houses and newer California splits. I was surprised to find her parents on the front porch when I arrived, smiling. All I knew about them was that they were both community college professors and, according to Dana, somewhat overprotective. Her mother had an Instamatic camera and she demanded to take pictures of Dana and me, leaning us against opposite sides of their porch railing. It was weird but okay with me. They told me to say cheese. I said cheese. Her father shook my hand firmly, clapped my shoulder, and asked where I was planning to go to college.

"Well, I was accepted at the University of Washington," I said. "And then I want to go to law school somewhere."

"Outstanding," he said.

"Thank you," I said.

"Dana was accepted to Stanford," her mother said.

"That's what I heard," I said. "That's really something."

"Mom," Dana said. She rolled her eyes. "Please." Her dad burst out laughing for no reason. It startled me. I had never met such nice parents.

Dana's chestnut hair was pulled into a ponytail and she was wearing jeans and a tight T-shirt. I could see those breasts again, round and straining against her shirt. I wondered why she didn't dress like that more often at school. Dana's mom brought us some lemonade and we walked around to her backyard. Her parents watched us from the kitchen window, their arms around each other's waists.

"Before I start, you can say no if you want to," I began.

Dana laughed. "You don't have to worry about that."

So I launched into the story of Eli and me, our humiliation at the hands of Pete Decker and Matt Woodbridge, how Eli had saved me at the bus stop in elementary school, and saved me again the day my eye was shot out, about the moment in battle ball when Eli and I stood side by side and the day a few weeks later when he asked for my help, about my four-month project to rehabilitate him, to clean and clothe and cloak him in high school acceptability. I had told no one about Eli and me, and it felt good getting it off my chest, even if the effect on Dana was a bit confusing.

She listened for a while, smiling, then looked back at her house, then slumped against their swing set. She stared at the ground and nodded as I spoke. I told her about giving Eli my clothes and teaching him to walk and comb his hair, getting rid of his old glasses and practicing what to say to people. I told her how we met sometimes on Sundays and how hard Eli was working.

"That's nice of you," was the only thing she said, and it was so quiet I wasn't sure I'd heard her right. The whole time I talked, she never looked up at me. In retrospect, of course, I see my obtuseness as a kind of cruelty, but at the time I couldn't see past my concern for Eli, and I just kept talking. And talking.

I explained how impatient Eli had become, and how desperate he was to show people that he was more than they thought he was. But time was running out, and he needed something drastic. He needed a girl to notice what everyone else had failed to notice up to that point, someone to break the ice so that the other girls would see it was okay to date him. He needed a pretty girl, I said—Dana Brett put her hand over her mouth—a pretty girl whom the other guys wanted to date. He could ask a girl out on his own, of course, but he couldn't stand the weight of rejection. If the first girl said no to him, then no other girl would be able to say yes, even if she wanted to. He would be a lost cause, a goner.

"Why me?" she asked.

I looked back and saw her parents wave from the kitchen window. I waved back.

"Well," I said, "you're so much smarter than the other girls and, well, you're pretty and, I don't know, I guess I thought you'd understand."

"I do," she said.

"You probably don't remember this," I said. "But when we were kids, and Eli first got transferred into our class, you weren't mean to him."

"I remember," she said.

"So I thought you'd sympathize. And since you and I are friends . . ."

Finally she looked up at my eyes. "We are," she said, not as a question.

"You can double-date with Susan and me." I hoped she saw that by offering to double-date I was taking as much of a social chance as she was, driving to and from the dance with Eli. But of course that wasn't what she was thinking.

"Okay," Dana said, and she looked at me with down-turned eyes, and she seemed again like the smart, shy little girl from grade school. "Have him ask me. I'll say yes. But don't tell him you talked to me. It'll be better if it doesn't look like a setup."

"Thanks, Dana."

We walked back to the house and her parents came out to greet us, holding hands, her mother holding out a plate of cookies. I took four.

Dana walked right past them into the house. Her mother, seeing something was wrong, turned and watched her go inside. I took another cookie.

Her father was as clueless as I was. He stood there, still beaming at me. "What kind of law?" he asked.

"I'm sorry?"

"You said you're going to study law. I was wondering if you knew what kind?"

"Well," I said between bites of chocolate chip pecan cookies, "I don't know. Maybe contract law at first. But later I want to go into politics."

"Outstanding," said Dana Brett's father.

5 | THE DAVENPORT HOTEL

The Davenport Hotel was decked out and lit up for our prom, its once-grand second-floor ballroom littered with folding chairs and covered with green and blue streamers, shimmering paper fish, giant clamshells, and a trident that looked for all the world like a big dinner fork. At the last minute, however, the prom committee (Clark Mason, chairman) had rejected "A Night in Atlantis" as a theme, even though the decorations had already been purchased; and so a sign declaring the scene as BOOGIE WONDERLAND hung behind a foam-rubber faux grotto.

Boys stood around in little circles in their ruffled tuxedo shirts and flopping bow ties, the girls in candy-flavored lip gloss and taffeta dresses. Courage for this event was gathered outside in cars, from water bongs and ceramic pipes, from flasks and sixers. Unmufflered Chevelles and Novas pulled up in front of the grand hotel, windows shaking. Car doors opened and girls with piled hair and tight dresses emerged onto the sidewalk, shuffling feet while their dates went to park the wheels. Two girls who thought it would be "hilarious" to come to the prom in jeans and without dates sat silently in the lobby in big overstuffed chairs, the very portrait of second thoughts, while two guys in tuxedo T-shirts stood next to each other, hoping that their own bad idea could be divided in half. The rest of us strode into the hall in our shiny shoes and store-bought haircuts, parroting anti-quated adult behavior, rules handed down from some point deep in the past, utterly pointless rules like the required pinning of small flowers on shuddering lapels ("That's okay," Eli said when Dana told him she'd bought him a boutonniere. "I rented my own shoes"). Giving in to the mystique and the endless optimism of fresh testos-terone, boys rented rooms and upgraded their wallet rubber supply. Girls, too, had their delusions, their mimicking of wedding rites, their manicures and stylings, their practicing picture smiles in front of bathroom mirrors. The night itself was a letdown for most, but there were minor intrigues—surprise breakups, throw-ups, and feel-ups. But without a doubt, no one drew more attention that night than Eli Boyle and the lovely Dana Brett.

I spent the day with Eli, picking up our tuxes (black for me, white—to hide any rogue flakes of dandruff—for Eli), helping him get dressed, even combing his hair for him. His mother stood behind us in the hallway of their trailer, which I'd never been in before, and which smelled like the clothes of old people.

"Your hair's sticking up on the sides," his mother said.

"It's supposed to do that," Eli said. "It's called feather-ing."

"It's called sticking up. Those pants are too tight."

"They're supposed to be tight," he said.

"Where are your glasses?"

"I'm wearing contacts."

"Oh, God. Now you're putting shards of glass in your

eyes. And your chest and arms are so bloated. Is that from drugs?"

"They're muscles, Mom. From lifting weights."

"Well, it's not healthy. It's bad for your circulation."

I clipped his bow tie and straightened it and helped him into his jacket. I splashed Aqua Velva on his cheeks.

"You smell like a sailor," his mom said.

When he was dressed, she leaned on the back of a chair in their tiny kitchen—there was only room for the two chairs—and took his picture.

"My God, Eli," she said. "You're beautiful. I wish your father . . ." She turned away and started crying.

I drove. Eli and I picked up Susan, who looked a little too *professional,* and who didn't talk all the way to Dana's house, maybe for fear of cracking her makeup. At Dana's house, her parents didn't come out onto the porch this time. Eli went to the door and came back with Dana, who wore a silver dress with a deep neckline. She had a wrap pulled around her shoulders and when she shivered a little in the cold, on the way to the car, Eli offered her his coat. She took it and I sighed with relief. Her hair was swooped up on her head and spilled out on her forehead. She looked perfect, like an old movie actress. Susan hadn't been eager to double-date with two people so far removed from her social stratum, and when Dana walked out to my parents' Dodge Colt looking beautiful—and not in my date's makeup and hairspray way—Eli's coat around her shoulders, Susan mumbled something with the word "asshole" in it.

We had dinner at the Mr. Steak at the end of the mall, and at first, I have to admit, I worried about Eli's ability to pull this whole thing off. He sat next to me and echoed my every move, taking off his jacket and unfolding his napkin as I did, shooting glances at me every few seconds to pick up his next cue. He ordered the same food and drink that I did and looked at me for approval every time he spoke, which, in the first twenty minutes, was exactly once. ("So, do you like meat, Dana?") But as the dinner progressed he actually seemed to loosen up and even told a few good jokes at his own expense about grade school ("You probably don't remember me. I was sort of stuck up. Didn't talk to many people"). And while he didn't actually make eye contact with Dana, he was polite and stood when she excused herself to go to the bathroom.

By the time our food came, Dana seemed to be having a decent time—at least in comparison to my arctic date, who chewed her thumbnail and stared off into space as we began talking about college. I was looking at state universities. Eli couldn't afford a university, and his grades weren't high enough for a scholarship. He was going to start at community college, he said, build his grades up, and then hopefully transfer to a four-year school.

When Dana admitted she was going to Stanford, Eli's fork fell to his plate. "Wow!" he said. "Stanford. Are you sure?"

Dana smiled at her sirloin. "I'm sure."

Susan excused herself to go to the bathroom.

"Aren't you nervous?" Eli asked.

Dana looked up at him, surprised. "You know, I don't think anyone has asked me that. They just keep telling me how great it is."

"It is great, but that's the first thing that popped into

my head," Eli said. "I'd be scared to death. Everyone there must be so smart. And it's so far away."

"She'll do fine," I said, and waved a little plastic cup at the waiter so he'd bring me more sour cream for my baked potato.

Eli leaned back in his chair. "I just keep thinking college is going to be just like high school, but twenty-four hours a day. No escape."

"I don't know," said Dana. "I guess I've been assuming that's when life really gets going. In college."

"Really?" Eli asked. "You think so?"

"God, I hope so," said Dana. "If it doesn't . . ." She didn't finish.

There was a moment of quiet, and Eli took a deep breath. "I lied," he said to his plate. "My mom inherited some money that she put away for my college. I could probably afford a four-year school, at least in state. It just sounds so scary to me, I figured I should go to community college first. I'm a chicken."

"It's perfectly understandable," Dana said.

Eli laughed a little. "No, it's not," he said. He pounded his fork down into his ribeye and was about to cut it when he stood up, lifted his fork and his steak to his heart, and addressed Dana formally. "I pledge at this very moment, on this cut of meat, to take my two-point-five grade point average and enroll at Harvard."

Eli sat down and rubbed at the steak stain on his white tux as Susan returned from the bathroom, saw that she'd missed something funny, and glared at me. She mouthed that thing with the word "asshole" in it again and then sat down to finish her flank steak.

It's funny. I saw a basketball game on ESPN Classic

the other day, a game I'd first seen in 1979, the NCAA championship game between Larry Bird's Indiana State Sycamores and Magic Johnson's Michigan State Spartans. At first I was startled to have come across so important a relic of my teenage years, then I was giddy to watch my memories roll across the TV screen, then I was disappointed to see what a flat version it was compared to my mental picture of the game (the players were too slow; the game was a blowout; Bird and Magic rarely guarded each other). I had taken a very ordinary game and made it a seminal moment in basketball and my own development.

And perhaps my sweet memory of the rest of the prom, of Eli's near-total transformation, is a similar trick of mental editing and mythmaking. Because it certainly wasn't perfect. For instance, we hadn't had time for dance lessons, and so Eli's dancing during fast songs resembled nothing so much as a dog trying to escape a leash. The Mr. Steak stain on his tuxedo was quickly joined by punch on his shirt and a slice of cake in his lap and two unidentifiable stains that may have come from Eli himself. He head-butted Dana at one point and nearly chipped her tooth, and his hair eventually lost its feather and fell straight on his head; he looked like a pimply, red-haired Ringo Starr.

But these are minor blemishes on an otherwise sparkling evening. From the moment he and Dana strode in ("Who is that? Eli Boyle? No way") to the first slow dance (his mother had taught him a kind of box step; while the rest of us just leaned over and hung on our dates' asses, Eli and Dana actually danced) to his anticipating when to pull out her chair, when to get her punch, when to get her wrap, Eli was a gentleman, almost smooth, and I know that I am not imagining this part: more than a few girls found ways to cast looks over at the two of them. I can't say he and Dana clicked, really, but they seemed to have a fine time and I watched as Eli relaxed and began enjoying himself.

It was even his idea, after our regular dance pictures, to have one more taken, together, the four of us. Of course I see now the significance of this moment, not just for Eli, but for Dana and me and even Susan—for whom this was the penultimate indignity, the next-to-last straw, having to be photographed with the likes of Eli Boyle while our classmates stood in a queue. In the photo, Eli and I are standing behind our dates in the photographer's sea-foam grotto, lost in our tuxes, at the last minute our arms thrown over each other's shoulders and our heads dipped in, like war buddies about to ship, our dates standing at an angle in front of us, a cool distance between them, Dana smiling politely, Susan chewing glass. If you saw the picture, you would notice first this wide range of smiles: Dana polite and quite nearly believable, Susan snarling, me wary, and Eli positively buoyant standing next to me. I have a theory about pictures like that; they actually reveal more as time passes, and as the colors fade and the styles die, other things emerge, connections and motivations, and maybe even futures.

When the pictures were finished, Susan and I sneaked up to the room Tommy Kane's parents had rented for him on the ninth floor, where we guzzled T.J. Swan wine (*Steppin' Out*—the good stuff) and had quick, drunken, distracted sex (my tux pants at my ankles, her gunnysack dress around her neck). The wine made me sluggish and my hands felt like someone else's hands. After all the toil in her parents' Wagoneer, I wasn't as accomplished in an actual bed, and we weren't gone from the dance long.

I apologized all the way down in the elevator, but Susan was fixing herself in the mirror, as angry with me as I'd ever seen her. When we got back to the dance I couldn't see Eli and Dana right away, but then I spotted them over by the grotto. I immediately got nervous. Tommy Kane and his date, Amanda Rankin, were standing across from Eli and Dana; Tommy was too close, and I thought he must've gotten in Eli's face over something. I began to hurry across the room, ready to rescue Eli from trouble, but when I arrived I saw that everything was okay. Better than okay. Tommy was asking about the various stains on Eli's tux, and he was giving them a good-natured tour. They were all laughing. It was as if they were all friends. Eli beamed. Amanda Rankin, who had apparently gotten quite a bit of bottle courage before the prom, steadied herself on Dana's arm. And Dana didn't look unhappy either.

"There you are," said Tommy when he saw me. "Gimme the key. Eli and I are gonna take our sweet dates up to the suite and have a little sweet wine."

"Yeah boy! Fuggin' juice me!" said Amanda Rankin through eyes as uneven as my own. "I need more wine." This was a statement as untrue as any I have ever heard.

Eli looked nervously from Tommy to me and from me to Dana, whose face remained perfectly inscrutable, as if she were miles away.

"Whatever you want to do," Dana said to Eli.

"Great," said Tommy. "Let's go."

"Okay," said Eli, but the look he gave me was one of

terror. We hadn't gone over this possibility in our preparation. Drinking? A hotel room? In our wildest dreams, we hadn't come up with this scenario.

"We'll come with you," I said. This was the last straw for Susan, who yanked on my arm.

"I'd like to dance once at my prom," she said through gritted teeth.

"Go dance," said Tommy. "You can't hog the room all night, Mason. Give the rest of us a chance."

So Susan and I danced, a Led Zeppelin slow-fast-slow dance, then a Steve Miller Band guitar shake, followed by some disco instrumental that neither of us managed to catch on the beat. I kept watching the doorway of the ballroom, imagining all the trouble Eli could get into with a bottle of wine and a first-rate fuckball like Tommy Kane.

"Who are you looking for?" Susan asked me.

"Nothing. I'm just . . . thirsty."

We danced again, to "Bohemian Rhapsody," a song I thought might not end until sophomore year of college. After each song, I turned to leave the dance floor but Susan wouldn't budge, would just begin dancing again. So I'd stay for one more.

"Ready to go upstairs now?" I asked after Cheap Trick's "Surrender."

"No!" Susan said. "I am not."

"Come on. Let's go have a little wine."

"Fuck you, Clark!" Susan said. Then she burst into tears and ran out of the ballroom. A hundred pairs of eyes watched her go and then swung slowly to me, standing alone in this world I had created, this green, underwater Boogie Wonderland.

"Susan!" I ran after her and found her in the lobby, crying on the shoulder of one of the two girls who'd come in jeans and without dates.

"Asshole," said one of the jeans sisters.

"Susan. I'm sorry."

"Why don't you just go back in there?" said the other jeans sister. "Or go see your fucking girlfriend."

"Dana, please. Can I just talk to you?"

Susan's head turned slowly.

"I mean . . . Susan."

The two girls in jeans stepped back, as if Susan were a radiator about to blow. "I can't believe you just called her Dana," one of them said.

"Come on. I just messed up," I said. "Come on. Can't we talk?"

"You asshole. You fucking asshole."

"Susan . . ."

"You have been staring at her all night."

"No I haven't."

"Yes you have."

"It's not what you think," I said. "I'm trying to help Eli."

At the same time, all three girls' heads fell to the right, as if I'd just told them a terrible lie.

I could feel the desperation boiling inside, and that and the wine I'd drunk convinced me that I could make these dubious girls understand. "See, when I was a kid we both got picked on, but I grew out of it. Eli never did. I'm trying to help him."

Susan scoffed and turned to walk away.

My desperation bubbled to the surface. "See, our neighborhood was tough and there was this accident . . ."

And I don't know what made me do this, the wine probably, but I reached up and pushed on my eyelid until my prosthetic eye slid from its socket and I held it up to demonstrate . . . What? How he'd saved my life, maybe. Twenty years later, I can't really say what I hoped to achieve, but it certainly wasn't the result I got.

One of the jeans sisters—who, I later learned, had wolfed a half bottle of peach schnapps—vomited on the faded carpet of the lobby of the Davenport Hotel. The sound of her retching caused Susan to pause in the doorway and look back, at which point she saw: one of the girls in jeans covering her mouth, the other bent over, dumping a sour mixture of peach liqueur and stomach acid on the floor, while her boyfriend stood above them in a tuxedo, waving good-bye with his glass eye. And for just a second, I had the sensation that I could see with the fake eye that I waved around, the whole sad scene— me, the girls in jeans, a crying Susan, a few people lingering in the lobby, and the desk clerk, whose face betrayed nothing, as if such sights were so common here as to be dull.

I realized I could chase Susan and try to repair my own life, or I could go help Eli. It almost seems as if those two choices have been in front of me like this since elementary school, when Pete Decker first forced Eli and me to fight, when I first had the chance to rise above my own smallness and help my friend.

The door closed behind Susan. I put my magic seeing eye into my pocket and turned for the elevator. I'm coming, Eli, I said to myself, and the feel of that collapsed left eyelid reminded me of that day alongside the river, when Eli had rescued me, and I could hear the gurgle of that water and smell the smoking of my eyelashes. I can't say what I felt as I rushed to help Eli, some redemption perhaps, the emerging angels of my better nature.

The elevator stopped on every floor. My classmates got on or off and smacked me on the shoulder, asked why I was winking and said they'd heard that Susan was really mad at me. I ignored them all and got off on the ninth floor. I ran down the hallway. The door to room 916 was closed, and I couldn't hear anything inside. I took a breath, gathered myself, flattened my lapels, and patted down my hair, and then realized that with my left eye in my pocket I wasn't likely to pull off "gathered." I gave up and knocked on the door. I sensed someone looking through the eyehole and then the door opened and there was Eli, his tie removed, his hair a mess, his face ringed in sweat.

"Where have you been?" he whispered. He immediately began pacing.

I stepped inside the room and saw what looked like the results of a fierce battle. Two empty T.J. Swan wine bottles were keeled over on the coffee table. Amanda Rankin was asleep on the big double bed, her dress pulled down to reveal a padded black bra. There was no sign of Tommy or Dana.

"What happened?" I asked.

"I don't know." Eli careened around the room. "We drank a lot of wine . . . and Tommy turned out the lights and he and Amanda . . ." He pointed to Amanda Rankin's partially disrobed figure on the bed. "Dana and I just sat here. Amanda must've passed out, because after a minute Tommy turned the lights on and wanted to drink again."

166

I heard a sound from the bathroom like a sick person moaning. I looked over. The bathroom door was closed.

"Dana had a lot of wine. Tommy's in there with her."

I tried the door. It was locked. I pounded.

"Go away, Boyle," said Tommy. "We'll be out in a minute."

"Stop it," I heard Dana say, muffled, from the other side of the door.

My shoulder hit the door and I was surprised at how easily it opened. I suppose I hadn't hit anything that hard since I nearly killed the cheerleader during the basketball game. Inside, Dana was on her knees, bent over the bathtub, moaning and spitting, having just thrown up. Tommy was standing behind her, trying to pull her dress up.

"Hey, Mason," said Tommy, his eyes drunken slits. He smiled.

I pulled him out of the bathroom and pushed him across the room. He crashed into the bed and fell to the floor. As I stalked toward him, Eli slid past me into the bathroom.

Tommy was laughing. "Come on, Mason. She was giving me the eye, man." He looked at my collapsed lid and smiled. "Oh, sorry."

I pulled him up by his tux shirt and pressed him up against the wall. He pushed me back and I nearly lost my balance. "Come on. She don't like that fuckin' geek." He pushed me again, harder, and I staggered back, against the bed.

I grabbed him by the shirt and flung him across the room, and he knocked the television from its stand. It crashed to the floor next to him. "Jesus, Mason. What the fuck's got into you?"

Just then a key turned, the hotel room door opened, and in came the same desk clerk that I'd seen downstairs. He still had that stony look on his face, the most overwhelming case of boredom I'd ever seen. He looked around the room: One girl passed out on the bed. One boy on the floor next to the TV. The eyeball boy standing in the middle of the room. One girl getting sick in the bathroom. Another boy standing helplessly behind her. Empty wine bottles everywhere.

"Out," he said quietly. "Get out of here before I call the cops."

Tommy pulled himself up. "My dad rented . . ."

"I don't care if your dad owns the fuckin' hotel, kid." He said it like he was quoting us a price. "Get your things, get your girl, and get out of here."

Tommy walked to the bed. He pulled Amanda's dress back up over her bra and then shot me a glare. He wrestled with Amanda and got her to her feet. "I'm on TV!" Amanda chirped, then she slumped in his arms. Tommy staggered under her weight.

"I'll help," I said, and stepped forward.

"Don't come near me, you fuckin' one-eyed freak," Tommy said.

Eli came out of the bathroom and helped Tommy stand Amanda up. They carried her out of the room and toward the elevator.

"Get the other one and get out of here," said the desk clerk. Then he turned and followed Eli and Tommy and Amanda, who chirped, "What channel is this?"

In the bathroom, Dana had gotten to her feet and wiped her mouth on a towel. She smoothed her dress in back and turned to see me. "That's not very good wine," she said.

168

She fished around in the medicine cabinet until she found a small tube of toothpaste, put some on her finger, and rubbed it on her teeth.

"I was going to kick him as soon as I finished puking," she said. "But thank you."

"Sure," I said.

"Where's Eli?" she asked.

"Helping Amanda to Tommy's car."

I could hear engines growling and tires squealing on the street below. I checked my watch. It was midnight. The dance was over.

Dana looked out the window at the glittering skyline of Spokane. I've always thought it a strange city that way: a city of illusion, at night its downtown big and sparkling, but during the day small and decaying, with big gaps between the buildings. At night, you can imagine great things here. But daytime in Spokane is cold and real.

Dana reached out and touched the window. "Do you have any idea how many kids like me sit at home on Friday nights and fantasize about this, about what people like you and Susan and Amanda and Tommy are doing? Everything we want is inside rooms like this." She turned and smiled. "It's sad."

She picked up her wrap and draped it over her shoulders.

"Thank you for coming to this dance with Eli," I said. "I think it really meant a lot to him."

She got a faraway look. "You're welcome," she said.

I stepped forward and gave her a small hug and we separated.

"God," she said, and reached up to touch my face. "Your eye."

I don't remember much after that, how we ended up on the floor or when my hand found the neckline of her dress and one of her fine, new breasts, or how long we chewed on each other's tongues and ran our hands over each other's legs and sides and ribs and shoulders. What I do remember is the realization that someone was in the doorway watching us. And I remember being glad we hadn't gotten any further when I looked up from the floor and saw Eli Boyle—saw that look on his face that would remain with me forever, that look I would see again this week on his dead face, his eyes round and helpless, taking in more than they could bear.

I wish I could tell you how we all got there. Or what was said afterward. Honestly, I don't remember much beyond the look on Eli's face. I remember the carpet smelled like wine. I remember that Dana Brett's skin was a revelation. And I remember that it was just after midnight, the beginning of another cold, real day.

A foolish man is no more unhappy than an illiterate horse.
— Erasmus, *In Praise of Folly*

V

SIX MONTHS WITHOUT A DEAD BODY

I | IT'S THE EX·WIFE

It's the ex-wife. It dawns on Caroline as she reads Clark Mason's bitter divorce records, as it also occurs to her that this nice philosophical, theoretical discussion of crime may in fact refer to an actual crime—messy, banal, and ordinary, a new pile of old shit: Woman bangs everyone but her husband. Takes all the money from the divorce. Remarries before the ink is dry.

So he kills her.

Clark or Tony Mason—whatever he calls himself—why should he be any different from any of the slag-headed, short-tempered men who end up here? Most murderers kill someone close to them, and most murderers are men and most victims women—the unrequited, the girlfriends, the wives and ex-wives, women who spurned or cheated or simply didn't get dinner on the table in time. Caroline had wanted this to be different, wanted *him* to be different. But that's what happens when you go trolling for meaning in the truth. Fables are for children, parables for priests. All true stories are melodrama. Or noise.

The noise in these divorce papers is deafening. Caroline winces as she flips through the charges and countercharges recounting the three-year matrimony and acrimony of Clark A. and Susan A. Mason: *Complainant was unfaithful . . . Respondent forced complainant to quit her*

profitable job in Seattle and move to Spokane . . .
Complainant hid joint money in private accounts . . .
Respondent irresponsibly spent couple's savings, mortgaged
their home, and liquidated stock to run for Congress . . .
Infidelity . . . Impotence . . . Emotional abuse.

From the dissolution papers, Caroline learns that Clark
and Susan were married in December 1999 in Seattle
and divorced in January 2001 in Spokane. It was his first
marriage and her third. There were no children. In 1999
they left Seattle and moved to Spokane, and bought a
swanky, sizable house on Manito Country Club—with
cash. Caroline can imagine it. Stories like this seem apocryphal in Spokane, because they never happen to anyone
from Spokane. It's always a cousin in Seattle . . . or a
friend in the Bay Area.

Clark's story starts like all of those: Guy sells stock
holdings right near the high-tech peak. Sells a house in
the inflated Seattle market. Pulls a few million from investments and a million more out of a waterfront condo.
Comes to Spokane with enough money to buy half of
downtown, so it's a cinch to pick up a top-of-the-line
$500,000 house abutting the city's best country club—
with cash.

That's where this story diverges from the fairy tale.
Clark uses the rest of his dough to run for Congress, and
when he realizes he's losing, he starts draining the bank
account. When that's gone, he mortgages the house. The
wife is the kind of woman—Caroline can see her with
handled shopping bags climbing into her Lexus outside
the Bellevue Nordy's—who doesn't pay attention where
the money comes from, as long as her pedicure is paid
for. Clark loses the election, of course, and when she finds

out he spent all the money, well . . . the divorce lawyers are called in.

Apparently, there was some kind of settlement in which Clark was supposed to make payments to Susan, because the last court filing—and the probable spark for killing her—is from only a week earlier. Clark has missed a payment (*for the second time this year*, the papers note) and Susan's lawyer wants the court to garnishee his wages. Caroline can see the whole thing play out. He is served the court papers. He's listed as representing himself (ouch—a lawyer who can't even afford a lawyer). As he reads the court order (over and over) his face tenses up. The woman has cheated on him, bled him dry, and mocked his dream of running for office. He's all full up. So he whacks her.

It's hard for Caroline to admit, but if Clark's ex-wife is dead, then all his talk of contrition and nonsense about "nameless crimes" is just so much rationalization—the sound the guilty make when their mouths move.

Oh, I can name your crime, she thinks. And there's one other thing that worries her. Susan is apparently remarried. When the divorce papers were first filed, she was Susan Ann Hargraves Jennings Larsen Mason—a maiden name and three husbands—but in this last court order she is listed as Susan Ann Hargraves Jennings Larsen Mason *Diehl,* and Caroline worries for a moment if husband four, Mr. Diehl, is facedown in the same ditch as his new wife.

It also strikes Caroline in a moment of cattiness and self-abuse that this woman—who is her age, thirty-seven—has managed to snag four husbands in the time Caroline has gotten exactly zero.

The Diehls aren't listed in the telephone book, so Caroline checks the reverse directory. Doug Diehl is listed as having a house on Five Mile, a hilltop neighborhood of big, newer homes just north of the city. He's part owner of a Mazda and Ford dealership. No wife is listed, but they have probably just gotten married. Caroline calls Doug Diehl's home number.

"Hello!" Two voices answer together, in a terrible singsong. Caroline can imagine them bent over the answering machine as they recorded this, probably holding hands. "What's the *Diehl*?" asks the male voice. "We are!" says the female voice. "The real Diehls!" they sing together.

"We're not home right now," she says, "but if you leave a message for Susan—"

"Or Doug," he chimes in. He sounds older than her, and there's just a hint in his flat voice that these are her lines that he's reading.

"—we promise to call you back. So, do we have a Diehl?" she asks.

"We sure do," he says.

Caroline drops the phone into the cradle. "My God," she says aloud. Play that tape in court and Clark might just make a case for justifiable homicide.

She grabs her jacket, and on her way out peeks in the window of Interview Two. Clark Mason is rubbing his eyes, his pen still poised over the legal pad. It's eleven o'clock Saturday morning, fourteen hours since he began confessing. Maybe it's some sort of endurance test, she thinks, for him or for me. Or maybe it's an angle. After all, he is a lawyer. So what, he dresses and acts like a loon because he *wants* her to get fed up? Wants her to send him home so that later, when he's arrested for killing his ex-wife and her new husband, he can say that he tried to confess, but the police sent him away? It's a stupid idea, but it makes as much, or as little, sense as any of this—as much sense as a guy who wants to make a religious confession to a cop.

The confession has stretched now into its third shift. She tells the new desk sergeant there's a potential witness in Interview Two making a statement, and that if the guy wants to leave, to please call her. The sergeant promises to check on him, but he doesn't look up from the lurid paperback he's reading.

The drive north is quiet and peaceful, the early spring sun melting any last pockets of snow. Spokane lies in a long east-west river valley—pinched, it feels some days—and leaving downtown either to the north or the south takes a person up a progression of short hills blanketed with modest homes. Five Mile is one of the last and most drastic hills, where the houses lose their modesty, a steep three-hundred-foot tree-lined shelf, as if a huge cruise ship had improbably ground ashore at the edge of a city.

Doug and Susan Diehl's grand house is perched on three or four fenced acres on the starboard side of this ship. It is a new home of brick and cedar, three stories, with a massive attached garage that has four progressively larger doors: the smallest for a golf cart, the next two a standard two-car garage, the last door for a big motor home. The grounds are landscaped and fountained, covered in flowers, and there is a horse barn in back. Caroline parks behind an old, beat-up pickup truck with a metallic sign that reads JACK'S STABLE SERVICE.

Out of habit, she feels the hood of the truck. It's cold.

The white gravel crunches beneath Caroline's feet. She walks between flower beds to a big, arched front door, rings the bell, and waits. Nothing. She looks inside the window next to the door. The sunken living room is immaculate. White carpeting and white leather furniture and white lamps. It's like heaven. There are no bodies anywhere. That's a good start. She walks around back and sees no sign of anything suspicious, which doesn't prove a thing, of course. Doug and Susan could be in the basement, their heads crushed. *The Real Diehls!*

Sixty yards behind the house, the barn stands in a field of cut alfalfa. It appears to be new, painted bright red, with a white X on the door. A horse is grazing in the bunchgrass outside it. The barn door swings lazily in the wind. Caroline walks across the backyard toward the barn. Halfway, she bends over and picks up a woman's sandal. She walks through an open gate and keeps walking until she reaches the barn door. The horse looks up, sees her, and looks back over its shoulder, into the barn. Caroline follows its gaze to a bench across from the horse's stable and sees what appears to be Susan Ann Hargraves Jennings Larsen Mason Diehl, very much alive, and very much naked, astride what appears to be Jack of Jack's Stable Service, who looks about twenty and whose cargo pants are bunched up around the ankles of his cowboy boots. Jack must be pretty good at the service he provides in stables, because Susan's eyes are pressed shut and she is grinding her upper teeth into her lower lip. Caroline turns back to the horse, who turns back to her, as if he's going to speak, as if he's been waiting all morning for someone to come along so he could say what's on his mind—*Fuckin' humans*—and then he goes back to grazing.

She backs away and considers leaving or letting Jack finish his service (according to her fading recollection of such things, they are getting close), but then the answering machine echoes in her head—"We're the real Diehls!"—and she decides she can at least ruin the former Mrs. Mason's day. Caroline steps behind the barn door and knocks on it. The faint rustling sound—which she desperately wishes she'd heard before she looked through the barn door—stops completely now.

Susan whispers, "What was that?"

Caroline knocks again. "Ms. Diehl. Can I talk to you?"

There is a louder rustling now, back into clothes, she presumes. Caroline steps back from the door and waits. After a minute Susan Diehl comes out, wearing very small, very tight, very brand-new blue jeans, a western shirt, and one sandal. Her hair is blond and frosted and even after Jack's service she looks fit to entertain, with a good half-coat of makeup on her sharply featured face. She is tall and bottle-pretty, heavily produced, with vivid green eyes and long legs that go some distance in explaining what a guy like Clark saw in her.

Caroline offers her badge. "I'm Detective Caroline Mabry. With the Spokane Police Department."

Susan flinches. Behind her, a single eye watches through the crack in the barn door. Susan opens her mouth to say something to Caroline, but nothing comes out.

"I need to ask a couple of questions about your ex-husband." When Susan's expression doesn't change, Caroline realizes she's going to have to be more specific. "Clark Mason," she says.

Susan covers her mouth. "Oh my God. What happened?"

"Nothing. I just have some routine questions," Caroline says. "We're just trying to get some information."

Susan's eyes tear up.

Caroline is surprised.

"What did Clark do?" Susan asks. "Is he okay?"

"No, he's fine." Caroline smiles reassuringly. "I just talked to him."

"Oh." Susan reaches up and absentmindedly pulls a piece of straw from her hair. "Oh. Thank God. I worry about him."

"Why?"

"I don't know." Susan looks Caroline up and down, measuring her. They are about the same height, but that's the only similarity, and eventually Susan looks at the ground. "Habit, I guess."

Caroline looks down at Susan's one sandal. She hands her the mate she found in the lawn. Susan drops it in the grass and steps into it without apology.

"How is Clark?" she asks.

"He seems a little troubled," Caroline answers.

"You don't say."

They walk back to the patio. Susan steps inside, pours them each a glass of lemonade in green, stemmed glasses, and with little prompting when she returns, begins telling the story of herself and Clark.

"We started dating when we were sixteen," Susan says. "Clark was my high school sweetheart. We went to the prom together. The whole nine yards." She crosses her legs. Painted toenails.

"But you didn't get married until 1999?"

Susan nods. "We broke up at the end of our senior year. He went to college and acted like a—" She searches for the word. "—beatnik for a while. I married an older guy. Sort of like Doug, but a bit more—" She glances up at the barn. "—attentive. Clark and I lost track of each other. I was living in Seattle in '99. I'd just gotten divorced." She makes eye contact with Caroline. "My second divorce. My ex-husband had been a big political donor, and we were invited to a fund-raiser for some candidates, and I figured just because we were divorced didn't mean I had to lock myself away, so I went. It was at the Seattle Art Museum. There were all sorts of candidates milling about, and I watched one of them work the crowd and I couldn't believe it. It was Clark." She smiles at the memory. "Do you remember the first person you ever really loved, Detective?"

Caroline nods and thinks, not of high school, but of someone far more recent—she's surprised to find that she wants to call him right now.

Susan shrugs. "He swept me off my feet." She looks out to the barn, to where Jack is leading the horse back inside, and then looks down at her painted toenails. "Which is probably not that much of a trick, now that I think about it."

Caroline doesn't know what to say. She sips her lemonade. It is fresh squeezed.

"Our first date, he rented a Jeep Wagoneer and we drove into the mountains." Something about the memory strikes her as funny and Susan looks down at the ground. "We were married within three weeks. It just felt so right."

"And you moved back to Spokane?" Caroline asks.

"It's funny. At the fund-raiser, I just assumed Clark

was running in Seattle. It wasn't until I'd agreed to marry him that I even realized that the Fifth congressional was in Spokane. And by then, I was convinced that we were in love."

She shakes her head. "I spent my whole life trying to get out of this place, and now Clark drags me back with him. It was hard. I had a little boutique in downtown Seattle—nothing fancy, second-tier designer wear, last season's misses. But I was happy.

"And it wasn't just me. Clark had big clients and was writing contracts and bringing in business. He was considered a legal expert on high-tech companies." She smiles. "Which, in Seattle, was a pretty good position to be in. And I'm not even talking about the money, which was considerable. We were established. And he throws that all away. Says his name is *Tony* Mason now and he's running for Congress. Gives up everything, pisses it all away, to come back here."

"Why do you think he wanted it so badly?"

"I don't . . ." Susan leans forward, holds her glass in both hands and watches the lemonade swirl around the glass. "Actually, I've given that a lot of thought. I took it for granted because Clark always wanted to be in politics. He used to joke that he was president of his incubator. In high school, he ran for everything.

"But I don't think I ever understood just how badly Clark needed it. My therapist says running for office was his way of compensating." She glances sideways and then whispers, "Because of his eye."

Caroline nods. "What happened to his eye?"

"Some kind of accident when he was a kid." She shrugs as if it's not important. "I guess I always thought Clark wanted the power, or the fame, or, you know . . . to pass laws or govern or even, what . . . make a better world?" She says the words "better world" like a person might say "flying car." "But he doesn't want that shit. Fame, money. He sure as hell doesn't want power. You know what he wants?"

Caroline shakes her head no.

"He wants people to vote for him. Clark just wants them to pick *him*."

They are quiet. Susan leans back and crosses her legs, a move so elegant Caroline has to remind herself that only a few minutes ago those legs were riding the help.

"And you didn't want to be a politician's wife."

"No, I was into that part. Go to Washington, D.C., the parties and society there? In a minute. But even if he'd won, that was more than a year away. And when we got to Spokane, it was okay. We got a nice house, joined the Spokane Club and the Manito Country Club. I joined the Junior League. It was fine.

"Then, one day, I was at Nordstrom and I saw a girl from high school. I don't even remember her name, but she remembered mine. Do you remember so-and-so? she says. She's got three kids. So-and-so had an ovary removed. So-and-so works at the Safeway. Jesus—and it was like . . . My God. I can't live here. I mean, I lived in a two-million-dollar house on Lake Washington. I owned a boutique in Seattle. But here I was, just another stupid girl from the Valley, and no matter what I did, that's all I'd ever be. That's all I can be here." She finishes her lemonade.

"In the meantime, the party abandoned Clark. Sent him over here to run, and then cut off the money to the campaign. He won the primary, but he started out thirty points behind Nethercutt in the general and the people who said they were going to vote for him also would've voted for a potted plant.

"Then the attack ads started running, saying that Clark was a puppet, a Seattle guy coming in to take over Spokane. Clark . . . he went crazy. He should've given up, or run a cursory race. Even his campaign manager said that. But Clark wouldn't listen. He started spending our money. Without telling me. He sold all the stock—Microsoft, Cisco, everything but one stock: this idiotic Empire Game company that belonged to some guy he knew. He traded in his BMW. Tried to trade in mine. Took out a mortgage on our house. I arrived in Spokane the wife of a millionaire, and when we split up we had four thousand dollars and some stock in this worthless game company."

Caroline finds herself wanting to defend Clark. "In the divorce records, he accused you of having an affair."

Susan's eyes drift closed. Then they snap open, and Caroline sees something like determination behind the eye makeup. "I love Clark. In fact, he might be the only person I ever have loved. So go ahead and judge me if you want, Detective. I don't care. But don't think for a second that you know me. Because you don't."

Jack has finished in the barn and he walks through the gate and sheepishly toward the house. He is older than Caroline first believed, maybe thirty. He is skinny and walks with a limp, and his hair hangs long and greasy in the back. Caroline and Susan both watch him walk up to the house.

"Check's on the table," Susan says to Jack. "I'm sorry—" Again, she doesn't finish.

Jack nods and limps past them. From behind, Caroline can see that his knee seems to bend both forward and sideways and it's not hard to imagine a horse has fallen on that leg. When he goes around the front of the house, Susan stands and watches through the back of the house, her hands on her teardrop hips. Caroline hears the front door open as Susan moves along the house and watches through the back window, maybe to make sure he doesn't steal anything. The front door closes, and when Jack's truck starts, with a choke and a shudder, Susan walks back and resumes her story.

"The night before the election, we finally had it out. We yelled and screamed about all the things we'd done to each other. We each blamed the other for every problem either of us ever had. Grudges from high school. My divorces. His general unhappiness and lost ambition." Susan stares off past the barn. "I was crying; he told me that he'd never loved me. And finally I said, 'Clark, if I'm such a horrible person, if you never loved me, then why did you marry me in the first place?' Do you know what he said?"

Caroline shakes her head slightly.

"He said that he needed a wife, that people wouldn't vote for a bachelor. He said that even in high school, he thought I looked like a politician's wife." She shrugs and meets Caroline's eyes. "So you want to know if I fucked someone else? Yeah. I fucked someone else."

"Who?"

Susan flinches. "It doesn't matter."

"It may be important."

"It's not." She measures Caroline again. "Clark knows I had an affair, but he doesn't know who. I don't want him to know. It doesn't matter now."

"Look," Caroline says. "I'm going to be straight with you, Ms. Diehl. But I'd appreciate it if you didn't say anything to anyone about this. We think Clark might've hurt someone. Maybe even killed someone."

"Clark?" She shakes her head. "No. No way." Then she narrows her eyes and stares at Caroline but doesn't really see her, as if thinking about it.

"So let's say he found out who you were with." Caroline lets it hang in the air. "I'm looking for anyone he might have had a grudge with."

"The only person I ever knew him to hold a grudge against was Tommy Kane."

Caroline writes the name down. "Who's he?"

"Guy from high school. I don't even know what it was about. One day they were best friends; next day they hated each other."

"So what about the man you—" She can't find the word. "Did Clark know him?"

"Yeah. He knew him." She gives it some thought. "Look, I really don't want him dragged into . . ."

"Hey, if it turns out the guy's alive, I won't tell Clark anything."

Susan stares off toward the barn for a long minute and Caroline stares patiently at her, waiting her out. "Ms. Diehl?"

"I don't . . . Richard Stanton," she says finally. "His name is Richard Stanton."

Caroline writes the name down. "He lives here?"

She shakes her head. "Seattle."

"Have you talked to him recently?"

"It's been more than a year."

"Phone number?"

"No idea." And she offers no more information, just stares at the ground.

"Anyone else you can think of that Clark might want to hurt?" Caroline stands to leave and Susan stands with her, frowning.

She shakes her head. "Why do you think he hurt someone?"

"It's just . . . a tip," Caroline lies. "There's probably nothing to it."

Just then something occurs to Susan. "You thought it was me." This strikes her as funny and then, apparently, sad. She reaches for the door and opens it, then leans against it and looks at Caroline. "Clark didn't do whatever it is you're investigating."

"How do you know that?" Caroline asks.

She looks at the floor and a trace of shame fills her eyes. "Because if Clark was capable of it—after what I did to him two years ago—he would've killed me."

2 | HE SLEEPS PEACEFULLY

He sleeps peacefully, slumped over the table in the interview room, his face pressed against the stacked legal pads. Caroline watches Clark Mason through the slim window of the door, wondering if she could pull the pads out without waking him. She can't imagine what could be on all those pieces of paper.

Evan's fax from the newspaper is on the machine. The cover page reiterates that he has better things to do on a Saturday than dig through old files, and that not only does this make them even for the favor she did him, but she is now in his debt. She throws the cover page away and flips through the first pages—which consist of filings with the state and federal election commissions. It includes a list of donations from people and companies, everything from the teachers union to a downtown restaurant to long lists of individual donors. She circles a few, but nothing clicks, although one couple—Michael and Dana Langford—is listed as having donated twenty thousand twice. She writes down their names. Evan has noted on the filings that Clark wouldn't have been required to file records of his own money spent on the campaign.

Also in the fax are news stories from the paper, beginning with the story when *Tony* Mason launched his candidacy ("A 34-year-old political novice has stepped to the front of a weak field of Democrats trying to unseat four-term Republican Congressman George Nethercutt . . ."). The next story is a profile and Caroline skims it, sees that Mason grew up in the Valley, that he went to college in Seattle, got his law degree there, and (after a few years of "youthful meandering and exuberance") worked for a Bay Area technology company, then landed at a big Seattle law firm, writing contracts and representing high-tech companies. He made a good deal of money. He never left his Spokane roots too far behind, though, and according to the story, he serves on the board of a Spokane computer company called Empire Games.

Clark's teachers expressed no doubt he would one day run for office. "I'm surprised it's taken Tony this long," his old chemistry teacher is quoted as having said. In the picture that accompanies the story, Clark has shorter hair and no eye patch. He must be wearing a glass eye. He is staring straight ahead—lizardlike, as Evan remembered. Susan, much more relaxed in front of the camera, is hanging on Clark's arm. They are in the living room of a big house. Caroline is surprised by the detachment in the story—it offers barely more than the list of contributors—and both the article and the picture seem to her a kind of flat data, devoid of insight. There is a quality to the newspaper stories that intimates that "Tony" Mason is of a certain type—the young, idealistic politician, born to run for something—but this seems overly simplistic, leaves her with no better picture of who he is. His only issue seems to be "getting the technology train to stop in Spokane." She notices that every person who talks about him calls him Tony, and she imagines Clark prepping his friends and acquaintances, instructing them on what to say when the reporters call.

There are small stories about the Democratic primary and about campaign appearances. One story examines "Tony Mason's surprising challenge" of Nethercutt, and reports that his constant hammering of the "technology gap" between Spokane and Seattle has helped him gain twelve points in the polls. Yet he's still ten behind. Even so, Caroline can imagine the momentum he must've felt, and can imagine Clark stepping up to spend more of his money, desperate to get closer.

Then, two weeks before the election, comes another big story, headlined ADS TAINT MASON AS OUTSIDER. The story details an advertising campaign "charging that Tony Mason's strings are being pulled by party insiders from the west side of the state." The story reports that Seattle is about 60 percent Democrat while Spokane is about 60 percent Republican, and quotes television ads in which a deep-voiced announcer reads, "Until a year ago, Clark Mason was a rich Seattle attorney. Do we really want a rich, liberal west-side lawyer representing eastern Washington in Congress? Do we trust Seattle to take care of Spokane?" Apparently the ads never mentioned George Nethercutt, and the Nethercutt campaign denied any involvement. The story lists the sponsors of the ad as a political action committee called "the Fair Election Fund," which came into existence only a few weeks before the ads ran and apparently never cared about the fairness of any other election. In papers filed with the state, the Fair Election Fund is listed as having only two officers. Neither was available to be quoted, and neither had anything to do with the Nethercutt campaign. The ads cost $120,000.

Caroline writes down the names of both officers of the Fair Election Fund: Louis Carver and Eli Boyle.

The last news story is from the day after the election. Mason got more votes than anyone predicted, but he was never really close. The story has him planning to stay in Spokane, and to practice law and work on the computer game company, of which he was part-owner. The story goes on to say that he gave an emotional speech to a small room of supporters, and that he broke down twice. "You can be blinded by the glare from your own dreams," he is quoted as saying.

She jots down the names of the people quoted in the stories, although she isn't looking forward to a repeat of the pointless interviews with Pete Decker and Susan Diehl. When she is done, Caroline puts the news stories and election filings in a drawer in her desk and stares across the Major Crimes office to the door of the interview room. She thinks of Clark Mason sleeping in there, and realizes that she's tired, too.

She pulls a phone book from a drawer in her desk and opens it to the K's. There are three Kanes, Thomas, two Kanes, Tom, and one Tommy Kane. She tries that one.

"Hello."

"Tommy Kane?"

"Yes."

"I'm calling about Clark Mason."

"Look," he says, "I told the person who called last time. I'm not donating money to his goddamn campaign. I didn't vote for him last time and I don't care if he's running for treasurer of hell. I'm not voting for him. You understand? Take me off whatever list you've got there and leave me the hell alone."

Caroline considers correcting him, but she has gotten all the information she needs: Tommy Kane is not dead, and she doesn't really want to get bogged down in some twenty-year-old feud. "I'm sorry," she says. "We won't call again."

She checks her notes from the interview with Susan Diehl and looks for the name of the man she had an affair with—Richard Stanton. She tries the Seattle directory and comes up with six of them.

She looks back across the office, to the interview room. This is crazy. Maybe Susan is right; Clark couldn't kill anyone. After a moment she grabs the extra sandwich she bought, stands and walks to the door, opens it, and steps lightly inside. Clark Mason is breathing deeply; Caroline remembers the last time she watched another person sleep, five months ago, before her boyfriend moved out.

Clark Mason gulps air and shifts a bit. Caroline stands still. When he's breathing regularly again she edges forward and looks down at the third legal pad, open beneath his face. His handwriting is careful and neat, but he is covering most of it and she can only make out bits and pieces. Words are crossed out, entire sentences. She tries to figure out what he's writing about but can only make out that there are people in a hotel room, Clark and someone named Dana.

He stirs just then and Caroline steps back. Clark sits up, yawns, and rubs his hair. "Sorry," he says. "I fell asleep."

"It's okay."

"What time is it?"

"Almost three."

He nods. "Saturday afternoon," he says, not exactly a

question. He seems sluggish, slightly disoriented from his short, powerful nap. "I'm sorry."

She shrugs. "You can't quit now. I think you're close to the world record."

He rubs his temples and then looks down at the legal pad. "I can't tell if I was just dreaming or if I'm remembering because of the writing." He looks back at the pages he's written. "It doesn't seem real."

"What you did?" Caroline asks.

"Any of it."

"People always say that," she says. "You'd be amazed how many times I hear that. The first time someone fires a gun they always say it didn't seem real. Watching the person fall. The blood. None of it seems real."

"The blood," he says, as if in agreement.

She waits for him to say more, but he doesn't. He just looks at the sandwich in her hand. He seems groggy.

She slides the sandwich over in front of him. "You like turkey?"

"Mmm. Thanks."

She thinks about just dropping everything she knows on him: his ex-wife, Pete Decker, Tommy Kane, the election. Maybe it would shake loose his confession and get him to abandon this insanity. But she's not really sure what it adds up to. She'd rather wait until she knows more. She watches him unwrap the sandwich. The bottom piece of bread falls in his lap, smearing mayonnaise and diced lettuce all over his pants. It's strangely endearing, watching him try to clean up his pants.

"I shot a guy once," she says.

He looks up. "And you killed him?"

"Yes."

"Why?"

"He was coming at me. I thought he had a knife."

"Did he?"

"No," she says. "It turned out he didn't."

"Oh." He looks down at his sandwich.

She waits, to see if her own confession brings out his. But he takes a bite of sandwich instead.

"The reason I bring it up is that I was just thinking about what you said, how the victim wasn't really important, that the action itself is the . . . what did you call it?"

"The ideal," he says.

"Yeah, yeah." She tries to remember what it was that she wanted to ask him, something about motivation and justification, but it slips away and all she can do is stare, trace him with her eyes, his sharp jawline, the tangle of dark hair, and the strap from his eye patch that drifts in and out of that hair like a boat swamped by waves. "What happened to your eye?"

He says, between bites of sandwich, "BB gun fight. When I was a kid."

She's disappointed, somehow. She'd imagined some great story, the horn of a bull in Pamplona, a spear in New Zealand, but that's the truth of a thing like this. Parents warn you about sticks and BB guns, and when a person loses an eye it's generally because of a stick or a BB gun. *Things are entirely what they appear to be, and behind them—*

"Can I see it?" she asks.

He hesitates and then lifts the patch. The eyelid leans heavily down on the socket, but she can't see anything else. He lets the patch fall back.

She watches him chew the sandwich and she feels tired

all of a sudden, wonders if he'd mind if she laid her head down on the table and surrendered. The afternoon air is thick; it's difficult to hold her head up in it.

"The guy you shot?" he asks finally. "That's the only person you ever killed?"

"Yeah."

"But it's still with you? You still see it."

"Yes. But there are things I feel worse about." She pictures Rae-Lynn, the one she couldn't save, who spent her last six weeks fucking and doping and falling. Caroline bought Rae-Lynn a sandwich like this once; she can still see the tiny girl wolfing it down.

Clark nods. "There aren't even names for some of the crimes we commit."

It hits her like a kick to the side and she wonders for a moment if he can see right through her, to the bone. He is staring at her across the table, that one eye imploring. She would like to dismiss him, to let this whole thing go, pass it on to Sergeant Spivey to deal with Monday morning, and get some sleep. Sleep. But he says things like that and . . . Jesus. She puts her head down on the table and laughs bitterly.

"What's the matter?" he asks.

"I'm tired, Clark."

Then she feels his hand on the back of her neck, rubbing it, just underneath her hair. His hand is big and warm; the fingers find strands of tension in her neck and shoulders and he pushes, his hand constricting around the back of her neck. Caroline hears herself sigh. Then she pulls away, snaps upright, and stands.

He looks at his own hand, as if it has acted without his knowledge.

She's surprised to hear what's on her mind come out of her mouth. "Did you really kill someone, Clark?"

The question catches him. He looks down at the legal pads and runs his fingers along the pages, as if ordering the words, tidying them up. But sometimes there's nothing you can do. He gives up and his hands go back to his lap. He looks up at her and laughs. "If I hadn't, and if we had met some other way, do you think—?"

She sees the sandwich, the table, the legal pads, the pen, and his hands—a random collection, an idiot's still life.

"Yeah, probably," she says, without a trace of either flattery or flirtation. And when he doesn't say anything else, she turns and leaves.

3 | ALONE IS EASY

Alone is easy on the weekends. Usually by this time on Saturday afternoons Caroline Mabry has forgotten that other people even exist, and has settled in front of the television or the computer screen, finally at ease with herself after a week of awkwardness at the office. And so it comes as something of a surprise to see all of these people out on a sunny Saturday, hurrying in and out of their cars, into restaurants and shops. Everything seems so compact and tied down for these people: skis racked on top of their cars, children strapped into safety seats in the back. They all seem to be going someplace, the same place—some active, lively, family place—where everything is buckled down and safe. Compared with these people she feels untethered, flapping all over the place as she wanders through downtown Spokane, the melting snow puddled up on the streets beneath her.

Clark Mason's apartment is in Browne's Addition, a 130-year-old neighborhood of decaying mansions and grand family homes, most of them converted into apartments. She parks in front of Clark's building, an old two-story square, split into four apartments. There are four mailboxes on the paint-chipped front porch; she reads that C. Mason lives in A, on the first floor. One of the other mailboxes is covered with skateboarding stickers and another belongs to a girl named Lisa Miller, who has dotted the *i*'s in both her first and last names with crescent moons.

She peers through the window of Clark's apartment. There is no body. No blood. That's good. Or not. She recognizes the style of furniture as early college—ragged couch, bookshelves made from planks and cement blocks. There are books everywhere, and she feels a twinge, remembers his big hand on the back of her neck, and thinks, Great, I finally meet a guy who actually reads and he's either crazy or a murderer. Or both.

She walks around the side of the house and looks in the windows—a small bathroom with a soap-on-a-rope hanging from the shower, a bedroom with an open futon and a row of suits in a small closet—and then negotiates weeds and old lumber to make her way around to the back, where the porch is clear except for a bowl-shaped barbecue grill and a red picnic table. No blood, no feet sticking out of closets. If Clark Mason did kill someone, he didn't do it here.

When she comes back around to the front of the house, there is a man climbing the porch two steps at a time, an older man in slacks and a polo shirt, maybe sixty, dignified looking, with short gray hair and a day's gray beard. Caroline thinks about the skateboard stickers and the crescent moons and guesses the man isn't here to see those tenants. Sure enough, he walks to Clark's door and pounds on it. "Clark!" he yells. "You in there?"

The man turns around and sees her. He has sharp, washed-out blue eyes and that easy quality that attractive older men have. He also has the most drastically cleft chin that she has ever seen, like someone has taken one shot at splitting his head with a maul.

"Excuse me," she says. "Are you looking for Clark Mason?"

"Yes." The man eyes her suspiciously.

Caroline offers her badge. It takes a second to register with him, and when it does, he reaches out and grabs her forearm. "Oh, my God. Is he okay?"

"He's fine."

"Oh, good." He lets go of her arm. "He left a message on my machine yesterday. He sounded horrible. I was worried."

"Are you his father?"

"No." The man regains his dignified air. "I'm . . ." But he seems unable to tell her exactly what he is. "I was his campaign manager. Are you sure he's okay?"

"He's fine," Caroline says. "He's down at the station."

"Thank God," he says. "I've been calling him the last two days. Finally I just decided to drive over."

"Over?"

"From Seattle. I live in Seattle. Clark tried to reach me yesterday. He sounded so desperate. I was worried that . . . I don't know . . . he would commit suicide or something."

"Actually," Caroline says, "he says he killed someone."

The man's jaw drops.

"We found him in an abandoned building, and when we tried to ask him some questions he said he wanted to confess to a homicide."

"Who?"

"He won't say."

"No," he says. "That's not possible. Clark wouldn't hurt a flea."

Caroline extends her hand. "I'm Caroline Mabry. I'm a homicide detective."

"Richard Stanton."

It takes a moment for the name to register, for Caroline to remember Susan Diehl's reticence about the name of the man she was sleeping with when she and Clark were married. When Caroline had asked Susan if Clark knew the man, what had Susan said? *Yeah. He knows him.* Clark's campaign manager. That *is* cold.

"Can I talk to him?" Richard Stanton asks.

"He's down at the station, giving his statement. When he's finished, I'll let him know you asked about him."

"Look, there must be some mistake. It's inconceivable that Clark could hurt anyone, let alone kill someone."

"He said he was 'responsible for someone's death.' "

Stanton looks at the ground, concentrating, and then he slaps his head. "Oh, wait. I know what he's talking about. Jesus. That stupid, sweet kid."

Caroline waits.

"I'm sure it's not what you think."

She smiles. "How do you know what I think?"

"He's not a criminal."

"That may be," she says. "But if he is, and if you know something about it and you withhold information from me, then you might be in as much trouble as he is."

Stanton chews his lip, thinks about it. "Let me talk to him. I can straighten all this out in twenty minutes."

"Tell me what this is about and I'll let you talk to him."

They are at an impasse. He regards her, as if

measuring her resolve. "I can't. I'm sorry." Stanton looks away. "Can you take him a note?"

"Sure," she says, and offers a page of her notebook and a pen. "Put your phone number on there too."

He writes something, tears the sheet out and folds it, gives it to her.

"I'll have him call as soon as he's finished with his statement."

"Thank you," he says.

"So what happened?" Caroline points to the small apartment. "Guy runs for Congress and ends up in a shithole like this?" She tries to sound conversational. "That's a little weird, isn't it? Did somebody steal all his money?"

But Richard Stanton is spooked and doesn't want to talk anymore. "Look, my loyalty lies with Clark. I don't want to say anything until I talk to him or to his lawyer."

"Sure," Caroline says. "I understand." But something about the word "loyalty" doesn't sit right with her. She says, "I talked to Susan."

He flinches and looks up at her. Caroline keeps her face still, inscrutable.

Stanton doesn't look away, gives her a practiced smile. "How is Susan?"

"She's great," Caroline says. "Frisky as a colt."

Finally, Stanton has to look down. Caroline waves the piece of paper with the note on it. "I'll make sure Clark gets this. I'm sure he'll appreciate your loyalty."

"Thank you," Stanton mumbles. He starts to leave, hesitates, then walks quickly toward a car parked across the street: a BMW 700 series. He presses the keyless entry and the door chimes for him. It strikes Caroline that the candidate's wife seems to be doing pretty well and the candidate's campaign manager seems be doing pretty well. But the candidate himself is living like a freshman. The BMW pulls away.

In her own car, she opens the note. "He was sick. Nothing you could have done," Stanton has written. "Call me.—Richard."

She wads up the note and throws it to the floorboard of her car. Then she pulls out her cell phone and calls the front desk. The sergeant says he just checked on the Loon in Interview Two. "He's still at it."

"Thanks. I'll be back in a little while."

"So what's this about?" the sergeant asks. "What's he writing in there?"

"My resignation," Caroline says.

She hangs up the call and is about to drive back to the cop shop when she looks up and sees the sun at the horizon, maybe twenty minutes from setting. She's been at work now for twenty-eight straight hours. She looks down at the phone in her hand and taps out a number that she knows by heart but hasn't dialed in months.

"Hey," she says when a man answers. "Is this a bad time?"

When he says it isn't, she feels herself slump forward. "Look," she says, "I really need to talk. Is there any way you could meet me for coffee?"

4 | DUPREE IS WAITING

Dupree is waiting at the coffee shop, the same place she visited this morning. It feels like a week since she's been here, since she came downtown to see if Pete Decker was dead. The pierced girl is bringing Dupree a cup of coffee. She smiles when she sees Caroline: "Another chai?"

Alan Dupree stands up. He is wearing jeans and a T-shirt beneath a denim jacket. "Hey there." He's a little shorter than she is, and a lot balder. He has softened a bit around the middle since he took retirement from the police department six months ago. Even so, the blue eyes and the easy movement are the same as they've always been, the same as the day she met him thirteen years ago. And when he sits down she feels the old stuff, the sharp attraction in her throat, the desire to forget things she knows to be true.

She clears her throat. "Thanks for coming."

"My pleasure. You saved me from pinochle with the in-laws."

"How's Debbie?" Caroline asks. Dupree and his wife split up for a short time last year, just before Alan retired, and Caroline imagines their resuscitated marriage as tentative in some way, incomplete. Or maybe that's just what she likes to imagine.

"She's good. We're doing fine. She likes me better retired."

"And the kids?"

"They like me too. Staci asked me today what boys use their wieners for."

"Yeah, I've been wondering that myself."

"I told her nobody knows for sure."

"And how's the dark side?" Caroline asks. Since retiring, Dupree has worked as an investigator for a couple of defense lawyers, applying the same knowledge and energy to freeing bad guys that he once used to catch them.

"Great," he says. "The evil one gives great bennies."

Caroline has known other cops who retired and went to work immediately for defense lawyers, splitting from themselves, revolting against the framework that held them in place. She thinks about her own recent crisis and wonders if she could ever work for the other side like that. She doesn't think so.

"I don't think you called me down here to ask what boys do with their wieners."

"Actually . . ." Caroline tries to smile at his joke, but her eyes are drawn down to the table and her cup of tea.

Dupree reaches out and squeezes her hand. "Are you okay?"

"I don't know," she says. "There's this . . ." And she starts to call it a *case,* but she catches herself and suddenly it's all so ridiculous, so unlikely, she has the urge to simply drop it, go home and forget the whole thing. Perhaps she's known all along she was being obsessive and irrational, but it seemed harmless until now, when she can imagine the look of concern on Dupree's face.

"Tell me," he says.

And though she doesn't want to, she's too tired to not talk. She starts slowly, Friday at nine, and she can hear herself pronouncing the right words—*Davenport, eye patch, homicide, confession, legal pads, twenty-one hours*—but she can tell by the look on Dupree's face that the story is not translating, that he's not getting it—why she'd spend the whole weekend running down the people this guy knows, making sure they're still alive (she thinks it must sound like a normal murder investigation in reverse, starting with the killer and looking for the body). "I know it sounds crazy, Alan, but you can see how I got caught up in this, right?"

He doesn't say anything.

"You think I'm losing it," she says.

"When was the last time you slept, Caroline?"

"I know what you're thinking—"

"When?"

"Night before last."

"Two days without sleep. Are you drinking? Taking something?"

"No." She laughs, or makes that sound anyway; it feels like a cramp in her chest.

"You call Spivey at some point during all of this?"

"Yes," she says. "He told me he wouldn't authorize overtime."

"So you're not even getting paid for your breakdown," Dupree says. "Nice."

She laughs in spite of herself. "Look, this guy did something, Alan. I can feel it."

He is a believer in intuition too, and for the first time, he seems to consider her seriously. Or maybe he's just being nice. "You check girlfriends? Wife?"

"Ex-wife," she says.

"She alive?"

"Oh yeah. In fact, when I saw her, she was full of spunk."

"Who's with the lunatic now?"

"Nobody."

"You left him down there?"

"I can't charge him with anything. But he isn't going anywhere. I took his shoes and his belt."

Dupree looks confused. "He a suicide?"

"Probably not. I just knew he wouldn't go anywhere without his shoes."

For the first time Dupree smiles, and gets that look of pride, the one that used to sustain her. "Look, just send the guy home, Caroline. Before it gets any weirder. Tell Spivey to pick him up Monday and they can start over."

"Okay," she says, to placate him, to drop the subject. "You're right."

He takes a drink of his coffee. "You knew I was going to say that. You brought me down here to ask me something you already knew the answer to?"

"No." The breath catches in her throat.

Dupree just watches her.

"Look," Caroline says. "How many confessions have you heard? A thousand? We arrest a guy inside a house and he confesses to breaking in. Or he confesses that he killed the girl whose blood he happens to be wearing. We can see that. We call it a confession when some asshole describes for us the world we can see with our own fuckin' eyes.

"But this guy today . . . I mean, did it ever occur to you that there is another kind of confession, maybe a more important kind?

"What I'm trying to say is—" She's frustrated by her inability to communicate to him. "Maybe there's a whole other world, Alan. And maybe it's made up of all the intentions and the things we *don't* do, the things we don't say. The things we want. Maybe there's a place where all of our ideas go, our desires, and it doesn't matter whether we acted on them or not, in this other world they still have . . . power."

And finally she looks up at him and she can see that he wants to know, but he can't possibly. How can he when she doesn't even know.

"God, you need to get some sleep," he says quietly.

"Maybe there aren't names for the crimes we commit."

"What the hell does that mean, Caroline?"

"I . . . I don't know." She closes her eyes and thinks about Clark Mason and the way he uses that word "confession," the purity and freedom of it, the way he seemed to just cut loose, to talk—or to write, actually. "I wanted you and Debbie to split up," she blurts. "I never told you that. I never acted on it. But it's what I wanted."

"Oh, come on, Caroline," Dupree says. "That had nothing to do with it. You can't take responsibility for what happens to other people."

"Did you think when you left Debbie that we would get together?"

His answer catches in his throat. "That wasn't why—"

"Did you think we would get together?"

He looks down at his coffee.

"Then don't tell me it didn't have anything to do with it." She feels herself getting wound up. "Up here, in the world, we collect fingerprints and we make eye contact and we measure blood spatters and interview people who lie to us and we pretend like we don't want each other and that what we're doing has meaning. But what the fuck are we doing? You're with your wife. I'm alone. The dead stay dead. We bag 'em and take 'em away and clean up their blood and so what? We save some girl's life, and we're so busy patting ourselves on the back, we don't even notice that she's been dying since she was twelve. We just move the shit around up here, Alan. We don't change anything. We don't save anyone."

"Who told you we're supposed to save people?"

"Then what?" She cranes her neck.

"We make sure the other guys don't get away with it."

Caroline wants to sleep or to cry, she can't tell which. She looks past Dupree, out the front window of the coffee shop.

"You're tired, Caroline. That's all. You're a little burned out, and you're letting some nutcase get inside your head."

She's ignoring him now, staring out the window and across the street.

"You need to send this guy home. You need to get some sleep. You need—"

Caroline stands and begins walking slowly across the coffee shop.

"Where are you going?" Dupree asks.

She walks to the window and looks out. Across the street, behind the row of parked cars, she can see Pete Decker, wearing jeans and a T-shirt. He is yanking on something—the hair of the young girl who answered the door to Pete's apartment. Pete is dragging her by the hair across the sidewalk, toward the door of the apartment building. Two of the boys who were up in Pete's apartment earlier stand patiently on the sidewalk holding big stereo speakers and watching Pete pull the girl.

Caroline walks out the coffee shop door and begins to cross the street.

The girl says nothing as Pete drags her by the hair. Her face has the placid surface of the recently and frequently stoned. In fact, she doesn't resist at all until they reach the doorway, at which point she spreads her arms and calmly gets hold of the door frame. For a moment, Pete can't get her inside. He flicks at her face with the back of his hand and the girl crumples, and Pete gathers himself to finish dragging her inside when he looks up and sees Caroline striding across the street.

"Oh, hey," he says, and lets go of the girl. She slumps in the doorway.

Caroline reaches the curb without slowing. Pete steps out of the doorway and begins to sprint down the sidewalk, but she has the angle. She gets her arms around his waist and is dragged a few steps as Pete tries to run. He smells like cat piss and onions. He twists and punches at her the way he punched the girl; Caroline feels a weak blow glance off her head, and she slides off his waist and down his legs. He tries to run again, but she's got his ankles and Pete Decker crashes down on the sidewalk. He scurries a few feet with her holding his ankles before she can pull herself up and jump onto his back and crawl up, driving the ball of her kneecap between his shoulder blades. The air goes out of him, but he keeps trying to crawl forward. She grabs the scruff of his hair and pushes his face into the sidewalk. Pete continues to struggle, flailing with his arms and legs. Caroline wonders what the hell is taking Dupree so long.

And it's not until she gets one of his wrists and cranks it, and Pete finally gives up and slumps down on the sidewalk, that she looks up and sees Dupree standing there like a civilian, like a fucking tourist next to the gawkers and the kids with the stolen stereo. They're all staring down at Pete Decker, whose face is jammed into the sidewalk and whose nose and lips are bleeding. And they all have the same look on their faces.

"Jesus, Caroline," Dupree says. "You need to get some sleep."

5 | THE COLD RETURNS

The cold returns at night in Spokane, on just about every night in the winter, even nights like this, when the sun has lied about early spring. At dusk the air loosens, the pooled snow begins to freeze, and the grass shines like it's been sheeted with glass.

Across the street from the coffee shop the patrol officers have arrived. They carry the stolen TV from Pete Decker's apartment, along with plastic baggies filled with pipes and baking soda and allergy medicine and batteries and enough cooked methamphetamine to keep Pete and his young friends stoned until the real spring comes. A handful of people watch from the street. Dupree stands among them self-consciously.

Pete sits quietly on the sidewalk, hands cuffed behind his back, trying to reach the dried blood on his nose with his shoulder. When he sees two cops carrying the stolen TV through the front door, Pete tries to get Caroline's attention. "I was gonna give that back just like you said. You didn't give me much time to finish your list."

The father of the girl has arrived—a big man in work boots—and Caroline sees the girl cower in the lobby of the apartment building. Caroline pulls the father aside and points at Pete. "He's facing assault charges for hitting

211

your daughter," she says, and then shakes her head. "Make sure you keep her safe so she can testify. Okay?"

The father nods.

Caroline shakes her head. "What kind of asshole would hit a girl?"

The father looks down. "I don't know."

"Yeah," Caroline says. "Me neither."

The girl emerges from the building with a patrol cop, and the father opens his passenger door.

From the sidewalk, Pete cranes his neck and tries to laugh. "We was just screwin' around, huh, Amber? Tell the cops we was just screwin' around. Amber?"

Caroline walks over and crouches next to Pete so that her body is between him and the girl. Pete pulls back a bit, but when he realizes she's not going to hit him, he smiles. "You didn't give me very much time."

"No," Caroline says. She continues to fill out her report for the patrol cops.

"I could've used a little more time," Pete says.

"Sorry," she says, without looking up from her report.

Amber leaves with her father. Pete watches their car pull away.

The patrol cops come and stand Pete up. He rises easily; he's comfortable in custody, and the cuffs hang naturally on his wrists.

"Hey, I thought of something," Pete says.

"Yeah?" On the report, Caroline checks boxes for assault, possession of drugs, possession with intent to deliver, possession of stolen goods, and resisting arrest.

"Yeah," Pete says. "You asked if Clark ever had a beef with anyone. There was this one guy when we were kids."

"Tommy Kane?" Caroline asks without looking up.

"I don't know that guy. No, this guy was some kind of queer or something. He and Clark used to get into it at the bus stop. This kid named Eli Boyle."

Caroline ignores him.

"I used to have to break up their fights."

Two patrol cops grab Pete by his arms. "Yeah, I hope that helps you," he says. The patrol cops lead Pete away to the car. "Maybe helps me out too?" They push his head down, but he's done this often enough himself, and he slides easily into the backseat. "Maybe you tell my PO how I'm cooperating, okay? Okay?" The back passenger door closes and Caroline looks up to see Pete Decker settle back comfortably and nod to the cop in the front seat, as if he were Pete's driver. The car pulls away.

Dupree joins her on the sidewalk. "You goin' home now?"

"Yeah," she says. "I'll go down and get what the guy's written so far and tell him we'll pick it up on Monday."

"Good," Dupree says, and he looks down at his shoes. A decade ago, when she first started dreaming the old stuff—running away with him, a small town by a lake, kids—Alan's bald spot was the size of a nickel. Now it is a cantaloupe. She wonders if she has aged as obviously, or with her, if it's mostly inside, if there's a hollow spot, an emptiness that was a nickel and then a cantaloupe, and now is a beach ball.

He looks up from his shoes. "I was thinking about what you were saying. You know, about you and me? About that other world?"

"Forget it." Maybe that's what she's imagining, a place where all her daydreams went, and the people she cared about—all the good things that seemed to be in the future but were now beyond her. She reaches out and squeezes his arm. "I was just talking out of my ass, Alan. I'm just tired. Go home. See your family."

"Yeah, okay." He starts to go. "So are you seeing someone?"

"Mm-hmm," she says. "As a matter of fact, I am."

"That's great. What's his name?"

"Clark," she says.

"What's he do?"

"Lawyer."

Dupree smiles, a parent's reaction upon hearing that a misfit daughter has met a lawyer, a relief to see she's getting her life together. He seems genuinely happy for her. Or relieved that she's not his responsibility anymore.

"That's great, Caroline."

"Yeah. We've been seeing a lot of each other. We talk. It's good."

"Good," he says. He shuffles his feet once, reaches out and gives her a hug that she doesn't return, and starts for his truck. She watches him drive away.

Then she walks to her own car and drives back to the cop shop. She parks in the turnout, figuring she'll send the guy home and be back to her car in ten minutes or so. Inside the cave, the desk sergeant gives her a quick wave. "Good work down there. You can do the paper on Decker on Monday. You should go home. Get some rest."

Dupree has called.

"Yeah," she says. "I'm gonna do that. I just need to get something."

The thought of bed is overpowering. And yet, still, something is nagging at her, a name she keeps seeing and hearing. There is a point of fatigue that brings apathy, and if you can push beyond it, she thinks, another point that brings clarity.

She punches in the code to get into the hallway, and then uses her key card to get into the Major Crimes office. She looks in on Clark; he's still writing, of course, leaning back in his chair now, balancing the legal pad against the edge of the table. She goes to her desk, to straighten up before she kicks Clark out and goes home for what's left of the weekend. She takes the news stories and the list of contributors and is about to throw them in a desk drawer when clarity arrives.

She flips through the news stories until she finds it. The names of the two officers of the Fair Election Fund, the nonprofit PAC that laid out all that money on ads painting Clark Mason as a carpetbagger from Seattle. One of the officers is named Eli Boyle. She flips to the list of donors to Clark's campaign: five thousand dollars from Eli Boyle. So he's giving to the campaign and funding the ad campaign against it.

And what did Pete say: *Some kid named Eli Boyle.*

She goes to the reverse directory. Eli Boyle lives on Cliff Drive. She thinks of the grand old houses on Cliff Drive, overlooking downtown. The reverse directory also lists Eli Boyle's occupation. Founder, it reads, Empire Games.

That's listed, too, in the donations, for twenty thousand dollars and fifteen thousand dollars. And she finds Empire Games in her notes from the interview with Susan (. . . *sold all the stock except Empire Games* . . .) and in the news story (. . . *he's on the board of directors of a Spokane high-tech company called Empire Games* . . .). She looks up Empire Games in the reverse directory. Its address is the same as Eli Boyle's. She writes it on a sheet of notebook paper, tears it out, and stands. She walks across the room and opens the door to the interview room. "How we doing, champ?"

"Great," says Clark. "I'm almost done."

"Okay," Caroline says.

"What time is it?" he asks.

"Almost eight," she says.

He smiles, that easy smile, and she knows how Susan Diehl must've felt, seeing him after all those years. "I can't tell you how much this means to me," he says. "Your having faith in me like this."

"Okay," Caroline says.

Outside, she is surprised by how dark and cold it has gotten. She starts her car and drives across the river gorge and into downtown, curving along Riverside with a handful of other cars, and makes her way down wide streets built at the turn of the twentieth century for thick lanes of traffic that were long gone by the turn of the twenty-first. The buildings are stout and handsome— marble and brownstone, terra-cotta and brick. This city conceals more than some, its wealth and its power, its alliances and feuds, and even more, its grace. She catches a glimpse of the Davenport Hotel, lit up with construction lights. It's supposed to reopen later this summer. Spokane is old, and it is beautiful like old things are, lit from within by nostalgia and hard times. But so many windows are still dark, so many storefronts vacant. She envies the optimists here, but how can you ignore the taped and painted windows, the boarded doors? How can you not feel like a whole city of people waiting for it to finally be over, a whole city tending a parent's slow death?

She turns on Stevens and heads up the South Hill, once the concentrated prime real estate in Spokane. Cliff Drive is a short row of older houses at the first crest of the hill and Eli's house is at the far west edge, not one of the mansions but a grand home nonetheless, a nice, two-story Tudor style. The lights are off. She parks in front and steps out of her car. From here downtown appears bright and busy, and she can see across the river, across the valley, to the hills that used to frame the north side of the city, until streets and buildings sprawled over those and the next hills too, and the next, where the money has been moving, where Susan Diehl is sitting on white furniture in her own half-million-dollar house on her own ledge, drinking martinis with Mr. Diehl. It's a beautiful view, the lights like liquid coming down those ridges and the clouds set atop the valley, and she envies for a moment this Eli Boyle, with his high-tech money and his political donations and his Tudor house on this point, above all the shit.

Her feet clomp on the wooden porch. No one answers the doorbell. She presses a flashlight against the big picture window to cut the glare and peers inside. The living room is beautiful, dark wooded, with built-in hutches and cabinets, a fireplace, and a grand, curving staircase. But there is no furniture. She looks back to the front yard to see if she's missed a For Sale or a Sold sign, but she hasn't.

She walks along the wood porch to another window and peers in at a dining room, also empty. She walks all the way around the house, to the back, and looks in the kitchen. No appliances. Nothing. From the back porch she looks across the vast lawn. There is a garage, or a carriage house actually, on the side of the house. It is made of stone. River rock. A single set of dark wooden stairs winds its way up to the second floor. There is an apartment on top, or an office. These windows are dark too, but a dull blue light comes from one of the windows, like that of a computer screen.

The cold grass crunches under her feet. A hand-lettered sign on the carriage house reads EMPIRE INTERACTIVE. She shines her flashlight on the sign, then climbs the steps to the second floor and gets a slightly different view of downtown Spokane, with some perspective. From here, you can get it all in your field of vision. That's the thing. It really is a small city when you think about it, a city of coincidence and reoccurrence, of patterns and inescapable reputations. A man has dinner at a table next to his ex-wife in a restaurant he hasn't been to in two years and he shakes his head. "That's Spokane." A woman sees an old boyfriend picking out china with his new girlfriend at the Bon Marché. "That's just Spokane." But don't they also take some measure of security from that, too? Don't they all believe they know everyone here, that they are safe and gentle and good to one another? The devil you know.

She once went six months without a dead body.

But as she reaches the top step she recognizes that faint smell and it breaks her heart a little. Six months. And when she tries the doorknob to the apartment above the carriage house, it turns easily in her hand. Caroline Mabry takes a breath and pushes through the door.

The eyes may be confused in two ways . . . when they've come from the light into the darkness and when they've come from the darkness into the light.
– Plato, *The Republic*

VI

Statement of Fact

IV

I | WHO AM I

W ho am I to describe Eli Boyle's life, to trace its shape—the outside surfaces, the dates and places, the beginning and the end—when, admittedly, I never took the time to learn what existed inside that form, the truth of who Eli was, what drove him, what scared him, what he dreamed?

When this story comes out, the news media will not be so judicious, of course. They will sum up Eli's life with one false cliché or another: rags to riches to rags again, or the impersonal nature of computers, or the profane irony of a love triangle. And perhaps these stories are true; I honestly don't know what Eli believed, or what he thought about or—certainly—what his story *meant*. My own expertise lay simply in the horror of a shared adolescence, from its birth in humiliation at the Empire bus stop to its ending in betrayal in a wine-soaked room at the Davenport Hotel.

The world continued after the prom, of course, weightless days that left no imprint on me. True, my former friend Tommy Kane never spoke to me again, but that was of no great import—although I suspect it was he who threw my yearbook in the boys' room toilet. (A janitor fished it out; even today, many of the nineteen pages on which I was photographed remain wrinkled and stained.)

Dana and I did not get together after the prom. I'd like to believe this was because of our concern for Eli's feelings, but it likely had as much to do with a kind of inertia caused by the rigidity of our high school personas. At school, I was disheartened to see Dana retreat back into her loose clothing and pigtails, to see her stop wearing makeup. And I was equally surprised that my attraction to her could turn itself off so easily. I knew what lay under those baggy clothes, and yet she seemed too much like the old Dana, too bookish, too girlish, too logical in comparison to the curvy collections of fluff that I found attractive. I began to think of the girl in the hotel that night as someone else entirely. But this retraction wasn't entirely my doing. Something changed for Dana, too. She began to hesitate when she saw me, to blush when I said hi, to avoid me in the halls. It occurred to me that she might even see me as a mistake, as a blemish on her otherwise perfect school record, the B she never got. And when I read what she wrote in my wet yearbook (. . . *I'll always care for you. Be good. Dana*), I knew I'd been kissed off.

Susan and I were finished, too. She didn't sign my yearbook, but at school one of her friends handed me a note from her that read, in part, *We are fucking through*—although my teenage dyslexia transposed the last words to read *We are through fucking*—and I was understandably, or maybe just hormonally, heartbroken. I'd like to say that I was through with women built like Susan (all facade, no structural integrity), and that I had learned to appreciate the charming architecture of women like Dana (who am I kidding? There were none), but this is a story of weakness, not of strength.

I got no yearbook wishes from Eli. No notes or second-hand threats. I suppose I just stopped existing for him. I thought about apologizing, telling him that Dana and I weren't going to see each other, that it had been a mistake, but I worried about making it worse, making it seem like I'd stolen something I didn't even want, that I'd made out with his date just to spite him. While I tried to figure out what to say, one morning my shoes and jeans and T-shirts—the entire costume from Eli's ill-fated remake—appeared on my back porch, neatly folded.

School ended before I figured out what to say to Eli, or to Dana. Of course I could've picked up the phone anytime, but something had given way in me. With college looming, the final hours of my childhood held little interest for me, like the last, hot afternoon of grade school—report cards mailed, desks cleaned, every eye on the needle-thin second hand making its glacial sweep around the clock face.

Days lost their mooring and drifted, banged one into the next, and I moved within them in a languid, sun-bleached daze. Summer bled out beneath my feet. My life took on the quality of nostalgia, sweet and distant and beyond change, my family receding into an album of memories. I crafted a schedule in which I rarely saw them, working as a dishwasher in a restaurant all night and sleeping most of the day. I was about to become the first in my family to go to college, and my parents were overly respectful of this; they kept their distance, unsure how to treat me. They fed me and housed me but stayed out of my way, and I ate and rested and brooded like a climber the night before summit.

But Ben had no patience for this new state of affairs.

He'd just turned sixteen, and though he remained small (a shade over five feet six inches tall, broom thin), he was dealing with sprouts of hair beneath his arms and on his chin, and the divining-rod erections that govern most sixteen-year-old boys. I'd always been a sort of tour guide through his adolescence, and now that it was finally getting good, Ben couldn't understand where I'd gone, why I wouldn't drive to the lake with him or shoot baskets or talk about girls—why I wouldn't sit on the porch at twilight and laugh at things so familiar we barely needed to mention them.

"Let your brother sleep," our mother would say as I lay in bed all afternoon, the pillow over my head, trying to breathe in long, sleepy rises and falls, pretending I didn't know Ben was in my doorway. Eventually, he got the message; by summer's end, he'd just nod when he saw me. When I left for college, he was camping with friends.

So that's how my last summer as a child passed, in chrysalis hibernation, closed off to the people in my life, until the first day of September arrived and I emerged coolly into our driveway, a suitcase in each hand. My sisters hugged my hips. My mother cried.

My father handed me the keys to their old Dodge Colt, as if I'd just won a very bad game show. "I can't pay for very much college," he said. "But I can sure as shit get you there."

"Thanks," I said, and shook his hand. Then I climbed in the car.

I should have known, of course, that I was leaving behind unfinished business, not just with Ben, but with Eli and Dana. But all that summer, solitude had worked like a drug on me, and I happily allowed old intentions and obligations to fall away. I believed what TV teaches you—that change is only an episode away, the past is dead, and the only world is the one we're in.

I drove my father's car against the grain of late-summer clouds, drifting west on I-90, shadowing the river valley through the city of my birth, my arm resting on the open window, the wind rippling my sleeve. I crested Sunset Hill and saw Spokane recede in the rearview, a world beneath me, the last light glinting off the downtown buildings. The whole thing felt intimately familiar; the beginning of every daydream I'd ever had.

And that was it. September came and we did what people do—Dana and Eli and me. We went to college. More than a decade would pass before we would speak again.

Dana went to Stanford, just as she'd told everyone she was going to. She rarely came home from Palo Alto, but I heard through mutual friends that she joined a sorority and embraced the blossoming that she'd only flirted with in high school—tight skirts and torn jeans, filtered smokes and cheap well drinks. After this brief rebellion she cannily double-majored—she must've had a psychic student adviser—in management information systems and marketing. She became part of a group of Stanford grads and their friends that billed themselves as a sort of Bay Area technology salon—a tight community of young creative computer and business students who lived in and around Silicon Valley, "positioned," as they would say, to be the vanguard of all that was coming, and to become quite wealthy in the next few years.

In that first decade after high school, there would be

no canniness or blossoming or positioning for Eli. Certainly no wealth. He spent a year at community college but managed only a few credits before he dropped out to care for his mother, who had been diagnosed with Parkinson's disease. Eventually, he and his mother moved to a downtown apartment to be closer to the hospital where she received medical care, and Eli gave up on college altogether and took a job processing film at a one-hour photo. I saw him once during this time—walking downtown, wearing a photo-booth apron, his nose in a book, plying the sidewalk with his bent-legged shuffle, shoulders rolled forward and glasses at the end of his nose. I was with two frat brothers, privileged sons of Mercer Island professionals, and I am sorry to admit (amid a thousand sorries) that I did not wave or stop to say hi or so much as slow down.

For me, those first two years of college had been nothing short of epiphanic, fulfilling in ways I didn't know I could be fulfilled. Seattle was a land I had dreamed about without knowing it existed (let alone four hours away by car), and I happily left behind my hometown and its embarrassing, rigid poverty, its stunted ambitions, its daydreams that too often consisted of getting day shift at the aluminum factory. I thought of my home as a kind of childhood disease I had overcome, and I learned to despise it the way a thankless child despises his uncultured family.

The campus of the University of Washington opened for me like a pop-up book. Backpacked and Ray-Banned, I marched in Top-Siders and polo shirts with twenty thousand other soldiers of reinvention, from class to class in vast lecture halls, to intramural games along the lake, used bookstores on the Ave, keg lines in the district, breakfast joints in Wallingford, bars in Belltown. I crabbed and kayaked, rock-climbed and mountain-biked, threw Frisbees on cold beaches, drank Canadian beer, and learned to have sex with bulimia-thin girls in dorm room bunk beds and sorority house study carrels (though I never forgot my lessons with Susan, and was always on the lookout for a more vehicular hump). I studied. Got A's. Networked. Brown-nosed.

But most of all I ran for things. I started slowly, filing unopposed for sergeant at arms in my freshman dormitory ("Make it Mason!") until, by my junior year, I was in full campaign mode—vice president of my fraternity (and then a shoo-in for the top spot my senior year) and president of the campus chapter of the Young Democrats, as well as a lesser officer in six other organizations, everything from Junior Toastmasters to the Young Sierra Club. I fell in with a group of similar alpha achievers, and we worked our young résumés and our grade point averages with the same fervor that we chased tail.

At some point during my sophomore year, I stopped thinking of myself as being from Spokane. I was part of the torrent of people who were just then beginning to flood Seattle with our affections and affectations, with our arrogance: an unwitting conspiracy of transplants and entrepreneurs, hikers, bikers, and seekers, the regionally hip—a cult of casually dressed devotees of grubby Northwest realism. Over the next twenty years, we would ruin all that we found charming: old flop hotel lounges and Irish bars and Pioneer Square taverns. We discovered smoky dives filled with drunken hobos and cranky Norwegian fishermen and drank and smoked amid them, sucking their genuineness until we looked up and saw the hobos were software engineers and the fishermen bicycle messengers and hummus was on the menu. Coffee and chowder and punk trios became brand names and mall kiosks and dull pop. Tucked-booth greasy-spoon breakfast joints became tour-guided facsimiles of tucked-booth greasy-spoon breakfast joints, and only by listening closely ("We'll have the whole wheat goat cheese pancakes, the six-herb flan, and two cappuccinos") could a person tell the difference. We turned every gas station into a coffee shop, and by the time I left Seattle you could have four hundred flavors of coffee, but you couldn't find a decent gallon of gas.

We were beginning to love the place to death.

"Aren't you homesick?" my mother used to ask on the phone, at the outset of my affair with Seattle. Later, she was more direct. "Are you ever coming home?"

But how could I leave, even for a weekend? The sun might come out.

Spokane was only four hours away and yet it faded from my memory. I came home only three times each my freshman and sophomore years. "I'm really swamped" was my standard response to my mother's entreaties. This was the advantage of being the first in my family to ever go to college; they had no balance to my stories of round-the-clock studying, of mandatory poetry readings and guest lectures and spirit bonfires.

When I did come home I felt increasingly detached from Spokane, and from my parents, whom I lectured with the arrogance of a transplant, with the zeal of a religious convert. Every other sentence out of my mouth began, "The problem with this place—" I suggested that

Seattle's vitality revealed Spokane's failings: its aging population, its economic and political intractability, its lack of imagination and unrelieved shabbiness. "Spokane is Kmart," I famously said at Christmas dinner once. "Seattle is Nordstrom."

Mom and Dad were so proud of my A's and my smooth transition to college that they indulged my bouts of civic self-importance. My sisters, too, sat through my lectures. The only person who didn't put up with this shit was my brother Ben, who rolled his eyes at my newfound civic pretentiousness and missed no opportunity to mock me: "Spokane is a cup of piss," he said that same Christmas. "Seattle is a two-dollar cup of piss."

My parents were just beginning to worry about Ben during this time, that his unleavened cynicism was more than just a phase. He had graduated from high school and grown into a thin, caustic young man; with his short hair and raw features, he looked like a British soccer fan. He had abandoned his smoking jacket and pipe for a mode of self-expression he called "enlightened laziness," which consisted mostly of sitting around my parents' house in flannel pajamas, skimming old philosophy books, playing Atari, and drinking red wine out of Slurpee cups. When my father laid down the law and told him to enroll in college, Ben disrespectfully declined. He found an apartment and got a job mopping hospital corridors at night so that his days would remain open for sitting around in his pajamas, reading Nietzsche and Sartre, and drinking red wine out of Slurpee cups.

That fall—it was my junior year—every phone call home quickly devolved into a discussion of Ben's malaise. "He needs to get out of Spokane," I said. "It breeds apathy." But my mother convinced me that at least some of it had to do with Ben missing me, that he was aping my slovenly behavior during my last summer at home.

That's how, on a crisp, clear Saturday morning that October, I found myself driving across Washington State, through the serrated Cascades, through the channeled scablands, wheat fields, and scrub forests, until I descended into Spokane and all that I'd left behind. I drove straight to Ben's apartment, near Spokane Falls Community College, on a basalt-and-pine ledge north-west of downtown. His apartment was at the end of a wrought-iron-railed staircase—a basement studio with dark curtains hung over submarine windows. It was 11:00 A.M. and the apartment was dead quiet. I knocked three times before the door opened, and there stood Ben, in flannel pajamas, eyes half-opened slits. I followed him into the apartment and he went to the kitchen, poured himself a bowl of Cap'n Crunch and a tumbler of red wine.

"Isn't it a little early for Chianti?" I asked.

He rubbed his head and his brown hair remained where he'd pushed it, like Play-Doh. "You can't serve Riesling with Cap'n Crunch," he said.

The apartment was dark and fetid, damp like the inside of a shoe. "Mom and Dad want me to talk to you about college," I said.

"Barber college? Electoral college?"

We sat on the ratty couch in his living room and he gulped wine while we watched football on his twelve-inch TV. Dog-eared paperbacks lay everywhere; I picked one up—*Resistance, Rebellion, and Death,* by Albert Camus.

"You do the classwork, but you don't want the credits. Is that it?"

"You want me to pay someone to tell me what books to read?"

"Is that all school is to you—the books? What about the people? The experience? The social life?"

"Yeah, good point." He feigned earnestness. "Maybe I could join your frat. We can double-date-rape together."

"Look, I'm just here because Mom is worried about you. It doesn't matter to me what you do."

"That's a shock." Ben took a pull of his wine.

I talked him into getting dressed and going for a walk. I put on a windbreaker. Ben put on three sweatshirts.

We walked west, down Pettet Drive and across the river, and when Ben looked up, he saw that I'd steered us to the campus of Spokane Falls Community College.

"Subtle," he said.

"Sorry," I said. "I know you had your heart set on living in the basement of that crappy apartment building the rest of your life—"

"Actually," he said, "I'm waiting for something on the second floor to open up."

"—mopping floors, drinking wine, and playing Atari."

"I'm saving for a Nintendo."

"Don't you want more than we had growing up?"

"Actually," he said, "I want exactly what we had growing up."

We walked into the student union building. There were a handful of students in the cafeteria, studying and eating. "Doesn't this look better than mopping floors?"

Ben was unimpressed. "You don't think someone mops these floors?"

"I don't see why it has to be you."

"It has to be someone." He took in the students' dim presences and looked away. "Do you know what your problem is, Clark? You decide what you're going to see before you even look at things."

I was amused. "Yeah, why do you suppose that is?"

"You really want to know what I think?"

"Sure."

"I think you're so busy climbing you don't notice what's really around you."

"That's called success, Ben," I said. "That's called drive."

"Or running away."

"I run *for* things. Not away. You might think about that yourself." I pulled him over to a bulletin board near the front of the cafeteria. It had the word CLUBS written on top in big block letters. "There's a whole world out here—"

"There's a whole world in here." And he pointed to his head.

I ran my hand over the bulletin board, shingled with flyers and notices from three dozen campus groups, from the Gay and Lesbian Student Alliance to the Arab Student Union to the Spokane Climbing Community. "You know what this is?" I tore a phone strip from a campus philosophy group and handed it to him. "This is—"

That's when I saw something out of the corner of my eye that froze me.

"What's the matter?" Ben asked after a few seconds.

The club name was stenciled in green military-style letters on a white sheet of paper, but there was nothing explaining what the club did. There was only its name, the date and place of its next meeting—that very day, it turned out—along with a contact person and a phone number. I wonder even now, years later, what might have happened if I hadn't torn that small piece of paper away. Maybe none of this would have happened. Maybe that was the point from which all things diverged, the point at which we could've all continued forward, instead of eddying back to the place where I sit now, alone.

"Is that—" Ben began.

"I think it is," I said. I stood there with my little brother, staring at that tiny sheet of paper. On the paper was written a phone number, the one-word name of the club— "Empire"—and a contact person.

Eli Boyle.

2 | THE EMPIRE CLUB

The Empire Club met in a dark, smoky lounge called Fletts, on a street of old businesses just across the river from downtown. At night, the lounge burned easily through its fuel, a steadily dying clientele of heavy drinkers and smokers. During the day Fletts served up BLT's and patty melts at its small lunch counter, and the smoke was allowed to slowly dissipate in the lounge, which sat dark and empty—except on Saturday afternoons, when the lounge housed Eli Boyle's Empire club.

I sat on a stool in the restaurant, from which I could see down the length of the counter to the lounge. The meeting was scheduled for 2:00 P.M.; it was 1:30. I ordered a cup of coffee and a bowl of tomato soup and sat with a baseball cap pulled down on my head and my windbreaker pulled up high at the collar. Looking to my right, I could see down the lunch counter and across the hall, where Eli was scurrying around the lounge, pacing up and down a long table, stacking sheets of paper in a dozen piles. He looked pretty much the same, although a potbelly strained his button-down shirt and his hair had thinned. But what surprised me most was the look of intensity on his face.

"I still can't believe that guy kicked your ass," Ben said. He had begged to come, and now I could see what a mistake it was to have let him.

"It was a draw," I said.

"Are you going to talk to him?"

"I don't know."

The other members of Empire began dragging in. "Hello, honey," said the old waitress, or "Hiya, sweetie." The first was a gawkishly tall young man with dark hair and a storklike nose, followed by a frail young boy leaning sideways in a wheelchair, pushed by an older woman I assumed was his mother. Two girls came in together, their steps synchronized, a good four hundred pounds between them, and then a pale young man. They all carried thick black binders with the word EMPIRE stenciled on the front, and they were eager, as if they had a great story to tell and couldn't wait to get inside to tell it.

Five minutes before the meeting was to start, I felt a poke in my side.

"Clark friggin' Mason."

I turned and looked up, half expecting to see Eli, even though the voice was higher pitched, and coming from a man less than four feet tall.

"Louis!"

"Do I look different?" he asked me.

He looked about the same, a blunt curl of hair over wide fun-house features.

"I grew two inches since high school," he said proudly. As soon as he said it, I could see that he was bigger, and that by dwarf standards he must be quite tall.

"You look great," I said.

"You too."

"Are you in this . . . thing, Louis?"

"Empire?" He smiled and waved a binder like the other

members carried. "Yeah. It's really great. Eli has a real gift. Are you here for—"

"No," I said, "we just happened to stop in—"

"What are the odds?" Ben said next to me.

"—for some soup," I continued.

"We love us some soup!" Ben said.

I elbowed Ben and turned back to Louis. "So what is this thing?"

"Empire?" Louis looked unsure, as if it wasn't his place to say. "It's hard to explain."

"But it's a club?" I asked.

"No," he said, "more like a game, one of those interactive, character-driven things." He quickly corrected himself. "Eli doesn't want us to call it a game."

"What does he call it?"

"He used to say it was an 'alternative world.' Now he just calls it Empire. He says defining it is the first step to killing it."

"So it's like a role-playing thing?" Ben asked. "Like Dungeons and Dragons?"

Louis chewed on his bottom lip. "I really think you should talk to Eli about it."

"I'll bet it's more like Risk," I said. "Or Axis and Allies." I remembered the way Eli always drew tanks, and the charge he'd gotten from tug-of-war and battle ball. "One of those games where you have wars and conquer each other and take over land?"

"Yeah, there's some of that. But you know, you should really ask Eli."

I looked into the lounge. "I don't know if he'd want to see me," I said.

"Yeah," Louis agreed. "He doesn't let go of things easily."

I was surprised that Louis knew about the rift between Eli and me. "Maybe I'll stop by next time I'm in town."

I could see Louis was relieved. "Sure," he said. "Next time."

The waitress saw Louis then and brought him a Coke. "Hey, big guy," she said.

"Hey, toots," he said, and turned away from me. "What time you get off?"

"Couple minutes after you touch me," the waitress said.

This tickled Louis. "On my worst day," he said. While he flirted I tried to get a look at the folder he was carrying, but he held it close to his side. There were about ten other people in the lounge now, and I could see Louis was eager to join them.

"Could you do me a favor and not say anything to Eli?"

"Sure," he said. "It was really great to see you, Clark."

Once Louis was inside, the waitress carried a tray of glasses and two pitchers of soda into the room. Eli held up a pocket watch, made some announcement, and the lounge erupted in noise and activity, like a small stock exchange. Ben and I craned our necks to watch. The group was spread out at the tables, shuffling paper, stacking things, and exchanging what looked like Monopoly money back and forth, making trades, shuffling fake money and papers from their folders back and forth across the tables. People were relaxed and smiling, but they were also working hard. At the front of the room Eli was not smiling. He paced and collected paper from people, handed paper around, talked and gestured with his hands. Every few minutes, he'd turn around and move pins on a big map behind him.

"This gives me the creeps," Ben whispered.

Eli worked with such energy it was hard to take your eyes off him. At one point he wiped sweat from his brow. A few minutes later he castigated one of the girls about something, and she looked down at her shoes in shame.

We watched for ten or fifteen minutes more and then we paid for our soups—Ben hadn't touched his—and walked out, taking the opportunity to look closely into the lounge. At the door, we could hear people yelling: "Two over here!" "Calling out!"

We started walking back toward Ben's apartment. "That was weird," Ben said. "Watching someone who didn't know we were watching him."

I knew what he meant. There was something odd about Eli, the way he could detach from himself physically. "He's always been like that," I said. "I think there's always been this gap between the way he sees himself and the way we see him."

"So which one is real?" Ben asked.

"What do you mean?"

For the first time that day, Ben was engaged. "I just wonder, which is a truer view of reality, the way we see ourselves or the way others see us. Is Eli king of that room, king of the fat girls and albinos? Or is he what we see—the same old awkward guy from our neighborhood, whose only claim to fame is that he once kicked your ass?"

"Eli is what he is."

"But I'm not just talking about Eli." Ben stopped walking and leaned against the chain-link fence of a park. Behind him, kids were shooting baskets on hoops with no nets. "I'm talking about all of us—about me," Ben said. "I imagine I'm living an ascetic's life, stripping myself of everything but my curiosity. But you show up out of the blue and all you see is a guy wasting his life drinking wine and watching TV."

Ben rubbed his hollow cheek and seemed to be chasing something around in his mind. "Or you, with your frat-boy friends and your law school haircut imagining you're more evolved than the rest of us."

I didn't deny it. "So what do you see?" I asked.

Ben's eyes hitched once on the way from my face to the ground. "That's not the point I'm trying to make."

"Sure it is," I said. "What do you see when you look at me?"

"It's not important," he said.

"Come on," I said. "What do you see, Mr. Ascetic? Mr. Chianti. Mr. Curiosity."

"Well," he said. "Okay. I see someone so focused on the way he's perceived that he forgets who he is. And where he's from."

I grabbed him by the sweatshirts and pushed him against the fence. "I'm only going to tell you this once," I said. "Eli Boyle did not kick my ass."

I smiled, and then he did, and I let him go. But for a few minutes afterward I still felt his louvered ribs in my hands, and the echo of what he'd said in my head. We walked slowly back to his apartment, the wind swirling garbage before us, our progress marked by the sagging clapboards of our hometown. I looked around Ben's neighborhood. Every other car window seemed to be covered with plastic or cardboard or duct tape. "Is there no glass in this town?" I asked. We passed a couple of children playing in a patch of dirt that passed for lawn. One of the kids sat in a bathtub, weeds coming through the drain, while the other kid made thundering swats against the bathtub with a stick.

Ben sighed. "You make the classic elitist mistake."

"What's that?"

"Believing that people choose to be poor."

I looked around at the neighborhood, which was not much different from the one Ben and I had grown up in. For the first time it occurred to me that no matter how many times I sat at an outdoor café on Capitol Hill, how many beers I had in Pioneer Square, Seattle might never be my home. If that is true—and I have come to believe that it is—then I suppose it's also true that no matter how many interesting and progressive and attractive people I met in my life, I was always alone in some fundamental way when I wasn't in the company of my little brother.

"You'd better get back," said Ben when we reached his apartment.

"Yeah," I said, distracted. "I got this thing tomorrow."

"Sure," he said.

"We okay?"

"Sure."

"And you'll at least think about school?" I asked.

"Every day," he said.

We hugged awkwardly and I started for my car. I thought of something I wanted to say—that he was wrong, that I could tell the difference between what other people thought about me and what I knew about myself—but when I turned around Ben had disappeared, gone back into his cave.

3 | MY BROTHER DIED

My brother died suddenly, or so it seemed to me, embedded as I was in the ephemera of fraternity politics, classwork, and stretch-panted sorority girls that constituted the fall quarter of my junior year. My brother died on November 19, 1985, one month after I saw him, in the hour it took me to finish an exam in Principles of Government—an hour that he spent slipping in and out of consciousness, lifting his head, swearing at a nurse, pulling his IV tubes out, asking for our father, breathing fitfully for a few minutes, and finally going still. My brother died in spite of the fervor of a team of nurses and doctors who arrived with a crash cart and tried shocking and drugging and beating him back to life. My brother died two hours after his first treatment of experimental chemotherapy drugs and high-dose radiation—a *double double,* one of the techs called it—sparking in my family a perpetual distrust of the medical community, as if the doctors had hastened his death. (Years later, my father still referred to doctors by his clever pet name for them: "heartless sons of bitches.") My brother died twenty-four days after being diagnosed with Stage IV extradonal Hodgkin's lymphoma—the fastest "outcome" his doctor had ever witnessed for that particular late-stage illness, or so he would tell us later. My brother died a week after turning nineteen.

You might wonder, Caroline, why I've waited until this late point in the narrative to mention something as important as my brother's cancer, why I would attempt to understate it this way, to slip it into the text like any other detail in here, as if an element like that has the same atomic weight as a first kiss, a driver's license, the joys of college. My only defense is chronology, which we cling to the way we cling to faith, in the vain belief that if we obey the order of things, the universe might not go to shit, time might not pile up around us and we might not become buried by random events, ruined by confusion and grief.

But it happens anyway.

A week after I left, Ben's boss called my mother to say that he had missed two straight days of mopping. Mom found him unconscious on the floor of his apartment, in his pajamas, a spilled mug of wine on the linoleum. He was sweating and feverish, his neck and shoulders horribly swollen. She had seen his glands do similar, smaller versions of this trick over the last two years, and she thought about the years of chills and sleeping problems—*That boy's always got a bug.* She said his name and touched his forehead, and her hand jerked away, hot and wet.

I don't know whether, in those first days, my parents shielded the severity of Ben's illness from me, or the doctors shielded it from them, or I simply didn't get it. But from across the state, the progression was impossibly fast, marked by confusing telephonic pronouncements from my mother: *The doctors think it's The Exhaustion. They're testing him for The Cancer. They think it's in The Limp Nose. They think it might be The Hotchkiss Disease.*

Apparently, it's matzo-sized, which sounds fairly big. They think it's in the fourth stage. I think that means he's almost better.

I don't blame my mother for any of this. She'd suddenly been dropped onto a planet with a completely different language, and doctors who couched my brother's death sentence with passive and misleading terms (*late-term systemic, marginal outcome, radical treatment, negligible recovery rate*), terms that forced her to ask questions she didn't even know the words for and certainly didn't want the answers to. And she had to bear this alone. My father couldn't bring himself to step into a hospital, and my sisters were too young to help. I planned to come home when the quarter ended, of course, but I was too late.

Afterward, the doctors said that Ben's body had rejected the experimental drugs. But they insisted that the drugs had been his only chance. He was lucky, they said, because he wasn't lucid at the end and had very little idea what hit him. I have a tough time thinking of Ben as lucky, of all things. Ben had a mathematician's sense of the world. He was fascinated by probability, interested in the play of numbers against events. "What are the odds," Ben was always saying, although like most people interested in defining luck, he seemed to have very little of it himself. Growing up, he would gamble on anything: ball games and stock prices and elections and how many kids were in the new neighbor family, whether it would rain tomorrow. He loved stories of rare and marvelous fortune: the lottery winners and people who find free money, the man who falls from an airplane and lives, the woman who finds a Van Gogh in the attic. "What are the odds," he'd say, and this wasn't just a figure of speech for Ben; he genuinely wanted to know. "One in a million?" I'd say. "Three million," he'd say; the longer the odds, the deeper Ben's interest. I think he would've been morbidly fascinated to find out that his kind of blood cancer had an occurrence rate of less than one in two hundred thousand, that 80 percent of Hodgkin's sufferers can be cured, but that the percentage with Ben's combination of factors who had a sustained remission was so small as to be—as the doctors liked to say—negligible. Of course, Ben wouldn't have settled for a sloppy word like "negligible." Ben believed there was a number that corresponded with everything in the universe and everything in people—not just our height but our courage, not just our weight but our grief.

I had just returned from my government test when one of the guys in the frat said someone was waiting on the phone for me. The phone was sitting off the hook. When I put it to my ear and said hello, there was a pause and I didn't recognize my father's voice at first. "Clark? It's Dad." He sounded rickety and unsure, as if he were speaking from a chair balanced on one leg on the ledge of a skyscraper. "Ben passed away an hour ago."

In my memory the grief is beyond description, without shape or size—my apologies to Ben—and is everywhere, filling rooms and cars and conversations. But again my sorrow is not the point of this story, and so I won't dwell on days and weeks that, frankly, I don't recall anyway, aside from the keening of my mother and the way my father's hands hung at his sides; he was not a man accustomed to helplessness. The funeral was—as funerals for young people always are—unbearably sad, and made maudlin by some of Ben's old high school friends, who stood to blow their noses in front of the congregation and offer that Ben was "like, cool." I remember wishing I could make eye contact with him then so we could revel in their idiocy and in the silliness of such a spectacle. Ben would've liked it.

In fact, Ben would've relished everything about his funeral—the melodramatic grandeur and hypocrisy, the way slim acquaintances treated their sadness as a kind of commodity, the way they invented relationships with the deceased and tortured us with empty memories and platitudes. I imagined how Ben would've loved watching people sidle up to me after the service to recap for me what had happened.

"So sudden," they said, shaking their heads.

"Yes."

"Your only brother," they said, apparently thinking that hadn't occurred to me.

"Mmm."

"And for you, to not make it home from college."

"Yes."

"The fact that you never even got to speak to him."

"Right."

"You must be devastated."

"Mmm."

And then, shuffling their feet, summing up: "And someone so young."

"Yes," I said. "What are the odds?"

After the funeral I spent the night at my parents' house, but it was dark and ghostly and I knew I had to leave. The next day I drove back to Seattle with the radio off and the windows down, icy air blowing through the car. I stopped at the tiny town of Vantage, at the crossing of the Columbia River, got a cup of coffee, and stood on the banks watching the black mass carve a path to the ocean. Where I'm from, everything flows east to west. So that's what I did. I kept driving, until I dropped down out of the Cascades and into the Puget Sound clouds.

All that week the weather sat heavy on Seattle, gusting rain and acres of wet fog. I slept in my car the first night rather than returning to the fraternity house. The next day, I checked into a motel and I sat there all weekend. I ate only potato chips and drank only water. Then, on Monday, the sky suddenly cleared and the mountains emerged from fog and the brick and ivy of the university seemed almost too sharp, too focused.

I knew I had to get back to my life, and so late that morning I walked to my first class in a week, the sun on my neck and shoulders pushing me on. I slumped down in a chair in my Principles of Government class. After a few minutes the other students began filing in; the professor came over, arms crossed on his chest like sagging bandoliers.

"Mr. Mason?" he said. "You missed a few days."

"Yes," I said. It seemed like enough.

He nodded. "Well, we're still on the Greeks." His name was Richard Stanton—a former lawyer, weekend television anchor, public relations man, and state legislator. He would also become my mentor, my campaign manager, my best friend.

Professor Stanton was in his late forties, silver haired and handsome to the girls in class, although his deep-clefted chin drew him the nickname Dr. Assface. He was one of those men discomfited by age; he'd gone in for a small stud earring and had recently begun keeping his neat gray hair a few inches past professional. Each morning he gathered the back, which was short of his collar, and tied it in a desperate ponytail, and although there couldn't have been a half-inch of hair on the south end of the rubber band, I think it was meaningful for Dr. Assface to have that ponytail.

He was the kind of professor dismissed as a lightweight within the academic community (what he used to call "the nest of fucking vipers"). He attributed this to jealousy, although it was true that he rarely published and it was heavily rumored that his only book, the eighty-four-page, widely spaced *History of Political Progressivism in the Pacific Northwest*, was both vanity published and mostly cribbed. But his claim of being the subject of professional jealousy made sense too, because his teaching style made him tremendously popular among his students. He had two speeds: the slow, thoughtful academic—leaning back in his folding chair, a look of deep contemplation on his face, his index finger jammed directly into that bunghole of a chin; and the eager spider monkey—springing around the room, climbing on the backs of chairs, sitting on desks and tables, folding his legs over, crouching a few inches from our faces, and otherwise artificially engaging us with movement so as to agitate us into some measure of intellectual curiosity. He broke the spider monkey out when our energy flagged, which was often, and I always thought his motivation was a magician's motivation, creating a flourish with his left hand so that we wouldn't notice him reaching his right into his sleeve, creating a small explosion to hide the doves he pulled from offstage, creating a ruckus with his body to disguise the dexterity of his mind.

I had declared political science as my major the spring before and this was one of my first upper-level classes—filled with thirty students, many of them, like me, former high school student body presidents and DECA club parliamentarians, Eagle Scouts and Daughters of the American Revolution, students who had always run for things and run things, future wonks and activists and candidates. But I must say, as a group, we were not the most dynamic thinkers in the world. Most of us achieved without thinking, earning A's through rote and habit. Still, we expected to run for all manner of offices in the future and to win, to rise effortlessly to the top of whatever worlds we chose.

Dr. Stanton taught Principles of Government more like a philosophy class than a government class. He started with Moses and the idea of a lawgiver, and was supposed to continue through the Greeks to the Romans, Cicero and Seneca; Saints Augustine and Thomas More; through Rousseau, Thomas Paine, and de Tocqueville; Hobbes, Locke, and Marx; Thoreau and Malcolm X. But Dr. Stanton was far more interested in antiquity, and he rarely made it much further than the Romans, or occasionally the saints, sometimes summing up four centuries of political thought with one day's lecture: "And Thoreau's *Civil Disobedience* leads us into Gandhi, and of course Dr. King. Any questions?"

So when I returned we were still on the Greeks, Dr. Stanton's favorites, the Big Three: Socrates, Plato, and Aristotle. But he was low key on this day and I drifted in and out of the class, my eyes stinging, my mind wandering, sloughing along and kicking aluminum cans down the road.

That's when it happened. I hesitate to qualify *it*, to explain it away as a religious moment or a realization or anything else, because it simply is *it*—a flash, an awakening.

It occurred at 11:48 A.M., two minutes before the end of class on November 29, 1985, on one of those sunny fall days—the last of the season, as it turned out—that make you feel itchy and bored, like a nine-year-old two hours from recess. Dr. Stanton was talking about Plato's *Republic,* specifically the section in which Plato has Socrates propose that "until philosophers are kings . . . cities will have no rest from their evils—no, nor the human race." He was sprawled across his desk, on his side, his legs entwined like sleeping lovers. He was nudging us toward the ramifications of the philosopher-king, but like everything the Big Greeks posited, like everything we learned, we filtered it through minds ruined by television. So my classmates fixated on whether a dreamy, goatee-wearing, dope-smoking nihilist in a microbus—Shaggy from *Scooby-Doo*—would be able to lower the deficit. Dr. Stanton grew frustrated with the flatness of our thinking and our halting "um" and "like" dialogue, until one of my classmates said, "I don't get what Pluto means," at which point Dr. Stanton leapt off the desk, landed on his feet, yelped, sprang into the air, and windmilled his arms, performing the wild finale to all his classroom magic tricks. "Read book seven!" he screamed. "Now!"

I turned gingerly to book VII of *The Republic* and began reading. It started as dully as the rest, with an allegory so elaborate and unlikely I had trouble following it: Plato had Socrates propose a deep cave in which prisoners were raised from birth. In this cave, the prisoners could see neither the sun nor anything else of the outside world; the only light came from a fire burning far above and behind them, so that they saw only the shadows of things on the wall, not the things themselves. "The prisoners," Plato wrote, "would believe that the truth is nothing other than the shadows."

Of course, I'm hardly the first student to be struck by Plato's simple ontology, to make the short leap of imagining my life as a cave, society as empty and illusory, and all that I had been conditioned to want as nothing more than fancy lies. Success, fame, money, women? Shadows. Just shadows.

But if my epiphany was that of a million other disaffected, twenty-one-year-old state school philosophers, it was also that of a young man who had just buried his brother, and I must say—I went a little crazy that day. Behind me, the sun slanted through a window in the classroom and bits of dust danced in its light, a Milky Way of mites and bits and loose particles. How can we still pretend that heaven is *up there* when whole universes— tiny heavens and hells—can exist in a single beam of sunlight.

"Mr. Mason?" Dr. Stanton stepped toward me, and as I looked up from the sunlight to him I felt myself passing, as Plato said, from one realm to the next, from belief to knowledge. Even now I can't say just what it meant except that I was overwhelmed, a parched man suddenly up to his knees in cool water.

"Mr. Mason?" Dr. Stanton asked again.

For the first time in my life I could see. Or I was blinded. Or there's no difference. I slapped my head. The other students looked up at me.

"I don't—" I cast around, looking at the ruffled paperback of *The Republic,* at the students around me, just like me, dreaming our stupid little dreams, competing and succeeding and living and dying by rules that we didn't make up, rules that made no sense. I reached into the sunlight. Nothing was there.

"What is it, Mr. Mason?"

"I don't—" And I saw myself on Empire Road, that narrow gash of houses, that stretch of failure—the cruelty of Pete Decker at one end, the frailty of Eli Boyle at the other. That would always be *my* universe, *my* galaxy of dust in *my* beam of sunlight. Tears streamed from my eyes—the bad and the good. Grief is a release and—

"Mr. Mason?" Dr. Stanton said. "What is it?"

"I don't—" Every dream is an escape.

"Mr. Mason!"

The really shitty thing is this: When someone dies, you never get to see him again. Never. How can you possibly deal with the unfairness of that? How can you deal with the death of the best person you know, the death of everything true and good?

I looked up at Dr. Stanton. "I don't—" I wiped my eyes. "I don't believe in God."

4 | WHAT I MEANT

W hat I meant to accomplish with this confession was not a recounting of the grief-induced, sophomoric insights (though technically I was a junior) that I had in college but something more, something transcendent.

I am a failure even at being sad.

So again, I apologize, Caroline. I only wanted to make the point that I wasn't always like this—or rather like the obnoxious young politician who was handed his hat in the 2000 congressional elections, the desperate man who drove to Eli Boyle's house two days ago with murder in his heart, who walked gingerly across the lawn to Eli's carriage house, who climbed silently up those steps.

At least for a short time, beginning in the fall of 1985 and ending more than eight years later, in the spring of 1994, I was free.

Though I hadn't known how to express it that day in class (atheism not really being the point), the combination of Ben's death and Dr. Stanton's class transformed me, untethered me from all that I'd believed.

I moved out of the frat house and into an apartment above a garage in Wallingford. I quit all my campus posts and all the self-serving organizations I had joined. I gave the Dodge back to my parents and bought an old ten-speed bicycle. I grew my hair out, stopped shaving, and started wearing secondhand clothing; I favored army fatigues and flannel shirts. I stopped wearing my glass eye and went back to the eye patch—a bit self-consciously at first, but old habits die hardest. I sat for hours on the Ave on lotused legs, reading poetry and smiling at strangers. I became one of those people you step around on the sidewalk, a step removed from panhandler.

Strangely enough, this didn't affect my social life as much as I feared it would. I didn't get involved seriously with anyone, but I screwed constantly. It turned out there was no shortage of girls who were looking for sad, hygienically challenged men, girls who smelled like patchouli or clove cigarettes, nice girls who seemed like the sort that Dana would've become, the sort that Ben would've dated, girls who didn't really comb their hair, who majored in comparative literature and international studies, who carried string-tied journals in their worn backpacks and rode bicycles for transportation, girls who talked knowledgeably about rain forests and dominant cultures and art-house movies.

I went almost six years without seeing a shaved armpit.

I exchanged the politics of me for the politics of them. And there were plenty of them to help. I raised money for AIDS patients, African famine relief, and Central American refugees. I volunteered at schools and community centers in Seattle's Central District and at shelters downtown. Free of the strictures of my self-loathing and its corresponding ambition, I ambled in good conscience about the campus, and the city—a better man. Of course, the cynic might look at me now—disgraced politician, low-rent attorney—and doubt the sincerity of this transformation. For them, I offer this one proof:

For ten years, I did not run for a goddamned thing.

"You know, it's possible to go a bit overboard with this kind of thing," Dr. Stanton finally said when I showed him the tattoo on my lower back—the Chinese symbol for compassion (at least that's what I was told; I found out later it was actually the symbol for *compensation*, the word right next to "compassion" in the illustrated dictionary my tattoo artist used). Dr. Stanton was uncomfortable with my rebirth, I think, because he worried about his role in it, and specifically, that he was now my mentor.

"Look, I'm not really the mentor type," he said. "I'm sorry about your brother and I'm glad you found something meaningful in my class, but that was Plato. That wasn't me. I don't even *like* Plato."

I was amused and impressed by his protests, which seemed in keeping with the modesty and intelligence that a great mentor should have. Still, it was he who encouraged me to continue along in my previous poli-sci/ pre-law track ("Don't throw the baby out with the bathwater"), insisting that my brother would've wanted me to be a lawyer and that I could do more good as a lawyer than "playing bongos on some street corner."

So I spent three years getting my master's in sociology at the University of Washington and then found my way into a lesser law school, not so much out of some deep desire to practice law, but out of a much deeper desire not to leave college, the brick womb of my rebirth. I lingered in law school as long as they would have me, taking a few classes here and there, constantly changing my emphasis.

Dr. Stanton finally gave in to my need for a mentor, and he and I met once a week for lunch, during which time I would share with him some new plan for using my law degree to bring about unlikely social change. I was forever trying to earn his respect, and forever getting his good-natured scorn instead. I will list a few of my ideas and Dr. Stanton's responses, ideas that I should really have registered with the Patent Office's Department of Hubris. I planned to:

Open a nonprofit legal services clinic for indigent elderly men ("There's a great deal of money to be made in hobo law," Dr. Stanton said); establish a safe house and law office for battered women; use the same house to care for and represent homeless children and orphans; organize a team of lawyers to sue for third-world debt relief and the international removal of land mines ("I do like the idea of sending lawyers to blow up old land mines"); create a pro bono law firm to research old Indian treaties and then sue the government over them; and offer free representation to the families of executed prisoners ("Yes. Help Dutch's family get his handguns back from the coppers").

Richard Stanton was—and remains—the finest and truest person I know in the world. We would meet at one of the bars near the campus, spend the first half of our lunch with me fantasizing about my conscience-clearing law career and the second half with Dr. Stanton complaining about the poli-sci department and the university as a whole. He felt no respect from his colleagues; he was mistrusted, he said, because of his television and private-sector background—"Nobody likes a convert, Mr. Mason"—and at the same time, he was seen as something of a simple traditionalist within more progressive academic circles because he rarely published and insisted on teaching forms that had been long taken for granted and left behind. He drank more and more during these lunches, and often stayed to drink alone after I left, although he was the kind of drunk who knew he was ingesting a depressant and so he grew quieter and more reflective with each glass of draft beer—no raised voices or lampshades for him. At the end of our lunches, he always seemed on the verge of tears. Somewhere in there I became aware of a horrible event in his past, right around the time he went in for the earring and the pony-tail, something that caused him tremendous guilt and sorrow. He left a woman behind, I think—his wife, prob-ably, but it seemed to be more than that—and either he assumed that I knew the details or he believed the details were beside the point, because he only ever made glancing reference to it ("my collapse," or "the big fuck-up") and thwarted every attempt I made to find out what happened. ("What *happened*?" he responded when I asked him directly. "You think this shit just *happens*? Like the weather? Wake up and smell the self-determination, Mr. Mason. Put down the bong and take a hit of reality.")

This was my life in the late 1980s and early 1990s, a satisfying mixture of college, grad and law school (seventy-two thousand dollars in student loans), sodden lunches with my mentor and friend, and the occasional vegetarian Birkenstock Ten Thousand Maniacs girlfriend.

I finally graduated from law school in 1993—at the age of twenty-eight and near the bottom of my class—and, while I waited to take the bar exam, got a job working with Max Gerroux, Dr. Stanton's best friend, a former liberal appeals-court judge who'd given up the bench as part of an elaborate plea bargain over the butt of a joint that a state trooper saw in his car ashtray one day, a plea bargain that allowed him to continue practicing law and smoking joints. The latter he did with far greater passion and frequency than the former. Every time I knocked on his door, Max would grunt, "One moment, please," like someone who has been punched in the stomach, then let out a great exhale, spray something around his office and answer the door with narrow, red eyes. "Clark!" He always seemed surprised that I was there.

"There" was a small office on the second floor of a brick storefront in the funky Fremont neighborhood of Seattle, above a Greek restaurant, behind a door marked simply LAW OFFICE. The office smelled like feta cheese and tahini sauce, and was decorated with metal filing cabinets and a horrific nude self-portrait of Max in oil colors (Dr. Stanton called the painting "greasy gnome porn"). Max was barely five feet tall, with jet-black hair. He was half Flathead Indian and half Jewish—"the first and last of my people"—and he credited this background for creating his heartbreaking sense of humor and his preternatural ability to abide suffering and deflect bullying.

Luckily, these were just the sorts of law he liked to practice.

"Look," he would say over the phone when some prosecutor was playing hardball on a plea bargain. "I am a Flathead Jew. You're welcome to keep busting my ass, but you'll have to forgive me if I *don't fucking notice!*"

He represented drug cases almost exclusively, and twice he came under investigation for taking his payment in product. Our office was even hit once. During the raid I stood next to Max, who smiled as filing cabinets and

257

drawers were emptied on the floor. He wasn't a great lawyer, but the man knew how to hide a stash.

Unlike Dr. Stanton, when I confided in Max my plans for pro bono and legal social work, he beamed with pride. He got positively giddy about the hobo clinic and the Native People's Justice Center and the rest, nodding and grinning and planning right along with me. "Yes, I see it. We should get right on that, Clark. I know some influential people who will demand to fund this idea of yours. We'll have this thing up and running by the first of the year." I don't think he really knew any influential people—they certainly never came to our office—and anyway, we barely made enough on his drug cases to pay for our spot above the Greek restaurant, let alone do pro bono work.

I passed the bar, and by the spring of 1994, when I got a letter that would mark the beginning of this recent trouble, I was a bearded and ponytailed practicing lawyer and a junior partner in the two-person progressive law firm of Max Gerroux Law Offices. But before I detail the contents of that letter, I should make one more thing clear about Max, a detail that explains both Max and my deep loyalty to him.

He was dying. A snakelike tumor had taken up residence in his spine. It was wrapping around the bone and working its way through his body, wearing a kind of Ho Chi Minh Trail from his brain to his testicles. He had long ago given up on the doctors' ability to beat the tumor, saying that it seemed more natural to have the cancer kill him than the doctors. Everyone knew he was dying. He used this fact most effectively in court, pushing for speedier trials and expediting plea bargains and cutting through reams of legal bullshit ("We all know I won't be here to appeal this. Don't make me go through the motions of something I'll never see to the end").

If this sounds manipulative, you will just have to take my word that he didn't wield his illness cynically or unnecessarily. In fact, he talked about his painful and insidious cancer so plainly and without affect that to this day, I consider matter-of-factness a form of courage. Some days we would be going over paperwork and he would make a small groan or squeeze his eyes tight—"Clark, I need to make a quick phone call"—and I would understand that he needed to get high to fight off the intense pain. It was also understood between us that I needed to protect my future as a lawyer by leaving the room, that I was to never witness his drug use—in case the cops returned to finish their raid. I honored the small deception and usually went for a walk down to Lake Union when I knew he was getting high. I was with Max for six months before I realized why we represented drug dealers: partly because Max honestly believed that the police violated civil rights in drug cases and partly because Max needed to be paid in dope.

As for me, I suppose I cared for Max out of a surrogate loyalty toward Ben, and as I watched Max's cancer progress, I concentrated on every detail, every wince and groan, those things I'd missed nine years earlier with Ben.

One day in the late spring of 1994, Max and I were working on an appeal, the paperwork spread out before us on his pressed-board desk. My mind was elsewhere, specifically on the aforementioned letter, which my parents had forwarded to me the day before. And so I didn't notice that Max was making small huffing noises, as if he was being punched in the rib cage. Finally, when

I looked up, I could see that he was glistening with sweat and having difficulty breathing. His eyes were pressed shut.

"You need to make a phone call," I said.

He winced with pain. "I don't know if I can."

"Let me help," I said quietly.

"I don't think you should—"

"It's fine," I said.

"No."

"Please," I said.

He pointed to the oil painting of himself naked. I was shocked that it would be in such an obvious place. Even the cops had looked behind that painting. I took the painting down but there was nothing behind it on the wall, no safe or false panel. "Frame," he muttered. "Lower right-hand corner." I pulled the frame apart and saw it was hollowed out. A small ceramic pipe, matches, and a sandwich baggie of rich green marijuana slid out. I loaded the bowl and slid it between his quivering lips. I waved the match in a circle around the bits of green bud, and he inhaled with short, raspy breaths; the buds sparked red and burned away, and a line of gray-blue smoke issued from the pipe. Max's eyelids fluttered and he held the smoke in his lungs as long as he could, then let it seep out. A quiver of something—pain or relief, I'm not sure there was a difference—rolled through his body.

I refilled the bowl and held it out for him again.

"Thank you," he said, and smoked the second bowl. When we were done, I helped him lie on the couch in his office and I left to go for a walk. I walked through Fremont and down to the lake. I sat on the bank and watched some sailors working on an old crab ship, the hull rusted and streaked. I could hear them across the water, talking and laughing. I pulled the letter out of my pocket and read it again, for the tenth time that day. I will not recount it from memory, except to say it started with a plain, friendly greeting and an apology for not coming to Ben's funeral all those years ago. There was some business about how I hadn't been at the ten-year reunion and congratulations on becoming a lawyer. The rest of the letter I *will* quote from memory, because it is seared in my mind:

I'm going to be in Seattle on business next month and I thought maybe we could get together, if you want to. There's something I'd like to talk with you about.

I've been thinking a lot about you lately.

With love,
Dana

5 | SHE WAS BEAUTIFUL

She was beautiful, even more than I'd remembered. Her hair was short and spiky, cut so that it framed her round face and dark eyebrows, her slender nose and round eyes, and made each of these features appear singular—as if they had been invented specifically for her face. But even more than her physical appearance, Dana Brett had acquired a comfort with herself, with her body; she wore a long, tight print skirt with no sign of her old smart-girl self-consciousness, and watching her walk in it, a man could be forgiven if he thought of trading everything—family, career, self-respect—for one day spent tracing that skirt's gentle roll over hips and thighs, to the calf, where a glimpse of smooth, tanned ankle revealed a simple silver bracelet, a dizzying piece of jewelry that was impossible to ignore, to avoid imagining it as the only thing left on her, gleaming in the light from a bedroom candle.

You may surmise by this description that I had been pining away for Dana during the twelve years that we were apart, but that's not exactly the truth. In general, I don't pine. As I have said, I continued to date, though it's true that Dana had never been far from my thoughts. And it was only at that moment, staring at the vision of Dana Brett outside the restaurant Cyclops (I know . . .

but the food was good), that I understood why I'd dropped my habit of trophy blondes and had gone out of my way to date girls who were approximations of Dana, best-guess estimates of what she would be like now: smart, liberal, funky girls who wore hemp bracelets and crocheted hats and read poetry chapbooks and talked of saving sea mammals. When Ben died I lost the chance to live through his eyes, and while I didn't imagine that I loved Dana during those ten years, I think I did start to live through her eyes, to imagine that my new self might please her, as strange as that may sound. I always thought I would see her again, and part of me wondered if I would feel the way I eventually did feel that afternoon—pained, stricken, for the first time in my life, in love. I wasn't really surprised to feel like that, but I *was* surprised to find that the surrogates for Dana that I'd been dating were nothing like her, and had no more in common with her than with those sea mammals. For Dana wasn't simply another progressive arty chick. She was, as I said, singular, and no cheap granola knockoff could've captured her combination of natural beauty and self-confidence, all of these disparate elements held in place by the binding heat of her.

She stood on the sidewalk in Belltown and looked far too sophisticated for the funky Cyclops, with its Jell-O–mold exterior, the entire wait staff in black-rimmed glasses and Doc Marten's. I parked and walked down the side-walk, and when she stepped forward I knew that my life had come back to this point for some reason, that our ten-year orbits had finally circled back around on us because we were meant to be together.

I keep searching for another word, but she was simply

beautiful. Beautiful. And I wasn't the only person to think so. Her husband seemed to agree with me.

"Clark," she said, kissing me on the cheek. "It's so good to see you! This is Michael Langford, my husband. Michael, this is my good friend Clark Mason."

He stepped forward and stuck out his hand. He was tall.

I held up my hand and pretended to cough so I wouldn't have to say anything until I could get my wits back. The wind blew dust along the sidewalk, and I pretended to have something in my good eye while I waited for the flush to leave my face.

Inside the restaurant, they sat on one side of a small glass-topped table, holding hands in her glorious lap. I sat on the other side, my hands in my own lap. Dana kept staring at me and smiling.

"I can't believe how different you look," she said. "I like it. The rugged look."

I flicked reflexively at my ponytail, which now reached the middle of my back, and stroked my beard. "That's what I was going for. The ragged look."

"You look great," she said, and I could hear the tone in her voice that said I didn't look great, that I looked pretty awful. And that was when I fell apart, when nine years of progress fell away and I was the boy on the bus again.

The menus came and I snuck a hateful glimpse at Michael as he read the entrées. I hadn't had a chance to take him in, but as I looked I felt myself blush again. He looked a little like me. Not the me in the restaurant that day, the roadie for a Southern rock band, but the me I might have been if I hadn't had the epiphany in Dr.

Stanton's class, if Ben hadn't died. And for the first time, staring at them—neat and clean in their NorCal money-light way—I hated my Platonic rebirth, and began to think of it as nothing more than some kind of irrational, extended grief.

Michael Langford had short dark hair, a solid build, and a square jaw. He was tall and athletic, the kind of capable, white American male upon whom this country was built, the kind cast in old World War II movies and westerns, the kind adept at selling big-ticket American items—cars and condos and congressional agendas. The kind I always wanted to be. You recognize your own kind, of course, and I could see this guy was what I had been once, an achiever, a success junkie, a salesman of the first order, a runner for things, a politician—perhaps not in practice, but certainly in bearing. While I was working to make myself the kind of man I thought Dana would love, she fell in love with the kind of man I used to be.

When the waitress came, I had the briefest urge to order a skewer of irony. I looked down at my hands and wondered, What the fuck happened to me?

"What kind of law do you practice, Clark?" asked Michael after we'd ordered.

"For the time being, I'm doing some criminal law," I said. "First amendment cases. A lot of pro bono." I wanted to stop talking, but my tongue was operating freely. "Illegal searches. Civil rights violations. I recently started a nonprofit legal aid service for homeless children." Shut up, I told myself. "And the elderly." For God's sake. "And battered women." I tailed off right around that point, though I may have mentioned orphans and illegal aliens and widows and land mines and slavery reparations.

"Wow," Michael said.

Dana blushed.

"I'm fielding offers from some big firms in town, though, thinking of going corporate." I was amazed at the lies that were spewing from my mouth. I couldn't get a job parking cars at a big firm. But these were more than lies. I was drowning, prattling on helplessly, hoping I might say something that would make me feel better. "I'm also considering international law. Working abroad." Abroad? I was considering working abroad?

"Really," Michael said. "Where?"

I was curious, too. "Portugal."

We were all quiet for a moment, as I geared up to talk about the complex Portuguese legal system and the demands there for civil rights lawyers. I prayed for my food to arrive so I could shove it in my mouth and shut myself up, so I could divert myself and stop staring at Dana's piercing eyes, so I could stop lying like a husband at three in the morning. "So when did you two get married?" I asked desperately.

"Three months ago," Dana said. "At a winery north of San Francisco. It was spur of the moment. I didn't even tell my parents."

"That's great," I said. "Three months." We didn't see each other for twelve years and I missed my chance by three fucking months. I tore at a piece of bread and crumbs shot into the air. "I'm engaged myself . . . about to be engaged."

"Oh, what's her name?" Dana asked.

"You don't know her." Course, neither did I.

"What does she do?"

"Pilot."

"For an airline?"

"Mmm." I chewed on some bread. "Yeah."

"What'd you say her name was?"

I chewed and swallowed my bread. "Megan. She's out of town. Megan."

"I'd love to meet her sometime."

"She's out of town."

Dana smiled. "It really is great to see you, Clark," she said again.

"So you both work in computers?" I asked.

"We work for a small finance firm, sort of like an investment bank, but lighter on its feet, committed to emerging tech companies. In fact, that's what we wanted to talk to you about. You see, Clark," Michael began, as if I were buying a vacuum from him, as if he'd just dumped crumb cake on my carpet to demonstrate the beltless sucking power of the R-690 Clean Machine, "what we do is function as a kind of a buffer, a go-between for Charlie and—"

Dana touched his arm lightly, and that simple touch filled me with such deep longing and regret that I felt the last part of my new self tear away. "He's not going to know what Charlie means," Dana said gently to her husband.

Michael rolled his eyes at himself, like he'd been stupid to imagine that I might know what Charlie was—and even though I had no idea, I couldn't stomach the conde-scension of having him actually tell me.

"I'm sorry," he said. "I forget I'm not talking to industry people sometimes. We call venture capital people 'VC,' you know, like the Viet Cong. Charlie? VC? So the people who put up the money are Charlie."

"Sure," I said, and looked toward the kitchen for my soup. "Charlie."

"Well, if a small company needs seed money," Michael said, "we put him in touch with investors. Charlie—the money person—tends to be in his fifties and sixties, while Chad—what we call the idea person—tends to be in his twenties. We fill the gap between Charlie and Chad. We explain Charlie to Chad and Chad to Charlie, the money to the idea and the idea to the money." He winked. "And we take a piece of both."

"It sounds dry," Dana said. "But it's fascinating. And creative." It occurred to me that she was working as hard as I was to impress, and I thought about how she'd changed too, how she must think that I—brave defender of indigent pregnant Indian hobos who'd stepped on land mines—saw her, perhaps that I would judge her as having lost something of her idealism. I thought about Ben's question to me about perceptions: which is truer, the way we see ourselves, or the way others see us. We always imagine that we know ourselves, but in truth, we can only see out. We can't see in.

"Tell him about the virtual grocery store," Dana said.

"No," Michael said. "I've gone on enough."

"Please," Dana said, as if anxious to show me she hadn't sold out completely, that she was still the same smart, idealistic Dana.

"Well," Michael began, and then he raised an eyebrow as if he was about to propose something a little bit risqué, a threesome among the Jell-O molds. "What if, at six o'clock, you decided to make fish tacos for dinner. But you have no fish. You have no tortillas. You simply touch a computer screen and a company fills your entire order, swings by the fresh fish store and the grocery store and delivers your entire order to your door within twenty minutes. And what if the computer knows you and knows what kind of milk and bread you like, and what if it's hooked up to your refrigerator, and it instantly checks every store in the city until it finds the best prices for your particular milk and bread, and what if you are delivered *your* personalized groceries for less than you would have paid to gather them yourself? What would you say to that?"

"I'd say . . . What are the odds?"

"Exactly!" Michael said.

Dana must've caught my sarcasm because she looked down at the table.

"We tell investors that we aren't just interested in making money," Michael said. "We're idea farmers. We plant them, grow them, and water them. We want to build a forest of ideas, up and down the West Coast. And that's where you come in."

"I come in?" I asked.

"We're well positioned in the valley," Michael said. "We've worked with eighteen start-ups, linked them with venture capital and larger investment bankers. We've already had two successful IPO's. But there are two axes of technology on the West Coast and, frankly, we have no penetration in Seattle at all."

"Penetration," I repeated.

"We're looking to expand, looking for someone to help us identify and contact start-ups here." He leaned forward, as if he were about to confide something in me. "I was assuming we'd find someone with a tech background, but Dana pointed out that we have the tech backgrounds. What we need is a lawyer, someone who can write contracts. And then she thought of you. She said you were always a real go-getter in high school."

I shuddered like an addict when he said "go-getter."

"I know it's probably not as rewarding as fighting for Indian tribes or going to Portugal, but it could be exciting. And profitable.

"I'm not just talking about a job," he said. "I'm talking about a chance to maybe find the next Microsoft, to be in the center of the next big thing. I'm talking about changing the world, Clark, charting a course into the twenty-first century."

I must interject that this was 1994 and such metaphors were being mixed up and down the West Coast; idiot utopians were emerging everywhere, and a fair number of them were becoming profanely rich. As for my own actions that day, I was not motivated by money, even though that lunch would end up making me—making us all—a great deal of money. No, what I said next was really no different from my lie about practicing constitutional law, or moving to Portugal, or getting married. I was just trying to impress an old flame and her new husband, trying to reclaim something that I'd lost in Dana's eyes, trying to be part of another club—the club of high-tech entrepreneurs. I could have said, No, I'm committed to moving to Portugal, but instead I began talking out of my ass.

"I represent a company like that," I said.

"Here?" Michael asked.

"No," I said, panicking, thinking they'd want to see it. "In Spokane."

Dana looked up suddenly, as if I'd finally gone too far.

"A start-up?" Michael asked, and leaned forward on the table.

"Yes," I said, making a mental note to find out what that meant.

He leaned forward. "Anything you can talk about?"

"Michael," she snapped. "Slow down. He doesn't work for us yet."

I made eye contact with Dana then, and it occurred to me that she wasn't really irritated with Michael, but was trying to keep me from digging this hole any deeper, that she knew I was lying, that I'd been lying since we sat down at lunch, that I could no more do the job they were talking about than I could speak Portuguese. I saw the old disapproval in her eyes, and I guess it pissed me off.

"No, I don't mind," I said, and cleared my throat to give myself some time to invent a high-tech company or two. "Well," I said, and like an angel, our waitress arrived with our food and I had another minute to think. And I don't know why the solution popped into my mind just then. Maybe it was seeing Dana or thinking about the last time I'd seen Ben, or maybe it was Plato's fault.

"It's a game," I said. "A character-driven, interactive thing."

"VR?" Michael asked.

"Virtual reality," Dana translated.

"No," I said, and when Michael looked disappointed, "Not yet, anyway." I went on to describe a game in which people's real lives intersected with the game, until the lines blurred and it was anyone's guess which realm was real.

Michael was intrigued. "How long until it's ready to test?"

"Oh, they're playing it now," I said. "A test group."

"Really," he asked. "What's it called?"

"Empire," I said. "It's called Empire."

6 | WHAT HAPPENED NEXT

What happened next could only have happened in those money-drunk, speculative, E-topian days of the mid-1990s. Based on my ridiculous description, Michael and Dana agreed to come to Spokane in two weeks to have a look at the progress that the Empire research and development team was making. If things went well, they said, they knew an impatient investor who desperately wanted to give seed money to some kind of new interactive, character-driven game, something more involved than Duke Nukem, and more ambitious and darker than the recently released Sim City and Myst, a game that could be accessed at some point in the future by way of something I later found in my notes scribbled as the "Inner Nut."

You might assume that a young man living in Seattle in 1994 would have at least a working knowledge of computers—if he wasn't already toiling away on his own start-up. I offer no apologies for coming late to that party. Yes, I lived in Seattle, but that was no ticket to awareness by itself. There are auto mechanics in Seattle, too. Hell, I'd also missed Nirvana (I prefer my punk smart and clean—R.E.M. and the Talking Heads). At that late date of spring 1994, I still owned no stock in Microsoft or Intel or AOL. What did I own? A 1974 Audi Fox, a bicycle, several shelves covered with books, four suits, some other clothes, a coffee maker, and a couch. But I had no stocks, no computer, and, like most people in 1994—even in Seattle—I couldn't have found the World Wide Web if you spotted me two W's and a backslash.

So I was relieved to find that Eli at least owned a computer—even if it was an ancient Radio Shack TRS-80. And I was happy to find that Empire was still being played, nine years after Ben and I had eavesdropped on it, although only two original members were left (Louis being one of them). Total membership had increased by only six in all that time, from fourteen to twenty.

"I do appreciate your interest, Clark, and it sounds like a great opportunity," said Eli as we sat outside the Orange Julius he was managing then. "But Empire isn't even a game, let alone a computer game."

"But you just said you use a computer."

"Yeah," Eli said. "I store the information on it, but there are no graphics or anything. Empire is up here," he said, tapping his head. "It's just a series of actions and reactions and decisions, and then we record everything that happens—mark territory, assaults, and retreats on a map. Stuff like that. People buy and sell land and weapons. They hoard food and destroy crops. They get involved romantically and betray each other, make war and have to surrender and build up from scratch. It's all very ethereal."

"It sounds perfect," I said. "Just what this company is looking for."

"Do you understand that the action isn't even *managed* by the computer?"

"How is it managed?"

"By me," he said. "If you let a computer do it, then it just becomes a measure of hand-eye coordination, a series of tricks that you perform to get from one level to the next. If a computer does it, then the people will cheat. They won't learn a thing."

Eli was becoming exasperated; his pocked cheeks shone red. "I don't think you appreciate how important this game is to me," he said. "This is ten years of my life we're talking about, Clark."

The truth of this struck him like a blow. He laughed and rubbed his head and looked away. "Ten years," he repeated. Eli had probably gained forty pounds since high school, and he'd finally completed his switch to wire-rim glasses, just when black frames had come back into style. He'd gone mostly bald and his pipe-cleaner arms cantilevered from a flat chest and round stomach. He'd never married. When I'd called him at home, he was wary, but here in person, on his break in his orange and brown uniform, he'd seemed genuinely glad to see me—though surprised by my beard and long hair and eye patch. Soon it was as if no time had passed at all, as if there had been no falling-out between us and we were back on my porch trying to make him look cool, instead of sitting in the mall outside a hot dog stand trying to save my face.

"It's just—" He turned to face me. "—this is all I have, Clark."

"I know," I said. "Listen, in ten days Dana and Michael are coming here, and I'm supposed to show them a computer game. Just help me get through that meeting. I promise I'll make sure nothing bad happens."

He looked up and down the bright wide aisle of the mall—music and surf wear and big salty pretzels, a tight orbit of vacant worlds, all paying eight bucks an hour. Then he looked back at me. "What would we have to do?"

For the next ten days Eli, Louis, and I worked nonstop transforming Empire into a computer game. We hired a computer coder named Bryan, and he and I got a quick tutorial in the strategy and what Eli called "the purpose" of the game. From what I could understand—and I don't know that I ever *got* Empire—it imagined an ancient land of forest and mountains and deserts and lakes and seas. Players started as noblemen or -women—lords, as they called themselves—with a small plot of land and a certain number of serfs to work the land and to form an army when the time came. ("You can even imagine that you're sleeping with your serfs!" Louis proclaimed, much to the embarrassment of all.) The goal was not only to take over land and serfs, to defeat the other players and become emperor of more lands, but "to exist on this plane," Eli said, "to live and grow in this world."

There was a random aspect to the game—a spinning wheel and dice determined plagues and famines and earthquakes and the like; this was the quickest fix, replaced by computerized random choice—but most of the *action* was generated by decisions and reactions that the players made, by their aggressions and their lust, their treaties and their double-crosses, their clashes and battles and betrayals. All of this was overseen and arbitrated by Eli Boyle. The game worked best when players bought into the realism of the game and started looking for options and ideas that hadn't even occurred to him, Eli said. In fact, he told me, recently two players had married in the game to double their holdings, and a few months later, they were married in real life.

"That's what makes Empire work," Eli said, "human nature. Not a bunch of flat pictures drawn by some computer."

We bought four new IBM PCs, and the coder set about replacing many of the easier manual functions of the game with computer functions and transferring the data—the history of the game—from the floppy disks of old TRS-80 to the hard drives of the new computers. He warned us that there simply wasn't time to re-create the game on computer, though—the graphics and the story lines, the countless loops and switches that a computer would require to truly simulate and manage a game this complex.

"What you're talking about is an immersive, interactive digitized world in which players can link to one another electronically and can not only interface but overlay actions and reactions. And you want all of this done fluidly, in real time," said the coder, Bryan, a thick, bearded guy who usually had more than one cigarette burning in the ashtray next to his computer. "You do realize there are companies with coders and writers and illustrators that have been working around the clock for years on shit like this. And you want me to make your game in two weeks?"

"Nine days," I said.

"Nine days," he said. "We might have to take a few shortcuts."

Nine days later I stood in the Spokane International Airport, watching people deplane from an Alaska Airlines flight from San Francisco. Dana came off first, in jeans and a sweater, and fell into my arms. Something about the way she fit against me made her feel different from any woman or girl I'd ever been with. My eyes closed as she pressed against me, as I felt her thighs against mine, her hand on the back of my neck, her voice in my ear. "Clark, I'm glad we're doing this together."

She stepped away and looked at me. "You cut your hair," she said quietly, ruffling my collar-length hair. "And you shaved." She smiled as if I'd done these things for her, which, of course, I had.

"I see your eye's better," said Michael. He and I shook hands.

"It's a glass eye," I said. "I just took the patch off."

"Right," and Michael looked around at the small, odd-shaped 1960s airport terminal. "Very quaint," he said. "Very Jetsons. I like."

The third member of their party stood next to Michael, swinging his head around impatiently, as if he'd expected our presentation right here in the terminal. He was the investor they had spoken about: "Charlie," they had called him, whose name, it turned out, was actually Charley. He was in his early fifties, edgy and flustered in his gray suit, with thick black eyebrows poised above his dark eyes. Apparently, he had made his money in southern California in the lucrative business of water-slide parks.

"This is all very unusual," he said to me in a machine-gun voice. "I don't like it. You're supposed to come to me; I'm not supposed to come to you. All the stories say you come to me. This isn't how it's supposed to work, me coming to you. I don't like it."

"Well, I appreciate you coming," I said. "I think you'll be glad you did."

"It's all graphics," he said to me. "In *Forbes*, they said

gaming is all about the graphics. Are the graphics top-notch? Because if the graphics aren't top-notch, I should just turn around and get back on the plane."

Dana took him by the arm. "Charley, relax. Let's get something to eat."

I took them to the lounge of the Spokane House restaurant and hotel, at the top of the Sunset Hill, leading into town. Four of Eli's most computer-literate Empire players were there, along with four more . . . attractive people I'd arranged to have present to balance the field a little bit in front of our potential investor, who might not be very encouraged by the spectacle of a game that appealed mostly to dwarves and fat people.

Four computers were set up on tables facing the front of the room; the old Empire binders were nowhere to be found.

The Spokane House lounge was paneled and dark (my primary reason for choosing it) and overlooked the city, which loomed below in the tree-filled valley like an overgrown garden. "Pretty town," Charley said. "What's the real estate picture like?"

"Very affordable," I said, finding myself speaking in Charley's quick staccato. "Cheap. Practically free. Good place for development."

"Excellent," he said. "Very good."

I stood at the back of the room with Michael and Dana and Charley. Eli stood at the front, as if he were about to teach a class. The four real players and the four actors sat in front of him, facing him, their backs to us. Dana and Eli acknowledged each other with a small nod. Dana smiled. Eli did not. When I'd told her over the phone that Eli Boyle was my partner in this game, Dana had seemed pleased—not so much for the game as for me, as if it were a good sign for me, for my soul or something. Eli had reacted to her presence in this whole thing with nothing but a grunt.

At the front of the room he paced nervously in corduroy pants and an old sweater that strained to cover his growing gut. He'd combed his hair, putting some lines in the greasy top, but the back and sides winged out like exploding waves. I watched Charley stare at Eli, measuring the creator of what we were about to see.

"I like that guy," he whispered. "That's what *Newsweek* said they look like."

"What who looks like?" I asked.

"Computer people," he said. "You know, entrepreneurs, geniuses, nerds, that kind of thing. They don't have time to shower. Too creative. You know, like him." He nodded his head at Eli again.

The four real players turned on the computers, as we'd practiced earlier. Their screens buzzed to life and they began typing letters and entering numbers as I explained the game to Michael and Dana and Charley. I told them about lords and serfs, about treaties and wars, about double- and triple-crosses. The old Empire map came up on the screens. When Charley or Michael asked questions I didn't know the answers to, I made them up.

"How do you win?" Charley asked.

"You defeat other players' armies, vanquish them, take over their land."

"Good, good," he said. "Is there violence? The *Wall Street Journal* said that kids like to see blood. Is there blood?"

Eli and I made eye contact and he looked out the door

and into the hallway, to where Bryan the coder was sitting. Then Eli turned back and nodded at me. "Come on," I said. "Let's pick one player and I'll show you how Empire works."

We had set Louis up at the far end of the room. I pretended to pick him at random, and put my hand on his shoulder. From there we couldn't see any other computer screens, just his.

"After a few minutes of routine decision making by the player," I began, "land swaps and weddings and treaties and the like, updating the map, that sort of thing, the player proceeds to what we call 'the shadow world' and begins living the results of the decisions he's made, where he'll get to make new decisions based on the actions and reactions of the other players."

"The shadow world," Charley repeated significantly.

"Louis," I said. "What's going on with you?"

"Oh," he said, "Dave and I are allies, but I want his access to the ports, and so when we get out to sea I'm going to turn on him and attack him, try to defeat his navy and get him to give up his port town." One of the fake players, Dave, gave a friendly wave from across the room. Louis typed some letters and hit return on his keyboard.

I watched Charley's face drop in wonder as the computer screen leapt to life, and two animated ships were sailing next to each other on a meticulously drawn sea. The computer focused on the deck of one of the ships, and there was a dashing, dark-haired, strangely futuristic-looking man—Asian in appearance—at the wheel of one of the ships. Louis kept working the keyboard until the ship swung sideways, came abreast of the other ship, and fired its cannon. There was no sound.

I nodded at Eli, who nodded at the phony player Dave. "Hey!" Dave yelled. "What are you doing, Louis? I'll get you!"

Michael and Charley didn't seem to notice Dave's delivery, which struck me as over-the-top. They watched intently as the two ships engaged in a rousing sea battle, firing cannons and—anachronistically—lasers at one another, the angles and views shifting back and forth as Louis pounded the keyboard and leaned back and forth as if learning to ride a bike.

"The player controls the camera angles, everything," I whispered. "We're having some trouble with the sound."

Michael edged closer, an odd look on his face, as if he were trying to connect Louis's frantic typing with the carnage he was seeing on the screen. Blasts hit Dave's ship and sailors were blown off left and right, until corpses littered the water. That's when another ship appeared.

"Damn it!" Louis said right on cue. "He's made a deal with another player. Samantha!"

"Ha!" yelled Samantha. "I got you, Louis!"

On the screen, a beautiful, Asian-looking woman commanded a roundish, pink ship that looked a little bit like an animated panty shield and fired lasers and cannons across the bow of Louis's ship.

"Jesus Christ," Charley said.

Michael's mouth was wide open; he stepped even closer to get a better look.

That's when all the computer screens flashed, hummed with static, and went black.

"Ah, shoot," I said. "We did it again. We blew up the network."

"Damn it, Clark!" yelled Eli from the front of the room, on cue. "I told you it was too soon. I need more time."

"This is why he hasn't wanted to get any investors," I whispered. "He's such a perfectionist. He takes it personally. He's been working on this game for years."

"It shows," said Charley.

Eli stomped to the back of the room and turned off the computers. "We're not ready, Clark. I need six more months." And he stormed out of the room.

I apologized and we sat in the room for a few more minutes, talking to some of the real players about how much they loved Empire. "We'll get these bugs worked out," I said. "I'm sorry you didn't get to see the other realms, the land and the mountains, and all of it." That night I had dinner with Michael, Dana, and Charley and we talked generally and specifically about the game and its potential. Afterward, I drove them back to their hotel. In the hotel lobby Dana hugged me again, and Charley pumped my hand as if my arm might bring oil. Michael patted me on the shoulder. "Nicely done," he said flatly; then he took Dana by the hand and dragged her toward the elevator.

There was a message waiting for me in my hotel room. Dana, I thought, and my nerve ends felt alight. I hit *play*. It was from my mentor and best friend, Richard Stanton.

"Clark? It's Dick Stanton. Look, I don't know how else to tell you this, but Max died this morning. He took some pills. The pain—" Dr. Stanton sighed. "They found him in his office. I just thought you'd want to know. You meant a lot to him."

I tried to call Dr. Stanton, but there was no answer. I could imagine the bar stool where he was sitting. I left the hotel and stood outside, tried to measure the depth in the night sky. I'd been home for ten days and hadn't been out to see my parents. It had been about four months since I'd seen them. They didn't even know I was in town. I started my rental car and drove east on the freeway, through industrial areas and down Trent to my old neighborhood. My parents still lived in the house on Empire Road and I parked across the street, watching Mom and Dad through the front picture window. She brought him a beer. They watched TV together. I hadn't seen much of my parents in the last few years, in part because I believed that they blamed me somehow for Ben dying. I might've convinced them they were being irrational if I didn't believe it so strongly myself.

After a few minutes of watching them watch TV, I drove downtown and went back to my hotel room. I didn't sleep. The next morning, I drove Michael, Dana, and Charley to the airport. Charley said he was going to think about it, talk to his partners, and then we'd have a conference call in a week. "Very impressive," he said. "Top-notch."

Every time he said something like that, Dana smiled at me.

At the airport bar Charley bought us all a drink, and then excused himself to go to the bathroom. He and Michael made eye contact before he left. Then Michael asked Dana to give us a few minutes alone. When she was gone, Michael reached in his suit pocket and came out with a slip of paper.

"Charley likes your game very much," Michael said.

"We're going to talk more about it when we get back, but he wanted me to tell you his initial reaction."

He slid the paper across the table to me. It said, simply, *$1.5*.

"Is that—?"

"Million," Michael said. "Seed money. You draw up the papers."

"Jesus."

Then Michael leaned forward and his lips slid back over his teeth. "Look, you can cut your fuckin' hair and put in your phony eye, but I know what you are. I've always known what you were. *Portugal. Land mines.*" He sneered. "You're a fuckin' low-rent bottom-feeder lawyer. You work for the biggest drug lawyer in Seattle. You don't think I check out the people we work with?"

He took the slip of paper back. "And I know Japanese animation when I see it."

I took a drink. It had been Louis's idea to pretend that a Japanese cartoon was, in fact, the graphics to Empire. We used one of his favorites, Samurai Sea Battle Number 9, and Louis practiced until he could simulate the action in the cartoon. The VCR out in the hallway wired in to Louis's computer, the TV encased in the computer screen, the phony players, Bryan cutting the power before they got too good a look, Eli's creative fit—the whole drama had worked. Or so I'd thought. But Michael had seen through all of it.

"Are you going to tell him?" I asked.

Michael's eyes narrowed. "No," he said. "Dana likes you. And Charley likes your weird-looking friend. A million-five is a million-five. And even though you're two years away from having anything worthwhile, there's something there."

He reached out and finished his bourbon.

"Anyway, it's always better to have the crooks working *for* you." He waved his drink to the bartender and turned to face me full on. "But I want in. I want shares. And if you ever pull something like that again and I'm not in on it, I will make sure you go to jail and I will feed your law license to my fucking dog. Do we have an agreement?"

Dana and Charley were walking back together.

"Do we have an agreement?" he asked again.

"Yes," I said quietly.

They arrived and Charley picked up his drink. "To Empire!" he said.

Dana squeezed my arm.

"To Empire," said Michael, and he put his arm around Dana's waist, pulling her away from me.

He nuzzled her neck and she blushed and turned in to him. And it was at that moment that I first pictured it. It only takes one thought like that, the door opening a crack, and you start imagining how it would work, what you would do, how you might get away with it. It was at that precise moment that it first occurred to me that the world would be a simpler and better place if Michael Langford were not in it.

Everyone dreams the thing he is.
– Calderon de la Barca, *Life Is a Dream*

VII

EVEN ASSHOLES DESERVE A BREAK

I | THE DEAD GUY

The dead guy is lying on his side, as if he's just fallen out of his chair. He is heavyset, with a round face and wire-frame glasses that are still hooked over one of his ears. His thinning red hair is furrowed with perfect comb lines, except around the ears and back, where it curls like a clown's hair. He is wearing blue jeans, the cuffs rolled up, and a gray T-shirt, and he is barefoot, his legs crossed at the ankle, one of his feet wedged into the carpet—toes down. The room is quiet, and lit only by the humming computer above the corpse, its screen saver alternating pictures of Napoleonic soldiers with idyllic sketches of forested lands and two scrolling messages in big bold letters: EMPIRE. MORE THAN A GAME and EMPIRE. MAKE YOUR OWN RULES. She breathes heavy, through her mouth, and the room seems to close around her and the body—a forced, sad intimacy.

Caroline reaches for the light switch but stops herself before disturbing any prints. She removes her flashlight from her belt and shines it down on the body and the carpet. It's a tight weave, so footprints are unlikely unless the killer—who is she kidding—unless *Clark* tramped through blood on his way out.

Blood. From the doorway she can see it spattered everywhere that her flashlight lands: on the computer keyboard, on the ceiling, on a coffee cup on the desk. The main current of blood is on the floor, and it's been here long enough to have its own history, of flow and desiccation, soaking outward from the body, flooding the forest of carpeting, and finally lapping onto the linoleum in the kitchen, where it dried brown and hard like taffy.

She pulls out her phone, punches in the number for the desk sergeant, but doesn't hit the call button. Not yet. The first rule of a crime scene: Don't do anything that might disrupt evidence. But she's also supposed to check for a pulse, and even though the smell and the gallon of spewed blood don't make that very likely, she can always say later that she wanted to make sure the stiff was . . . well, stiff.

So she puts her gloves on, slides out of her shoes, and steps carefully into the room, letting the door close behind her.

As she walks toward the dead guy, the beam from her flashlight moves across his body and gives the illusion that he is rolling over to face her. And even though she knows it's a trick of light, of perception, she looks away, raising the flashlight to take in the carriage house apartment. It is so sparsely decorated as to feel temporary. Half the apartment is made up of this small office, which is maybe twelve by twelve. A desk is pushed against one wall. The other walls are lined with bookshelves, and these are covered with fantasy and historical novels, stacks of computer magazines and binders with the word EMPIRE written on them. There's a file cabinet just to the left of the doorway, and she thumbs through some papers on top of it—financial documents, investment reports, quarterly statements. She finds a bottom line on one of them. *Balance last period: $45,108.44. Balance this period: $2,062.05.* There is also a computer-printed airline ticket for a flight Friday night: Spokane to Seattle, Seattle to Los Angeles, L.A. to Belize. The name on the ticket is Eli Boyle.

Just beyond the desk is the door to the kitchen. The stiff fell to his left, pitching slightly forward, and since Caroline doesn't want to step over the body, she shines the light over him, into the kitchen: boxes of sweetened cereal on the kitchen counter, a tower of dirty bowls in the sink. Next to the kitchen is a bedroom, with a futon and a television on the floor. Just to the left of that is a small bathroom.

Looking around the cozy apartment, Caroline forgets, sniffs once through her nose, and almost vomits. She covers her mouth and nose with one hand, and with the other rummages through her bag until she finds a stick of flavored lip balm. She applies it to her upper lip, and the cherry smell under her nose helps calm her stomach.

When the nausea has passed, she opens her eyes and looks down at the cell phone in her hand, the number for the desk sergeant still on the screen.

She looks around the legs of the desk and the chair but doesn't see the gun anywhere. One time in fifty the shooter will panic and drop the gun where he used it, but not this time. She looks down at the desk: two sips of coffee left in a cup, a brown apple core sitting on top of a book about Web design, sunglasses, another cup with pens and pencils in it. The chair has spun back and away from the desk, as if the stiff stood up too quickly. She tries to imagine how it happened:

He's sitting at the computer. Clark comes in and the stiff stands and turns.

No. He fell facing away from the door. He didn't turn. He was sitting, or standing, at the computer when he was shot. She shines the flashlight on the ceiling again, at a small hole in the drywall surrounded by spattered blood. Right above the desk. Why would he stay at his desk unless he knew the person coming in? Unless he was expecting him? *Clark comes up behind the guy and—*

But the angle is wrong. According to the blood and the wound, the angle of the shot is almost straight through the head, from the right side up. That means the killer had to come in the door, step to the right, and *shoot up.* It's more of a suicide angle.

Unless . . . *Clark wants something from the guy at the computer. He nudges the guy at the desk, jams the gun into his cheek, demanding, pressing the barrel into the side of his face. Naturally, the stiff tilts his head to the left, away from the gun.* Caroline draws a line with one hand and uses the other to simulate the gun, lining it up to match the chair and the hole in the ceiling. Or maybe the stiff reaches over and knocks the shooter's hand down and the gun points up and goes off. Yes, a struggle. *The gun goes off accidentally.*

Great. She's inventing scenarios in which Clark Mason is innocent.

Finally, she crouches next to the body.

In the past she's had to search for fatal wounds, but this one is so obvious as to be gaudy: she traces with her flashlight a stark, bone-and-blood gorge running from the man's teeth to the top of his head. The wound on-ramps through his cheek, leaving a ghastly sneer where it uncovers his upper molars, then tunnels behind his cheek-bone, bursts forth and takes his right eye, then goes under-ground again, a thick, straight, dark bruise beneath the dull putty of his forehead until it exits—volcanic, meaty—at the seam of his thinning hairline.

She looks up and shakes her head in sympathy.

The bottom side of the entry wound has a dark burn ring, meaning the gun was right against his head when Clark pulled the trigger. If it wasn't an accident, it was vicious and angry, unimaginable.

The phone number for the desk sergeant is still on her phone.

"Damn," she says aloud. This is all going to get away from her the minute she makes the call. The process will take over. It always does. The place will crawl with cops. The lieutenant will want a briefing, the public informa-tion officer will want something for the vultures, the deputy ME will pronounce death (Aren't you being hasty? someone will joke), and the rubber-gloved evidence techs will come in like ants on a Popsicle, securing the crime scene, marking, collecting, and tagging evidence, dusting light switches and telephones and countertops and door-knobs, measuring indentations in the carpet, checking the driveway for tire tracks, the whole thing reduced to a series of photos and spatters and latent prints, too many people moving too fast, making misjudgments and bad decisions, disturbing Caroline's quiet measure of this thing.

Certainly the confession will become moot, a simple confirmation of what they already know, and not what Clark has promised. Meaning? Context? Forget it. There will only be one real question: Where's the gun?

Motivation is a nice bow, but that's a package for someone else to wrap: reporters crafting stories, prosecutors choosing between first and second degree, judges reading mitigation reports. Cops don't care what a thing means. Or, more accurately, they don't believe it. They know there's only one reason this shit happens: somebody wanted. Sex, money, revenge, drugs, what does it matter? It's all the same. The first crime is the wanting.

What did you want, Clark?

The courts will need those details. What you wanted (motive), when you wanted it (premeditation), and how you went about getting it (mitigating factors) can make the difference between twenty years and life. And if you wanted something too much and too soon or too often, or went about getting it the wrong way, they might even put you to death. In Washington State, they used to be thoughtful enough to give you a choice: needle, juice, or rope. Needle would be harsh, confining, strapped down like that, a mockery of what that gurney is usually used for, medicated to a darkness that must feel nothing like sleep. But no matter how bad the needle, it's better than the juice. The juice scares her. There is a picture they used to show tight-lipped suspects, a picture from the late fifties of a guy in Georgia whose chair misfired, sparked, and caught, a guy who didn't die until his nuts and armpits burst into flame and he burned from the inside out.

Even so, for Caroline, nothing would be worse than the rope. And not for the reasons that death penalty opponents go on about—the pain and inhumanity of having your neck snap that way, the indignity of shitting and pissing your last moments away. No, what gets her is the fall. She hates those dreams, the ones in which her feet scramble for ground and it's just not there. To have that be her last conscious thought, falling like that—Jesus. That would be unbearable.

What did you want, Clark?

She looks down once more at the phone in her hand. She goes through a mental list of all the rules she's broken this weekend, from the minute Spivey told her to go home. Where does it lead? Finally she raises her thumb and hits the call button.

The desk sergeant's voice shakes her from her tired stupor. "Spokane Police Department. Sergeant Kaye."

"Dennis. It's Caroline Mabry."

"I thought you were going home."

"Actually, I went to interview a potential witness first, and I, uh—" She looks down at the stiff. "I came across a DOA. Gunshot wound."

"No shit. Suicide?"

"Not unless he ate the gun after."

"Got you a homo-cide?"

"Looks like."

"Make and model?"

"White male. Approximately thirty-five to forty. Headshot."

"I'll get some units en route," he asks. "You want me to call Spivey?"

She shines her flashlight from the body to the chair and finally to the computer, where the screen saver has just shifted to a digital soldier holding out a sword, challenging her, preparing to run her through. The soldier fades, replaced by a drawing of pastureland, a rock fence, a flock of sheep, a castle in the distance, and the words EMPIRE: MORE THAN A GAME. Something about the screen saver sticks in her mind.

"Detective," Sergeant Kaye says, "did you want me to call Sergeant Spivey?"

"No," she says. "I already did." It is a big lie, in cahoots with so many smaller ones this weekend. Who knows how much time it will buy? But that's all she wants now, a little more time before this whole thing gets away from her, a little more time for Clark before all of this comes down around him. She bends in closer to the computer and reads the scrolling message of the screen saver: EMPIRE. MAKE YOUR OWN RULES.

At home, her screen saver alternates pictures of mountains from the Northwest. The mountains are relentless; they don't care whether she's composing a sonnet or a grocery list or a suicide note. After five minutes, the mountains rise and cover everything, and the words recede into the black.

"What about your guy in the interview room?" asks Sergeant Kaye. "Is he connected to the DOA? You want us to read him?"

And yet, she reminds herself, beneath the mountains nothing changes. The words are still there; all you have to do is touch a key and the screen comes alive.

"I don't know if he's connected," Caroline says, measuring her words, the lies coming easier now. "Put a guy on the door and I'll talk to him when I get back." She gives Sergeant Kaye the address and hangs up the call. Then she turns off her phone.

Caroline takes a breath, leans over the keyboard, and uses her flashlight to press the space bar. The screen saver disappears and up comes an e-mail program. There is an open message in the inbox from deadeye@empire.com.

Eli—
   Don't do anything. I'm coming back there. Don't move. I need to talk to you.
   I lied about everything. There is no more money. I'm sorry. For everything.
   It's going to be okay.

   Clark

Her head falls to her chest and the hope goes out of her. Why not just videotape himself? She's shocked at how badly she wants Clark not to have done this.

Of course there is another world. Just below this one. It is undisturbed. Perfect. Our intentions go there, and the things we can't have. Regrets. Promises. Wishes.

When we dream we are falling, this is where we go.

She leans forward and, with her flashlight, turns the computer screen off. The e-mail fades as the picture pulls in on itself, universe collapsing, and then black. Caroline stares, as if she can't believe she just did that. Okay, she thinks, now you've got some time.

She backs carefully to the door, looks once more at the room, perfect and undisturbed. She can already hear the first siren, still blocks away. She slides her shoes on, backs out the door, and pulls it closed behind her.

2 | THE DWARF LISTENS

The dwarf listens intently, but with very little reaction, as Caroline explains that they haven't positively identified the body, but she has every reason to believe that Eli Boyle is lying dead in the small apartment above his garage.

"No shit," says Louis Carver. He shakes his head. "Wow. He actually did it."

Caroline tenses. She's said nothing about Clark Mason. "Who?"

"Eli. He used to talk about it all the time, in this totally detached way, like it was just the most normal thing. We'd be talking about investments or what kind of car to buy and he'd just blurt out, 'I could jump off a bridge.' Or 'What do you think of hanging?' Just out of the blue, like that."

"No," Caroline interrupts. "Eli didn't kill himself. Somebody shot him."

They are on the porch of Louis's house and he's standing in the doorway, holding the screen door open as if she's selling something he doesn't need. He falls back against the door frame. He is about four feet tall, bowlegged and thick through the chest and trunk. He wears khaki pants and a sweatshirt that reads, simply, COLLEGE. His features are pleasant, though slightly crowded. A spit of brown hair covers his forehead; he is graying at the temples. "Eli was murdered?" he asks.

"We think so."

"Who did it?"

"We don't know," Caroline says. It occurs to her that Louis Carver does not seem terribly upset that his old friend and business partner is dead.

She was feeling claustrophobic at Eli's carriage house apartment—watching the evidence techs start to dismantle the room—when she remembered Louis's name from the Fair Election Fund. She got his number from information, apologized for calling at ten o'clock, and asked if she could stop by to talk to him for a minute. She left Eli's house without telling anyone, turned her phone off, and drove here, to this tidy daylight rancher in the Shadle neighborhood, on a street of honest, working-family houses.

"Murdered. No shit," Louis says again.

A short, attractive woman—still, a foot taller than her husband, with ink-black hair—sticks her head around the corner of the doorway. She is wearing flannel pajamas and looks as if she just woke up. "Is everything okay?" Mrs. Carver asks.

"Eli Boyle is dead."

If Louis reacted inscrutably to the news, his wife's face registers outright disdain at hearing Eli's name. "Oh."

"He was murdered," Louis tells his wife.

"That's too bad," she says flatly. A baby begins crying behind her, lost and sleepy. She puts her hand on Louis's shoulder and turns around to go get the baby.

"Do you know if Eli had any family?" Caroline asks.

"No," Louis says. "Just his mom, and she died several years ago."

"Do you remember the last time you saw Eli?" she asks.

"Sure." He rubs his eyes. "Two years ago. November of 2000."

"Before or after the election?"

"After," Louis says, seeming surprised that she knows about the election. "You must've talked to Clark already."

"That's actually one thing I wanted to ask you about. How would you characterize the relationship between Clark Mason and Eli?"

"They're best friends. They—" Louis tries to read her face. "You think Clark had something to do with this? Clark *Mason*?" He covers his left eye. "One eye? Tall? Occasionally runs for Congress and gets his ass kicked? That Clark Mason?" Louis shakes his head violently. "No way. Clark wouldn't do that. He couldn't. The guy opens the window to let flies out of his house. He spent the last eight years baby-sitting Eli. What reason would he possibly have to kill him?"

Caroline climbs a step, bringing her closer and to eye level with Louis. "Your name was listed with Eli Boyle's as one of two officers in a political action group." She looks down at her notebook even though she knows the name. "The Fair Election Fund? You paid for the ads that called Clark Mason a carpetbagger?"

Louis comes all the way out now and lets the screen door close behind him. "That was a long time ago and we all—" His face is red and his eyes narrow. "Look, I didn't even know . . ." He lowers his voice. "I just signed where Eli pointed. We had given so much to Clark's campaign that I just assumed we were starting a fund to help him. When I saw in the paper what it was, I was furious. I was a hell of a lot angrier than Clark, if that tells you anything. I sure as shit wouldn't have forgiven Eli for that. But there was Clark, a week later, telling me he couldn't have won anyway. He was actually trying to get *me* to forgive Eli. He went on about how Eli took all this punishment when they were kids. What a hard childhood Eli had. Finally, I couldn't listen anymore. I said, 'Clark, you're talking to a fucking dwarf here. I'm probably gonna need more than a tough childhood.' "

"And you left Empire right after that?" Caroline asks.

He nods. "Two weeks later. Sold my stock back to Eli at the option price. Walked out the door with about eighty grand and never looked back. If I'd sold a year earlier, before the crash, I could've gotten probably ten times that."

"How many partners were there?" she asks.

"Four minority partners: myself and Clark, Bryan, who was our tech guy, and Michael Langford, this investment and finance guy from the Bay Area. We each had five percent of the shares, and since Bryan and I worked there, we also got salaries. Twenty-nine percent was divided among the investors that Michael brought in. Eli retained the other fifty-one percent. That was Clark's doing, too. Eli was terrified that he was going to lose control of the game, so Clark set it up so that Eli's share of the company could never drop below fifty-one unless Eli sold his stock, which of course he never did."

"So you left Empire because of the Fair Election Fund?"

Louis looks past her. "And I had some real problems with the way Eli ran things." He seems wary of saying more.

"Look," Caroline says, "I'm just trying to figure out

who killed your friend. I don't care about anything else. So tell me, why did you leave Empire?"

"Well, for starters, there *was* no Empire. Not the way we were selling it. Not like it was supposed to be." He leans back and searches for the words. "After we got the money everything was different. We got an office, hired illustrators and writers and coders. Every six months, we'd put on a show for the investors, tell them what they wanted to hear, let them see whatever real progress we'd made. Then we'd fake the rest. They want the game on CD-ROM? We put the preview on CD-ROM. They want it on the Internet? We put the preview on a Web site. They want streaming video, multitexturing, 3-D graphics, photorealistic rendering? Fine. As soon as we finished a presentation, we'd go back to work on the next presentation.

"But the game never played. It didn't work. We kept putting options on the car and hoping the investors wouldn't realize there was no engine. We spent all our time making presentations for the venture capital people, and in the end that's all we produced: presentations. You know the key to getting rich back then?"

Caroline shakes her head no.

"Never finish. Always be six months from shipping. That's when you have the most potential, when you haven't messed up yet. Every year I kept thinking they were going to pull the plug when they realized we didn't have a game, and every year some new idiot stepped forward with another million.

"Meantime, Eli was getting this reputation as a genius, going on and on about the realms and the levels of being, about how people wouldn't *play* Empire, they would *live* it. He sounded like some kind of guru. And the game was like a ghost, a rumor. You'd see it referred to in *Red Herring* and *Wired* and *The Industry Standard,* a sentence here or there— 'sources say that when Empire is ready, it will change the entire perception of gaming,' that kind of shit. All the insiders knew about it. Once I read that some company was working on 'an Empire-style interactive game.' " He laughs.

"Eli was so secretive and controlling, that just fed the whole thing, made it seem that much more mysterious and cutting edge. *Because* the game never appeared, I think it actually got better and better in people's minds. Like a striptease. You show people a glimpse and they put the rest together in their minds. By '98, everyone wanted to license our game, or buy us outright: Microsoft, Sega, Nintendo."

"But you didn't sell?"

"Eli wouldn't even consider it—maybe because he knew there was nothing to sell. And he wouldn't go public, which we needed to do if we were ever going to raise enough capital to really develop the game. And every time he said no, it seemed to increase the demand and the interest by VC investors."

"What did Clark think of all of this?"

"The rest of us wanted to sell—Bryan, me, Michael especially. It drove Michael crazy, especially when Eli started acting so paranoid and insecure. Michael even suggested we have Eli committed at one point. But Clark never wavered in his support for Eli. He was going back and forth between here and Seattle and California, doing legal work for other start-ups, doing real well for himself. But no matter how much money he made, he always came back here and took care of Eli.

"They were like brothers. It was Eli who talked Clark into running for Congress. Clark said that maybe he should go for a smaller office first—city council or state legislator—but Eli told him to go for the whole thing. Paid for half his campaign."

Caroline stares at her notes. Something is missing. "So if it was Eli's idea and he was financing the campaign, why spend the money trying to defeat him?"

"I don't know," Louis says carefully. "I never talked directly to Eli about it."

"But you have an idea?" Caroline asks.

Louis rubs his bottom lip. "At the end of '99 everything was going great. We were making progress on the game. I was even starting to think we might actually have it up and running by the following year. We had offices and a warehouse, fifteen people working for us. It was a year before the election, and Clark went back to Seattle to raise money for his campaign. When he came back he brought that woman with him, and that's when everything seemed to change."

"Susan."

"We went to high school with her—although she'd probably deny it. Clark was completely different after they got married. All of a sudden he's hanging around at the Manito Country Club, acting like *one of them*. Part of it was the campaign—Clark needed the support of those people, I guess. But to Eli, it was a betrayal. Pure and simple. And if there was one thing that Eli couldn't stand, it was disloyalty. He was always sort of distrustful, but he was getting paranoid. After a while, he even accused *me* of working with Michael behind his back, trying to sell Empire out from under him."

Before Louis can finish, his wife shows up at the door with a round, red-faced baby boy, maybe three months old. "It's cold, Lou. Why don't you come inside?"

"We're almost finished," Caroline says.

Beaming, Louis opens the door and takes the baby from his wife.

"Oh, Louis," says his wife. "I don't think the detective came here to look at babies." Her hand rests on Louis's shoulder.

"Eighty-fifth percentile," Louis says proudly. The baby pulls his fist to his mouth and starts sucking, and Louis hands him back through the doorway.

When his wife and baby are gone, Louis turns back to Caroline. "That's the other reason I left, right there. I met Ginger about the same time Clark got married. It made Eli crazy. He said I was abandoning him. He had this investigator that he hired every once in a while, and he had the guy follow Ginger because he was convinced she was a plant hired by another game company to steal our secrets. I just laughed. 'Secrets, Eli? What secrets? We don't even have a game.'

"You know what he said? He said, 'Come on, Louis. Why else would she sleep with you? Don't you think she'd rather fuck a normal-size guy?' This was right around the time he spent all that money to defeat Clark. I'd finally had enough of his paranoia and viciousness. So I left. Took a bath on my shares and walked away."

Louis chews on his lip. "There was a time when I would have told you that Eli Boyle was my best friend, when I would've done anything for him. But a few minutes ago ... when you told me that he was dead ... to be honest? I didn't feel a thing."

305

"But you don't know any reason why Clark would kill him?"

"Absolutely not."

"Well," she says, "someone had a reason. Did he have enemies, anyone who might have wanted him dead?"

"You could start with about two dozen investors," Louis says. "There's me. Bryan, our old tech guy—Eli drove him out. Michael, the money guy."

Then something occurs to Louis. "You said enemies? That's funny. I only heard Eli use that word once to describe someone. It was 1998, I think. Eli was in his office, reading the paper, this big grin on his face. I asked what was up, and he showed me this little newspaper story about a guy arrested with a bunch of cocaine in his car. Eli said he'd had the investigator find the guy. I said that was quite a coincidence, and Eli gave me the strangest look. Really creepy. You know? Like it was no coincidence.

" 'See this?' Eli said. 'This is what I do to my enemies. Remember that.' "

"What did he mean?"

"I wasn't sure I wanted to know."

"Did you know the guy?"

"Oh, sure," says Louis. "We went to high school with him. Mean, wiry asshole, used to terrorize Eli at the bus stop."

3 | PETE DECKER SCOWLS

Pete Decker scowls when he comes into the county jail interview room and sees who has interrupted his sleep. Scraggly haired and yawning, in the jeans and T-shirt that he was wearing this afternoon when Caroline tackled him on the sidewalk, Pete turns back to the guard.

"What'd they do, assign me my own cop?" he asks. Then he turns to Caroline. "You ain't done enough for me today?"

She had a hell of a time convincing the jail commander to let her talk to an inmate late Saturday night, but Caroline finally persuaded him that Pete had vital information in a homicide investigation and that she didn't have time to go through normal channels.

Her cell phone vibrates. She looks down. Spivey. He must've finally been called out to Eli Boyle's house. It won't be long now. Caroline reaches down and turns off her phone.

"I just need to ask you a couple of questions," she tells Pete.

He crosses his arms. "I don't like when you ask me questions."

"You mentioned someone, a guy that Clark used to fight at the bus stop when you were kids."

"Yeah." Pete finally sits down.

"Eli Boyle."

"Yeah, that's him. Weird fuckin' kid."

"When did you see him last?"

Pete shrugs. "I don't know. Twenty years? About the same time I saw Clark the last time." He gestures toward the jail guard standing at the door behind him. "I don't bump into too many people from the old neighborhood."

"Uh-huh." She looks down at her notes from the interview with Louis Carver. "Do you remember anything about your arrest in '98?"

"Did three and some at Walla Walla for that shit. 'Course I remember."

"In the arrest report, you said that you *found* five hundred grams of cocaine outside your apartment."

He shrugs and tries to smile. "Yeah. That's a good one to try in court, huh? Fuck I was thinking? *I found it!* Stupid-ass motherfucker."

"So did you?"

"Did I what?"

"Find a half-kilo of cocaine outside your apartment?"

He stares at her and his eyes narrow, as if he's trying to figure her angle. "What the fuck is this—"

"Look, I'm just asking a question."

"Bullshit."

"You don't want to tell me what happened in '98?"

"You're fuckin' with me."

"I'm not."

"You won't believe me."

"I might."

"Okay. You want to know?" He chews his bottom lip. "I'd been out two months, but I was straight. The one good thing about state time is you can get off the shit,

308

you know? You probably don't believe me, but I was pissin' clean those two months."

He looks down at a crudely drawn tattoo on his arm, as if it would finish the story for him. "Had a car, a little apartment downtown, a job washing dishes. Most times that shit don't work for me—goin' straight. It's boring. But Walla Walla changed everything. I hated that place so much, I'd have washed every fuckin' dish in the world to stay out.

"Then one afternoon, I come out of my apartment to go to work, and there's a car parked next to mine. Brand-new fuckin' Mercedes-Benz. Beautiful car. Charcoal-colored ragtop. I mean . . . we didn't get us a lot of Benzes parked outside my building. Nobody's around and the top and windows are down. No other cars in the alley. So I looked in. I mean, how could I not? Be like some chick sitting topless on your sidewalk, you know? You gotta look. Don't mean nothing. Just means you looked."

He wipes his brow at the memory.

"It was sitting right there in the driver's seat. Half a brick. I never had that much weight myself—not in coke—but I seen guys cut from packages like that. Shit. I don't know if the guy was coming back for it, if it just fell out, if it was a drop. I don't know shit except it's sitting there on the driver's seat, like everything I ever wanted in my life, like someone left it just for me. Like God or something just woke up that day said, 'You know what, Pete, ol' buddy, even assholes deserve a break some-times.'

"I don't even remember grabbing it. Next thing I know, I'm driving away, checking my rearview mirror, that thing in my lap." He cradles his hands as if holding a baby. He

309

smiles. "I made sure no one was behind me and then I cut a seam and did a line while I was waiting for a red light. Oh! Pure as a hug from your mama. Shit was amazing." He laughs and his eyes roll back. "Best four minutes of my life."

"Four minutes?"

"That's about how long I drove before the cops swarmed me. Uniforms. Four rollers. I figured they was watchin' the Benz, but when I told 'em I found it in that car, they just laughed at me." He shakes his head. "They got a big kick out of that. 'He found it! Motherfucker found it!'

"I said, 'You mean you guys wasn't watchin' that Benz back there?' They just laughed at me. 'What Benz?' they said. I swore so much that's what happened, they drove me back down the alley to check it out. But the car was gone.

"In court, the cops said that some dude had called in, said he saw a guy in a gold Nova driving north on Division with a big bag of coke in his lap. Bang, strike three, judge gives me a fuckin' nickel. You know, I've had bad luck, but to have some fucker call in when I'm doing a line in my own car? That shit's unfair."

Pete shrugs, as if he's bored with his own story. "Yeah, yeah, so poor me, huh? What's this got to do with Eli Boyle?"

Caroline looks down at the Department of Motor Vehicles report for Eli Boyle that she just printed out. She slides it across the table.

Pete picks it up and reads it, his lips moving as he does.

She watches Pete's face as he reads that Eli Boyle has

registered only one car in the last four years, a gunmetal gray 1998 Mercedes-Benz SL500 convertible. Pete looks up from the paper, his face blank, as if he can't comprehend this, as if he's never imagined that such patterns could be at play in his life, that he could be subject to such elaborate forces, the shadows, the world beneath this one.

Maybe that's what's going through his head, Caroline thinks, or maybe that's just me. Because all Pete says is, "Motherfucker."

"He hired an investigator to find you," Caroline says. "I guess he knew what time you went to work and he parked there, figuring you wouldn't be able to resist."

Pete shakes his head and reads the DMV report again. "Why?"

"I don't know. I was hoping you could tell me."

"I don't . . . I don't know," he says quietly. She watches the disbelief on his face become something else, sadness over those lost three years, maybe, or the wonder over whether he could've stayed clean. Then his face changes again, and this new emotion is unmistakable—cheeks reddening, eyes narrowing, lips closing in.

Caroline stands and motions to the guard. She takes the report from Pete. "Listen, I'll put in a word with the prosecutor," she says. "Tell him you helped me. Maybe they'll give you a break."

The guard comes in, but Pete is staring off, miles away.

"Oh, and if you're thinking about paying Eli a visit when you get out," Caroline says, "you're about three days too late."

4 | SHE'S LOST CLARK

S he's lost Clark. Of all the terrible things that could happen now—and there are others—this is the most terrible; Caroline has no idea what to do next. She stands in the doorway of Interview Two and stares, unbelieving, at the empty chair. No legal pads. No pen. No coffee cup. It's as if he were never here. Now that she could finally sit across from Clark and say, *Look, I know what happened*, there is no Clark to sit across from.

She'd come back to drop the whole thing in his lap that way—Eli Boyle and Pete Decker and Louis Carver, all of it—to tell him that his time was up and his confession was over. Oh, it's over all right. She steps out into the hallway to look for the uniform that Kaye was supposed to post on the door, but there's no one. Fucking Kaye. She begins moving toward the front desk.

"Caroline!"

She turns. Spivey is at the other end of the hall, coming out of the bathroom, wearing jeans and a Mariners sweatshirt, with his cop haircut and that ridiculous caterpillar of a mustache on his thin upper lip. "Where the hell have you been? I've been trying to reach you."

"There was a guy in Interview Two—"

"Mason?"

"Yeah," Caroline says. "You know where he is?"

"I cut him loose."

"What?" She begins stalking toward Spivey. "When?"

"I don't know. Fifteen minutes ago. After I finished questioning him."

"You questioned him?"

Spivey laughs bitterly. "Yeah, that's what we do with witnesses. Remember? We don't throw them in a room and disappear for two days. You want to tell me—"

"You didn't charge him?"

"Who?"

"Mason."

"Charge him with what? Being a fucking nut job?"

"What about the body? Boyle?"

"What are you talking about, Caroline? The suicide you found?"

"Suicide? There was no gun."

"Sure there was. We found it in the lawn, right where Mason said he threw it. Said he freaked out, grabbed the gun, opened the door, and threw it across the lawn. Kept saying he was responsible. But don't worry. I took care of him. Put the fear of God into him, told him we could charge him with evidence tampering if he didn't put down his pen and cooperate."

She falls back against the wall. "Suicide?"

"Yeah, the vic had powder residue all over his fingers. His prints were all over the gun. From the angle, the ME said it had to be self-inflicted. Straight up through his noggin." Spivey puts his forefinger against his cheek, elbow tight against his side, to demonstrate. "We tested Mason's fingers just to be sure. No powder residue. Besides, he's got an alibi. Boyle's neighbors heard a gunshot at four P.M. Friday. Your boyfriend was on an airplane at four. It's all here." He waves a single sheet of paper.

Caroline grabs it and reads. Spivey has typed it up. Clark has signed it.

Statement of Clark A. Mason:

I certify that the following statement is truthful and complete. I arrived at Spokane International Airport at approximately 4:10 P.M. on February 10, 2002, after a personal trip to San Jose, California. Worried about the emotional state of my friend Eli Boyle, I proceeded immediately to his residence on Cliff Drive, whereupon I found Boyle dead, having shot himself in the head with a .38-caliber handgun. Running to the body, I picked up the gun, went outside, and threw it across the lawn. I was nervous and emotionally agitated and I left the scene without notifying authorities. Later, I was approached by Spokane police officers at the Davenport Hotel, and I agreed to tell them what happened.

Clark A. Mason

The statement falls to her side. It's not right.

"So what the hell got into you?" Spivey is not finished lecturing. "Letting that poor wack job sit in here sweating all weekend, convincing himself he's a murderer?"

Caroline ignores him. "The thing he was writing. His statement. Did you read it?"

"Oh, I looked at it—four notebooks of crazy shit about growing up with the dead guy and going to the prom.

Listen, you are not a psychiatrist, Caroline, and no matter how much you want to help someone—"

"Where is it?"

"What?"

"The statement. Where is it?"

"He said he wanted you to have it. I put the whole thing on your desk."

Caroline turns away from Spivey, walks into the Major Crimes office, and switches on the light. She finds the four legal pads stacked neatly and begins flipping through the first one, looking for . . . what? She can feel adrenaline, and for a moment, she forgets that she hasn't slept for two days.

"Listen, Caroline," he says, "I'm serious about this. You really fucked up this weekend. I'm gonna have to write this up, you know."

She sets the first section down and starts flipping the pages of the second legal pad, Clark's handwriting loosening as he gets tired. The words pour over her like water; none of it sticks. Maybe Spivey's right; Clark is crazy.

"I don't know why you didn't just call me," Spivey says, "why you have to make everything so difficult all the time."

She sets the second legal pad down and starts skimming the third. More rambling. She's about to set it down when the last sentence catches her attention. ". . . *the world would be a better and simpler place if Michael Langford were not in it.*"

"Where's the gun?" she asks without looking up.

"What?"

"The gun. You said you found the gun in the grass. Where is it?"

315

"On my desk. God damn it, Caroline—"

She brushes past him, reaches for a box of surgical gloves on the counter, and grabs one as she stomps past the cubicles to Spivey's glass-walled office.

He follows her in. "I'm not kidding here, Caroline! You really fucked up—"

She can take no more. "I fucked up?" She spins on her heel and up into his face. "Patrol found this guy on the twelfth floor of a vacant building. Staring out a window."

Spivey shrugs. "So?"

"So before you kicked him loose, did you consider why a depressed guy might go up to the twelfth floor of a vacant building by himself?"

Spivey takes a step back. "Oh."

She turns away, reaches into the plastic bag, and removes the black handgun, an evidence tag wrapped around the trigger guard. "Or did you ask yourself why, when Mason's friend is lying there dead, his first thought is to pick up the gun?" Caroline releases the pin and flips the gun open. She holds it up and stares at Spivey through the empty chambers. "Two," she says.

"What?"

She holds out the gun for him to see. "There are two empty chambers. One slug went through Boyle. So where's the other one?"

It is remarkably quiet in these offices at one-thirty on a Sunday morning. Caroline's eyes drift from Spivey to the gun and finally to the stack of legal pads, on top of which Clark has written, in big block letters, STATEMENT OF FACT.

. . . the less honest I was, the more famous I should be. The very limit of human blindness is to glory in being blind.
– St. Augustine, *The Confessions*

VIII

Statement of Fact

I | YOU'RE PROBABLY WONDERING

You're probably wondering how a man falls so far so fast—how an idealistic, socially conscious lawyer one day finds himself planning a murder, of all things, how a man who's never broken any laws (okay, there were a few narcotics statutes) skips over all the other felonies and misdemeanors and goes straight for a premeditated murder. Of course, the explanation begins with my over-powering ambition and, especially, my unfailing blindness to the desires and motivations of people around me. But there are two other forces at work here, and between them, these two hard cases are undoubtedly the cause of more criminal acts than all the other suspects combined:

Love.

And politics.

This is the shape of my confession, then, a dark story of love and politics, a reckoning, a cautionary tale of how far one man can fall in this world. And to describe a fall, of course, one must start with height.

So let me just say this: I was rich.

I use this as the measure of my success because it is the gauge of my generation, a generation which will fade from even the shortest history because we contributed so little in the way of art and politics and bravery, because our currency was . . . well, currency. We were an entire cut of people in their twenties and thirties still running creative and procreative juices but spending the current of our days discussing stock options and price-to-earnings ratios and small market capitalization and "What's in your 401(k)?"

Since profanity is nothing without a tease—a glimpse of flesh beneath the satin—it is a fair question to ask: How rich was I?

At the peak of my wealth, in 1999, I had seven million dollars in various checkbooks, savings accounts, stock portfolios, retirement accounts, and pants pockets. I had a condo in downtown Seattle, a new BMW roadster, a new Range Rover, and a vintage Harley-Davidson motor-cycle. I was shopping for a boat. Now by the standards of the founders of Microsoft and Amazon and countless other late-century techno-thieves, my portfolio was little more than cab fare, but to me it was as much money as existed in the world.

I remember the first time it occurred to me that I was rich: in 1997, when I was making one of my rare visits to see my parents. I stood in their driveway as my father paced around my Harley.

"It's a beaut," he said. "How much was it?"

"It really wasn't too expensive."

"How much?" he asked.

When I told him that it cost thirty-two thousand dollars, he laughed giddily, but then his face set and he cocked his head. "Huh," he said, and he didn't have to tell me that it was more than he'd earned any year of his life.

I won't bore you with the details of my windfall, the picks and splits, the mergers and offerings, the good fortune that I convinced myself was good analysis. Suffice it to say that after I helped Eli get Empire off the ground (at least conceptually; in other ways, that Spruce Goose would remain forever grounded), I returned to Seattle and threw myself into the hunt for technology start-ups, to show Dana that I could succeed in her world or, rather, in her husband's world. I worked nonstop, hounding the city for raccoon-eyed computer geeks, for Microsoft drones looking to break off from the mothership, for coders and programmers, dreamers and brainstormers, people with the slimmest ideas as long as they involved somehow hunching over a keyboard and staring into a glass box. I read newspapers and trade magazines, hung out at cyber cafés and the technology departments of local universities. I beat the bushes until, by 1998, I'd flushed three dozen successful start-ups out into the open for Michael's venture capital riflemen, and written the contracts and done the various other legal work for five successful IPOs. You have probably heard of some of these companies, and may have even owned their stock, the most noteworthy being CybSysTechTronic (CSTT—the nation's premier producer of data cap transponders and backup port regulators for wireless modem and data recovery chips) and Myonlineshoestore.com, which was, for eight wonderful months, the number two online shoe store *in the whole country*.

Not all of my companies were successful, of course, and after the crash a certain newsmagazine looking to describe the irrational frenzy of the late nineties listed among the heavily funded and lightly considered tech businesses one discovery of mine: MousePants (later MousePants.com), which manufactured computer-friendly clothing, beginning with cargo pants with small mouse pads on the thighs (I suppose we should've stopped production once we saw the ubiquity of laptop rollerballs and touchpads, but even without the eponymous gimmick this was a good-looking, comfortable pant).

From the outside, the legal part of my job was not glamorous—a daily diet of IPO's, recaps, mergers and acquisitions, management buyouts, divestitures, bridge financing, debt and equity placement, credit lines, reorganizations, and countless other functions that were simply a shifting of money from one pocket to another. First for Michael and Dana, and later for one of Seattle's bigger law firms (I will not tempt action from those carnivores by mentioning the partners on their letterhead), I worked as a buffer, as Michael said, between Chad and Charlie, drafting paper maneuvers that ensured Charlie would give Chad an endless supply of money and Chad would give Charlie "a position" in some emerging tech business. Any guilt I felt over our . . . exaggerated display of Empire quickly faded when I saw the speculative prospects that brought in millions in seed money and made our game seem as established as Monopoly, when I saw that the point of this new economy was not some finished machinery, but the money that greased it so fully that it would take five years to realize the machine was running only on that grease.

But most of my wealth came not from my legal work, but from tips and insights I gleaned about start-ups and new products, buyouts and takeovers. Each time I bought stock for myself, I picked up a few for Eli, too, and while he spent most of his money paying back investors and genuinely trying to turn Empire into a computer game, he managed to do pretty well alongside me, two unlikely success stories from Empire Road in the Spokane Valley.

But while it is the most obvious, money wasn't the only measure of my success, and not even the one that motivated me. I am a perception junkie, always have been; my drug is the way people see me. I had kicked the habit briefly during my ascetic phase following Ben's death, but now I was back on the shit. And all of Seattle seemed to be tripping with me, a full-blown collective high.

My own symptoms were so acute I began to doubt that I even existed when no one was there to see me. I craved that fleeting moment when I stepped into restaurants and people looked up, or meetings when it was my turn to speak. I dated every girl who would go out with me, always eager for new eyes in which to see myself. When I pulled to a stop at a traffic light I looked around for my reflection in the windows of buildings, my forty-dollar-trimmed hair, my tailored suit, my glass eye and sunglasses— near-perfection encased in a black BMW.

I was chained again to this self-addiction, and it wasn't long before I began to imagine the black tar of my particular habit—politics. I joined a few groups, a taste there and here—the Jaycees, a Bar Association committee on technology, nothing too extravagant. I got involved with the Democratic Party, and donated money to a handful of candidates. But the little tastes made me want more, until I found myself having the old daydream: a podium, bunting, my name on a banner behind me, a crowd of supporters: *Mason. Mason. Mason.*

During those days, older, established lawyers occasionally sought me out to explain this new world of high-tech business, and I developed something of a reputation as an expert in my field. I spoke at conferences to rooms full of gray-haired lawyers about the speed and dexterity with which we would need to practice contract law to keep up with the demands of an industry that seemed to change by the minute. During these presentations I sometimes began sentences with the words "In the future," and I rambled on about the day when client conferences would be video-streamed over broadband, when computers would automatically read through a trial transcript and make the appropriate appeal, when entire hearings would be held on the Internet and the lawyer would never have to leave his office (except, I suppose, to jetpack home to have sex with his robot girlfriend in his cryogenic sleeping portal).

That's how it happened that, in April 1998, I accepted a request to speak at the first annual "Spokane Technology Symposium" with various civic leaders, elected officials, and local entrepreneurs (always shy about such things, Eli had given them my name when they tried to recruit him for the symposium). The whole endeavor smacked of desperation, as the local leaders tried to spark the kind of twelfth-hour high-tech boom that had transformed Seattle and Portland—and much of the rest of the country—but passed Spokane by like a long-haul trucker on bennies.

The symposium was held in the conference room of an airport hotel. We sat at round tables as waiters brought us fingers of chicken left over from some canceled flight, and a salad that consisted of cottage cheese and Jell-O. At each table sat a member of the city government and several representatives of the technology elite of Spokane.

At my table was a frowning, buzz-cut retired air force corpsman who had recently been elected to the city council and who wanted to make sure the library computers weren't being used to access porn; a junior high school student with razor-wire braces who won a computer science contest by using his laptop to graph local marijuana prices; the furtive founder of a local keyboard manufacturing company that was in the process of moving to Belize; and the manager of one especially cutting-edge firm called Jocko's Soft Tacos: "We just got a new computer for our drive-thru window that has cut in half the number of Mexi-Bobs that we throw away."

I also spoke to the mayor, a nice older gentleman who had retired from "the carpet industry, myself," and who ran for office because he was tired of gardening with his wife all day. He admitted that he was catching hell for failing to bring technology companies to Spokane, and for allowing sharp minds such as mine to escape.

"My kids like the computers," he said. "Me, I wouldn't know how to turn the goddamn thing on if you put my hand on the crank." He struggled to frame the problem, using his fingers to put quote marks around every eighth word. His opponent in the upcoming election claimed that to "attract" certain kinds of industry, cities must offer "incentives" to help convince entrepreneurs that a certain "atmosphere" existed.

That's true, I said. Tax incentives, growth districts, infrastructure—there were things a city could do to attract technology companies.

"And how long does it take, all of that?"

"Well . . . it can take years," I said.

"Yeah," he said. "That's no good. I only got three months."

I suppose that's when it first dawned on me that my newfound success connected at some point with my old dream—that I could be a kind of visionary figure, a political candidate for the twenty-first century. It would be more than a year before I would do anything about this vision, though, and even that day, I got drunk and didn't give any more thought to my political career. And beyond that flash of inspiration, I suppose Spokane's first technology symposium isn't very important to the core of my confession—except for one other detail.

After dinner (barbecued ribs and coleslaw) and several drinks, I staggered to the elevator fairly drunk—and not quite alone. That night, in a small room on the fourth floor of a hotel built into the hillside over my old hometown—the lights of Spokane sparkling below us like a lake of stars—I had sex for the first time with Dana Brett.

2 | IT WAS UNBELIEVABLE

It was unbelievable to me that Dana could've fallen in love with such a sneaky, coldhearted, lying bastard as Michael Langford. She seemed oblivious to his manipulation of her, his cheating of clients, his double-dealing with colleagues and competitors. She also seemed oblivious to his intense dislike of me. Oh, when we were around other people, Michael was friendly, but when it was just the two of us he berated me, called me a fraud, and taunted me with the fact that he had married the only woman I have ever loved.

"Hello, Mason," he would say when I answered the phone. "Who are you bilking today?" When I would say something he disagreed with, he'd say, "Mason, are you looking through your bad eye again?" When he didn't return my calls right away, he'd say, "Sorry I didn't get right back to you, Mason. I was nailing my wife."

Michael's company was called Techubator. (He and his partners thought it was a clever name for a tech company incubator; I always thought it sounded like a machine to help jack the fatty.) I only got involved with Techubator in the first place to spend time with Dana, and with Michael's constant disdain and vicious barbs it was the only reason I stayed as long as I did. But as I got deeper into the business, Dana's role kept decreasing. Then, in early 1998, she left the firm entirely to devote herself to creating Web sites for nonprofit agencies.

I was frantic. I tried to dissuade her through e-mails and phone calls, but she was adamant that it was time to move on. On her last day I flew down to Techubator head-quarters in San Jose for her going-away party, and when the cake was gone and the chino-wearing staff had wandered back to their cubicles, I saw Dana sneak outside the office and found her on a park bench on a sidewalk in the business park.

She said the pace had gotten to her. "We're running on a treadmill. We never get anywhere. We start these companies and then move on to the next one before we know what happens. It's like giving birth and never getting to see the babies grow up."

"We had three IPO's in the last six months, Dana," I said. "We have three more in the works. How much bigger do the babies have to get?"

She had grown her hair longer; it was brown and straight, and she pushed it back out of those cinnamon eyes. "I don't mean financially, Clark," she said. "All of the things that were supposed to happen . . . the trans-formation of our economy and our culture. What happened to all of that?"

"My economy's been transformed," I said.

She ignored me. "Besides, it'll be easier on me person-ally."

I perked up, put my hand on hers. "Things tough at home?"

She looked up. "No," she said, not convincingly. "I just think it's not good for a couple to live together and work together. And frankly, I'm sort of bored, Clark. I need a new challenge. I need something more."

In the time I'd spent at Techubator, Dana was always friendly toward me but she'd maintained a slight reserve. And yet, at meetings, I'd feel her eyes on me and I'd know she was thinking the same thing I was—that we'd somehow missed each other in the crash and whorl of our lives.

That's what I felt sitting on that bench. With the words "something more" hanging in the air, I looked into her eyes. She didn't look away. The space between us seemed charged. Dana's mouth opened slightly.

"Dana—" I began.

"There you are," said Michael, an edge in his voice.

We both looked up from the park bench.

Michael came into the courtyard, bent down and kissed her full on the mouth, then rested his hand on her neck and looked down at me. "We're so glad you could come, Clark," he said. "Did Dana tell you all about our plans?"

I said yes, and how impressed I was with her nonprofit Web site plans. Before coming to work for them, I reminded them, I'd done quite a bit of charity work myself.

"Oh, right. In Portugal," Michael said evenly, nearly masking his sarcasm. "Did she tell you the best part? In a year or so, we're going to start having kids."

"No, she didn't mention that part."

"Or two years," Dana said.

Michael squeezed her shoulders. "I can't wait."

A few weeks later I left Techubator and accepted a job with the Seattle law firm. I still remained involved with some of the companies funded through Michael's venture capital contacts, and we were both still shareholders of

Empire—which was chewing up seed money with no hope of having a real game in the near future—but I knew I couldn't stand to have any more regular dealings with Michael Langford.

For four months I could think of no excuse to call Dana. But I found myself thinking about her every day, and I felt a charge, a gap in my breathing when I'd see her small oval face and those placid eyes.

Then, in April of '98, I was invited to the technology symposium in Spokane. I agreed to go only if they included a presentation on what I said was the fastest-growing segment of the industry—Web pages for nonprofits. I told them I knew the perfect expert to come speak on that topic, and that coincidentally this person had lived in Spokane, too. And then I made an anonymous donation to the symposium to pay for this expert's airfare. For her part, Dana seemed excited to be back to Spokane, and to see me, and that's how Dana and I ended up together in the lounge at the Airport Ramada Hotel and how we found ourselves at a corner table, laughing and throwing back White Russians and Cape Cods, as if we might drink enough booze to float us over the locks between us, which is, of course, the only really good thing about booze.

I told her that her presentation had been great. (In fact she'd alienated the crowd a bit, contending that for every dollar a city spent attracting private technology firms, a city was morally required to spend a hundred dollars on computers for schools and other public projects.) I also remarked on the sorry state of affairs in Spokane, compared with new economy centers like Seattle and San Jose.

"Oh, they're better off without all that shit," Dana said, raising her glass to ask for another Cape Cod. "Sometimes I think this is the last real place on earth, Clark. Sometimes I think I haven't been right since I left here."

"Spokane?"

"If Michael would do it, I'd move back here in a minute. Have a bunch of kids."

"What would Michael do here? There's no technology base. There's nothing."

She shrugged. "He could be a waiter. He was a waiter when I met him. A *good* waiter. He could hold nine water glasses." When she was drunk her right eyelid fluttered, and it occurred to me that if the left eyelid got going too, she might just lift off the ground. "That's something. Bringing people water. That's basic goodness. Someone is thirsty. You bring them water. What has any of this technology"—she pronounced it teck-nodgy—"really done for anyone, Clark? Does it make them less thirsty?" She swilled her drink. "We used to go to the mall to buy our CDs. Now we buy them at our desk. What's really changed?"

"The whole world," I said. "The whole world has changed."

"Is this what you saw us doing when we were young?" she asked. "We were idealistic. We wanted more than this, Clark. Remember? Remember what you wanted?"

I stared into her fluttering eyes. "Yes," I whispered. "I remember."

She stared back at me, confused, and then it seemed to register, what I was talking about. She laughed, tossed her head back, and snorted. "I don't mean that, silly." She waved her hand dismissively and knocked my drink into my lap.

331

I jumped up and slapped at my crotch, where the Kahlúa had doused whatever had begun to smolder down there.

"I'm sorry," she said. "I'm a dope." Then she took her drink, looked at it, and dumped it in her own lap, the vodka and cranberry juice making a small and inviting pool in her skirt. We both watched as the booze seeped into the small triangle between her thighs—until all that was left were six of the most fortunate ice cubes I've ever seen.

"There," she said. "Even."

Ten minutes later we were in her hotel room. I would like to say that the next eight minutes constituted one of those life-altering, transcendent moments that can occasionally occur when two people do what we attempted to do, but far too much liquor had crossed the breach for anything more than a boozy tumble. (*Ow. Ooh, not there. Mmmph. Are you okay? Sorry.*) We certainly did nothing to make good on the promise and longing of all those years.

And yet, when it was over, we held tight and I spent the next hour staring at the tiny blond hairs on her temple, listening to her breathe on my neck, and we lay all night like that in each other's arms, slowly sobering up, but not saying a word, not wanting to waste a second with talk or sleep, our fingertips lightly tracing each other's bodies until dawn began to nudge at the curtains and we could stand it no longer and, aching, we pressed together again, and then all morning, clenching and arching and falling away. And I doubt that such things can be controlled, but the last memory I hope to indulge on this earth is the weight of Dana's hand on my neck and the gust of her voice on my ear as she whispered, "*Clark. Oh my God, yes.*"

When I finally gave in, it was to the deepest sleep I can ever remember. When I awoke, about three that afternoon, Dana was sitting in a chair across from my bed, talking on the phone. "No," she was saying. "It was fine." She listened for a few minutes. "I'm flying out tonight." She listened again. "Clark?" She looked up at me. "Yeah, I saw him a little bit. . . . Well, we didn't make any plans, but if I see him, I'll tell him hi."

"Okay," she said. "Love you too," and hung up the phone.

"Hi," she said to me.

"Hi."

She smiled sadly, and I had the inexplicable feeling there was someone else in the room with us—some version of our pasts or vision of our futures, some overwhelming sadness. "You have the worst timing of any person I've ever met," she said finally.

We showered separately, dressed, and drove into town. She wore a print dress that reminded me of the things she wore as a kid. She kept pushing her hair over her ears. We ended up at the Davenport Hotel, which was just then beginning another renovation, and I stood quietly in kinship with it, my insides long ago gutted and abandoned, dead for fifteen years and now, against all reason and odds, crying out for rebirth.

We drove out to the Valley, to her parents' old house, in the apple orchards near the Idaho state line. They'd moved to Arizona a few years earlier, and Dana didn't want to disturb the new owners. She sat low in the passenger seat of my rental car and traced the white porch

333

railing on the car window. "We're kids for such a short amount of time." She turned and looked at me. "But forever."

Dana had never been to my house when we were in high school, and I said nothing as we drove past it. My mother was in the yard, her back to us, bent over a flower bed along the sidewalk in front of their house—her shoulders a little narrower, her hair a bouquet of gray. I passed behind her, a ghost in a rental car.

"Where is it?" Dana asked a few blocks later. "I thought we were going by your house."

"It was back there," I said.

At the airport, I ordered a drink, but Dana didn't want one. We sat at the end of the terminal, watching mothers preboard with their babies.

"Have you thought about how you're going to tell Michael?" I asked.

"Tell Michael?" She cocked her head.

I stared at her for a moment and then said, "Oh." Understanding fell in my lap like a White Russian. "You're not going to tell Michael."

They announced her section of the plane and Dana stood. "Oh, Clark," she said. "I'm sorry. It would kill him." She kissed me. "This was nice. Maybe even something I needed. But I have to get back to my life now."

This was nice. I lurched and burned and swayed and watched her walk all the way down the tarmac, until at the very end, just before she stepped on the plane, I swear I saw her glance back.

I got drunk that night, and again the next night and pretty much every night for the next six weeks. I have always tried to drink moderately, but as you may have noticed by this point in my confession, I have a somewhat compulsive personality. So for me drinking moderately is akin to fucking moderately, or jumping moderately from a cliff. Either you do or you don't. And after watching Dana get on that plane, I did. I got drunk on the plane back to Seattle, got drunk at the airport bar after I landed, and then—when Dana wouldn't answer my e-mails—set about humiliating myself in a different bar each night for a month and change. I have fond memories, and fonder blackouts, from this time (one Saturday afternoon I staggered from a Pioneer Square bar and led a tour of the Seattle Underground to the water, where, thankfully, I was stopped before I could perform any baptisms). I will not indulge these lost evenings, these nights in which I was potted, canned, screwed, smashed, soaked, bottled, and blitzed; instead I'll skip to the last night of this long hot binge, when I was summarily thrown out of the Triangle Pub for standing on a stool and asking for help measuring the bar's hypotenuse.

After I was led outside I promptly fell over on the sidewalk, looked up into the drizzle, and saw a girl's thin face staring down at me. She was young and lithe in her Deadhead sundress, her braided red hair and worn backpack. I immediately recognized her as one of the girls I'd slept with during my bohemian days.

"Tamira," I said.

"No," she said. "Kayla."

"Oh. Kayla. You look like a Tamira."

"Yeah. I just came out to tell you, it doesn't have a hypotenuse."

"What?"

"The bar. It's an isosceles triangle. Doesn't have any right angles. So you can't measure the hypotenuse." She peered into my eyes. "What's wrong with you?"

I asked her to marry me. We went instead to a late-night breakfast joint where I told her the whole sordid story while she ate ginger french toast and tofu sausage with one of her turquoise-ringed hands and smoked Lucky Strikes with the other.

"So you're saying you spent the last three years trying to be like the guy that this Dana woman married?" she asked.

I thought about it. "Yes," I said. "I guess I did."

Kayla took a drag of a Lucky Strike. "Well, there's your mistake. The last thing some married chick wants is a guy like her husband. You should go back to yourself."

In a flash of understanding I saw that Kayla was right. Go back to myself. The problem was this: which self?

Two days later I was back in Spokane, at a cemetery downriver from the city. I crouched down in front of a small stone, set flush into the ground. I ran my finger over the letters, BENJAMIN T. MASON, and those cruel dates, NOVEMBER 12, 1966–NOVEMBER 19, 1985. I know there are people who go to such places to talk to the person who has died, but I couldn't bring myself to do it. (I also refuse to say that a person has "passed," as if he has simply processed a rich meal.)

Mom had left plastic flowers on Ben's grave, and a wooden hummingbird whose wings windmilled frantically in the wind. I straightened the flowers, wiped the grass clippings from the headstone, and wished that Ben could tell me what to do now. I remembered his saying that I really only lived in the perceptions of others, and suddenly it seemed painfully true. I couldn't think of a time when I'd acted on my own, when I wasn't driven by my grief for Ben or my love for Dana or my desire to show up Michael Langford—or, for that matter, the tyranny of Pete Decker or the suggestive looks of girls in high school. I wondered if I even had a self.

"I miss you," I said aloud. Surprised at myself, I looked around to see if anyone had heard, but no one was near.

I left the cemetery and drove into Spokane, to the northeast end of downtown, to a brick storefront that had been an antique and junk shop until six months ago, when it became the offices of Empire Interactive.

This was at the beginning of Eli's compulsion about security, and he'd recently installed an elaborate key card system on the door. In addition, the windows were tinted so no one could see in. I pounded on a window, unsure if anyone inside could see me.

Finally the door opened and out came Louis Carver, beaming. "Clark! What are you doing here?"

"I came to check on my investment."

Louis patted me on the small of my back. "Come in."

I followed him through the door into a narrow

337

anteroom, where a security camera monitored our progress, then through another key-carded door into what looked like a cafeteria: tile floor, long tables where a half-dozen people sat working intently on computer terminals. At the far end of this room were three small offices, one for Bryan the tech guy, one for Louis, and one for Eli.

He came out of his office wearing wrinkled slacks and a striped shirt with a salsa stain near the collar, his glasses slightly askew. "Clark!" he said, and then his piggy little eyes shifted around the room, as if embarrassed by the excitement in his voice.

"Hey, Eli." I reached out and he took my hand reluctantly, gave it a soft, fleshy shake, and then turned back toward his office.

Louis gave me a lingering stare and then went back to work.

I followed Eli into his office, a simple, white-walled room, with a long computer table and the old Empire binders stacked on bookshelves along the walls. He looked out the window at the people in the office. "I don't trust them," he said. "I don't like the way they look at me. They're ingratiating. They smell money. They pretend to hang on every word I say. They pretend to like me."

"Maybe they do like you," I said.

He turned to me, one eyebrow raised, as if I'd just suggested that he become a male model or an exotic dancer. Then he turned back to stare into what they called the Game Room. "I just don't know why we had to hire so many," he said.

"We've got to get this thing off the ground, Eli," I said. "If we don't start earning money pretty soon, the investors are going to get antsy."

338

"I don't care," Eli said. "I'll pay them out of my own pocket."

I had to beg him to show me what they were working on, including an e-mail component that would allow characters (Eli still wouldn't call them players) to contact each other away from the instant messaging of the game—to allow more backstabbing and double-dealing. "That's the key," Eli said: "treachery." I hadn't been by the office in more than three months, so he showed me the newest graphics, which were—as our team of young testers assured him—"killer." He was especially excited about a prison for miscreant and broken characters—a rocky island covered with catacombs, tunnels, and torture chambers, straight out of *The Count of Monte Cristo*.

But he was leery of showing me much else, including the game engine that he and Bryan were constantly tinkering with, the "brains," the basic system that ran the shadow world, took the information and the actions of the characters and translated them into the movements of people on the computer screen.

"It's not that I don't trust you, Clark," he said, "but you come in contact with a lot of other companies. I'd hate for something to end up in the wrong hands."

It was late in the afternoon. Eli had recently moved into the house on Cliff Drive (that place of horrors, now) and he invited me over. I said we could take my rental car—I knew Eli hated to drive—but he smiled wryly and pulled a single, plastic-coated, black key from his pocket. I followed him out back, and there it was: a new, dark gray Mercedes-Benz convertible, and the only extravagant thing I ever knew Eli to buy.

I followed him up the South Hill to his house, but after we parked he led me away from the main house to the small carriage house in back, where he was living. There was very little furniture in the carriage house, and his clothes were still in his suitcase. Apparently he only ate pizza; the boxes were stacked against one wall. "You want a beer?" he asked.

I explained that I'd been drinking too much lately, and that I'd recently had a kind of pre-midlife crisis. Yet after what had happened at the prom, I didn't figure he'd sympathize with my attempts to steal Dana from another guy, so I spoke generally about my desire to find some part of myself that I'd forgotten. "I just can't help feeling," I said, thinking of Dana, "that there are things from my past I need to confront."

Eli stared at me for a long moment. "Come here," he said finally. "I want to show you something." I followed him into the kitchen. He opened a drawer. Inside was a bulging folder with the word DONTES written across the top. Eli reached in the Dontes folder and pulled out a thin file, then slid it across the counter to me.

A name was typed on the file: Pete Decker.

"Open it," Eli said.

There were three black-and-white glossy surveillance photos, taken through a car window, each showing a thin and tired-looking Pete Decker coming out of a downtown apartment building in jeans and a T-shirt and a dishwasher's apron. The last picture showed him climbing in a beat-up Chevy Nova. He'd aged considerably, and not very gracefully, in the twenty years since I'd seen him.

Eli stood over my shoulder as I looked at the picture. "I hired an investigator to find him. He's been in and out of jail." Eli grinned. "He just got busted again a few days ago for cocaine. Isn't that great?"

"You hired an investigator to find Pete Decker?" I asked.

He must've registered the discomfort in my voice because he took a step back. "Yeah, like we were talking about. Unfinished business. I mean, you of all people must've wondered what happened to Pete Decker."

I was curious, but honestly I felt nothing as I looked at the pictures of this skinny, smoked-out guy, hands in his jeans pockets, a cigarette butt dangling from his mouth.

"Yeah," I said. "I don't mean there are scores to settle. It's more about myself, like I got sidetracked, like I've forgotten who I was supposed to be." Again, I thought of Dana. And Ben. "Like I've let people down."

Eli smiled and took the pictures back. When he put them in the drawer I saw something black and metallic and it was only later that I realized that it was a handgun. And if I make this discovery sound casual on my part, a fleeting image, know that later, when hatred and revenge filled my chest, I had no trouble remembering exactly where that gun was located.

"Come on," Eli said. "I want to show you one more thing."

I followed him out the door and down the stairs. We crossed the dry lawn to the main house, dark and empty. He juggled some keys until he found the right one. He turned on a light and half the bulbs lit up in a huge chandelier in the foyer. I followed him into the big open living room, pillars on either side of the door and a curved staircase climbing to the second floor. The windows were topped with stained glass and the wood floors were polished and immaculate.

"Beautiful," I said.

"It's too big. And there are so many windows. It feels so . . . exposed. I don't feel like I fit here, like my life hasn't caught up with this house. So I haven't put any furniture here. I haven't hung anything on the walls." He gestured to the fireplace. "Except that."

It took me a moment to recognize the framed photograph that hung above the mantel. There were four people in the picture and they were so young, their faces lineless and blameless and unafraid. The two girls in front were pretty, especially the petite dark-haired one, who smiled shyly, as if she knew something the others didn't. The other girl clearly didn't want to be in the picture and she contributed little beyond a bland attractiveness—blond hair, blue dress, baby's breath corsage. But it was the two boys in the flaring tuxes who caught my attention: the taller one with the feral hair and uneven eyes, his arm thrown around the shoulder of the short awkward boy, who beamed like this was the high point of his life.

I felt Eli over my shoulder. "You were fearless," Eli said. "You did whatever you wanted. Played sports and dated cheerleaders and ran for everything. I thought you could do anything you wanted."

I turned back to Eli Boyle and it occurred to me that, outside my family, he'd known me longer than anyone in the world.

"I remember who you were going to be," Eli said.

I looked at the prom picture again.

That's when he pulled a pen and a checkbook from his back pocket, leaned against the wall, and wrote out a check. He turned and handed it to me. It was a check for ten thousand dollars. It was made out to "The Committee to Elect Clark Mason."

"I can help you," he said.

And even though it was preposterous, seeing my name like that—*The Committee to Elect . . .* —it sparked something in me, something primal and powerful. I tried to laugh it off but I could not take my eyes off the check. "Elect me to what?"

"Whatever you want," he said. "Something big."

And that was it—the genesis of my half-witted plan to become Representative Clark Mason (later, Eli and I agreed that a candidate with two last names might be a meal too rich for Spokane voters and I went with my middle name, Tony), my plan to pick up my ambitions at the place where I'd left them fifteen years before. Eventually Eli and I settled on the U.S. House of Representatives as my best big shot. The current lifer in that seat, a prosaic Republican named George N——, was vulnerable for the first time because he'd defeated the previous lifer, Tom F——, an equally prosaic Democrat, solely on the issue of term limits—specifically, limiting candidates to three terms. Now, of course, faced with his own fourth term, George N—— had changed his mind and decided term limits weren't such a good idea after all.

We talked about it all that first night and the next night and every day for the next two weeks. We were taken with the millennial excitement of the 2000 campaign, the opportunity to present a new kind of candidate— progressive both socially and technologically—and over the next few months Tony Mason was born.

My God, I was invigorated. It was as if clogged blood

vessels had been cleared to my head and my heart. But if I was happy, Eli was positively exuberant, and he attended the details of my impending campaign as if we were both running.

"Butch and Sundance," he said one day, out of the blue. "Together again!" I mostly laughed this kind of stuff off, but it was a recurring theme for Eli in those early days of the campaign, this idea that the election was about him and me. "It's good to have someone who will always be loyal to you," he said one day.

"You bet," I said.

"You know, Clark," he said another time, as we priced office space for my campaign headquarters, "in my whole life, I never made another friend like you."

I thought about our fight at the bus stop, the way I avoided him at school and made out with his date at the prom, the way I used him and Empire to try to get Dana back into my life, how I went weeks, months, even years without talking to him. And he thought of *me* as his best friend. But again, I was too self-absorbed to really register Eli's loneliness, or to imagine what he got out of helping me run for office. All I could think about was the campaign; all I could think about was the candidate.

Even though the general election was still two years away, my contacts in the Democratic Party were clearly intrigued by me. Conservative Spokane was a tough sell and anyone who had a plan—and, especially, his own money—was welcome to run. After getting the party's blessing, the very first person I called was my old professor, Richard Stanton.

"Maybe you ought to just go straight for president," he said.

I explained my theory, why I thought George N——— might be vulnerable this time, how I was going to bring economic development to my old hometown, how I would run as the first true candidate of the twenty-first century.

He said he hadn't heard me this excited since I was imagining my stupid nonprofit legal service ideas. "Good to have you back, Mason," he said.

That's when I asked him to be my campaign manager.

Dr. Stanton burst into laughter. "No way in hell."

I figured I could change his mind later. In the short term I began fund-raising, calling some of my old business contacts. Finally, after a week or so, I called Michael and Dana Langford at home. It had been two months since I'd slept with Dana.

"Mason," Michael said. "Tell me: how is it that you're not in prison?"

I heard someone else come into the room with Michael. "Hey, baby," he said. "It's our old friend, Clark Mason."

I patiently and evenly explained what I was doing, and said that if he and his wife would support my candidacy in any way, I would be eternally grateful.

He put his hand over the phone and I could hear him telling Dana. After the word "Congress," he burst into laughter. Then Dana came on the phone.

"Are you really?" she asked. I was thrilled at the things I heard in her voice—pride and envy, hesitation and urgency.

"Yes," I said. "I am."

"That's great," she said. "Of course we'll make a donation."

"Hey, tell him *our* news," Michael said in the background.

"I was going to," she said, another strain in her voice. "Clark, do you remember in Spokane, when you and I were talking about timing?"

"Of course I remember," I said quietly. "You said mine was bad."

She cleared her throat. "Well, I didn't know for sure then, but now I do," she said. "I'm pregnant. Michael and I are going to have a baby."

4 | RUNNING FOR OFFICE

Running for office is nothing like you assume it's going to be, nothing like the discussions of public policy and government ethics that we engaged in during college poli-sci classes. I could write for days about the disappointment of politics.

And yet we have precious little time left, Caroline. We both know that. No time to waste wading through the billion trivial details that make up a modern political campaign: endless debate over what colors to use on buttons and posters ("Since George N—— is using *red and blue,* I think we should go *blue and red*"), what I should wear ("No cowboy boots? You're running for Congress from eastern Washington and you don't own cowboy boots?"), and the tone of commercials (it took four people two weeks to choose "Isn't it time for a change?" over "Aren't you ready for a change?").

The thing that surprised me most was how little I actually had to do. We were perhaps a little *too* successful in raising funds early on, because before long we had an eighty-dollar-an-hour expert for every aspect of the campaign, and nothing was really required of me other than wearing the right tie with the right suit and remembering to stare straight into the camera. ("That eye," said the director of my commercials the first time he met me,

347

as if I weren't even there. "What am I supposed to do with that goddamned eye?") There turned out to be very little market for the speeches I'd daydreamed of giving, and the handful of addresses I did deliver were written by pros. ("Small words! Big ideas!") I certainly wasn't expected to formulate policy or fine-tune my stances on issues; they had poll numbers to tell me which of my beliefs were popular enough to mention, and if I couldn't duck a certain issue, there were copywriters to rewrite my more liberal opinions. ("Each student has the right to pray in school. What I'm saying is let's protect the students' right to *not pray*.")

After a few months of this, you end up feeling more like a product than a candidate, like a toilet cleaner or an especially moist cake, and when the TV lights flicker and the makeup begins to heat up, you can actually feel the talking points and last-minute instructions start to bake in your mind (*Stare straight ahead; say farm equity, not farm subsidy*). Early on, I was fine with this state of affairs. After Dana dropped her bomb it dawned on me fully that I would never be with her and I was happy to just stand there and wave, cut ribbons, pat schoolchildren on the head, and not think about the woman I loved having the baby of my sworn enemy.

In fact, I felt a real kinship with Empire. By early 2000, we were both fully funded and fully imagined, yet we were, at best, half realized—sketchy products with limited prospects and very little application in the real world.

I recall only one moment of transcendence during the eighteen months I ran for Congress—one day when my candidacy was about something more than my candidacy. It was early on, a gathering of the four Democratic hopefuls in front of twenty or thirty people at the Spokane Public Library. Eventually we ended up talking about the causes and possible solutions for Spokane's double-digit poverty rate and its fifty-year economic slump. (I wonder: after fifty years, isn't a pothole simply part of the topography?) In the end, this is the only issue in Spokane. Everything else—high crime, the meth epidemic, declining downtown, bad roads and services—spirals out from the one thing about Spokane that no politician in the last fifty years has ever come close to solving: it is poor.

The other candidates each seemed to have a pet cause for this state of affairs, and so we spent some time talking about the long decline in mining and other natural-resource-based industries, the geographic isolation, the inability to transition to other kinds of business, the city's insidious, uncaring power base, and what one candidate called "an unending cycle of regenerative failure."

As I listened I had the sense that we were staring at a vast, flooded valley, trying to decide which molecule of water was to blame.

"Those aspects of the problem are valid, of course, and we should do everything we can to address them," I said. "But let's be honest. That's not what the voters really want." I allowed that to hang in the air for just a moment and then I leaned back into the microphone. "What they want is for this to be a place that their kids don't have to leave. What they want is to stop gathering at the back fence to tell the neighbors how well the kids are doing in Seattle or Portland or San Francisco. I'll tell you what these people want from government—they want us to bring their children home."

I looked backstage and saw Eli, his fists balled up in front of his face, nodding enthusiastically, as if he'd been waiting for me to say that very thing.

If a campaign can be defined by one moment, then in that one I rose slightly above a mediocre slate of Democrats and stopped being simply a political upstart, the "New Economy Guy," the youngest of the four Democrats trying to unseat George N——. In that moment I became the prodigal candidate, the pied piper, and the hard subtext of my candidacy was cast—*Vote for Mason. He'll bring your kids home.*

In the winter before the election, Dr. Stanton took a leave of absence from the university to come aboard—"If you're really serious about wasting your money, I want to help"—as my campaign manager. He urged me to loosen up and be myself ("*Tony* Mason? Who the fuck is Tony Mason? Sounds like a gay rib joint"). The campaign was hitting on all cylinders, and yet I could sense in Eli some distrust of Dr. Stanton and the other political operatives surrounding me.

Our strategy was simple: spend money. It's almost unheard of for a first-time candidate to outspend a sitting congressman, but I sure as hell gave it a run. Ours became far and away the most expensive campaign in eastern Washington history. I spent the little bit I'd raised before the campaign even got going, and the paper-route allowance the party gave me barely paid for billboards and antenna balls, so it wasn't long before I was breaking out my own checkbook to cover expenses. By the end I spent about two million dollars of my money and about $300,000 of Eli's, plus quite a bit directly from—I found out later—the coffers of Empire

Interactive. I probably would've spent even more—honestly, I'd have spent every cent he and I had—but at the same time the campaign was draining one end of my bank account, the long-dreaded flameout of the speculative technology market was draining the other end.

I suppose I should mention one other event that occurred during this period and that was connected in its own way to the campaign: I got married. Again, I don't want to derail this confession with my personal mistakes, and I certainly don't wish to enflame my ex-wife's very capable legal team by going into details—which would be in violation of at least one court-issued gag order anyway—and to be painfully honest about it, the entire thing exists in my memory like just another detail of the campaign, managed and measured, without much involvement on my part. So I will simply say this: I had known the woman before, and had even had a short romantic history with her. I can't say how much of my decision to marry her was based on politics, but I will say that as a young candidate in a conservative district, having a wife lent me a certain gravitas that I had lacked as a single man. In fact, everyone saw her as an asset to the campaign—"You can't go wrong with big-titted arm candy," Dr. Stanton said—although the thing I found most attractive about her this second time through was that she did absolutely nothing to remind me of Dana and the heartbreaking feelings that I still carried for her.

Unfortunately, though, this woman was accustomed to a certain lifestyle, and that presented a challenge to my financial solvency and led me to a few lifestyle changes (full membership at one of Spokane's two country clubs, for expensive example).

It was around this time that Eli started pulling back, too. What had once been a campaign focused around the two of us was now a huge machine with me at the center and several layers of publicity and press and strategy people between Eli and me, not to mention my new wife, a self-centered snob who'd gone to high school with Eli and who still had no use for him. Eli sightings became scarce around the campaign, and to my deep shame, I did nothing to bring him back into the fold.

And so it was that by the summer of 2000, with the election only months away, I found myself in the troubling position of having done exactly the opposite of what I'd set out to do, what the young visionary Kayla advised me that morning while she ate breakfast: *Go back to yourself*

Instead I chased the weakened version of an expired daydream, formless and without meaning. I became a politician. For someone allegedly seeking self-awareness and redemption, it would have made more sense to have my soul surgically removed and replaced with chipped beef.

I knew I was betraying myself in some fundamental way, but my addiction was in full bloom; I couldn't stop. I became more depressed and scattered as the campaign wore on. I butchered a swing through the small farm towns of the Palouse, south of Spokane. (At the Colfax library I was supposed to deliver the line "It's time to get government off the backs of the small farmer," but what came out of my mouth was somewhat off-message: "It's time to get farmers off their fat asses.")

"What's the matter with you?" Dr. Stanton asked me. "You actually have a shot here." After that, he bowed out of rural campaign swings with me; he worried that he was making me nervous. But I screwed up when he wasn't with me, too, and at one stop I called George N—— "a chinless dickball, an ethics-challenged, steaming bowl of fuck."

Dr. Stanton was irate. He said that if the media had happened to be at that event the campaign would be over. He asked if my verbal slips were caused by problems at home. "A campaign is tough on a young couple, especially if you've just gotten married. Why don't I talk to her? You want me to talk to her?"

"No," I said. "That's nice of you, but it's not her." And still, Dr. Stanton was a good enough friend to realize that my marriage *was* part of the problem, although I don't think he understood the larger problem. Just as Ben had foreseen, my weakness had finally played itself out; I had turned myself over completely to the perceptions of others, the voters, members of various country clubs and organizations, my campaign staff, the media covering the race, the state party, everyone but myself. And these verbal mistakes, these Tourettic slips of tongue, were my real self trying to get out.

But the more successful Tony Mason the candidate became, the further *Clark* Mason receded into the background, until one day in September, seven weeks before the election. I was sitting on the couch in our house, staring at furniture that my wife had chosen for us from catalogs and stores in Seattle. I looked down and saw that I was wearing clothes that a campaign consultant had chosen, sitting on a couch I'd never seen until it showed up in a living room that someone else had decorated.

"Tony?" my wife said from the kitchen. "Can we go

somewhere warm for vacation after the election?"

"Sure," said Tony. "We can go wherever you want." And just like that, Clark Mason was officially dead.

As I said, this is ultimately a story about a fall, and that is what happened in that autumn of 2000. So as not to clutter this up further with my emotional state, I'll draw on the cold organizational skills of my legal background to tell you what happened. And so I hereby duly report the following: that within a six-day period in October 2000, these events did occur in the City of Spokane, County of Spokane, Washington State:

I. I met with my accountant and was apprised of the following:
   A. Despite his repeated and unheeded warnings—something about all my eggs and one (1) basket—my entire portfolio consisted of emerging technology stocks.
   B. The bubble had officially burst and technology stocks were down some 200 percent. My particular stocks were down even more. A full third of the companies that I owned no longer even existed.
   C. I could try to redirect my investments, but I had spent too freely on the campaign, my house, my wedding, and countless other things.
   D. I was broke.
II. I met with the state Democratic Party chairman, who informed me:
   A. The party was impressed with my showing, but projections showed that I couldn't win.
   B. They were worried about rumors that my

campaign was partly funded by unwitting investors of a shadow company called Empire.
   C. The party wasn't inclined to spend any more money on the campaign.
   D. I was fucked.
III. Upset about these developments, I came home unexpectedly after canceling a campaign appearance and found:
   A. My wife lying naked on the bed, reading a book.
   B. Another man's pants lying next to the bed.
   C. Said man in my shower. (In hindsight, I wish I'd bothered to find out whose pants were on my floor and, more important, what sort of range stud could drive my pinhead wife to such heights of ecstasy that she actually wanted to read a book. But I needed to get out of there, so I walked out of the house and didn't stop until I was downtown, standing in front of the Davenport Hotel, of all places.)
   D. I was alone.

Unraveling can make one of two sounds: the long sigh of a balloon losing its air, or the dull flapping of a tire blowing out on the highway. An unraveling candidate makes both these noises, and nothing can be harder than to put back together a candidate who has come apart. I kept campaigning after the collapse—I couldn't think of what else to do—but it was over. My paid staff left when they were no longer actually paid, all except the loyal Dr. Stanton. I'm still touched by the way he kept apologizing for everything that happened, as if he could've done something to stop the deflation.

Like any wounded animal, when the last blow came, I found it a relief. It happened at the end of October. I was at the hotel where I'd recently moved, watching late-night TV, when I saw the ad: a picture of me from several years earlier, when I still had long hair and the eye patch. I didn't remember choosing that particular picture for an ad, and I was surprised that my formerly high-paid staff would allow it. Then the voice-over: "Until a year ago, *Clark* Mason"—I sat up at the mention of my real name—"was a rich Seattle attorney. Do we really want a *liberal,* rich west-side lawyer representing eastern Washington in Congress? Do we trust Seattle to take care of Spokane?"

My first thought was fairly detached: *Now that is an effective piece of advertising.* There were three such ads, all with the same theme and the same deep, movie-preview voice-over. They seemed to run every six or seven minutes on various channels. If there had been any hope for a last-minute reversal, that series of ads certainly took care of it.

A few days later, I read in the newspaper that the ads had been paid for by a political action committee called the Fair Election Fund, and that the officers of this fund were my friends Louis Carver and Eli Boyle. Louis called me immediately and said that he'd known nothing about it until he read it in the paper that morning; Eli's paranoia and delusions, he said, were getting out of control. I told Louis that it was okay, and that he should forgive Eli, that Eli needed him.

Later that day I talked to the press, halfheartedly

defending myself against the charges that I was a carpetbagger. "One thing I can tell you, I'm certainly not a *rich* Seattle lawyer anymore," I said. I liked that joke—it was the first thing I'd written for the campaign in a while—but I think it came off sounding self-pitying and arch.

When the press conference ended, I watched the TV cameramen pack up their equipment; it was a bittersweet feeling, knowing I would never feel their hot lights on my face again, that their attention would move elsewhere, that I had run my last campaign.

It was two days before the election. I bought a fifth of whiskey, drank half of it in my car, and brought the rest to my campaign headquarters, which was in the process of being dismantled. (We were three months behind in rent.)

There was only one person in my office, a young volunteer named Lara. She cried as she watched movers pack up desks and computers, boxes of pins and bumper stickers.

"Mr. Mason," she said. "I'm so sorry."

"Thank you, Kayla," I said, and patted her on the head.

"Who is Kayla?" she asked.

"Hmm?"

"You called me Kayla."

"I did?" I thought about that clear-eyed girl, Kayla—who had magically appeared on the sidewalk outside the Triangle Pub, with that most basic of geometry solutions and the kind of advice Ben might have given: *Go back to yourself.*

I walked right past Lara, went outside, and looked up into the sky. I got in my car and drove east, across the river, to my parents' house on Empire Road. I parked in front

357

and walked to the front window. My father was still awake. I could see him watching TV. Mom slept next to him on the couch. Dad saw me, got up, and opened the door. We stood on the porch looking at each other from opposite sides of the screen door. He had aged so much; I'd seen him a dozen times over the last decade, but I realized that I hadn't *seen* him in so long, hadn't *seen* anything. His calm blue eyes seemed to float in almond-shell lids; the creases around his mouth were dusted with gray whiskers.

"I lost," I said.

"Yeah," he said. Then he held the screen open for me. And finally, I went inside.

5 | AFTER THE ELECTION

After the election, I stayed in my parents' house for a few months, resting and getting my affairs in order, an exercise that mainly consisted of filling out stacks of paperwork chronicling various failures: divorce, bankruptcy, the sale of my house and other property, defensive filings with the Federal Election Commission and the IRS. But I also found time to talk to my parents about Ben, to explain my guilt and apologize for not being around all those years after he died.

My father mostly listened. My mother fed me. And the banks, creditors, and lawyers bled me, asset by asset, cent by cent, until there was nothing.

"They get the motorcycle, too?" my dad asked.

It was actually the last thing I had left. It was stored in a friend's garage in Seattle, and I had forgotten to list it in my dwindling assets. The next weekend I took the bus to Seattle, rode the bike home, and gave it to my dad. He tried to make me take it back, or sell it, but I insisted. The very next day he rode it to work. Unfortunately, it was only three months before the lawyers tracked the motorcycle down and took it away. I apologized to Dad, but he waved his hand.

"I didn't like it anyway." He never mentioned the bike

after that, but my mom said he rode it to work every day while he had it.

I continued to put my life back together. I hung a shingle in Spokane and began to practice law again—wills for people with nothing to leave behind, divorces for people with nothing to split. I got a little bit of contract work, enough to start paying my ex-wife, to get a very small apartment and an old Honda Civic. I stopped wearing the glass eye and put my patch back on. I grew my hair a little bit longer. I breathed. Ate. Walked. Talked a little. Was I better? I believed so. I made the mistake of thinking the trappings were my problem, the symptoms were my disease. I was poor, I thought, so I must be on my way to being whole again.

Then, more than a year after the election—this January, just a few weeks ago—I finally went to see Eli Boyle. Honestly, I wasn't angry with him. In some important way, I believed I deserved what he'd done. And yet I hadn't wanted to see him until then.

We imagine that time has qualities of its own, a weight and a girth, powers of redemption and recovery. We believe that time will fix or heal, or at least resolve. But sometimes the time just passes. The days go by and nothing changes, nothing.

I drove up the face of the South Hill. I turned on Cliff Drive and drove past the mansions to the end of the cliff, where the lesser homes clung to the tawny slope like billeted climbers. Eli's lawn and trees were over-grown, the house empty. This was all that was left of Empire Interactive. The employees had all been fired by Eli or had wandered away. Louis was the last to go, almost a year before. Since then, Eli had moved everything he could carry up to his carriage house apartment, where he still lived. He had painted EMPIRE INTERACTIVE on a small sign and posted it outside his door. Unlike me—and Michael and Dana, it turned out—Eli had been selling his technology stocks along the way, and he was keeping Empire on life support from the last of the money that he'd saved, hoping like all the surviving tech companies to make it through the long night until the money rose again.

I climbed the stairs and knocked on the door. Dead bolts slid, hooks were lifted, keys turned, and finally the door opened and he was standing there, shifting his weight from foot to foot. I hadn't seen Eli in sixteen months. He'd gotten heavier, his hair thinner, a dusting of red whiskers across his cheeks and chin. And there was something in his eyes, that darting; when he blinked it was like he was in pain, like he was trying to force glass from his eyes. He backed into his apartment. He had this way of scrunching up his nose to push his glasses up. He did this, they slid back, and he did it again. The room smelled like coffee, pizza, and body odor.

"I didn't want to do it, but you gave me no choice—"

"I know," I said.

"The whole thing, you running in the first place, it was my idea—"

"I know."

"And you brought that woman in—"

"I know, Eli."

"It's always you and me and then you always forget, you always forget—"

"I know, Eli. I won't forget anymore." I walked slowly around the apartment, Empire reduced to these stacks of boxes and binders at our feet. He grimaced as he backed slowly to his computer, still unsure, I suppose, just what I meant to do to him.

"It was . . . you . . . betrayed . . . I—" Eli seemed unglued, his eyes darting back and forth. "I couldn't let it go. You have to stand up sometimes. Fight back." His voice had no modulation, like an idling engine, and I could see that he was sick in some way.

"I'm not here to talk about that," I said. "That's all in the past."

He nodded unsurely and made a small whistling sound.

"I tried to call you, but your phone has been disconnected."

"It was tapped," he said. "I kept calling to have them get the bugs off, but they wouldn't so I finally just disconnected it." He pointed at the computer. "I have e-mail, but I think they're watching that, too."

"I'm here to see the game."

"It's not a game," he said. Again, the painful blink.

"I want to see it."

"It's not ready."

"I know it's not ready. It's never ready. But I need to see it, Eli."

He watched me for a few moments, then turned on his computer, opened a couple of files, and the game engine began loading. "It's very rough. Still having trouble with the transitions. It doesn't go very far into the action yet." He talked as he worked the keyboard. "Bryan left the pixel shaders in a terrible state, and . . . and—" He looked down through his glasses at the screen. "Just when I think I've finally gotten it to be organic, I see some other thing I didn't anticipate. It's that Michael Langford. I know there's more venture capital, but he won't release it—"

The computer screen went black and then opened on a pastoral scene, a village in the distance. The graphics were nice, if a little flat, already out of date, passed up two years earlier by the 3-D photorealistic real-time rendering stuff. Even so, there was a quality to the graphics that was soothing and familiar. Tiny electronic birds chirped, and white puffs of sheep sailed in the distance. Eli used the mouse to move us forward, and we glided, from his character's point of view, across the field, the village growing in our vision. But the computer stopped and the scene lurched and was replaced by a close shot of the village gate. "I hate that," Eli said. "That hiccup. That's what I'm talking about; it's very rough. And I'm telling you, it doesn't go very far into the scene yet."

"I want to see."

On the gate were the words USER NAME: ___ and PASS-WORD: ___.

Eli turned to me and it took a second before I realized that he wouldn't type his password until I turned away.

"Dontes," I guessed, thinking of the name on the Pete Decker file, the *Monte Cristo* prison he'd constructed, and most of all, of the elaborate way Eli had helped me build up my dream of a political career, before pulling it out from under me. "Edmond Dontes," I said.

Eli looked at me in horror. "How did you know that?"

I didn't answer. After a moment, he typed his password. The gate opened, and Eli's alter ego entered his village. Children and maidens rushed up to greet him. His computer-generated arms extended stiffly on either side of the screen, rubbing the kids' heads and taking flowers from the women. Then the image on the screen swung around slowly and there was Eli Dontes himself, tall and muscular, with a bushy mustache and curly brown hair, square of features and back. Eli saw me look from him to the vision of him on the computer, and he blushed and looked down. And then, the computer screen went blank, the picture replaced by strings of code.

"There are a lot of other scenes, but we're having trouble getting them to flow together."

"That's it?" I asked. "That's all you have?"

"Like I said, it's a little rough. Some glitches. If Michael would just release the rest of the investors' money—"

"That's actually why I'm here," I said. "Michael has someone who wants to buy Empire, or the concept of it, anyway." I reached in my briefcase and pulled out Michael's fax. "They want whatever you have, all development and research materials, all rights to the name and the likeness of the game."

"It's not a game," Eli said quietly.

"I doubt they're going to still want it once they see it," I said, "but it's an offer, Eli. Any offer is good. Especially given the climate and the game's . . . limitations."

He glanced over, then went back to reading the fax. When he got to the price, he laughed. "Two hundred thousand dollars? Is he serious? That's offensive."

"At least it's something," I said. "And this isn't just you. Michael and Dana. Me. We could all use the money, Eli."

"That sneaky asshole," he said. "I know what he's doing."

"You've been using your savings to keep the thing

afloat. How much longer can you do that?" In front of his house, the Mercedes had a For Sale sign on it.

"Michael's wanted this from the beginning," Eli said. "He's wanted it for himself from the very beginning." His eyes narrowed again.

"Eli," I said, "if you run out of money, they'll take your house, everything."

He waved his hand toward the house, across the lawn. "They can have the house."

"At least consider this."

"Tell Michael I want my money." Eli continued to stare at the fax.

"Listen to me. Michael doesn't have your money. He's as broke as you and me. Everyone's broke, Eli. You have to sell the game."

"Not a game!" He waved the fax around, then relaxed. "Don't call it a game." Then I saw the look on his face that I'd seen when he showed me the photos of Pete Decker, and I couldn't help thinking of him up here eighteen months earlier, during the election, pacing around, cursing me for betraying him again, for letting him get close and then pulling away. "Tell Michael to give me more money and I'll finish the game."

"Look," I said, "I have to be honest with you. The game isn't worth *two thousand dollars,* let alone two hundred thousand. Three years ago, maybe. But technology has passed it by. The things you're trying to do—wristwatches do that now."

Eli wasn't hearing a word I said. "So Langford thinks he can get Empire out from under me. I should've guessed. The levels of treachery, that's the thing. Your true enemy is always the last one to reveal himself."

"Eli, just think about it. Please."

"Don't worry," he said, "I can take care of Michael Langford."

When I left I could see him in the window above the garage, the small curtain pulled back, the lenses from his glasses reflecting the light as he watched me drive away.

That evening I called Michael to tell him that Eli had refused even to consider selling the game. Dana answered. I hadn't talked to her since the frenzy of the election, when I'd called to tell her I was getting married. Now she said she was sorry about the election, and about my divorce. We small-talked. I told her I was practicing law again, that I was going to stay. I could hear in my own voice the sense of settled defeat, of fatigue. "Maybe you were right about Spokane," I said.

"What did I say?"

"You said it was the last real place."

She laughed. "And is that a good thing?"

"Yeah, it is," I said. "You've got to be tough here, a realist. For me, yeah, that is a good thing."

She said she and Michael were at a kind of equilibrium. They'd had to sell their big house in Los Altos and were living in a smaller place in Sunnyvale, but they were clearing away the debt and Techubator was flirting with profit again.

"There's this sense among all the people down here," she said, "that if we can make it a few more months, the money will start to come back."

"You'll make it," I said. "You're too smart, and Michael's . . . relentless."

"Yes," she said. I could hear noise in the background. "We're having Amanda's birthday party," Dana said, and then she sighed. "Oh, Clark—" and I could hear in her voice a shadow of the huge longing that I felt.

"I'll get Michael," she said after a moment.

As I waited I could hear children laughing in the background, and Dana asking who wanted cake. That's when I started doing the math in my head.

"Congressman!" Michael said into the phone. "Oh, wait, but you lost, didn't you? Well, at least you have your wife to comfort you. Oh, wait, you lost her too."

"Eli won't sell," I said.

"He has to."

"I tried to tell him that, but—"

"Try harder." And then he hung up to go back to the party.

I sat with the phone on my shoulder, clicking off the months with my fingers. Amanda was four. The date was January twentieth. Go back four years and nine months: April 20, 1998.

I couldn't speak for that entire month, but I could account for one day. On April 16, 1998, Dana was with me, laughing and kissing my neck, sliding out of her booze-soaked skirt in a hotel room in Spokane.

6 | WE NEVER LEARN

We never learn anything. Our lives circle back around endlessly, presenting us with the same problems so we can make the same mistakes. We pretend we are moving forward but we live on a globe rotating on an axis, orbiting a burning sphere that is itself orbiting with a million other round hot stones. In a universe of circles, movement is just the illusion that comes from spinning, like a carousel—the faster it spins, the faster the world moves around it.

How else to explain what began to form in my mind? How else to explain how a man could lose all that I'd lost—a childhood, an eye, a woman, an election, a fortune, a brother, maybe even a daughter—and still believe that, in the end, he might win? How else to explain how I could look at my sick friend Eli Boyle, who had wanted nothing his whole life except my help, and begin imagining him as the instrument of my treachery? If I have not been standing in this very spot for thirty-six years, spinning in a tight circle, how else to explain my position today?

When I went back to see Eli, the whole thing was already taking shape. It would be horrible, but defensible, if all I did was fail to stop Eli before his delusions got worse, before he got dangerous; if I just stood by while he paced and ranted and the black metallic handgun hummed and vibrated in that drawer. I would still feel responsible, but at least I could have some technical deniability, that weak measure of conscience of someone who looks the other way in the presence of evil. What I did was inexcusable.

I showed up at Eli's house breathless and frightened. I lied to him. I told him that he was right, that Michael was holding millions of dollars from us, that investors were clamoring to get back into Empire, but Michael wanted the game for himself.

"He's jealous of you." I held up the two-year-old copy of *Wired* in which Eli was quoted ("The future of gaming is in giving up the illusion of the game"). I told him that Michael said that if we didn't sell Empire, he would sue us and send us to jail.

"Can . . . is . . . can he do that?"

"Sure," I said. "We faked those presentations. We funneled investors' money into the campaign without their knowledge. We'll go to jail, and he'll end up with the game."

"Not a game!" Eli seethed, and his eyelids tried to squeeze the world away.

I went up there every day for the next week and watched him pace and rant and vow revenge. "We should've never gotten involved with Michael. He's a thief."

"He's sitting there in California with all that money," I agreed, "all that money the investors wanted to go to Empire. He's sitting there laughing at you.

"He's going to steal the whole thing," I told Eli. "He's going to steal it and ruin it and make millions and he's going to laugh at you the whole time."

Eli shook and sputtered with anger. "He can't . . . I . . . won't . . . It's—"

I could feel myself giving in to something dark, something I'd always known was inside, but had always tried to suppress. I remembered Pete Decker on the bus, goading me into fighting Eli. *Kill that faggot motherfucker!* "He'll change the characters," I said. "He'll make it a bunch of princesses, or set it in the future. He's going to turn it into just another game, a stupid test of hand-eye coordination. Ms. Pac-Man."

After a few days of this, Eli's sputtering and shaking began to go away, and I could see the thing forming in his mind—as clearly as if it were my own mind—until one day we sat together at the lunch counter at Fletts, speaking in low voices over cups of clam chowder.

"You can't have anything to do with this," he said.

"If you say so."

"It has to be me," he said. "I'm sorry."

"Okay."

"From here on out, don't ask me any questions."

"I won't."

"You need to be out of town."

"Why?"

"Why do you think?" he snapped, as if I was an idiot. "We have your political career to think about."

I stared at my soup.

"Call Michael," he said. "Tell him I want to set up a meeting for two weeks from now. Tell him the meeting has to be kept secret, and it has to be in Spokane. Tell him Empire is ready."

"Okay."

"I'll e-mail him the details of the meeting."

"Okay."

"If he asks, tell him I'm really losing it. Making crazy demands."

I had to look away. "I'll tell him."

"And listen. Afterward, you're not going to see me for a while. I may have to go away. Don't worry, I'll contact you when Empire is ready." He smiled. "We'll have the money for you to run for Congress again. We'll do it right this time. Just you and me. Not all those outsiders from Seattle. No women."

"Right," I said.

Then Eli took a bite of soup and pointed the spoon at me. "He's going to hurt like he's never imagined someone could hurt. He's going to hurt the way you and I hurt."

I didn't answer.

After lunch, he asked me to take him to the general store. Eli went in alone. He came out with a sack and I could tell by the shape that it contained a box of shells. "Don't ask," he said. At his apartment I sat in the other room, pretending to read a magazine, but I could see through the doorway into the kitchen as he loaded the shells into the gun, one by one, until all six chambers were full. I wish I could say that it filled me with dread, that it snapped me out of this craziness, but I watched with fascination.

When he was done, Eli put the box of shells and the handgun back in the drawer. He took a deep breath and came back in. I pretended to be reading the magazine.

"Don't worry," he told me. "This is going to work. I'm going to take care of everything." He walked me to the door.

I went down the stairs, but he stayed on the landing above me.

"Thanks," Eli said.

"For what?"

"For coming back, even after . . . I shouldn't have spent that money against you, Clark. I shouldn't have done that."

"It's okay," I said.

"We always come back, huh?" He scrunched his nose and raised his glasses and looked like the boy at the bus stop, the boy who'd come across me bleeding alongside the river. "We're like—" He shivered and then he smiled. Eli had trouble expressing emotions. He began to fidget and to shift his weight. "We're like best friends."

"Yeah," I said. "Sure we are."

He grinned like a kid at a birthday party. Then he paused.

"And we'll never go against each other again."

"No," I said.

He smiled again and went back inside.

When I got home I called Michael and told him Eli was ready to sell but that Michael had to come to Spokane. He didn't want to do it, but finally he agreed. "The game had better be ready," he said. "Otherwise, the deal's off."

"The game is ready," I said.

"One more thing, Mason," Michael said. "When this is all over, I don't want you calling here. It makes Dana nervous when you call. I don't like to see her upset."

Outside the snow was swirling, and I imagined being lost in it, lying down and letting it blow and drift around me until I was buried, gone. "Okay," I told Michael. "I won't call after this."

The next day, Eli sent me an e-mail.

Senator—
Have a nice trip. Get an early start. I'd go too but
I have a meeting that day, February 6, at 10:00 a.m.
Everything will be great after that.
Your best friend,
Eli

I bought an airline ticket for February 5, the day before Eli was going to . . . do it. I caught the last flight out. I got to San Jose about 10:00 P.M. and slept at a hotel near the airport. All night I tossed and turned, until the sheets and covers were like ropes binding me. In the morning I grabbed a taxi (a receipt, I was thinking, and a witness) and gave the driver Dana's address in Sunnyvale.

"That's gonna cost," he said. "You could rent a car for what it's gonna cost."

"I know." I stared out the cab window at the surging, pointless suburban northern California traffic—millions of cars and no sign of a downtown anywhere. The clouds were light and formless, a white-gray haze above us. I felt a detachment from myself—a defense mechanism, I suppose—self-denial over what we . . . what Eli was doing.

But it's his plan, I protested my own guilt. I didn't buy the gun. I didn't buy the shells. I didn't load it. I didn't tell Michael to come to Spokane.

"Gun?" the cabbie asked.

"What?"

He gestured to the eye patch. "Your eye. BB gun?"

"Oh," I said. "Yeah."

"It's always a stick or a BB gun, ain't it?" He turned and smiled, his own right eye milky, the pupil spilled out like the punctured yolk of an egg.

I looked back out the window. Cars swirled around us on the freeway, and every eye seemed to stare at me. A little boy perched on a safety car seat looked at me and shook his head slowly, and we stayed even with the little boy's car until I wanted to yell at the cabbie to go faster or go slower, anything but driving alongside that boy.

Calm. Cold. There is a synapse in the brain that connects brilliance to brutality. It is the oldest part of the brain. And so I felt better when I thought about the details, when I reveled in my criminal genius:

I had found a way to murder my enemy without incriminating myself, without even lifting a finger. The brilliance of it overshadowed any misgivings I might have. Even if Eli were caught, he would say I had nothing to do with it. The motive would always be his disagreement with Michael over Empire. My motive—Dana and our daughter—would stay secret forever. And since I would be with Dana when it happened, my motive would also be my alibi.

Perfect. Cold. I could hear my own breathing.

The cab left the freeway for the flat prosperity of Sunnyvale: small stucco war-era houses remodeled and expanded until they threatened to burst their small lots; new apartment complexes and condos and low-slung business parks where fortunes had been made and lost and were slowly being made again; an anachronistic villagelike downtown shaded by the condos and apartments rising around it. I was suffocating.

There was some kind of street fair going on and the cabbie had to detour around it—blocks of Berkeley vendors unloading knit hats and bracelets from Volvos and microbuses, and I thought I might choke in the back of that cab. The heat.

I had found a way to murder my enemy. What are you doing? Nothing! Settle down. You're just seeing an old friend.

"Seeing an old friend?" the cabbie asked. "That's great."

Was I talking out loud? Jesus. "Yeah," I answered. Was I really doing this? I checked my watch. Almost ten. The *meeting* would be any minute.

The cab stopped in front of a small, one-story stucco house, leaning out over two painted posts onto a lawn pocked with oranges from a small, leaning tree. No garage, just a cloth carport over a blue minivan. A tricycle sat on the front porch. My daughter's tricycle. My wife was in that house. The air was shallow and sharp in my chest; I couldn't get it to go any deeper, my lungs pressed beneath some weight.

I paid the cabbie and walked up to Dana's door. And that's when I knew I couldn't do it. My God. We were going to kill Michael. I'd told myself that Eli had lost his mind, but it was me. "My God!" I said aloud. "We can't do this." I rang the bell over and over. We had to hurry. We could still warn him. Michael's cell phone number! Maybe we still had time.

My first thought when Michael answered the door was relief: *Oh, thank God. I didn't do this.* Then a little girl came up and peeked around his hip. She was beautiful, round faced and pigtailed, wearing pajamas with

Belle from *Beauty and the Beast* on the front. Amanda.

"Who is it, Daddy?" Behind them was the house not of a Silicon Valley mogul, but a struggling, working couple: a box of Cheerios on the dining room table, papers and bills spread out, toys and pillows on the carpeted floor.

"What the hell are you doing here?" Michael asked me.

I couldn't look away from the girl. "Is Dana here?" I asked.

"Mama's gone," said the girl.

"She's in Spokane," Michael said. "That freak friend of yours said he didn't trust me. It had to be Dana. I don't know why I ever got involved with you crooks."

I just stared at that little girl, at Michael and Dana's little girl. She held out a picture she had drawn. I took the picture and looked down at it. It was a stick-figure girl with stick-figure pigtails. "That's me," Amanda said. "What's on your eye?"

"It's . . . it's a patch," I said. My legs felt weak beneath me. I thought of what Eli had said. *He's going to hurt like he's never imagined someone could hurt.* Oh my God.

"Are you a pirate?"

"He sure is, sweetie," said Michael. "What do you want, Mason?" Behind him, his telephone rang.

7 | WHAT ELI WANTED

What Eli wanted was the money he believed Michael owed him, the venture capital he was convinced Michael was holding back: $500,000, according to the ransom note Dana read over the phone. Michael listened with his hand on his head, making little moaning sounds every few seconds. I set Amanda's drawing down on the dining room table and stood next to Michael, my head next to his so that I could hear what Dana said.

" 'Get the money and fly to Spokane,' " Dana read. " 'There is a flight out of San Jose in ninety minutes. That gives you just enough time to go to the bank and get to the airport. The flight lands in Spokane at three-thirty. Exit the airport and walk to the garage. On the top floor, near the elevator, you will find a gray Mercedes-Benz with the top down. Put the money in the car and then go back into the airport and sit at the pay phone directly adjacent to the escalator. When Eli has the money, he will call and tell you where to find me. I'm in a cabin in the woods. If you do everything right, he won't hurt me. But if you call the police or don't bring the money, he will kill me. If you bring the police, he will never tell them where I am and I'll—' " She stopped. "What's that word?"

"Starve," said Eli in the background.

"It looks like swerve."

"No," he said. "It's 'starve.' How could you swerve to death?"

"Yeah, I didn't think that made sense," she said, and I couldn't believe how matter-of-fact she sounded, as if they were just chatting. " '*Starve* to death,' " Dana said. " 'You have until four o'clock. If Eli doesn't have the money by four o'clock, he will kill me.' " The phone went dead.

"Dana!" The phone dropped out of Michael's hand. "Jesus. This isn't happening!" He tried Dana's phone again, but there was no answer. While he listened to it ring, he suddenly pushed me in the chest. "Did you have anything to do with this?"

"Of course not," I said. "I love Dana."

He just stared at me. Then he threw his phone across the room and put his face in his hands. Amanda started crying. "Daddy?"

Michael picked her up and comforted her. His hand was on her head. It fit perfectly between her pigtails. He was crying, too. He pressed her hard to his chest, and her little legs swayed side to side. She had frills on her socks.

So perfect. So cold.

"Listen," I said. "Nothing is going to happen. I'll take care of this, Michael. I'll make sure nothing happens. Eli isn't violent. He's just confused. He'll listen to me. I'm going to get Dana back and get Eli some help. I knew he was losing it. I knew—" I couldn't finish. I couldn't tell him that I had pushed Eli to this point.

"I don't have that kind of money," Michael said. "We gotta call the cops."

"No," I said. "Not yet. Don't force his hand. I'll fly

back up there. I'll talk Eli down. Don't worry. I won't let anything happen. He's just confused."

"What if he hurts her?"

"He won't," I said. "Look, you can call the police if you want. But please. Let me fly up there and see if I can stop this. Get me on the plane and then it's up to you. Call the police. I don't care. But give me a chance to make this right."

Michael considered me. I'd always thought we looked alike, but as I looked into his teary eyes I felt so much smaller than him, so much less.

"Okay," he said.

He let me on his computer and I signed onto my e-mail and wrote Eli a quick note, just in case he checked.

Eli—
    Don't do anything. I'm coming back there. Don't
move. I need to talk to you.
    I lied about everything. There is no more money.
    I'm sorry. For everything.
    It's going to be okay.
    Clark

We ran out to Michael's minivan, parked under the cloth carport. His hands shook as he worked the keys— hung on a long gecko key ring—and he beat on the dashboard as we sat snarled in traffic, trying to get around the street fair and the construction. The drive took forever, Michael yelling at drivers and squirreling the minivan from lane to lane. Throughout, Amanda sat in a child's seat strapped in back, staring at me.

"Does it hurt?" she asked.

"Does what hurt?"

"The thing on your eye."

"Sometimes." I turned to face her full on. "So you just turned four?"

"Yeah," she said.

"When's your birthday?"

"December nine."

I turned to Michael, my mouth dry. "You had her party late."

He looked perturbed. "What?"

"Her birthday party. When I called in January you were having her party."

"My parents were out of town for her birthday so we had a second party when they got back," he said, incredulous that I would ask about such a thing at a time like this. I did the math again. Less than eight months.

"My sister just had a baby," I said carefully. "She was almost a month early. Was Dana early like that?"

"No. She was three weeks late. What the hell is this, Mason?" Seven months.

We pulled into the airport turnout. As I got out of the car, Michael put his hand on my arm. "Please."

I said good-bye to Michael's daughter and ran into the airport.

I bought a ticket and was the last person to board. I settled in, panting and sweating, between two businessmen, who leaned away from the frantic, one-eyed passenger who sat between them. The plane had to land in Seattle before continuing to Spokane. The Seattle leg seemed to take forever. I'd check my watch, and only two minutes would've passed. I'd sit for an hour, snap my arm up, and check my watch again. Two minutes. I stretched and leaned and craned my neck. Out the window the clouds were stretched and striated, not enough to cover the snow-scarred ground beneath us.

In Seattle the passengers deplaned slowly, as if they were marching to their deaths. "For God's sake," I muttered. Both the businessmen got off and the Spokane passengers got on, families, students, and short-sleeved businessmen, ladies in tan slacks, a couple of drunk golfers. The new passengers sat and we waited, quiet except for the low rumble of conversation from the back of the plane and an occasional cough. I checked my watch: 2:45. And still the plane didn't move. I buzzed a flight attendant and asked what the problem was. "It's just a minor delay, sir. We'll be taking off shortly."

We didn't take off until just before three. It was a fifty-five-minute flight to Spokane. There wasn't enough time. Eli had said to put the money in the car by four or she would die. I was having trouble breathing again. *Like he never imagined someone could hurt.* Eli didn't have a phone, so I tried to call Michael from the phone on the plane, but it wouldn't work. I slid my credit card over and over, but *it fucking wouldn't work.* I tried the phone in the row in front of me. None of them worked. Maybe Michael had called the police. Maybe it would be okay. At 3:55 we made a pass over Spokane, but there was low fog and the pilot said we had to circle. Always circling. We banked and straightened and I saw in a flash my own death, like a carousel ride, faster and faster, around and around, the same faces spinning at the bus stop and high school and the prom and Empire—Dana and Eli and me, and even Ben, until he couldn't hold on anymore and he let go of the railing and fell away. I knew then that I couldn't hold on much longer either (the plane banking, my head sliding against the seat, the tears falling from my eyes) and it occurred to me that I was dead already, that I had been dead since that day by the river, that Eli had put his hand on the chest of a corpse, had comforted a dying boy, and I thought, We are all just loose piles of carbon and regret.

When the fog cleared and the plane stopped circling and I stopped spinning, there was nothing holding me together; when we finally landed, at 4:10 P.M., I felt as if I would dissolve in the air.

As I got off the plane, I half expected to see police meeting me. There were none. I ran through the airport, waded through the other passengers, and sprinted across the terminal, over the sky bridge and into the parking garage, up the elevator to the top floor—low-roofed concrete and round pillars. No cars. The Mercedes was gone. My voice echoed in the garage. "No! Eli!" I ran down three floors to my own car, which I'd left in the garage the night before. My tires squealed coming down the ramp, and I sped away from the airport and across town.

It took me fifteen minutes to get to Eli's house. The Mercedes was parked out front, the For Sale sign still on it. I ran up the stairs to the carriage house apartment. "Eli!" The door was unlocked. He would never leave the door unlocked.

My old friend Eli Boyle was lying on his side. Blood was barely moving, in a slackened flow outward from the wound, across the carpet, onto the kitchen floor. Lying there on the ground he seemed so small, just like when we were kids and I saw him walking to the bus stop, the braces rattling around his knees, drawn into himself, as if he could keep the world away. And I remembered feeling his hand on my chest that day, comforting me, the pellet from Pete's gun burning in my eye.

I suppose there are worse things than rest. "I'm so sorry, Eli," I said. I crouched down next to him. Blood wept from his head.

The gun was next to his body. I picked it up. The shades were pulled in the apartment and it was dark, so I carried the gun out onto the porch. I pulled the pin the way I'd see Eli do it and rolled the chamber out. There were two bullets missing. I slammed it closed, threw the gun across the lawn, and screamed out: "Dana!" And then I looked up at the main house and—

Caroline? Another police officer is here. A Sergeant Spivey? He says you have gone home. Is that right? He says I have to stop writing. We almost made it, didn't we? Just close enough to know what we've missed . . . if that's not the shape of life—

I've been trying for two days to imagine the words I would use to close this, to finish—I have dreamed for you the profoundest words, Caroline—poetry to temper the sorrow and the longing, to somehow make this life beautiful.

But there are no words. No poetry. And only one thing left for me to do.

Rest now.

Clark

What kind of people have committed suicide because they were tired of life?
– Erasmus, *In Praise of Folly*

IX

ANYTHING YOU SAY

I | SHE FINISHES READING

She finishes reading and sets the last legal pad down in her lap. Spivey is a pad behind—reading with a confused and cross look on his face, mustache twitching as his lips move with the big words. It's three-thirty in the morning. As she slides the last pad over to Spivey, she remembers what Clark said: *There aren't even names for the crimes . . .* Caroline stands, walks across the office to her desk, sits down, and calls information.

"Sunnyvale. California. A listing for Michael and Dana Langford." As she waits to be connected Caroline's attention drifts to the top of her desk and a photo of her parents on their wedding day. It is the only picture she has on her desk, and the only picture she has of them together—a small three-by-five in which her mother rests one gloved hand against the black tuxedo on her father's chest. It is such a sweet, simple moment—her mother's got something funny to tell her father, and he can't wait to hear it. She's tried to imagine it a million times, what her mother might've said at that moment, and she still has no idea. All she knows is that after fifteen years that's the only thing she would take from her desk.

A woman answers on the fourth ring, "Hello?" Airy and easy at three-thirty in the morning. Either Dana is alive or her husband moves on quickly.

"I'm trying to reach Dana Langford," Caroline says.

"This is."

"My name is Caroline Mabry. I'm a police detective in Spokane."

There is a pause and Caroline hears footsteps and a door easing closed, as if the woman has gone into another room. Then Dana says, in a hushed voice, "Look, I have no interest in pressing charges. You can't do anything if I don't press charges, right?"

"Actually, we don't need the victim to press charges, no."

"Please," Dana continues. "It was just a misunderstanding between friends. No one was hurt. Did my husband call you?"

"No, your husband didn't call."

"I just don't want anything bad to happen to Eli," Dana says.

"Anything bad," Caroline repeats, and thinks, She doesn't know he's dead. "Look, Ms. Langford, if you could just answer a couple of questions—"

"I won't get Eli in trouble?"

"You have my word," Caroline says. "We won't be charging Eli with anything."

Dana starts slowly and Caroline has to draw her out with questions. But soon enough, she's just talking, telling the story of herself and Eli and a friend named Clark Mason, who all went to school together. As Caroline jots down notes, Dana explains Stanford and Michael, how they recruited Clark to find high-tech companies, how Eli's interactive game, Empire, came to be one of their companies. It is a strange feeling, hearing Clark's story from this angle, and as Dana begins to describe what happened the day Eli tried to kidnap her, Caroline imagines that her scribbled notes are a kind of staccato ending to Clark's long confession:

Last Friday at 0600, Dana flew up from San Jose to meet Eli re: selling Empire. 0945 Eli picked her up at the airport. He was "edgy, nervous." He drove her to his house "for meeting." She was surprised: no furniture in house. Empty except prom photo above fireplace. Empty house, Eli's pacing gave her creeps. At 1010 Eli borrowed her phone. Called Michael. Handed her the phone. Gave her note to read. Wanted money or would "hurt" her. Said she was in cabin in woods.

At first, Dana was confused. "I was not frightened." Eli never threatened her with gun. She never saw gun. After she read note, they had a "friendly chat." Felt she could walk away anytime. Didn't try. They sat in empty living room, talking. Eli agitated. "I was worried about him. I'd never seen him like that." She convinced Eli there was no money. No investors. They talked about high school. He started crying. Under great deal of stress. Eli: "I have nothing, no friends." Dana cheered him up: "That's not true. What about Clark?" 1115 Eli gave her phone back and she called Michael. Told him she was fine. Begged him not to call police. Eli drove her to airport. 1235 Dana caught flight back to Oakland/Alameda. 1645 Landed. Husband picked her up.

"And that was essentially it," Dana says.

Caroline looks back at her notes. There seems to be so much missing, and yet she's not sure what it could be. "Did you talk to Clark at some point that evening?"

"Yes," she says. "He called right after I got home. He must've heard from Eli. He was quiet. He seemed concerned. I asked him to make sure that Eli got some help, and he promised that he would."

So Clark didn't tell her that Eli was dead, or about the plan he'd set in motion between Eli and Michael.

It seems funny to her: Clark is sure of what he knows, and Dana is sure of what she knows, and yet we all live in a world that is partly imagined. We see some things, and the rest we fill in—motives and reasons as imagined as a joke shared between newlyweds on a wedding day forty years ago.

Caroline sets her pen down. "Can I ask you something personal?"

Dana hesitates. "Of course."

"Why didn't you and Clark get together?"

There is a long pause; Caroline is sure this woman must be wondering what kind of police officer would ask such a question.

"I don't know," Dana says. "Maybe it was timing. Or maybe it was just safer to imagine that we could have been good, without actually taking the risk. Sometimes I think we blew our only real chance back in high school."

"Why—what happened in high school?" Caroline asks.

There is another hesitation. "It was at the prom," Dana says. "Eli and I went together, but at the end of the night Clark and I ended up kissing in a hotel room."

"Eli was jealous," Caroline says.

"Clark and I just felt so badly that I think we stayed apart. It seems kind of ironic now, that Eli kept us apart and then later brought us together."

"Do you think that's why Eli let you go on Friday?" Caroline asks. "Because he still had feelings for you?"

"For me?" Dana seems confused. "Eli doesn't have feelings for me."

Now it's Caroline's turn to be confused. "But I thought—"

"Eli loves Clark," Dana says. "Always has."

And suddenly there it is: Eli turning Empire into a computer game to appease Clark; pushing Clark into politics to get close to him, then trying to defeat him when Clark married Susan; and the cruelty of that final note, on Eli's e-mail when he returned from taking Dana to the airport.

"Did Clark know how Eli felt?"

"I don't know," Dana says, and she chooses her words carefully. "Sometimes Clark could miss things like that. It's another reason we never got together, I think. He doesn't always see what's right in front of his face."

When they are done Caroline thanks her, and hangs up without telling her that Eli has killed himself and that Clark tried to engineer the death of her husband. By all rights she should tell Dana, but something—maybe just fatigue—prevents her from doing it.

She thinks about how many times as a police officer she's had to deliver news like that, telling parents that their children aren't coming home, telling a wife that her husband has been in a car accident. For a while she would just blurt out the bad news because she couldn't stand the look in their eyes as they tried to think of some good reason that a cop would come to visit. Then she learned to go slowly, to let the person gird himself for what was coming. But this time . . . hell, she just doesn't want to do it.

When she sees Spivey go to the bathroom, Caroline

walks into his office and takes the four yellow legal pads. Then she returns to her desk and takes the picture of her parents. Caroline stares at it for a moment, her mother's hand on her father's chest, everything she dreamed as a little girl, and then she slides the photograph into her bag and walks out the door. Spivey has just returned from the bathroom; she hears his voice behind her. "Caroline?" But the door closes and she is outside.

It's still dark, an hour before sunrise, and the air has a February chill, but it will be warmer this morning than yesterday, and warmer, she supposes, tomorrow. She climbs in her car, starts it, turns off her radio and cell phone, drives quietly through the dark city and up the South Hill to Eli's house. She parks on the gravel between the house and the garage. The scene has been processed, the body removed; she imagines it in the slick plastic bag, cold and dark. Everyone has gone home. Police tape still blocks off the stairs to the carriage house. By tomorrow, even that will be gone.

She goes past the carriage house and walks up to the main house, shines her flashlight on it and catches dark wood and gabled eaves. The back doorknob turns in her hand and Caroline steps inside. She's not sure what she's looking for, just that there is one shot to account for. Her footfalls echo in the empty house and she shines her flashlight around—dusty hardwood and old flowery wallpaper, bookshelves and pillars. She comes into the living room and is amazed at the view through the picture window, the city lights laid out full beneath her.

On the wall behind her, then, she sees what she came for and starts to put it together: Eli in this room with Dana, nervous, paranoid, and yet still the same odd, shy kid who can't even bring himself to show his gun to the woman he's supposed to be kidnapping. As they talk he loses his nerve, sees that she is telling the truth, that there will be no money. He drives her to the airport, and when he arrives home he goes up to his apartment and checks his e-mail. And there he finds the message that Clark sent from San Jose—*I lied about everything. There is no more money.*

And then—

Caroline shines her flashlight above the fireplace where a bullet hole—round and jagged, unmistakable in the plaster—is framed by the square dust outline of a picture frame.

She finds the picture itself on the floor in front of the fireplace, blown off the wall by the gunshot. The glass is shattered but the frame is intact. Caroline picks it up and turns it over in her hand, expecting to find the nickel-size bullet hole through Clark's young face. But his face is still there, smiling, his arm thrown around the eighteen-year-old version of Eli Boyle, whose head is now gone, a small, ragged hole in the crisp paper of a faded photograph.

Jesus, even at the end, after all he'd done, Eli didn't have it in him to hate Clark as much as he hated himself. She can imagine him staring at the photograph on the floor, then walking back outside, his arm limp at his side, going upstairs to the carriage house, sitting at the computer and reading Clark's message over and over: *I lied about everything.* Is it spur of the moment, a shudder, a frenzy, a delirium, a dream? She tries to imagine it; maybe it's because she hasn't slept all weekend, but Caroline can only see it as a kind of fatigue, of giving up, the gun falling against his cheek, eyes pressed shut. Enough.

393

Rest now.

She is close, too close to stop now. And only one more thing to do. Caroline slides the prom photo into her bag next to the legal pads and walks toward the door. And she thinks maybe it's all we can do sometimes to save ourselves.

She finds him at dawn, sitting on a ledge atop the Davenport Hotel, staring out at the city. She sees him from the car as she drives up, sees his feet first, dangling from the terra-cotta molding that rests like a crown on the twelfth floor of the old brick hotel. Apparently he doesn't see her, and in Spokane on a Sunday morning there is no one else on the street to see *him;* no movie crowd has gathered to crane their necks to see if the loon really jumps, no firefighters stand below with nets, no priests or uniformed cops lean out the window to console, cajole, and capture. She sees only a single man, hair licked by the wind, 130 feet off the ground, staring out from the top of a building.

She parks and steps out of her car. The Davenport Hotel rises dark and empty before her, burning at its base from the glow of construction lights. On these lower floors, behind braces of scaffolding, the restored terra-cotta gleams like new teeth.

She could climb the scaffolding to an open window. That's probably what Clark did. Instead, she peers through the automatic double doors. A janitor is working inside, wearing headphones and running an electric mop across the marble floor, no doubt cleaning up from one of the parties or wedding receptions they have here on the weekends in the restored ballroom. The hotel is four or five months from reopening and already people are straining to get in, to glimpse the history and the promise, to see for themselves if it's really coming back.

Caroline pounds on the glass, but the janitor can't hear her. She waits until he swings the sweeper her way and then she waves her arm. The janitor looks up, then shakes his head: No.

Caroline presses her badge against the glass and finally the janitor comes over. He reads her badge through the glass, then searches the ring on his belt for the proper key. He opens the door without saying a word. She explains that they picked someone up at the hotel two days earlier, and she just needs to have a look around.

The janitor shrugs and goes back to his mop. Caroline walks past the elevators and peeks into the lobby—she is not above longing, herself. She looks up at the paneled skylights, at the ornate railing on the second-floor walkway overlooking the marble-floored square, a fountain at its center. She closes her eyes and tries to hear the water trickling, the crowds, bellhops and porters, tropical birds, the cars motoring up to the door, Lindbergh and Earhart and Fairbanks sitting in chairs in the lobby. And Thomas Wolfe, downing his Scotch, grabbing his hat, preparing to leave Spokane "through land more barren all the time."

She opens her eyes on the dark, empty lobby—maybe a person can only spend so much time in empty buildings composing elegies. Caroline walks back and presses the button for the elevator. She is relieved when she hears the car coming down. The stairs might've killed her. Forty-eight hours without sleep.

The elevator is framed in gold-leaf pillars, oak leaves

and clusters, but inside it is pure freight, the walls and railings papered and taped, a carpenter's sawhorse left in the center of the car. She rides up leaning on the sawhorse, the elevator motor and cables mumbling about morning and sleep, until the doors open onto the top floor of old rooms and Caroline emerges into a dusty hallway where the remodeling is still mostly theoretical. The first sunlight streams in from the east bank of windows onto a floor in which the lath-and-plaster walls have been removed and what remains is the bones of these rooms, framed in new honey-colored two-by-fours and a few old, gray beams and headers. She feels the breeze from the open window and walks toward it.

He is sitting on the ledge, his back to her, sky beginning to turn in front of him. She sticks her head out and feels the cool air, gasps a little. Spring comes with a hangover in Spokane—late, regretful, sometimes staggering back to bed. She slides her bag out onto the ledge and then begins to climb out the window, bracing herself on the window frame. She feels his ice-cold hand on her arm, helping her out on the wide guttered ledge. She sits next to him, shivers against the cold.

"You found me," he says.

"I found you."

They are facing north. Before them is downtown Spokane and the river channel, beyond that the gently sloping hills blanketed with homes and a simple, honest grid of streets. The whole thing is flatter than she would think. When you're on those streets the hills seem imposing, but from here it is a graceful and good incline, like a man propped on a pillow in bed, reading a book.

She looks past Clark, to the east, where the sky is clear and the sun streaks down the long river valley all the way from Idaho, framed by long straight rail lines and a bolt of freeway. Then she looks west, to where the dark sky is trying to hold on to threats.

"It's beautiful," she says. "I hope I didn't interrupt anything."

"I was just trying to get up the nerve," he says.

"What were you waiting for?"

"Sunrise," he says.

They both turn and look at the sun, still cradled in the foothills to the east.

"You wait long enough you might freeze to death instead."

"I probably don't have the nerve for that, either."

Caroline reaches in her bag, takes out the legal pads, and sets them down in front of Clark. Then she gives him the prom photo.

"Did you tell Dana?" he asks.

"No," she says. "I didn't tell her about Eli and I didn't tell her about you."

Clark stares out to the north again, leans back against the brick, and closes his eyes. "Do you know the worst part? Eli never told her it was my fault, that it was all my idea. He let me off the hook."

A jet tears across the clean sky above them, east to west, high and noiseless, its stream carving the blue until it hits dark clouds and disappears. Caroline picks up the yellow legal pads. "So is that it?"

"Hmm?" He turns to face her.

"The confession. Is that all of it?"

"Yeah. I guess it is."

"What now?"

"I don't know," he says. "What do you normally do?"

"What do we do?" She shrugs. "If someone turns himself in to the police and admits that he intended to commit murder? Committed acts furthering that crime? Entered into a conspiracy? We usually say you have the right to remain silent. That anything you say can be used against you. That you have the right to an attorney, but if you can't afford one we'll give you an overworked one who just got out of law school and will go into private practice the week your case goes to trial."

He smiles a little bit. "Am I under arrest?"

"I haven't decided," she says. "My sergeant thinks you fucked this up so much, there's probably nothing to charge you with. He thinks we should try to have you committed."

"And what do you think?"

"What do I think?" Above her, the jet's slipstream is already dissolving in the violet sky. She sets the legal pads down, presses her thumb against her lips, then reaches over and touches his forehead. It is ice cold. She doesn't even remember if this is how it's done. But she makes a small cross of absolution on his cold forehead. Clark closes his eyes. "I think this world is enough," Caroline says.

And then she leans back and rests, stares out across her city, just beginning to stir, the houses coming to light among the timbers and the first cars gliding along the hillsides—the entire valley bathed in sun—dark ridges of pine and fir holding it in timeless embrace: Clark leans against her and morning settles over them.

· JESS WALTER

OVER TUMBLED GRAVES

Spokane, Washington, a bustling city split by hurtling white-water falls. One afternoon a young woman's body is found buried in a riverside park – then a second body, then a third. Before the week is out Caroline Mabry is plunged into a full-blown hunt for a serial murderer her colleagues have nicknamed the Southbank Strangler.

Caroline and her troubled mentor, Alan Dupree, bridle under an investigation overrun by headline-grabbing specialists and bean-counting statisticians. As they close in on a suspect, Caroline and Alan confront dark truths about the killer-hunting industry and about their attraction to each other. And in the end they come face-to-face with an evil very different – and far more alarming – than the one they thought they were chasing.

CORONET BOOKS
Hodder & Stoughton

MARCO  POLO

KU-773-919

MA DEI RA

PORTO SANTO

ATLANTIC

OCEAN   PORTUGAL

Azores (Port.)

Madeira
(Portugal)   MOROCCO

Canary Isles
(Spain)

Western
Sahara

THE
TOURING APP

shows you the way...
including routes and offline maps!

FREE!

GET MORE OUT OF YOUR MARCO POLO GUIDE

IT'S AS SIMPLE AS THIS

1 go.marco-polo.com/mdr

2 download and discover

GO!

WORKS OFFLINE!

SYMBOLS

 Insider Tip

★ Highlight

●●●● Best of ...

☲ Scenic view

Ⓒ Responsible travel: fair
trade principles and the
environment respected

(*) Telephone numbers
that are not toll-free

**PRICE CATEGORIES
HOTELS**

Expensive	over 100 euros
Moderate	60–100 euros
Budget	under 60 euros

Prices per night for two
persons in a double room
with breakfast in season

**PRICE CATEGORIES
RESTAURANTS**

Expensive	over 18 euros
Moderate	12–18 euros
Budget	under 12 euros

Prices for a meal with starter,
main course and dessert,
without drinks

CONTENTS

**MAPS IN THE
GUIDEBOOK**
(128 A1) Page numbers and
coordinates refer to the road
atlas
(0) Site/address located off
the map. Coordinates are
also given for places that are
not marked on the road atlas

(*A–B 2–3*) refers to the
pull-out map

INSIDE FRONT COVER:
The best Highlights

INSIDE BACK COVER:
City map of Funchal and map
of the bus routes on Madeira

The best MARCO POLO Insider Tips

Our top 15 Insider Tips

INSIDER TIP **Live music after a spot of golfing**

So much for the stuffy golfer hang-out: At the *Hole in One* there is groovy live music in the evenings and everyone is in high spirits. Both locals and tourists frequent the comfy pub and the secluded outdoor area → **p. 42**

INSIDER TIP **A drink in the "mill"**

For the local cocktail made from lemon juice, sugar-cane spirit and honey, Madeirans come from far and wide to the *Bar Moinho* (mill), where the *poncha* tastes terrific → **p. 57**

INSIDER TIP **Swimming spot – small but impressive**

You have to walk right down to the end of the coastal promenade, but it is well worth the effort: in the *Poças do Gomes*, you can take a wonderful swim between the rugged cliffs, watch fish or hire a deckchair → **p. 41**

INSIDER TIP **Raid the garden**

In the organic orchard and vegetable garden of the *Quinta do Cabouco*, hotel guests are allowed to help themselves for free, and their hosts are happy to explain what the exotic fruits are → **p. 58**

INSIDER TIP **Unspoiled view**

A wide-ranging panorama from the *Ponta Vigia* lookout point on the north coast of Madeira → **p. 66**

INSIDER TIP **Aloe vera cosmetics**

A secret tip for sunburn or strained muscles: aloe vera gel. Give your hair a special treat with shampoo made from the moisturising lily of the desert. Made in Madeira! → **p. 31**

INSIDER TIP **Sail to a desert island**

On a day trip to the uninhabited nature reserve of the *Ilhas Desertas* you can spot sea birds, dolphins, whales and sometimes even monk seals → **p. 108**

INSIDER TIP **Snorkellers' paradise**

When the beach of Porto Santo is too crowded, snorkellers go down to the remote *bay of Zimbralinho*, in which they find turquoise water and peace → **p. 85**

INSIDERTIP Horsepower on Porto Santo

Discover the expanse of the hilly countryside: *Porto Santo Horseriding Tours* also offer tours on horseback for children and beginners → **p. 85**

INSIDERTIP Celebrating nature

With many outdoor activities, the island celebrates its nature for a week in autumn → **p. 113**

INSIDERTIP Glittering stones

While visiting the *Jardim Tropical Monte Palace*, do not forget to look round the enormous collection of minerals (photo left) in the onsite museum! Let yourself be dazzled by the unique wealth of sparkling precious stones and minerals → **p. 48**

INSIDERTIP Idyllic and remote

Not many tourists venture as far as the small coastal strip *Rocha do Navio* near Santana which you can whizz down to on the cable car → **p. 64**

INSIDERTIP Museum with a view

On the roof terrace of the *Madeira Story Centre* in Funchal, delicious specialities are served with a fantastic panorama view over the roofs of the old town as an added extra → **p. 38**

INSIDERTIP Calheta from above

Take courage to try something new – you will have fantastic views over the south-western part of Madeira floating through the air on a paragliding tandem flight → **p. 53**

INSIDERTIP Wine trail

A breathtaking hiking route leads from the *Quinta do Furão* near Santana along the steep coast lined by vineyards and descending in hairpin bends down to the Calhau of São Jorge (photo below) → **p. 65**

BEST OF ...

● *A garden to die for*
The *Quinta Splendida* hotel in Caniço has a wonderful garden in which many plants are labelled. Hotel guests as well as the general public can enjoy its beauty and the ocean view (photo) → p. 46

● *Live like Asterix*
The village of *Santana* is reminiscent of a Gallic settlement with its red doors, blue-framed windows with green shutters and drooping thatched roofs. The historic houses make the past come alive – like a trip to a museum, but for free → p. 64

● *Learn about what creeps, crawls and swims around Madeira*
There is usually an entrance fee to see the exhibits on Madeira's flora, fauna and geology at the *Museu de História Natural*. But, on Sundays, you can visit the museum and the aquarium for free → p. 37

● *A beacon of light at night*
Lighthouses always seem to have a certain kind of appeal. Madeira's most attractive one stands at the tip of the Rocha da Vigia in *Ponta do Pargo*. Originally constructed in 1922, it lures visitors inside to see its photo exhibition depicting the other beacons of light around the island → p. 55

● *Sweet treats from cane sugar*
At one time, sugar cane made the island's plantation owners rich. Today, there are only a few sugar cane mills still in use on Madeira. One of them is run by the *Sociedade dos Engenhos da Calheta*. In this mill, you can see how rum and honey are made – and give them both a try → p. 52

● *Above the abyss*
The Skywalk at *Cabo Girão* offers you a breathtaking panoramic view from one of Europe's highest steep cliffs with only a glass floor and 580 m/1903ft of air between you and the ground. What is even better: the spectacular vantage point is (still) free of charge → p. 44

●●●● Dots in guidebook refer to 'Best of ...' tips

● *Colourful and varied delicacies*

Flowers in glowing colours, exotic fruit, delicious vegetables and fresh fish – these are the treasures of Madeira. Vendors tastefully display their wares in the *Mercado dos Lavradores* in Funchal where you can try the best that the island has to offer. Friday is the liveliest market day (photo) → p. 36

● *Island of eternal spring*

In Funchal's *Jardim Botânico* you will quickly discover why Madeira is called the island of eternal spring. More than 2500 tropical and subtropical plants present themselves in all shades of green → p. 47

● *Sleds without snow*

Take one of the famous basket sleds on runners, propelled by the muscles of strong men, along the road from Monte down towards Funchal → p. 48

● *Along the levadas*

Walk alongside ancient irrigation channels through woods of eucalyptus and laurel, past dizzying gorges or along broad forest tracks. You will never forget the paths on the *levadas* of Madeira, for example on the *Levada do Furado* → p. 73

● *Favourite delicacies: Espada and Espetada*

Madeira's national dishes are true delicacies – try the famous black scabbard fish in *Serra e Mar* in Santana. The traditional *Espetada*, juicy beef on a skewer, can be enjoyed at *A Carreta* in Ponta do Pargo → pp. 64, 56

● *Set sail on the Santa Maria de Colombo*

Christopher Columbus lived on Madeira for a few years and planned his voyages here. On a replica of his ship, built true to the original, you can feel like an explorer yourself → p. 110

● *Pools made of volcanic rock*

The surf crashes on the black rocks a few metres away while you take a relaxed swim in the natural *lava pools* in Porto Moniz. An extraordinary experience! → p. 62

BEST OF ...

● *Retracing the steps of CR7*
Not only fans of World Footballer Cristiano Ronaldo will be excited: At the *CR7 Museum*, the life story and road to success of Funchal's most famous son are presented in a vivid and interactive manner → p. 36

● *Inside the volcano*
In *São Vicente* you can take a guided tour through a fascinating system of 890,000 year old lava tunnels. The visitor centre provides more background information on Madeira's fiery past → p. 68

● *See the fish without getting wet*
What used to be a fort in Porto Moniz is now home to the *Aquário da Madeira*. Specimens of the marine life of Madeira cavort before your eyes in a variety of pools and tanks (photo) → p. 62

● *Shop like a local*
Madeira Shopping seems to be where the whole island comes to shop. Mix among the locals in the over 100 shops, cinemas, cafés and restaurants located in Madeira's largest shopping mall in Funchal → p. 40

● *Art and culture in Calheta*
Mudas. Museo de Arte contempôranea has attracted much attention for its intriguing architecture. It's also home to exhibitions, an innovative cultural programme and an excellent café-restaurant → p. 52

● *Unwind with a tea*
When rain coming from the Atlantic blankets the island, the *Loja do Chá* in Funchal is the perfect harbour. This inviting tea house also offers apple pie and scones. Their cosy wicker chairs are ideal to help you while away an afternoon → p. 39

RAIN

RELAX AND CHILL OUT
Take it easy and spoil yourself

● *Pure wellness*
The wellness and spa facilities at the *Quinta Splendida* in Caniço are the most extensive in Madeira. Book a wellness programme here if you would like to be really pampered. → **p. 46**

● *The sound of mandolins*
During the summer season Madeira's *mandolin orchestra* gives a concert every Wednesday evening in the Centro de Congresso next to the casino The sound has enchanted many a visitor over the years → **p. 42**

● *It's tea time!*
Follow the example of Winston Churchill, George Bernard Shaw and Empress Elisabeth of Austria by enjoying the legendary after-noon tea on the terrace of *Reid´s* in Funchal – enjoy a one-of-a-kind experience with scones and cakes before a magnificent panorama (photo) → **p. 44**

● *Fine dining within fortress walls*
Exquisite dishes, a historical ambiance and a relaxing view of the sea ensure for a truly enjoyable dining experience at the *Restaurante do Forte* located within the walls of the São Tiago Fortress in Funchal. Sit back and savour the regional and international cuisine → **p. 40**

● *A room with a view*
The *Hotel do Campo* sits on a overhang slightly above the Ribeira Bra-va and offers more than just breathtaking views. Along with a peaceful night's sleep and a good dose of relaxation, guests can enjoy all the comforts and advantages of a certified eco hotel → **p. 58**

● *Set sail*
What could be more excit-ing than to feel the wind blowing through your hair as you sail aboard a yacht and dream of the endless waters of the ocean? The two mast-ed *Bonita da Madeira* sails with the dolphins past the island's most beautiful bays → **p. 108**

INTRODUCTION

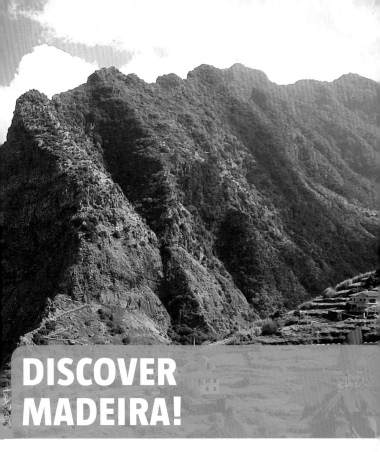

DISCOVER MADEIRA!

What about taking a holiday in Madeira? But all there is to see are flowers and pensioners! At least that is what everyone says. Admittedly, the Portuguese island in the Atlantic did gain a reputation for many years as a favourite island for *holidays and winter sojourns* for British and German senior citizens, but these are no longer the only visitors! You will now see young people on honeymoons and active and trekking trips, families with young children who go on boat trips to see dolphins, mountain bikers, trail runners, diving groups and many other active tourists. Madeira has much more to offer than *flower beds* (although they are really beautiful – there is nothing wrong with the wonderful parks and gardens!): the island is a paradise for everyone who loves marine and mountain landscapes and enjoys strolling through charming villages and mingling in the crowd at lively celebrations. And anyone who prefers a relaxed beach holiday can take the ferry over to Porto Santo where there is plenty of sand. The fact that Madeira does not offer Balearic beaches is no shortcoming, but more an advantage. The majority of holiday makers are here for the *natural beauty* of the island, the friendliness of its inhabitants and good food and not so much for Sangria. But anyone who thinks that

Flowers and a fountain adorn the courtyard of Funchal's city hall

nothing is happening in Funchal should walk through the old town in the evening – the Madeirans certainly know how to celebrate in style.

Madeira is however not only famous as the *Island of Flowers*: in travel brochures it is frequently named the 'green pearl in the Atlantic' or 'island of eternal spring'... But is that really true: is it always spring on the archipelago? Things are not quite that simple. Nowadays the summers are pretty hot and dry (thanks to climate change – forest fires are sadly also on the increase). In the winter, the island is mostly pleasantly mild and with a bit of luck you can catch a phase with sunny days and a temperature ranging between 15/59 and 20° C/68 °F. But at some point, there has to be some rain, otherwise the *Pearl of the Atlantic* would not be so green. Rainy periods can

1351
The Isola di Legno (wooden island) first appears on an Italian nautical chart

1419–20
The seafarers João Gonçalves Zarco, Tristão Vaz Teixeira and Bartolomeu Perestrelo take possession of Porto Santo and Madeira for Portugal

from 1456
Exports of sugar bring art, wealth, merchants and slaves to Madeira

1703
Portugal and England sign a treaty on commercial relations. As a result, the wine trade on Madeira falls under English control

occur at any time in autumn, winter and spring (you may think: what a pity). The good news is however: be relaxed about it! First of all, the island needs the rain otherwise you would not find all the colourful fruit in the market hall and the gardens would only feature cactus plants... What is more, if it is raining and windy on one side of the island, the weather can still be good on the other side! The damp *Passat clouds* prefer to congregate around the northern face of the island mountains while there are perfect weather conditions on the southern side or in lower lying areas. This explains the verdant scenery, particularly in the north of the island. The *laurel forest* of Madeira is such an outstanding feature that it was declared a world heritage site by Unesco in 1999. This unique so-called laurisilva still covers around 20 per cent of the island and is a relic of the laurel forest vegetation which was also found in Central Europe before the Ice Ages.

The first settlers on the island arriving in the 15th century were quick to recognise the influence of the differences in altitude and the northern and southern orientation on *agriculture* and above all on irrigation facilities. They began channelling water from the higher regions in the north to the sugar cane plantations and terraced fields in the sunny southern regions, which were, however, frequently too dry – this was the birth of the *levada* system! The settlers lost no time in creating daring water courses through the rocks to direct valuable rain and spring water from A to B. Thanks to its *levadas*, Madeira is today an ideal *island for hiking*. The *levada* maintenance tracks created an extensive network of paths leading not only the *levada* workers but also enthusiastic tourists into the depths of the green heart of the island with its wild gorges and rock formations that are millions of years old. Every twist and turn reveals a new breathtaking panorama, especially when you are hiking through the fantastic laurel forest.

> Madeira's laurisilva forest is a World Heritage site

Whether you have come to the island to hike through the narrow *levadas* or historical *veredas*, old cobbled connecting paths, or for golf, hang-gliding, surfing, climbing, canyoning or mountain biking – a plunge into cool water will do you good, not necessarily into the hotel pool, but also in the Atlantic Ocean. Now there are a few golden *sandy beaches* on the volcanic island – even if they have

1801–07
British soldiers are stationed on Madeira during the Napoleonic Wars

1960
Opening of the airport on Porto Santo

1964
Inauguration of Santa Catarina Airport on Madeira

1974
On 25 April the Carnation Revolution in Portugal ends the dictatorship of Estado Novo, which began in the 1930s under António de Oliveira Salazar

1976
Madeira becomes an autonomous region

only been artificially created with sand from Morocco. Up until a few years ago, it was really only possible to build proper sandcastles on the neighbouring island of Porto Santo. Today you are free to choose whether you would prefer to spend a day on the golden sandy beaches in Calheta or Machico, walk along the seaside on shingle beaches or black sand, for example in Funchal, Seixal or Prainha, or access the sea or natural *lava pools* using one of the numerous ladders to swim in the Atlantic. If you are genuinely on the search for miles of long sandy beaches, your best bet is to go to Porto Santo. The sister island is only around two hours away by ferry or a short hop by air. Along with the Ilhas Desertas around 30 km/18.6 mi further south and the also uninhabited Ilhas Selvagens about 250 km/155 mi away, the unequal island pair form the archipelago Madeira.

> **Attracting lava pools and sandy beaches**

In the early 19th century, it was primarily the wealthy British settling on Madeira who competed with each other to create the most beautiful and extraordinary *jardins*. This explains the famous *gardens and parks* which were created around their properties – you can still walk through some of these today and admire the spectacular borders and flowerbeds. The British certainly made their mark with their gardens, particularly making a distinctive impact on the agricultural development of Madeira. It was not only the *wine trade* that flourished with the aid of the British, but also tourism. In the meantime, a large proportion of the 260,000 Madeirans live – directly or indirectly – from the latter sector. Due to the lack of road connections on the island, tourism was initially limited to the capital city of Funchal, which experienced its first boom during the late 19th and early 20th centuries. For emperors, kings and artists alike, it became fashionable to spend part of the year on the Island of Flowers. Many came on the advice of their physicians as Madeira's *mild and damp climate* was considered as excellent treatment for respiratory problems, a weak heart and "nervous disorders". The Empress Elisabeth of Austria (known as Sisi) was probably one of the most famous of the island guests seeking recovery.

> **Madeira's gardens are world-famous**

1986
Portugal joins the EU

2000
Opening of the expanded Santa Catarina Airport and work begins to extend Madeira's motorway network

2013/14
A new cruise ship terminal is built in Funchal

2015
After 37 years in power, the authoritarian and patriarchal President Alberto João Jardim (PSD) resigns from office; the subsequent government tackles the reduction of debt and corruption.

2016
Forest fires destroy parts of Funchal

The purple flowers of the "pride of Madeira", which is endemic to the island

Today, wellness still remains a focal point here. New hotel complexes offering *spa facilities* are shooting up from the ground – not just in Funchal: thanks to new road connections, you now have swift access to all different areas of the island. Sadly not all infrastructural investments during past years have been characterised by sustainability: Alberto João Jardim, president of the island for many decades, unfortunately used EU funding to concrete over numerous areas on Madeira. The subsequent government is now attempting to find a balance between economic development and the conservation of nature.

Madeira is an archipelago full of contrasts and surprises: on the main island, you are confronted by a massively developed southern region and huge *national park areas* in the interior of the island and a largely unspoilt northern region. For many years now, Funchal has been considered the cleanest city in Portugal and all villages and towns are constantly smartening themselves up. There are no better-maintained front gardens and municipal parks in the entire country. You will experience heavy rainfall, but the sun will be shining in a clear blue sky only a short time later. You can hike through a dry headland one day, through luscious laurel forest the next day and wander through decadently blooming gardens the day after that. Allow yourself be enchanted by the beauty of nature on the archipelago, by its *cordial inhabitants* and their delicious recipes. And don't forget: if the weather doesn't live up to your expectations, simply travel to the other side of the island; somewhere you are sure to find your 'permanent spring'!

> **Now as then, everything revolves around wellness**

WHAT'S HOT

1 Design at the harbour

Creative interior designer The latest flagship of the Madeiran designer, decorator and painter Nini Andrade Silva perches on the massive Fortaleza da Nossa Senhora da Conceição, the so-called *Molhe*. The seafarer Zarco is also said to have lived on this fortified rock where an exhibition of designer furniture by the artist, a lounge cafeteria and the trendy restaurant *DC Atelier* currently occupy the stylish *Design Center (Estrada da Pontinha | Funchal | tel. 2 91 64 15 51 | www.niniandradesilva.com)* (photo right). Nini Andrade Silva is one of the most innovative interior designers in Portugal; she is hired by highly individual hotels to impress both guests and professional circles with her stylish interior designs. You can marvel at examples of her special design, for example in the hotel *The Vine (79 rooms | Rua das Aranhas 27a | Funchal | tel. 2 91 00 90 00 | www.hotelthevine.com | Expensive, photo above)*. She incorporated the theme of wine into innumerable decorative elements. She also selected a Madeiran tradition for the *Saccharum Hotel (243 rooms | Rua da Serra d'Água 1 | Calheta | tel. 2 91 82 03 00 | www.saccharumhotelresort.com | Expensive):* the hotel is a homage to sugar cane, molasses and honey!

2 Moda Madeira

Trendy evening dresses As the island gets a younger image, fashion designers have set to work to create stylish outfits suitable for clubbing. *Patrícia Pinto (Rua Nova de São Pedro 56 | Funchal)* offers a modern style with strong colours and see-through fabrics. *Lúcia Sousa (Palácio dos Cônsules, Rua da Conceição 23 | Funchal)* is known for her romantic dresses. Even the fashion-conscious sister of the football star Cristiano Ronaldo has opened a boutique in her hometown of Funchal: *CR7 (Rua Vale da Ajuda 90 | www.lojacr7.com)*.

Sounds in the air

Music to love When the disparate sounds of jazz and fado come together, the result is an out-of-the-ordinary kind of music that gets under your skin. At the recently established *Funchal Jazz Festival (www.funchaljazzfestival.org)* well-known artists such as Gregory Porter take to the stage for three days. The restaurant *House Jazz (Rua dos Aranhas 16 | Funchal)* has made a name for itself with live jazz. With a bit of luck, the star of the scene, *Vânia Fernandes* (photo), will put in an appearance. At *SCAT*, everything is also focused on music: top-quality live music is performed every evening in the *Funchal Music Club & Restaurant* on the Lido Promenade below the Hotel Meliã Madeira Mare: piano music accompanying dinner in a romantic setting with a sea view and then the fantastic in-house jazz combo till late at night with a wide and varied repertoire ranging from jazz and bossa nova to indie.

On the run

A fashionable mountainsports activity A new trend that ordinary mortals can only shake their heads at: trail running – a mixture of jogging and hiking, preferably on narrow, technically challenging routes with plenty of ascents and descents and along the edge of deep ravines. It sounds crazy, doesn't it? You can, however, see runners scampering through the landscape in all types of weather conditions. At the *MIUT – Madeira Island Ultra Trail (www.madeiraultratrail.com)* held at the end of April, thousands of athletes run 115 km/71 mi, 85 km/52.8 mi, 42 km/26.1 mi or 16 km/9.9 mi across the island and the *Skymarathon (www.madeiraskyrunning.com)* at the beginning of June features not only a 55-km/34.2-mi trail, but also a vertical sprint over 1 km/0.6 mi.

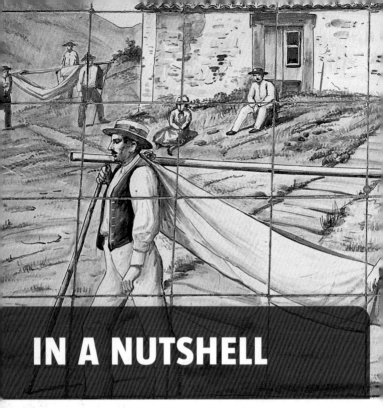

IN A NUTSHELL

FLOWERY DREAMS

No advertising text for the 'Island of Flowers' fails to mention the 'swimming garden in the Atlantic'. This raises the expectations of some visitors who get off the plane and expect to see a carpet of flowers as far as the eye can see, at best any time between January and December... That is not realistic, particularly on the heavily built-up south coast, so do not be disappointed. Thanks to irrigation however, many plants frequently found in subtropical and temperate climate zones grow on Madeira in the lovingly cultivated front gardens and park areas. Not everything flowers at the same time, but you are always sure to see something in bloom even in winter! Around 800 different native plants and over 500 imported plant types are found on the island: since the 1980s, two thirds of its area has been designated as a natural reserve.

In the terraced fields you can discover grape vines, bananas, potatoes and beans alongside a wealth of exotic fruits. Nearly all year long, aloe plants, hydrangeas and lilies of all types and colours line the winding roads and the aroma of wild herbs is omnipresent in the mountains in early summer. The absolute highlight for flower lovers is, however, the annual *Flower Festival* in May with its grand procession of brightly decorated floats and girls with flowers progressing through Funchal and the luscious carpets of flowers (which actually do exist!) under the lilac blooms of jacaranda trees.

Quintas, *levadas* or azulejos –
extraordinary and unique discoveries
await you on Madeira

THE MAINLAND INHABITANTS ...

Sometimes things are not so easy on the island. Occasionally, the Madeirans feel somewhat remote and isolated, even today, almost fifty years after Salazar's dictatorship. During this period between the 1930s and the Carnation Revolution of 1974, Madeira was left very much to its own political and economic devices. However, even in the 21st century there are still limitations: shopping in a well-known Swedish furniture store? This is only possible on the mainland. Going to rock concerts? They are only held in Lisbon which is 1000 km/621 mi away. Even now that there are low-cost flights and special ticket prices for island inhabitants and VAT is only 22% instead of 23%, a latent feeling of discrimination remains. Perhaps this is partly because the mainland inhabitants make fun of the islanders' dialect or that the central government in Lisbon controls all decisions made by the parliament on Madeira, despite the fact that the archipelago was granted the special status of an autonomous region in 1976 and has its own elected president. Admittedly, the former president, Alberto João Jardim who remained in power for decades, was not so popular with the inhabitants of mainland Portugal due to his blustering manner and secret mountains of debt; perhaps this can explain the certain degree of distance. Let us see what the future brings and whether the Portuguese of the mainland and the islands will become friendlier towards each other – perhaps also prompted by the tourism sector.

A close relative of our chaffinch: The Madeira chaffinch

PARTY PEOPLE

You will hardly find a single weekend without some sort of procession or harvest festival for a specific sort of fruit vegetable! The Madeirans will always find a reason to celebrate, whether it is the chestnut festival, a wine festival or a celebration for bananas, cherries or lemons. On top of that, there are frequent festivals for patron saints and for wind bands! As not that much else is happening on the island, a street or village festival provides some variety in life. These celebrations are accompanied with stalls selling succulent meat skewers and performances by folklore groups – and if you happen to experience the onion festival, you must not miss the fantastic onion exhibition set up by farmers!

WINGS & FINS

The extent of Madeira's fauna is fairly modest, as few types of animals succeeded in reaching the archipelago independently; in fact, only bats, insects and birds managed to make their independent way to the island. These were also joined by a few common wall lizards who multiplied in huge numbers, as you can observe today on sunny walls throughout the island. In picnic areas, you will also frequently be accompanied by the Madeira chaffinch waiting for some crumbs, one of around two hundred types of birds found on Madeira. Marine fauna displays much greater variety – ranging from black scabbard fish to tuna and cephalopods. Occasionally, whales and dolphins can be observed and even the previously endangered monk seals have returned to the island. You will rarely catch sight of most of the farming animals – which were all imported to the island: pigs live in their pigsties and cows and goats are normally kept in traditional huts with pointed roofs.

GLAZED WALLS

There is hardly a single church without *azulejos:* Portugal's ceramic tiles also belong to Madeira's building tradition. The oldest originate from the 17th century, but even today walls are still decorated with the weatherproof tiles that are much more than pure decoration. *Azulejos,* frequently patterned in blue and white but also sometimes colourfully decorated, are excellently suitable for protecting walls from damage through heat and harsh weather conditions.

NO BREXIT ON MADEIRA

Madeira almost ended up as a British island, but the English instead selected Tangier and Bombay as a wedding present for King Charles II on his wedding to Princess Catarina of Bragança in 1660. The British are however omnipresent on Madeira (and not only as tourists): they have exerted a great influence on wine-growing and still control almost the entire Madeira wine production. And who was it who made white embroidery and basket-making internationally popular? Involved not only in the wine trade, but also the biggest daily newspaper, numerous travel agencies and hotels, the British currently appear to own half of the island.

MANUEL'S ORNAMENTATION

If you have already visited Portugal, you will surely have heard of King Manuel I the "Fortunate", as the Portuguese experienced the zenith of its world renown and wealth during his reign (1495–1521) thanks to the successful voyages of discovery and conquest undertaken by Vasco da Gama and other seafarers. Madeira had already been discovered a few decades previously, and during this period an intense building phase commenced on the island. Manuel was able to finance the construction of magnificent monasteries, churches, towers and palaces ornamented with delicate maritime decoration across the whole of Portugal from the treasures he amassed through his maritime power.

You can still see churches and chapels decorated with typical symbols of the Manueline period: gateways are ornamented with stone decorations in the form of ships' ropes, algae and corals, balustrades are decorated with the Cru-

Church festivals such as here in Ribeira Brava are the highlights of everyday life

saders' Maltese cross and Manuel's own favourite symbol crops up time and time again – the armillary sphere, the navigational instrument which became well-known under Prince Henry the Navigator.

RONALDO AND THE GOLDEN BALLS

Whether you like him or not, you can hardly avoid encountering this character, primarily because the airport was named after him when the Portuguese national football team won the EM championship in 2016, so you will inevitably land at the Cristiano-Ronaldo-Airport. The international football player is also omnipresent in Funchal: in the form of the virile statue placed in front of his CR7 Museum (in which his "ballons d'or" are also exhibited), as a lifestyle hotel brand or an advertising icon on innumerable posters. Even his mother Dolores has now also become an advertising star in her own right. However controversial the narcissistic striker may be, Madeirans love their golden boy, not only because he was born here in modest circumstances and brings the island repeatedly into focus with his personality and makes generous donations after catastrophes, but simply because he is a fantastic footballer.

BEAUTIFUL LIVING

You will see *quintas* on many hillside locations in Madeira: grand mansions and properties which were chiefly constructed during the 18th and 19th centuries. This was the golden age of the wine trade when numerous British merchants settled on Madeira; they were presumably impervious to the frequently damp and clammy climate in Monte, Santo da Serra or other smart locations. They employed international architects to construct the latest stylistic trends and create exotic vegetation around these prestigious properties. Some of these magnificent parks can still be visited today and many of the *quintas* have now been converted into hotels. This exquisite architectural heritage stands in stark contrast to the extensive insular building mania chiefly funded by money from the EU – and perhaps you would genuinely prefer to stay in a restored *quinta* with a romantic garden than in a concrete box on the coast!

OVER THE HILLS

Imagine that you have been slaving away for years to produce a profit from your vineyards – and then your grapes are destroyed by phylloxera or mildew. You would then perhaps leave the area and make a new startsomewhere else. This is what numerous inhabitants of 19th century Madeira did who lost their vineyards through these blights,resettling in Brazil, Venezuela, South Africa, England and the Channel Islands. Madeira has been familiar with the phenomenon of emigration and return migration since the earliest settlements on the island (actually the "emigration" of the Portuguese from the poorer parts of mainland Portugal) – natural catastrophes, economic crises or changed working conditions have repeatedly caused the island inhabitants to seek their fortune elsewhere.

The current total population of the archipelago is around 260,000, but there are around a million "Madeirans" who originate directly or indirectly from the island. Some emigrants return after a period of time, frequently establishing a small shop (preferably a café) with the money earned abroad. If you see a magnificent new house next to a modest parental home in the villages, this is mostly a clear sign that emigrants have returned.

WATER CHANNELS

Some channels lead through the middle of settlements (even through Funchal) and flow alongside sloping vineyards and cultivated terraces while others run through deep valleys and dense laurel forestland or through narrow tunnels. You can take a relaxed walk chatting together alongside some of these water channels, but with others you have to be really careful not to lose your balance at narrow points where the path suddenly disappears – sometimes there is also quite a drop. These are the fantastic *levadas,* Madeira's greatest pride! Shortly after the island was discovered, slaves were charged with the task of creating these first artificial water channels to lead water from remote springs down to the sugar cane plantations. A large part of this network with a total length of around 2500 km/1554 mi was created during the 20th century. Some *levadas*

ra wine which has also found its way into our cuisine in various forms. This liqueur wine with around 20 % alcohol is made by adding brandy to stop the fermentation of the wine must, meaning that a large proportion of fructose is retained. The remainder of the se-

This *levada* path is lined with morning glories and Indian figs

are even connected to hydropower plants to generate electricity. The so-called *levadeiros* supervise the distribution of water to individual farmers and ensure that the water continues to flow right into the furthermost corners. And you can rejoice that the *levadas* have also created countless wonderful routes, permitting you to hike and walk along the working routes of the *levadeiros!*

RAISE YOUR GLASSES

An easy question for a quiz: name a typical drink from Madeira. The first answer is sure to be the tasty Madei-

cret is the storage in warm attics (the so-called *cantiero* process) or the heating of grape juice in steel tanks (Estafugem method). You will recognise which of these processes has been used to make your Madeira wine by the price and taste: you will pay at least 30 euros for wine from one of the types of noble grapes Sercial (dry), Verdelho (medium dry), Boal (medium sweet) and Malvasia (sweet) seasoned for 15 years in oak casks whereas a bottle of Madeira made from the common grape Tinta Negra Mole seasoned in steel tanks will only cost 3 euros.

FOOD & DRINK

Lovers of sweet wine lick their lips straight away when they hear the name Madeira: the island's wine makes a wonderful aperitif or after-dinner drink. A typical Madeiran meal usually starts with soup, which is followed by a hearty helping of the main course. In the island's *traditional peasant cooking*, "good" is synonymous with "plenty". With a little luck you will find tasty, down-to-earth specialities such as wheat soup or **INSIDER TIP** *watercress soup (sopa de trigo, sopa de agriões)*, tripe stew (do-brada), boiled kid (cabrito) and pork with wine and garlic *carne vinho e alhos* in a village pub. The cooks in tourist hotels and restaurants stick to *standard international fare*, while French, Far Eastern and crossover cuisine are the main styles

in gourmet restaurants. Apart from this, a good chef is able to conjure surprising culinary treats from staples like *bacalhau* (dried cod).

The *twin pillars of the island's food*, however, are *espada* and *espetada* – scabbard fish and skewered beef. Another popular main course is tuna *(atum)*, often served in a strong onion sauce. Swordfish *(espadarte)*, grouper *(garoupa)*, red snapper *(pargo)*, gilthead bream *(dourada)*, parrotfish *(bodião)* and *cavaco*, a kind of langoustine, often also feature on the menu. *Camarões* (shrimps) and **INSIDER TIP** *caramujos* (sea snails) are sometimes advertised on a notice on the door of little country bars as the day's speciality. Almost all restaurants serve limpets *(lapas)*. Fresh mountain trout

Rustic and plentiful – Madeiran cooking still revolves around down-to-earth dishes such as espada and espetada

(trutas) make a delicious change from sea fish. They are farmed in Ribeiro Frio. Madeirans prefer *frango* and *bife* – chicken and beefsteak – to fish, which is fairly expensive. At celebrations it is usual for dozens of whole **chickens** to be sizzling on the grill as an alternative to *espetada.* Unfortunately almost all the chickens come from intensive farming. Madeirans often eat their beefsteak in the form of **sandwiches**. A great deal of beef is imported – and the same is true of pork.

The main supplement to meat is ***potatoes***, boiled or as French fries. Sometimes sweet potatoes baked in their skins *(batata doce)* or *milho frito* also appear on the menu. The latter is maize polenta, seasoned with herbs and diced. *Inhame* is a member of the yam family. With a bit of luck you will be served this boiled root, which has a distinctive taste, as an accompaniment to meat dishes. As in the past this plant was often the only source of nourishment in times of hunger, it is still

LOCAL SPECIALITIES

açorda – clear, hearty bread soup with garlic and egg, ideally served in a big bowl from which guests can help themselves as often as they like

arroz de marisco – a stew made from rice, fish and other seafood, often garnished with prawns and large mussels, and seasoned with fresh coriander. Mostly available as a dish for two people, sometimes with spaghetti instead of rice *(esparguete de marisco)* (photo right)

bolo do caco – a round, flat white loaf, originally made from sweet potatoes but nowadays mainly from flour, which is browned on hot iron hobs

bolo de mel – a dark, spiced cake containing sugar-cane syrup

caldeirada – thick, spicy fish stew

carne vinho e alhos – diced pork, marinated for a long time in wine and vinegar with garlic and bay leaf or fennel, then braised

castanhetas – small fish like anchovies, fried and tossed in garlic oil

espada – the black scabbard fish features on the menu almost everywhere, often filleted and served with banana; however the locals also cook this fish with wine and garlic

espetada – the island's national dish. Traditionally the beef is freshly diced, rolled in coarse-grained bay-leaf salt and stuck on a skewer of laurel wood to sizzle over open coals until the meat is ready to eat

lapas grelhadas – limpets harvested fresh from coastal rocks are extremely tasty. They are prepared by cooking them with garlic butter and lemon juice on a hot metal platter from which they are then eaten (photo left)

poncha – the fishermen of Câmara de Lobos claim to be the inventors of this drink made from mixing clear sugar-cane spirit with lemon juice and honey

prego (no prato) – "nail *(on the plate)*" is the literal translation of the name for this combination of a thin piece of fried beef with a lettuce leaf and tomato. This trio of ingredients is popular as a sandwich between two halves of a roll

tremoços – preserved salty lupin seeds, served as an alternative to chicken stomachs or chopped pig's ears as a nibble with beer *(dentinhos)* regarded as food for the poor and turns up more often in home cooking than on the menus of high-class restaurants. When it comes to vegetables, **carrots and beans** from the island's gardens are much in evidence; sometimes a restaurant owner dishes up *pimpinela* (chayote, a kind of pale green gourd), which is often eaten at home. Many other types of vegetable are imported, often from Africa.

Beer, by contrast, is normally made locally. The leading brand on Madeira is Coral. If you want beer on draught, ask for an *imperial*. It is often mixed with lemonade to make *shandy*. The island's table wine, which enthusiastic wine makers have been producing for about ten years now, is still drunk relatively little, and wines brought in from Portugal are more common.

At festivals local **wines** – light-heartedly known on Madeira as *café de setembro*, September coffee – come into their own. They are usually served from plastic jugs, are rarely more than a year old and have been made privately in the traditional way. Their taste is somewhat between earthy and sour, which is why the Madeirans tend to mix them with lemonade. In Santo da Serra and Camacha there is another traditional mixed drink: *cidra,* i.e. cider, to which sugar or honey is added.

Quer sobremesa? There's no escaping the question about **dessert**, and on Madeira the answer is generally yes. Homemade cakes *(bolos)*, passion-fruit pudding, crème caramel or fresh fruit are the usual choices.

After a meal Madeirans always order **coffee**. If they like it small and black, they order a *bica* (espresso) or a *bica curta* (the even stronger version). If they prefer to dilute their coffee with a little milk, they ask for a *garoto*. A larger milky coffee is known as a *chinesa*.

A brew made from lemon rind and hot water is called *chá de limão* on the island. This drink, and coffee too, are available as *pingado* – with a shot of spirits, usually whisky.

When it's time to pay the bill, "one for all" is the guiding principle. It is not normal for each guest to pay separately: either the guests then divide the amount

‚Coral' is Madeira's best-known brand of beer

amongst themselves, or those who don't pay will take their turn next time the group eats out. If nevertheless you do wish to pay separately, when asking the waiter to bring the bill you should make the request with these words: *A conta em separado, se faz favor.*

The so-called **Couvert**, a starter which sometimes only consists of bread, butter and olives, but can instead include expensive cheese, ham or prawns can only be counted up in your bill if you have specifically ordered it. Some restaurants can attempt to include the couvert tacitly in the bill, but this is now officially forbidden.

SHOPPING

Madeira wine may be the island's best-known souvenir, but other items will also bring the flair of Madeira back home and keep fond memories alive. Why not buy some exotic fruit, honey (in prettily decorated jars), a *bolo de mel* (tasty cake from a local bakery is best), cherimoya or passion-fruit liqueur, or a bottle of *aguardente de cana* (sugar cane brandy)? Handcrafted traditional boots and sandals (or perhaps elegant Portuguese shoe creations from the designer boutiques in Funchal) will also bring the feel of Madeira to your doorstep. For a delightful, yet useful souvenir, pick up one of the coarsely woven pointed wool caps with earflaps and a bobble worn by men in the countryside to keep warm and dry. *Brinquinhos* traditional instruments reminiscent of a Turkish crescent with colourful wooden figures and castanets, evoke memories of merry folk festivals.

BASKETRY

As Madeira's basketwork does not yet have a seal of quality like that of the island's embroidery, you cannot be sure that every piece is a genuine local product. The best thing to do is to locate a basket weaver's studio. Alternately, you can place your trust in one of the cooperatives, such as *Café Relógio* in Camacha. Madeira's basket weavers sell a wide variety of items ranging from bottle baskets to garden seats, and bulky items can be shipped for you.

FLOWERS

Strelitzias, proteas, orchids and many other exotic plants are grown on the 'island of flowers' in a number of nurseries where they can be purchased or ordered directly. Quality retailers (even smaller shops) will pack these fragile plants for safe transport at little or no additional cost. If you want to grow your own flowers like Agapanthus, you'll find a wide variety of bulbs for sale in the market hall in Funchal. *Jardim Orquídea (Beco do Jacinto 1 | Santo Antonio | Funchal | www.madeira-orchid.eu)* offers orchids in particular, all kinds of flowers at *Florista Cattleya (Travessa do Freitas 9b | Funchal)*.

MADEIRA EMBROIDERY

Political leaders as well as leading fashionistas are in love with Madeira's authentic embroideries *(bordados)*. It was a British lady who turned the

Something with finesse, flair or flavour? Embroidery, flowers and Madeira wine are truly beloved souvenirs

traditional stitchery of local fishermen's wives into a refined craft and a blossoming commercial endeavour. Nowadays, only a few professional *bordadeiras* are left. The prices for bordados have skyrocketed as a result, which means that vendors are highly tempted to offer cheap, imported, machine-produced goods. When buying embroidery, check for the INSIDER TIP seal of quality of the I.V.B.A.M. *(Instituto do Vinho, do Bordado e do Artesanato da Madeira)*, which runs a fashion and design centre.

MADEIRA WINE

When buying Madeira wine, bear in mind the following rule of thumb: a good quality wine has aged at least five years. A fine old bottle of Madeira wine sometimes costs as much as the evening meal to go with it. But, the wine keeps for months or maybe years, even after it has been opened. At *Blandy's Wine Lodge (Av. Arriaga 28 | Funchal | www.blandys winelodge.com)*, you can learn about all steps in the production of Madeira wine and taste and compare wines from different sorts of grapes and degrees of sweetness.

PERFUME & COSMETICS

The production of perfumes, particularly from orchids and bird of paradise flowers, and the manufacture of INSIDER TIP natural Aloe vera cosmetics count among Madeira's newest business ventures. Once a year, the genuine Aloe flowers in an intense yellow and farmers can harvest three of the thick leaves three times a year. The leaves are then pulverised and processed to manufacture cosmetics. Made in Caniçal, creams and ointments that soothe sunburn, torn muscles or arthritis are becoming beloved souvenirs. You can find them in well-stocked gift shops, some supermarkets, pharmacies and health-food stores.

FUNCHAL

⬚⬚⬚ **MAP INSIDE THE BACK COVER**
⬚⬚ (138–139 A–D 4–6) (*① K–M 7–8*)

There is no better city in Portugal to explore on foot than Funchal: along the seaside promenade on the Atlantic, under the Jacaranda trees in the Avenida Arriaga, along the colourful back streets in the old town and through the magnificent municipal gardens – Funchal is a paradise for flâneurs.

Approximately 112,000 people, almost half of the total population of Madeira, live in the so-called "theatre", as the locals have named their huge bay. You can really see the "upper circles" which have progressively expanded up the hillsides. The view from above is even more beautiful, for example from the smart district of Monte looking down on the city centre and the cruise ship harbour.

> **CITY WHERE TO START?**
>
> **Old quarter:** with its narrow alleys, the old quarter of Funchal (*Zona Velha*) is a good choice to start a visit. On the western edge of this, the oldest district of the city, you can park in the Almirante Reis garage (*Rua Dom Carlos I*). The central bus station and terminus of the cable car to Monte are also here. The market hall (*Mercado dos Lavradores*) and the São Tiago fortress are very close by.

Everyone comes to the "bay of fennel" – Funchal is not only the capital, but also the vibrant tourist centre of the island

You can explore the historical city centre and the spruced up fishermen's quarter *(Zona Velha)* easily on foot. If you would prefer to be driven around, the commented tour (1.5 hours, also in English) with the double-decker open-top bus *(Yellowbus | 12 euros, hop-on-hop-off- ticket valid for 24 hours | departure point: Avenida do Mar, above the yacht harbour | www.yellowbustours.com)* will give you an initial impression. This tour will also take you to the western part of the town with its extensive modern hotel area with only a few banana trees. Originally, wild fennel was the principal plant in the bay – this explains why Zarco, the discoverer of the island, simply named the town Funchal, i.e. fennel grove.

SIGHTSEEING

AVENIDA ARRIAGA

The elegant promenade runs from the Cathedral to the *Praça do Infante* with the monument to Henry the Navigator. When the jacaranda trees are in bloom in late spring, you feel as though you are walking beneath a lilac canopy. You pass through the Neo-Classical Municipal The-

metre of rubble to fall into the sea and the "reclaimed land" was transformed into a new cruise ship mooring place

An inlaid ceiling, blind arches and delicate carvings: the Sé cathedral

atre *Teatro Municipal Baltazar Dias*, built at the beginning of the 20th century, the former Chamber of Commerce with its blue and white azulejo tiles and the tropical *Jardim Municipal*. This was formerly the site of the garden belonging to the Franciscan monastery where today you can taste and purchase the famous Madeira wine made by the vintner family Blandy: *Blandy's Wine Lodge (tours in English Mon–Fri 10.45am, 14.45pm and 15.45pm, Sat 10.45am | 45-minute tour with wine tasting 5.90 euros | Av. Arriaga 28 | www.blandyswinelodge.com)*.

AVENIDA DO MAR

The seafront promenade in Funchal has been the site of substantial rebuilding during the past years: in 2010, heavy storms caused more than a square kilo-

and the park *Praça do Povo*. Parallel to the main road with its many bus stops, you can now walk alongside the water's edge, enjoy "people-watching" in one of the cafés or watch the giant cruise ships leaving the harbour. The imposing *Fortaleza de São Lourenço* is situated on the other side of the street and is now a government building. The island parliament meets next door in the hemispherical structure, which is the former customs house, the *Alfândega Velha*.

CASA MUSEU FREDERICO DE FREITAS

This 17th-century villa is filled with valuable furniture, old azulejos, religious and Chinese art. Its former owner also collected drawn and painted views of his Madeiran homeland. *Closed Sun/Mon | admission 3 euros | Calçada de Santa Clara 7*

CONVENTO DE SANTA CLARA

If you want to visit the convent which houses a cornucopia of art treasures, you first have to ring the bell and wait until one of the nuns opens the door. When the convent was built in the late 15th century, it was inhabited by the Poor Clares, but now one of the Franciscan nuns who have lived here since 1896 and run a nursery school in the old buildings will let you in. She will show you the special altars and chapels, the cloisters and the interior of the church whose walls are completely tiled with azulejos dating from the 17th century. The church also houses the graves of the two daughters of Zarco who discovered the island and their father is possibly also buried there. *Closed on Sundays | admission 2 euros | Calçada de Santa Clara 15*

FORTALEZA DO PICO DE SÃO JOÃO

● ﹅

High up on the 111 m/364 ft Pico dos Frias, this fort, which was built early in the 17th century under Spanish rule, commands one of the best views of the city centre of Funchal. Unfortunately, you are not (yet) able to visit the inside of the old fortress, but the Rua dos Frias will take you to the INSIDERTIP *Café da Fortaleza (Rua dos Frias | Budget)*, situated behind the old building. Right next door, a new viewing point has been created, permitting you to enjoy stunning views of western Funchal.

CATHEDRAL (SÉ)

King Manuel I ordered the construction of Funchal's leading place of worship. The church was completed between 1485 and 1514, and is one of the city's few surviving examples of Manueline architecture *(visits daily 9am–11am, 4pm–5.45pm | Largo da Sé)*. Its name derives from *sede do bispo*, the seat or

throne of the bishop. Its steeple is clad in multi-coloured roof tiles, while in the plain stone-built façade a majestic Gothic doorway catches the eye. The architecture at the eastern end of the church with the apse is more playful: turrets twist like screws, and the balustrade is elaborately decorated. The finest feature inside is the 16th-century wooden roof in the Mudéjar style, which is inlaid with ivory. The best place to get a ﹅ good view of the Cathedral is from the Rua da Sé as it leads towards Columbus Square with its yellow houses and pretty street cafés.

MARCO POLO HIGHLIGHTS

★ **Mercado dos Lavradores**
The market halls are a treat for the eye, nose and palate
→ p. 36

★ **Quinta das Cruzes**
An enchanting garden surrounds the old mansion house with its artistic treasures → p. 37

★ **Cable car**
A trip over the roofs of Funchal
→ p. 38

★ **Reid's Palace**
Enjoy afternoon tea or cocktails at twilight → p. 44

★ **Basket sleds**
The traditional way of descending from Monte – and no snow in sight → p. 48

★ **Palheiro Gardens**
Abundant greenery – some wild, some cultivated – in a truly beautiful park → p. 49

From cabbage to potatoes: the cornucopia of vegetables at the Mercado dos Lavradores

MERCADO DOS LAVRADORES ★●

The Art Deco Market Hall built in 1940 is a festival for all the senses! It smells of flowers and fruit (apart from the fish hall where there is naturally a slightly fishy scent), the colourful fruit stalls and scary-looking scabbard fish are crying out to be photographed and many of the fruit stallholders are only too keen to offer you tasty samples of passion fruit or other exotic delicacies to tempt you to buy these expensive fruits.

On Fridays, the courtyard is full of farmers offering their fresh fruit for sale. If you would prefer to escape the crowds, there is a welcoming INSIDER TIP café with comfortable wicker furniture. *Mon–Thu, 8am–7pm, Fri 7am–8pm, Sat 7am–2pm | Rua Latino Coelho*

MUSEU DE ARTE SACRA

What are Flemish paintings doing in Funchal? How did they get to an Atlantic island? You can admire a unique collection of Flemish paintings, which came to Madeira during the 16th century when the sugar barons were paid for their precious commodity with works of art. *Closed on Saturday afternoons and Sundays | admission 5 euros | Rua do Bispo 21 | www.museuartesacrafunchal.org*

MUSEU CR7 ●

Die-hard Ronaldo fans come to Madeira to get to know the home turf of Portugal's most famous football star. But a visit to the museum, which was opened by the famous man himself in 2013, is also worthwile for sceptics or secret admirers. Ronaldo's life story and road to success are impressively presented; alongside many other trophies, you can see his four "Golden Balls" (as of 2017) here. *Mon–Sat 10am–6pm | admission 5 euros | Av. Sá Cameiro | Praça do Mar 27 | www.museucr7.com*

MUSEU DE HISTÓRIA NATURAL ●

Funchal's municipal museum is somewhat old school and perhaps a little fusty, but is really not bad if you want to find out more about Madeira's flora and fauna or need somewhere to go to brighten up a rainy day. What is more, the aquariums provide an impression of the archipelago marine world. *Closed on Mon | admission 3.86 euros, free on Son | Rua da Mouraria 31*

NÚCLEO MUSEOLÓGICO DO I.V.B.A.M.

This is certainly anything but a stuffy location! In the Embroidery Museum housed in the State Institute for Wine, Embroidery and Applied Arts, you can admire the stylishly embroidered objects dating from the 19th century and the Art Nouveau period presented alongside tapestries. *Closed Sat/Sun | admission 2 euros | Rua Visconde de Anadia 44*

PARQUE DE SANTA CATARINA ☆

You can go for wonderful walks in St Catherine's Park with its exotic trees, colourful flower beds, a Baroque chapel dating from the 15th century and fantastic views over the harbour and watch the local kids playing or become inspired by the young pairs of lovers who have arranged to meet on the park benches. At the upper end of the elongated park, the rose-coloured walls of the *Quinta Vigia* shimmer through dense and sumptuous plants. This historic mansion built in the 17th century was the official residence and guesthouse of the president of the regional government. You can visit the *Park (Mon–Fri | admission 1 euro)* attached to the Quinta with its aviaries. A few steps closer to the hotel area, a bronze statue of Sisi commemorates the sojourn in 1860/61 of the Austrian Empress Elisabeth on this site:

today the Casino designed by Oscar Niemeyer is located on this spot.

PRAÇA COLOMBO

What does Columbus Square have to do with the famous seafarer? Not very much, as he probably only spent a few days here to conduct some business in 'sugar town'. During the 15th and 16th centuries, the 'white gold' on Madeira triggered a boom: this explains why the city's coat of arms created as a mosaic at the centre of the attractively renovated square contains five sugar loaves. In the *Museu Cidade do Açucar (Closed Sat/Sun | admission 3.86 euros | Praça de Colombo 5)*, you can find out about the history of the sugar trade. The palatial mansion belonging to the Flemish sugar trader João Esmeraldo (actually called Jean d'Esmenault) once stood here. The museum displays archaeological finds including ceramic moulds for sugar loaves.

PRAÇA DO MUNICÍPIO

Standing on the square with its black-and-white cobblestones you can see three of Funchal's significant historic buildings. At the end of the square is the former town residence of the Counts of Carvalhal. Since the late 19th century this Baroque palace with its magnificent, *azulejo*-adorned courtyard has been the home of the *city hall*. The northwest side of the square is dominated by what used to be a Jesuit college and is now the *University of Madeira* with an impressive church, the Igreja do Colégio. Opposite the church, the Bishop's Palace now houses the Museum of Religious Art.

QUINTA DAS CRUZES ★

The home of João Zarco is said to have occupied this site. Today's residence, however, dates from the 18th century and is a museum, where you can get to know the lifestyle of rich citizens of Madeira in the past. Sometimes INSIDER TIP concerts of classical music are held here. The quinta lies within an archaeological park with exotic plants and stone Manueline windows, as well as a fragment of the 15th-century pillory *(pelourinho)* of Funchal. *Closed Mon | admission 3 euros, Sun and garden free | Calçada do Pico 1 | www.museuquintadascruzes.com*

Manueline fragments in the archaeological park of Quinta das Cruzes

SANTAMARIA DISTRICT (ZONA VELHA)
You will be charmed by Funchal's old town: the semi-ruined fishermen's quarter has developed into a fashionable night-life area with numerous bars, restaurants and Fado houses during the past few years. A special attraction is offered by the brightly painted doors in the

district which have been designed by local artists thanks to the art project *artE de pORtas abERtas (www.arteportasabertas.com)*. Having said that, if you ascend with the ★ ☆ cable car *Teleféricos da Madeira to Monte (daily 9am–5.45pm | 10 or 15 euros return trip | www.madeiracablecar.com)*, you will also notice that several buildings dating from the 18th and 19th centuries are still awaiting restoration. Despite a great deal of refurbishment, the narrow streets still exude an impression of the original atmosphere: you can still find quaint little corner shops and traditional craft workshops alongside trendy boutiques.

The *Capela do Corpo Santo*, a brotherhood chapel built by fishermen dating from the Manueline period, is situated in the middle of this quarter. On the eastern edge of the old town, you should not miss the pure Baroque façade of the *Igreja do Socorro* dating from the 18th century. Opposite this building, a lift takes you down to the coastal bathing complex *Barreirinha*. The most striking building in the Zona Velha is the yellow-painted *Forte de São Tiago,* which was constructed as a defence against pirates from 1614 onwards: there are plans to house Madeira's archaeological museum collection there in the near future.

While on the subject of museums, if you are interested in the history of the island, you should certainly go on a journey through time in the interactive *Madeira Story Centre (daily 9am–7pm | admission 5 euros | Rua D. Carlos I 27 | www.madeirastorycentre.com)* – there is a lot to see ranging from the volcanic origins of the island to the archipelago's significant historical events. What is more, you have an amazing view of the old town from the highly recommended ☆ INSIDER TIP roof garden restaurant on the third floor!

FOOD & DRINK

INSIDER TIP A BICA

Have the courage to go down the inconspicuous steps: in this cosy restaurant next to the Market Hall, you can mingle with the natives, eat good food at moderate prices and take a look at the nostalgic photos of Funchal on the walls. *Closed on Sun | Rua do Hospital 17 | tel. 2 91 22 13 46 | Budget–Moderate*

A CUBA

On first sight, this snug adega looks like a wine storehouse: there are even a few tables standing inside a gigantic wine barrel. It is however well worth visiting, not only for its rustic atmosphere: here you can try Madeira's typical specialities such as tomato soup, scabbard fish, bolo do caco or meat skewers, but the excellent pepper steak is also recommended. Despite its central location, the prices are unbeatably modest, particularly if you order a dish of the day for lunch. *Closed on Sun | Rua do Bispo 28 | tel. 2 91 64 69 30 | Budget–Moderate*

BIOFORMA ⊛

A highlight for vegetarians even though the snack bar is on the lower floor of an organic grocery store and only serves lunch. The dishes are, however, very tasty and good value! *Closed on Sat/Sun | Rua da Queimada de Cima 31 | tel. 2 91 22 92 62 | www.bioformaonline.com | Budget*

DOCA DO CAVACAS

A fish restaurant by the sea – just the way it's supposed to be, and particularly romantic at sunset. The *Poças do Gomes* natural swimming pools located below the restaurant are also worth a visit. *Rua Ponta Cruz | Estrada Monumental | tel. 2 91 76 20 57 | Moderate*

LOJA DO CHÁ ●

The tea house in Funchal: in this inviting café, you can not only meet for tea, but also for tasty scones and snacks. Enjoy the hustle and bustle on the esplanade or the cosy living room flair inside. *Rua do Sabão 33–35 | tel. 2 91 22 13 09 | Moderate*

MERCEARIA DONA MÉCIA

With its delicious daily specials and cakes, this small terrace café located in the inner courtyard of an old-fashioned style grocery shop in the city centre is a local institution. *Daily | Rua dos Aranhas 26 | tel. 2 91 22 15 59 | Budget*

INSIDER TIP O REGIONAL

From the garlic bread with home-made dips to the luscious seafood stew with spaghetti, the dishes served here delight

LOW BUDGET

All the *museums* in Funchal open without charge on 18 May (world museum day) and 27 September (world tourism day). Additionally, many museums offer free admission on Sundays.

Many restaurants in Funchal serve a *dish of the day(prato do dia)*, usually at a price well below 8 euros, which often includes soup and a drink.

While most of the large gardens charge admission, some parks are free: *Santa Catarina* and *Jardim Municipal* parks, the *Jardim Panorâmico* in the hotel quarter and the *Parque Municipal do Monte*. The plants are marked with their names, and can be enjoyed while strolling on shady paths.

the palate, and the waiters with their traditional colourful waistcoats are helpful and warm-hearted. *Rua de Dom Carlos I 54 | tel. 2 91 23 29 56 | Moderate–Expensive*

RESTAURANTE DO FORTE ●

Are you looking for somewhere elegant to have dinner? In the tent pavilion in the São-Tiago fortress, local dishes such as scabbard fish are imaginatively interpreted and, should you wish, you can be driven there in a vintage car. *Rua Portão São Tiago | tel. 2 91 21 55 80 | forte.restaurant | Expensive*

RISO 🔆

Everything revolves around rice here. Portuguese classics are combined with the tastes of Asia, and are served in imaginative variations from crispy to sweet. If the weather is fine, you can sit on a wonderful terrace on the cliffs. *Rua de Santa Maria 274 | tel. 2 91 28 03 60 | Moderate–Expensive*

SHOPPING

ARCADAS SÃO FRANCISCO

In the centre of Funchal, there are several nice shopping arcades. The small shopping centre located in the grounds of the former Franciscan monastery is particularly attractive with boutiques, a flower shop and cafés. In the neighbouring *Blandy's Wine Lodge* (see p. 31) you can buy Madeira wine. *Closed Sun | Rua São Francisco 20 | arcadassaofrancisco.pt*

FÁBRICA SANTO ANTÓNIO

You can find home-made confectionery, jams, sorbets and biscuits in this historic shop. *Travessa do Forno 27–29*

MADEIRA SHOPPING ● 🔆

The largest shopping mall in Madeira is situated above Funchal with over 100 shops, a cinema, almost 20 restaurants and cafés and a *hipermercado* – an ideal programme for a rainy day. *Caminho de Santa Quitéria 45 | Santo António | www.madeirashopping.pt*

MERCADINHO BIO 🔆

Madeira's organic farmers sell their eco-friendly grown products on the Av. Arriaga.

BEACHES & SPORTS

BEACHES

Funchal does not have a white beach for sunbathers as in Calheta and Machico, but there are some attractive ways to get into the sea – via steps on the rocky coast or across the pebbles of a beach. *Praia Formosa* in the west of Funchal, much loved by young locals, is one such pebbly beach. Tennis courts,

restaurants and bars round off the fun. In Funchal's hotel district on the promenade, there are two pools that charge for admission *(Lido and Ponta Gorda, 5 euros each)*. In addition to steps leading down to the sea, they have proper swimming pools, paddling pools for children, spaces for sunbathing and sanitary facilities. The natural tidal pool **INSIDER TIP** *Poças do Gomes (2 euros)*, situated between Praia Formosa and the western end of the promenade by the Doca do Cavacas restaurant, is somewhat smaller, cheaper and has no man-made pool. In the historic quarter opposite the Igreja do Socorro, the *Barreirinha* pool charges 2 euros while a little pebbly beach next to the São Tiago fort costs nothing and is popular with the children who live close by.

ENTERTAINMENT

There is always something going on in Funchal: particularly at the weekend, the poncha bars and fado houses in the old town (Zona Velha) are full in the evening as well as the (rooftop) bars and pubs on the promenade in the Lido district and near the Pestana Carlton Hotel focused around the Rua Favila. Some cafés even transform themselves into popular music bars. Once midnight has passed, the clubs begin welcoming customers (the admission price frequently includes a drink) with DJ sets and live acts. Dancing to Afro and Latin rhythms is especially popular on Madeira.

CAFÉ DO TEATRO

By day tourists and locals drink their coffee In the theatre café; in the evening the trendy crowd takes over. There is a mixed, tolerant clientele: alternative-minded students, chic yuppies, and sometimes holidaymakers who didn't come to Madeira to sleep, dance the night away to DJ sounds or live music. *Sun–Thu 8am–1am, Fri 10am–4am, Sat 9am–5am | Av. Arriaga | www.facebook.com/cafedoteatro*

Open to interpretation: a casino in the shape of a crown of thorns

CASINO DA MADEIRA

Diners and clubbers, gamblers and architecture aficionados: all of these rave about the casino, an extravagant construction designed by the Brazilian cult architect Oscar Niemeyer in the shape of a crown of thorns that resembles the cathedral of Brasília. Night owls come to try their luck at the gaming tables and dance to live music in the Copacabana disco. The renowned ● *Mandolin Orchestra (www.madeiramandolinorchestra.com)* performs every Wednesday during the playing season in *Centro de Congressos the belonging to the Casino. Av. do Infante | www.casinodamadeira.com*

INSIDER TIP HOLE IN ONE
This café with its cosy outdoor seating area turns into a trendy music bar in the evening. The live performances by Portuguese and international musicians will delight a wide audience and not just the golfing crowd. *Daily 11am–2am | Estrada Monumental 238a*

TEATRO MUNICIPAL BALTAZAR DIAS

The municipal theatre is often used as a concert hall. Madeira's classical orchestra *(www.ocmadeira.com)* performs in the Neoclassical auditorium. *Av. Manuel de Arriaga | tel. 2 91 21 51 30*

TRAP MUSIC BAR

This lounge bar and disco in the hotel quarter is full of glitz and glamour. Live bands perform at weekends and the dancing goes on until the early hours. *Mon–Thu 8pm–4am, Fri/Sat 8pm–5am | Rua do Favilla 7 | www.facebook.com/trappub*

VESPAS

On weekends and before public holidays, this traditional disco at the cruise ship harbour plays house, electro and pop music for its youthful crowd. Women can enjoy a free drink and pay no cover fees on the regularly held 'Ladies Nights'. *Fri/Sat midnight–7am | Av. Sá Carneiro 7 | www.facebook.com/vespasclub*

INSIDER TIP VINTAGE BAR
In this popular bar in the Zona Velha, the spirit of the 1970s, 1980s and 1990s lives on. Accordingly, it's a favourite night spot for the over-thirty crowd. *Wed, Thu, Sun 7pm–1am, Fri/Sat 8pm–2am | Rua Santa Maria 23 | www.facebook.com/23vintagebar*

WHERE TO STAY

ALBERGARIA DIAS

You are just minutes away from the bustling old town, but can still enjoy a quiet stay in this family-run hotel. There is even a small pool. If you book a suite on the fourth floor or a room with a **INSIDER TIP** sea view on the third floor, you will have a fantastic view of the roofs of the Zona Velha across to the Atlantic. *35 rooms | Rua Bela São Tiago 44B | tel. 2 91 20 66 80 | www.albergariadias.com | Moderate*

HOTEL MONTE CARLO

Some would perhaps consider this hotel situated high above the city centre as old-fashioned, shabby and in need of renovation, but anyone who has a liking for authentically charming old buildings with Art Deco furniture and historical photos or would like to feel as if in a film dating from the 1960s, will love it here. And wait till you see the view! If you are interested in the fascinating story of a house over a hundred years old – the helpful family owners will only be too pleased to show you around and talk about the old days. *33 rooms | Calçada da Saúde 10 | tel. 2 91 22 61 31 | hotelmontecarlo-madeira.pt | Moderate*

The terrace of Reid's Palace in the morning hours – it fills up in the afternoons

PESTANA CR7

Admittedly, you will occasionally catch sight of a few photos of the brilliant but – should we say – sometimes narcissistic world-class football player in the stylish hotel personally opened by the star himself, but to tell the truth, it is really cool. Its location in the centre of the harbour is in itself fantastic. The artificial turf along the 100 m/328 ft long corridor invites you to sprint and the DJ sets at the rooftop pool provide a great excuse to have fun. And it is possible to train off the excellent breakfast (with smoothies) in the fitness centre or on your personal yoga mat in your hotel room. Nevertheless, a warning: guests who are not fans of Ronaldo will not enjoy their stay. *49 rooms and suites | Av. Sá Cameiro/Praça do Mar |* *tel. 2 91 14 04 80 | www.pestanacr7.com | Expensive*

PORTO SANTA MARIA

Do you dream of staying in the town and yet directly near the sea? This elegant and modern hotel offers you both! Warm colours, a sunny terrace, a small indoor and outdoor pool are just what you need to relax. *146 rooms | Av. do Mar e das Comunidades Madeirenses 50 | tel. 2 91 20 67 00 | www.portostamaria.com | Expensive*

QUINTA MAE DOS HOMENS 🌿

This charming and elegant historic house with a pretty garden and pool offers a view over Funchal. The 22 studios and apartments are ideal for self caterers. *Rua Mãe dos Homens 39 | tel.2 91 20 44 10 | www.qmdh.com | Moderate*

REID'S PALACE ★

A dream of a hotel – fulfilled in the building of this luxurious residence by William Reid at the end of the 19th century. Today it still remains the best (and most expensive) house on the square; the location of the palace surrounded by a sub-tropical park at the end of the bay of Funchal is unique in itself, not to mention the first-class restaurants and the spa. If you would like to experience a touch of nobility, the hotel's legendary ● Afternoon Tea (34.50 euros, please make a reservation) is also accessible for (correctly dressed) ordinary mortals. *158 rooms | Estrada Monumental 139 | tel. 291717171 | www.belmond.com/reids-palace-madeira |* Expensive

SANTA MARIA

This always seems to have been a colourful location with a focus on young persons – the boutique hostel in the town centre was once a primary school. Roomy dormitories are available alongside luxury brightly-decorated double rooms with vintage baths. In good weather, you can have breakfast in the brightly decorated courtyard, which is transformed into a popular fish restaurant in the evenings. There is a communal kitchen for self-catering guests and a lounge for those who want to chill out. The only disadvantage: at the weekend, it gets rather loud in the lively street. *11 rooms (both dormitories and double rooms with shared bathrooms are available) | Rua Santa Maria 145 | tel. 291649120 | www.santamariafunchal.com |* Budget

INFORMATION

POSTO DE TURISMO

Av. Arriaga 16 | tel. 2912119002 | www.visitmadeira.pt

Additional tourist office: *Centro Comercial Monumental Lido | Estrada Monumental 284 | tel. 291775254*

WHERE TO GO

CABO GIRÃO AND FAJÃ DOS PADRES
(137 D5 and E5)*(🕮 H7 and H8)*

There is a spectacular steep drop of 580 m/1903 ft at the so-called ☼ Cape of Return – only the ● glass platform of the Skywalk stands between you and the coast several hundred metres below. A breathtaking view – as long as you do not suffer from vertigo. You can see right to Funchal 13 km/8.1 mi to the west.

On the coast below, wine and vegetables are cultivated on the narrow fertile alluvial strip of land known as Fajã do Girão. If you would like to explore this area, you have to take the cable car (5 euros) in the district of *Rancho* slightly east of *Cabo Girão:* this is also how the farmers access their fields on the seashore.

Even more breathtaking is Madeira's newest ☼ cable car which takes you down 300 m/984 ft to the *Fajã dos Padres* in four minutes – a fantastic experience. At the bottom, a paradise awaits you where you can take a stroll through pergolas covered in grape vines, snorkel in the jetty area and go to the *Caribbean restaurant (tel. 291944538 | www.fajadospadres.com |* Moderate*). Cablecar Fajã dos Padres (Rua Padre António Dinis Henriques | Quinta Grande | daily 11am–6pm, in the summer Mon–Thu 10am–6pm, Fri–Sun 10am–7pm | return trip 10 euros)*

CÂMARA DE LOBOS (137 F5–6) *(🕮 J8)*

The town is located in a picturesque narrow bay 9 km/5.6 mi west of Funchal where colourfully painted fishing boats are jacked up, offering numerous photo motifs – sometimes you can see dried fish hanging in the sun. Winston

Churchill was a great fan of this idyllic harbour which he painted during his stay on Madeira from a small 🌿 panoramic terrace west of the harbour at the turn of the year 1949/50. A plaque commemorates the artistically gifted British statesman.

Câmara de Lobos (pop. 18,000) takes its name from the monk seals (Lobos marinhos) living here at the time of Madeira's discovery and had gained the reputation several years ago as a town with the most serious social problems (unemploy-

pel was built under the personal order of Zarco, the discoverer of the island, on the establishment of the town in the 15th century and was taken over and reconstructed by the charitable brotherhood of the fishermen at the beginning of the 18th century. The interior features paintings depicting fishing scenes.

After walking past numerous pubs and bars, you will come to the parish church *São Sebastião* decorated with blue and yellow Baroque tiles concealed behind a striking cliff which you can climb up us-

The harbour and fishing district is the heart of Madeira's second largest city, Câmara de Lobos

ment, alcohol and drugs). Today, however, you can take a wonderful stroll along the coast and through the old town. The walking and jogging path towards Funchal going past the swimming pool and remaining parallel to the sea is particularly attractive. In the fishermen's district, it is well worth visiting the *Capela de Nossa Senhora da Conceição*. The cha-

ing the steps on the coastal side. A further bathing area can be found east of the church below the newly renovated square *Largo da República*.

Next to the market hall, the light-flooded restaurant *Vila do Peixe (Rua Doutor João Abel de Freitas 30 | tel. 2 91 09 99 09 | www.viladopeixe.com | Moderate-Expensive)* offers excellent cuisine: you can select fresh fish to be cooked on the grill. Alongside fishing and small-scale boat construction, the wine cultivated in the heights of the *Estreito de Câmara de Lobos* provides one of the main sources of income. In gratitude, the **INSIDER TIP** *Festa do Vinho* is held annually to mark the wine harvest at the beginning of September. The lively festival celebrates the age-old traditions of Madeirans ranging from the procession of the winegrowers bringing the grapes to be pressed to the traditional treading of the grapes. You will find stylish accommodation in the modern area built around the historic mansion *Quinta do Estreito (46 rooms | Rua José Joaquim da Costa | tel. 2 91 91 05 30 | www.quintadoestreitomadeira.com | Expensive)* with a swimming pool, garden, gourmet restaurant and a cosy rustic tavern.

CANIÇO (139 E5) (*Ⓜ N8*)

Caniço de Baixo with its hotel complexes, restaurants, cliff bathing areas and the promenade leading to the pebble beach Reis Magos has become a popular holiday resort. The actual town centre of Caniço is 200 m/656 ft above sea level: during the past three decades, it has developed from a village cultivating onions (now only commemorated by an annual onion festival in May) to a town with a population exceeding 23,000.

There are only a couple of original features such as the modest parish church dating from the 18th century and a few surrounding houses, one of which is today an excellent grill restaurant *Central (Rua João Paulo II 30 | tel. 2 91 93 43 44 | Moderate)*. The hotel *Quinta Splendida (166 rooms | Estrada da Ponta da Oliveira 11 | tel. 2 91 93 04 00 | www.quintasplendida.com | Moderate-Expensive)* is set amidst lush botanical gardens below the church, offering generous ● spa

facilities, pool and a charming gourmet restaurant in the historical mansion. Even if you are not staying at the hotel, you can still visit the fantastic ● hotel garden with an attractive ◗◖ viewpoint and trees, flowers and herbs labelled with their botanic names. A guided tour in English is also offered once a week (dates available at the reception desk).

Don't forget to go and see the *Cristo Rei do Garajau*! This statue of Christ has been standing guard above the pebble beach of *Garajau* since 1927, making it older than its big brother in Rio de Janeiro! You can also enjoy the fantastic view of Funchal.

CURRAL DAS FREIRAS
(137 F2) (*Ⓜ J5–6*)

A trip to the valley of the nuns is literally breathtaking, particularly if you happen to meet a bus coming from the opposite direction on the drive up the narrow mountain road to the viewpoint ◗◖ *Eira do Serrado* (1095 m/3593 ft). The thrilling drive is however well worth taking: the view from Miradouro of the around 500 m/1640 ft lower lying "valley of the nuns" and the jagged mountain tops surrounding the almost circular valley basin is unique. The valley was formerly thought to be the crater of a volcano, although the landscape was actually created by the small rivulet now snaking through the ravine. There is no convent here although the name of the town – which translates as "stable of the nuns" – originates from the sisters of the Poor Clares in the Convent St Clare in Funchal who owned land (and stables) here.

The chapel erected by the nuns has now been replaced with a modern building. From the ◗◖ **INSIDER TIP** cemetery, you have a grand view over the lower part of the valley and the steep rock face on which an amazing hiking path (approx.

1.5 hours) with old paving ascends to *Eira do Serrado*. Specialities from the valley are available in the rural taverns: chestnuts in all variations. An especially good place to sit is on the terrace of the *Sabores do Curral (Caminho da Pedra | tel. 2 91712 57 | Budget)*. For an overnight stay, the comfortable ☆ *Estalagem Eira do Serrado (26 rooms | tel. 2 91710060 | www.eiradoserrado.com | Budget)* can be highly recommended with its sauna, indoor pool and restaurant.

JARDIM BOTÂNICO ●(138 C5)(𝄞 *L7*)
There is always something in bloom in the Botanical Garden thanks to the hard-working gardeners and favourable climate. During your tour round the different sections of the garden situated about 3 km/1.9 mi from the city centre, you will gain a vivid impression of the tropical, sub-tropical and native plants that flourish on Madeira. In the 19th century, the *Quinta do Bom Suces-*

so ("of good success") with its approximately 20 acres of land belonged to the hotelier family Reid: the first trees were actually planted in this period. Today, the old manor house houses a touchingly old-fashioned natural history exhibition. A small *café terrace* is hidden amongst the luscious greenery near the ☆ *miradouro*. The valley station of the *cable car (daily 9am–5pm | 8.25 euros, return journey 12.75 euros | telefericojardimbotanico.com)* spanning the *Ribeira de João Gomes* gorge and leading to Monte Is situated at the northern edge of the park. *Jardim Botânico: daily 9am–6pm, in the summer half-year until 8pm | admission 6 euros | Caminho do Meio).*

MONTE (138 C4) (𝄞 *L7*)
Up in Monte, the climate is generally slightly cooler and damper. During the 18th and 19th centuries, numerous elegant manor houses were built on the slope 8 km/5 mi above Funchal, many

From here, it is straight downhill: with the basket sledge from Monte to Funchal of which were inhabited by wealthy Britons and elegant families from other European countries. In 1921, Karl I, the last Austrian Emperor, even sought refuge in exile here and accepted the offer to stay with an acquainted family. It was probably the damp lodgings that brought on the bout of pneumonia that would be the cause of his death a year later. The now beatified Habsburg monarch is buried in the pilgrim church *Nossa Senhora do Monte*. The Baroque church consecrated in the 19th century is the destination of the largest annual pilgrimage to the Virgin Mary held on 15 August. In the main square below the church, the idyllic *Largo da Fonte* with the former valley station of the cog railway which was in operation between 1894 and 1943, the inhabitants of the island fetch healing water from a spring. The pretty *Municipal Garden (admission free)* stretches from here down to the valley along the ramp of the former cog railway.

In front of the church steps, the drivers of the ⭐ ● *basket sledges (Mon–Sat 9am–6pm | 30 euros for a double sledge and 25 euros for an individual sledge)* are waiting to steer their customers in these historical sledges *(carros de cestos)* around 2 km/1.2 mi down to Livra-mento where expensive taxis are waiting for them. This sledge ride without snow and between moving traffic is probably unique in the world and therefore a special highlight for tourists in Madeira. The (exclusively male) basket sledge drivers belong to a type of guild and wear their special white outfit with a blue jacket and straw hat. Their shoes are reinforced with a special type of rubber.

Equally spectacular is the 15-minute ride in the modern *cabin cable car* departing from the valley station next to the INSIDER TIP *Tropical Palace Garden* in Monte. Back in the 18th century, a villa already existing on this spot was transformed into the elegant *Monte Palace Hotel* towards the end of the 19th century, which, however, gradually fell into decay after World War II. In 1987, the wealthy South African José Berardo (Joe Gold) bought the overgrown property where he created the enchanting artistic and tropical garden *Jardim Tropical Monte Palace (daily 9.30am–6pm | admission 12.50 euros | Caminho do Monte 174 | www.montepalace.com)*. You can stroll among a fairy-tale jumble of laurel trees, palm ferns, azulejo tiles, terracotta soldiers and other art works, walking past koi fish ponds, Buddha

SLEDGING IN SUMMER

Who could have had the idea of pulling tourists in basket sledges on wooden runners down to the valley? It is said that a British merchant in the 19th century was looking for a suitable means of transport to bring him quickly and comfortably to his office in Funchal. Oxen pulled the wicker baskets for part of the way, but on the steep stretch from Monte down to Funchal the best method was two strong men who pushed off the *carro de cesto* and steered it swiftly down to the valley, braking at the end. Nowadays, the basket sledgers do not even have to drag their vehicles back up to Monte: the steep prices paid by modern tourists finances the return trip by lorry.

High above Funchal: the Oriental Garden, part of the Jardim Tropical Monte Palace

figurines and oriental doorways. You can also marvel at the largest vase in the world made on a potter's wheel at the Romantic swan lake. Do not forget to visit the *Monte Palace Museum* in the upper part of the garden: 1000 sculptures from Zimbabwe are exhibited on the top two floors and one of the largest private mineral collections can be found in the basement – the exhibition INSIDER TIP "Mother Nature's Secrets" displays a unique abundance of glittering precious stones and minerals.

PALHEIRO GARDENS ★
(139 D5) (*M7*)

On the old road to Camacha, 9 km/ 5.6 mi east of Funchal at 600 m/1969 ft above sea level, one of the island's most beautiful and varied gardens can be found: the Palheiro Gardens *(daily 9am–5.30pm | admission 10.50 euros)*. The *Quinta do Palheiro Ferreiro* once belonged to the Count of Carvalhal. In the 18th century, he used the grand house there as a hunting lodge, but his descen-

dants wasted the family fortune, and so in 1885 the estate became the country seat of the Blandy family, a British dynasty of wine merchants. They built themselves a new residence on the grounds. This private country villa is surrounded by a carefully planned English garden with superb subtropical plants. Behind the chapel, the garden opens out to luxuriant strelitzias and a water-lily pond; in front of the quinta the sunken garden unfolds a gorgeous world of colours. The Gardens are also famous for their camellias.

The shady *teahouse* is the place to rest after walking round the garden. It is situated between the golf course and the *Casa Velha do Palheiro (37 rooms | Rua de Estalagem 23 | São Gonçalo | tel. 2 91 79 03 50 | www.casa-velha.com | Moderate–Expensive)*. This luxury hotel stands within the walls of the former residence of the Count of Carvalhal. It has been extended through the construction of a spa and a restaurant that serves exquisite food *(Expensive)*.

THE SOUTH

Fishing villages by the sea, narrow terraces for growing bananas, a bare high-altitude plateau, vineyards and charming little bays – no more than a few miles from the island's lively capital you can experience the unspoilt natural beauty of Madeira's landscape.

From steep coastal rocks, waterfalls cascade onto little beaches and winding roads, dense growths of agapanthus line the wayside, houses are surrounded with colourful blooms, and shady picnic spots with grills for cooking *espetada* tempt travellers to take a break. Tourism may be on the up in the south of Madeira, but there are still plenty of opportunities to discover the region without joining the crowd. Especially on walking trails through the villages that lie above the coast you can gain a remarkable impression of how country people live here. Old women in headscarves labour on tiny potato fields, or men climb across the terraces carrying 80 kg/176 lbs of bananas over their shoulders.

This is all in great contrast to the scene in the coastal towns: the old trading port of Ribeira Brava, the Mediterranean-like community of Ponta do Sol, and Calheta, a former centre of the sugar-cane industry which now benefits from the bright sand of its beach, provide pleasant living conditions for their residents. In coastal villages such as Madalena, Jardim and Paúl do Mar, growing numbers of keen surfers who have come from far and wide rub shoulders with fishermen and banana farmers.

From the coast to the plateau –
the south of Madeira can be pretty
and lively, or rugged and sleepy

CALHETA

(134 C4) (*$\varnothing$ C–D5*) Unadulterated beach life! You can go swimming on the light sandy beach and stroll along the palm-lined coastal promenade at the yacht harbour in the largest town on the sun-kissed southern coast (pop. 3100).

Calheta spreads through a narrow river valley up the steep coast. A few brick chimneys and historical distillery equipment stand as a memorial to the significant role of sugar cane in this town. Even today, there is still a sugar cane festival after the (now much reduced) sugar cane harvest in the spring. The most spectacular art and cultural centre of the island was built high up on the cliff above the town – the *Mudas* Museum. Calheta also offers a special event around Christmas: every year, the church community sets up a wonderful **INSIDER TIP** nativity crib with life-sized figures and occasionally real animals.

CALHETA

SIGHTSEEING

IGREJA DO ESPÍRITO SANTO

In the parish church, you can still see attractive ornamentation on the gateway, a carved wooden ceiling in the Mudéjar style and a tabernacle made of ebony and silver on the high altar, which have survived numerous reconstructions since the 15th century.

MUDAS. MUSEU DE ARTE CONTEMPORÂNEA ●

The architecturally striking art gallery displays the museum's temporary exhibitions of contemporary art. You have an amazing view from the ☼ terrace of the museum restaurant INSIDER TIP *Mudas Arte e Sabor (tel. 2 91 63 07 16 | Moderate)*. The museum also includes a shop and a cafeteria. *Closed Mon | admission 4 euros | Estrada Simão Gonçalves da Câmara 37 | www.cmcalheta. pt/en*

SOCIEDADE DOS ENGENHOS DA CALHETA ●

Fans of poncha swear by the sugar cane spirit *(aguardente)* from Calheta that is used to mix the Madeiran mini-cocktail. It is produced here in one of the last remaining intact sugar cane mills on the island. You can take a look at the historical equipment and learn the history of the mill in the small *Museum*. Then you can try the finished product in the *Bar Adega*, preferably in the form of poncha or sugar cane honey – *mel de cana*. *Daily 8am–8pm | Av. Dom Manuel I. 29*

Cutting edge: the Mudas Museum building perfectly harmonises with its exhibitions of contemporary art

FOOD & DRINK

Modern restaurants with large terraces mostly serving native dishes can be found at the yacht harbour.

NEW ERA ☼

Here you can enjoy excellent octopus dishes – spicy on request – whilst

52

enjoying the wonderful view of the harbour. *Av. Dom Manuel I./Loja 8 | tel. 2 91 09 81 38 | Moderate*.

BEACHES & SPORTS

SWIMMING
There is golden yellow sand on Madeira's sunny coast! The two man-made beaches at Calheta attract a few tourists, but most of all Madeiran weekenders – and the beach that was created using Moroccan sand is seldom crowded.

MADEIRA PARAGLIDING
Up in the sky! The experienced paraglider Hartmut Peters offers INSIDER TIP paragliding tandem flights every afternoon (weather permitting): experienced leisure-time pilots are also permitted to use the take-off site in Arco da Calheta by prior arrangement. *Rua Achada de Santo Antão 212 | mobile 9 64 13 39 07 | www.madeira-para gliding*

WHALE WATCHING
You can approach these marine mammals without disturbing them either in the restored fishing boat "Ribeira Brava" or the speed boat "Stenella". The German-Madeiran team from *Lobosonda* are involved in the protection of whales and provide statistics for scientific research by passing on whale and dolphin sighting data to the Whale Museum in Caniçal. *Mobile 9 68 40 09 80 | www.lobosonda.com*

WHERE TO STAY

ATRIO
The very cosy house built in the style of a quinta is perfectly tailored for hikers: you can for example hire sticks and torches and begin your trip directly from the hotel. After your hike, you can relax in the heated outdoor swimming pool or at the fireplace bar. The hosts attach special importance to harmony with the environment: solar panels are used to heat the water and breakfast includes homemade specialities and herbs from the garden. *22 rooms | Caminho dos Moinhos 218 | Estreito da Calheta | tel. 2 91 82 04 00 | www.atrio-madeira.com | Moderate*

CASA DO CALHAU GRANDE
These eight meticulously renovated stone houses are situated among palm trees and green terraces on a sunny mountain slope above Calheta, each offering self-catering for groups of two to six. There is a fantastic view of the sea and you can swim in the pool at the lower end of the property. *Caminho do Massapez 10 | Arco de Calheta | mobile 9 64 89 46 32 | www.calhaugrande. com | Moderate*

MARCO POLO HIGHLIGHTS

⭐ **Atrio**
Stylish accommodation with the atmosphere of a modern country house in Calheta → **p. 53**

⭐ **Paúl da Serra**
A high-altitude plateau that feels like Scotland – with breathtaking views → **p. 55**

⭐ **Cable lift of Achadas da Cruz**
It descends almost vertically to the fields by the coast → **p. 56**

⭐ **Boca da Encumeada**
In good weather the view reaches both coasts → **p. 58**

CALHETA

WHERE TO GO

JARDIM DO MAR AND PAÚL DO MAR

These two remote fishing villages are among the oldest settlements on the island. *Jardim do Mar* (134 B3–4) (*øø B5*),

yard. *The Jardim do Mar (27 rooms | Sítio da Piedade | tel. 2 91 82 22 00 | www.hoteljardimdomar.com | Budget)* is recommended for an overnight stay. *Paúl do Mar* (134 A3) (*øø B4*), frequently neglected by tourists, plunges into the sea

Banana plants and old farmouses: Madalena do Mar

5 km/3.1 mi from Calheta, with its population of 200, is surrounded by the fertile land of a coastal plateau. From the main square in the historic centre a lane leads down to the sea, where a fort once stood and a modern promenade has now been built. You can reach there by passing through the crooked alleyways in the centre of the village. A small stone-built house right on the esplanada houses the *Portinho* restaurant *(Rua do Portinho | tel. 2 91 82 71 35 | Budget)*, which specialises in seafood. The waves break directly below the terrace to the delight of surfers. After surfing, everyone (including the water rats) congregates in *Joe's Bar (Vereda do Poco Velho | mobile 9 66 13 02 08 | Budget–Moderate)*, a cosy pub restaurant with a jungle-like court-

in front of almost vertical cliffs. A huge rubber tree provides shade in the village square of the elongated site with a population of around 900. The elder inhabitants like to meet in the square for a chat. At the harbour where the children of the village jump into the sea, a statue and the colourful fishing boats provide a reminder that the locals were once all dependent on fishing, some continue to be so. You can enjoy delicious fish specialities and a sea view at the simple restaurant ⭐ *Sol e Mar (Av. Pescadores Paulenses 80a | tel. 2 91 87 21 40 | Budget–Moderate)*

MADALENA DO MAR (135 E5) (*øø E6*)

Some wealthy residents of Funchal own weekend homes in this high-class coastal village (pop. 500). It is strung out on a long bay at the foot of steep terraced slopes used for growing bananas, some 3.5 km/2.1 mi from Calheta. Enjoy the outdoor terrace of the restaurant *Cantinho da Madalena (Av. 1° de Fevereiro 2 | tel. 2 91 97 22 35 | www.restaurantecantinhodamadalena.com | Moderate)* with its great view.

PAÚL DA SERRA ★
(130 A–B6) (F4)
This plateau, 11 km/6.8 mi northeast of Calheta, reminds visitors of a moor landscape in the uplands of Britain. Only sturdy plants like grasses, gorse and bracken can cope with the inhospitable climate at an altitude of over 1000 m/3281 ft. The ground here stores rainwater like a sponge and is the source of *levadas* which distribute water to many parts of the island and channel it to hydroelectric plants. Dozens of wind generators turn their blades here high in the sky. Strong winds often blow up on the plateau, and when, as so often, the winds are joined by fog, then it is easy to understand why plans to construct an airport up here were quickly shelved. In good weather, however, there are stunning views from the panoramic road. About halfway across the plain, a road descends to the valley of *Rabaçal*, where walks lead to the *Risco waterfall* and to a valley basin in the rocks named *25 Fontes* (25 springs).

PRAZERES (128 C6) (C4)
This village (pop. 700, 7.5 km/4.7 mi northwest of Calheta) is an excellent base for walking in the west of the island: on trails going down to Paúl do Mar, along a number of little *levadas* or up to the Paúl da Serra plateau. The only attractions are the *Quinta Pedagógica dos Prazeres* (p. 111), a botanical park run by the parish with animals and a shady INSIDER TIP café *(Budget)* and the *parish church* with its two towers. It dates from the 18th century, but was restored in 1940. For dining in cosy surroundings try the *Restaurante Chico (Rua Igreja 164 | tel. 2 91 82 28 36 | Budget–Moderate)*; for an overnight stay, check out the environmentally friendly hotel *Jardim Atlântico (97 rooms | Lombo da Rocha 1 | tel. 2 91 82 02 20 | www.jardimatlantico.com | Expensive)* with its sports and spa facilities.

PONTA DO PARGO

(128 A3–4) (A2–3) **The most beautiful lighthouse (*farol*) on Madeira is situated on the west coast and is the principle attraction of the community of Ponta do Pargo (pop. 900) widely scattered over six districts.**

LOW BUDGET

The *Casa da Cecília (10 rooms, 1 appartment | tel. 2 91 82 26 42 | www.houseofcecilia.com)* in the centre of *Jardim do Mar* is a welcoming B & B with an unbeatable view out across the cliffs to the sea. An overnight stay in such a spectacular location at such an attractive price (from 30 euros) is hard to find.

In the large, plain hall the *farmers' market of Prazeres* is not beautiful, but there are always a dozen local farmers here who sell fresh fruit and vegetables, as well as bread, honey and cake, at low prices.

PONTA DO PARGO

A beacon of light: the moon above the lighthouse of Ponta do Pargo

At the base of the lighthouse on the Rocha da Vigia completed in 1922, there is a permanent exhibition *(daily 9.30am–midday and 2–4.30pm | free admission)* featuring photos focusing on lighthouses on the island. You have a magnificent view of the steep coast dropping 312 m/1024 ft into the sea from the ⊱ square at the foot of the lighthouse. This village on the western tip of Madeira is named after a tasty kind of bream called *pargo*, which swim in abundance in the local waters. The modest village centre of Ponta do Pargo lies around the church of *São Pedro*, which possesses an attractive painted ceiling done by a local Belgian artist.

FOOD&DRINK

A CARRETA ●
Rustic espetadas and other typical specialities of the island are served at this simple guesthouse favoured by hikers. *Lombada Velha | tel. 2 91 88 21 63 | Moderate*

O FORNO
The Bennett family will cater to all their guests' culinary needs, whether you choose a juicy steak from the open wood fire or a vegetarian dish. You must try the *poncha*, which is fantastic! *Closed Mon | Estrada Ponta do Pargo 316 | Salão | tel. 2 91 09 83 41 | Moderate*

WHERE TO STAY

There are no hotels in Ponta do Pargo, but a number of attractive holiday apartments.

QUINTA DO ESPIGÃO ⊱
A private house beautifully situated on a cliff surrounded by trees (minimum stay: 1 week). *Caminho de Portela Abaixo 1 | Serrado | mobile 9 65 88 23 17 | quintilha.com | Moderate*

WHERE TO GO

ACHADAS DA CRUZ
(128 C2) *(ⓜ B–C 1–2)*
A modern ★ cable car (*teleférico*) is the principal attraction of the little village Achadas da Cruz (pop. 160) 10 km/6.2 mi northeast of Ponta do Pargo, which has a sleepy air. The cabins of the cable lift sway downward, seemingly vertically, to cover the difference in height (300 m/984 ft) to the fields by the rocky coast below. Apart from the farmers, few tourists visit this location. *Outward and return journey 3 euros*

FAJÃ DA OVELHA ☀ (128 B5) *(∅ B4)*
12 km/7.5 mi south of Ponta do Pargo, this settlement (pop. 1100) is perched on a raise high above the Atlantic. The church of *São João Batista* with its lovely bell tower dates from the 17th century. A few typical old houses remain in the village itself. Fajã da Ovelha commands a fine view of the cliffs, with Paúl do Mar at the bottom. For the INSIDER TIP best *poncha* in this area go to the snack bar *Moinho (tel. 2 91 87 21 81 | Budget)* in the district of Maloeira. Although often tightly packed at the weekend, this bar has a rustic charm all its own.

RIBEIRA BRAVA

(136 B–C4) *(∅ G7)* **The "wild river" *(ribeira brava)* has created a dramatic valley in which there is not a lot of free space alongside the now tamed river and the connecting road to the north coast.**
The inhabitants of the valley regularly lost their homes and properties when the river swelled up to a roaring torrent – on the other hand, the village Ribeira Brava (pop. 6600) owes its very existence to its location at the intersection of the trading routes between the north coast and Funchal. The attractive village opens out on the sea: the clean streets, a charming coastal promenade with cafés and trees bringing shade and the swimming spot on the shingle beach are so inviting that it is tempting to stay there for a longer time. On 29 June, a huge festival is celebrated in honour of St Peter (São Pedro) whose highlight is a procession of boats along the coast.

SIGHTSEEING

OLD QUARTER
The historic core of the town can be found on either side of the pedestrianised *Rua do Visconde*. Here, little shops supply everyday needs, and some of them have even incorporated a bar to serve drinks. The *Câmara Municipal (town hall)*, a pink-painted quinta dating from the late 18th century, lies hidden behind the tall old trees of an attractive *park*.

What would you give for a deckchair? – the pebble beach at Ribeira Brava

RIBEIRA BRAVA

IGREJA DE SÃO BENTO

The most conspicuous feature of the parish church is its steeple with a blue-and-white pattern in tiles and a globe (an armillary sphere), the symbol of the Portuguese explorers. The foundation stone of the church was laid as early as 1440, which makes it one of the oldest places of worship on the island. During the Baroque period, however, it was given a completely new look. The original furnishings include a baptismal font donated by King Manuel I of Portugal in the chapel to the right of the entrance and the Manueline pulpit.

MUSEU ETNOGRÁFICO DA MADEIRA

Madeira's folk museum is housed in a fine 17th-century residence. The exhibitions in these stylish surroundings document traditional crafts, means of transport and methods of cultivating and harvesting crops on the island. In the little souvenir shop you can buy woven fabrics that were made in the museum. Part of the museum is used as a gallery to display changing exhibitions of contemporary art. *Sun/Mon closed | admission 3 euros | Rua de São Francisco 24*

FOOD & DRINK

RESTAURANT & GRILL MURALHA

Genuine works of art are created on your plates: your mouth begin to water as soon as the dishes are brought to the table. The fish and seafood are simply magnificent! What is more, you have an excellent view of the sea from the ☘ terrace. *Closed Mon | E. R. 220 1 | tel. 2 91 95 25 92 | Moderate*

WHERE TO STAY

HOTEL DO CAMPO ● ☺ ☘

The certified eco-hotel situated high above the town offers many comforts ranging from the outdoor pool in the garden, jacuzzi and sauna and a lounge bathed in light. This is a place to spend a quiet relaxing holiday with an amazing view. *34 rooms | Estrada da Banda de Além 25 | tel. 2 91 95 02 70 | www.hoteldocampo.com | Expensive*

INSIDER TIP QUINTA DO CABOUCO

The restored mansion house is surrounded by a flourishing garden with exotic fruits, which you are welcome to eat. There is a distinct family atmosphere in Filomena which has created its own small picturesque oasis with meticulous attention to detail above the Ribeira Brava: many friendships have been forged around the large round breakfast table, on the fully-glazed veranda and in the well-equipped kitchen for guests. *3 rooms | Caminho do Cabouco | mobile 9 18 69 69 96 | www.quinta docabouco.com | Budget*

INFORMATION

TOURIST INFORMATION
Forte de São Bento | tel. 2 91 95 16 75

WHERE TO GO

BOCA DA ENCUMEADA ★ ☘
(137 D1) (*H4*)

13 km/8.1 mi north of Ribeira Brava and some 1000 m/3281 ft above sea level, this "mouth" (*boca*) in the mountain range opens up to provide a thrilling panorama ranging across the north coast with São Vicente, the plateau of Paúl da Serra, the valley of *Serra de Água* and the wild heart of the mountains with their ravines and peaks. A number of demanding hikes start from the pass – over Pico do Jorge and Pico das Torrinhas to Pico Ruivo, for example.

The accommodation options here include the cosy and elegant ☆ *Pousada dos Vinháticos* with its log cabin annexe located a bit below the *Boca da Encumeada (21 rooms | Serra de Água | tel. 2 91 95 23 44 | www.dorisol.com | Budget)* or the hotel ☆ *Encumeada (49 rooms | Serra de Água | tel. 2 91 95 12 82 | www.hotelencumeada.com | Budget),* which also offers a superb mountain vista as well as hearty dishes from the grill and regional cuisine.

PONTA DO SOL (136 A4) (*E–F7*)
Between two high rocky capes, the town (pop. 4500, 3.5 km/2.2 mi west of Ribeira Brava) rises from the sea to the sky. The old heart of the settlement consists of the church and a couple of dozen houses – and beyond that terraced fields of bananas. On the coast, a beach of grey stones fringes the bay, which draws the locals in summer. On the coastal promenade, there are two hotels and several friendly pubs in the tiny centre of the village. Especially popular is the *Old Pharmacy (Rua Doutor Joao Augusto Teixeira 23 | mobile 9 27 79 38 66)* which is transformed from a comfortable café bar with a vintage souvenir shop during the day to a cool cocktail bar in the evening where the drinks are sold as "antidepressants"!

A great place to stay overnight is the *Estalagem Ponta do Sol (54 rooms | Quinta da Rochinha | tel. 2 91 97 02 00 | www.pontadosol.com | Moderate–Expensive)* situated on a high rock cliff high above the coast, a puristic new site surrounding a historical manor house with pool and popular bar. Or how about camping in tents between banana plants, fruit trees and a waterfall? In the remote mini tent site **INSIDER TIP** *Canto das Fontes (Caminho dos Anjos | www.cantodasfontes.pt | Moderate),*

In Ponta do Sol the church was built on the slope

nature lovers can slumber in one of two tepees, a yurt or even a cave. 100 m/328 ft below Roberto's organic plantation, the waves roll constantly over the shingle beach – an amazing soundtrack!

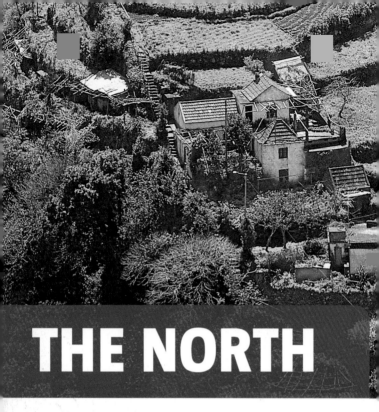

THE NORTH

Between Porto Moniz and Porto da Cruz the island's rugged side becomes apparent: the coast is steeper, the ocean is wilder, a strong wind often blows, great waves come rolling in to delight surfers, and almost twice as much rain falls as in the south. However, there is a wealth of spectacular sights and experiences to make up for the weather.

A narrow cliff road winds along the coast, often right beside the waves. Nowadays bypass tunnels have been drilled through the rock in many places, but the drive is still an adventure – if only for the wonderful views and the waterfalls that tumble down from the heights. The scenery also features bizarrely shaped towers of rock and natural pools of lava that cooled and solidified thousands of years ago – and almost ev-

erywhere walls have been added to them to make modern swimming pools. In some places terraces of vines cling to the rocky slopes, while elsewhere fertile valleys open a way into the heart of the island and climb up to the mountain ranges with their pointed rocky peaks, barren upland plateaus and jungles of laurisilva forest.

The inhabitants of the villages along the north coast lead a quiet life, almost independent of the world around them. For a long time they could reach the south only by sea or via paths across the mountains. This led to the emergence of strong, coherent village communities with all the facilities they needed to exist. Today tunnels connect them with Funchal, and many people commute there each day to their jobs. However, life in the villages has kept

Crashing waves, wonderful views, pools in lava rock – the rugged north of Madeira is a landscape full of adventure

its rural character – and those who live here are not easily roused or flustered, not even by the tricks that the weather plays on the side of the island where the trade winds blow.

PORTO MONIZ

(129 D1) *(ⁿ D1)* **Famous for its volcanic swimming pools, the pretty coast-** **al community Porto Moniz (pop. 1700) pulls in crowds of visitors in summer and at weekends – especially Madeirans.**

Porto Moniz has now been smartened up, not only by renovating the *piscinas naturais*, which wind and waves formed over thousands of years. The harbour too has been extended, the old fort restored, a helicopter landing pad built and a seaside promenade constructed. This promenade, the *Passeio Público Marítimo*, is the site of the modern science centre called *Centro Ciência Viva (daily 10am–*

PORTO MONIZ

Splashing around to your heart's delight – the lava pools offer relaxation next to the raging sea

6pm | admission 3.50 euros | Rotunda do Ilhéu Mole | www.portomoniz.cien ciaviva.pt) as well as the ● Aquário da Madeira (daily 10am–6pm | admission 7 euros | Rua Forte São João Batista) with more than 70 species of marine animals. Settlement in Porto Moniz began around 1574, when Francisco Moniz, whom the king of Portugal had appointed to administer these lands, came to live here. Until the 19th century, the town was a whaling station and trading port – and could only be reached by sea. The first coastal road was not built until the mid-20th century.

The historic centre of Porto Moniz lies above the port, around the 17th-century church of Nossa Senhora da Conceição. If you arrive from Ponta do Pargo or Paúl da Serra, don't miss the superb view down to the coast from the ⬥ Santa viewing point on the road above the town centre. A few bends before you get there, in Lamaceiros, a square with a mill, grill huts and toilets marks the starting point of the Levada da Ribeira da Janela, which flows 25 km/15.5 mi to Fonte do Bispo.

FOOD & DRINK

Numerous restaurants along the coastal promenade offer customary Madeiran cooking, particularly fish and lapas grelhadas (limpets). Many offer seating directly above the beach such as the popular ⬥ Sea View (in the Hotel Aqua Natura | Rotunda da Piscina 3 | tel. 2 91 64 01 00 | Moderate). The cuisine is slightly more rustic in the ⬥ Restaurant Salgueiro (Lugar do Tenente 34 | tel. 2 91 85 00 80 | Moderate), but there is still a view of the sea.

SWIMMING

You can swim all year round in the ★ ● lava pools (Piscinas Naturais) (admission 1.50 euros) with numerous concrete areas for sunbathing, even in winter when the sea is slightly cooler. There are also onsite changing rooms and (cold) showers. Although these facilities are not available at the pool at the restaurant Cachalote (admission free), you will probably see more fish here which are splashed over the wall at high tide if you have a face mask and snorkel. In the past, these natural traps were used as a method of catching fish: the sap of a euphorbia plant that is poisonous to fish but harmless for humans was added to the water in the pool, so that the fish floated on the surface and could simply be collected. Today the pools are a poison-free and refreshing place to swim; on busy summer days sunbathers lie cheek by jowl on the concrete surfaces.

WHERE TO STAY

AQUA NATURA ◉ �

There is nowhere else on Madeira where you can stay overnight closer to the sea than here! You have great views of the cliffs and Atlantic, even from the whirlpool. What is even better is that the young hotel is aiming for comprehensive sustainability. *25 rooms | Rotunda da Piscina 3 | tel. 2 9164 0100 | www. aquanaturamadeira.com | Moderate–Expensive*

INSIDER TIP CASA DO RIBEIRINHO

A 100-year-old house between the sea and the mountains with ten beds for self-caterers. *Sítio do Ribeirinho | Santa do Porto Moniz | tel. 2 9185 0140 | www. casaribeirinho.com | Budget*

INFORMATION

TOURIST INFORMATION

Opposite the piscinas naturais | tel. 2 9185 30 75 | www.portomoniz.pt

WHERE TO GO

RIBEIRA DA JANELA (129 E2) (⌘ D1)

In the course of millennia, the water of this river, which flows into the ocean here, has carved out a magnificent, deeply cleft valley with rock walls that have a

low cover of laurel forest in places. The ravine is an amazing sight. The village (pop. 230, 2 km/1.2 mi southeast of Porto Moniz) and the river take their name from a finger of rock in front of the river mouth, at the tip of which a window-like opening *(janela)* has been formed. At the edge of the village a road and the INSIDER TIP *Levada dos Cedros* lead inland to *Fanal* (129 E–F4) (⌘ D–E3), one of the most unspoilt and greenest parts of the island.

SANTANA

(132–133 C–D 3–4) (⌘ L–M 2–3) **Santana is the best-known town (pop. 3500) on the north coast of Madeira, thanks to its old wooden thatched houses.**

About 100 of these ★ ● *casas de colmo* still exist in and around the town. A few of them have been reconstructed next to the modern town hall; behind its colourful façade one contains original furnishings and a craft workshop, for example

---

★ **Lava pools**
Swimming among the volcanic rocks – natural pools in Porto Moniz → p. 62

★ **Casas de colmo**
Thatched and brightly coloured: almost like the world of Asterix and Obelix → p. 63

★ **Pico Ruivo**
Madeira's highest summit is accessible to walkers → p. 65

★ **Grutas de São Vicente**
Take a walk into the bowels of the island → p. 67

MARCO POLO HIGHLIGHTS

Living (housing) history: *casas de colmo* in Santana

for linen weaving, and another houses the tourist office. Anyone who is reminded of Asterix and Obelix at the sight of these brightly coloured little houses is not far wide off the mark: they probably have a Celtic origin. Families occupied them until a few decades ago, living here in extremely spartan conditions. In the lower room there was space for a bed, a seat and a washbasin. Children slept under the pointed roof, which could only be reached from outside, through a skylight. Family life took place mainly outside the house. Today a few *casas de colmo* have extensions and are still occupied.

Below the church of Santana a sign points to the INSIDER**TIP** *Rocha do Navio*, a nature reserve established to protect endemic coastal plants and rare sea birds. At the weekend, a lift runs several times a day for the farmers, also transporting holidaymakers *(return trip 5 euros)* from the cliff down to the tiny beach, next to which there are a few little fields. Not far from the village centre, you will find the *Parque Temático da Madeira* (see p. 111), whose Madeiran cultural attractions are primarily focused on families.

FOOD & DRINK

CANTINHO DA SERRA

This rustic country inn offers a cosy interior which is particularly welcoming in winter when the open fire is crackling. The portions of rustic dishes such as octopus with onions and braised kid in a clay pot are so substantial that they are often enough for two. *Estrada do Pico das Pedras | tel. 2 91 57 37 27 | Moderate*

SERRA E MAR ●

The traditional family restaurant serves marine delicacies such as black scabbard fish and mountain cuisine. The prices are moderate and the portions very generous – no wonder that it also enjoys such popularity with the local villagers. *Rua Baixo da Igreja | tel. 2 91 57 38 95 | Budget–Moderate*

WHERE TO STAY

QUINTA DO FURÃO ☼

Enjoy the stillness of nature! This friendly hotel is situated in remote tranquillity on the edge of a steep cliff, surrounded only by vineyards and vegetable fields. There are magnificent views along the north coast, the hotel restaurant offers top-class cuisine and the clean rooms, heated pool and cosy fireplace bar are further comforts. An attractive INSIDER TIP steep coastal hiking trail runs straight from the hotel, leading parallel to the sea to São Jorge. *45 rooms | Estrada Quinta do Furão 6 | tel. 2 91 57 01 00 | www.quinta dofurao.com | Expensive*

INFORMATION

TOURIST INFORMATION
Sítio do Serrado | tel. 2 91 57 51 62

WHERE TO GO

FAIAL (133 E4–5) (*M–N3*)
Amidst terraces of grapevines and orchards this charming village of 1600 residents, 9 km/5.6 mi southeast of Santana, nestles at the foot of a mountain by the sea – the *Penha de Águia* ("Eagle Rock", 600 m/1969 ft). Ospreys are said to have nested there, and seen from the right angle its western flank looks like a bird's head – hence the name. From the ☼ summit, you have an amazing view along the north coast, but it is a pretty arduous ascent to the top.

If the prospect of trout in bacon with a mountain of vegetables and sweet potatoes sounds enticing, stop at the *Casa de Chá do Faial (Lombo do Baixo | tel. 2 91 57 22 23 | Moderate)*. The locals as well as tour operators appreciate this restaurant with its furnishings of wood and basketwork and a great vista from the ☼ INSIDER TIP roof terrace.

PICO RUIVO ★ ☼
(132 A6) (*K4*)
Madeira's highest mountain (1862 m/6109 ft), 10 km/6.2 mi southwest of Santana, is the last stop on a wonderful hike via Achada do Teixeira. If the weather is kind, the panorama from the summit is breathtaking. The ascent to the peak on a paved path is not difficult and takes no more than one hour. The mountain hut is not currently open.

Walkers who are fit and well equipped can press on to the 1818 m/5965 ft *Pico do Arieiro* (138 B1) (*K5*). In early summer a unique display of endemic alpine flowers can be seen here, e. g. yellow Madeira violets. In very dry summers, this vegetation suffers due to forest fires, but the always wet winters climate enables nature to recover fairly quickly.

PORTO DA CRUZ
(133 F5–6) (*N4*)
The port *(porto)* of the cross *(cruz)* that was erected by the first inhabitants is one of the oldest settlements on the island, today with a population of 2600, 12 km/7.5 mi southeast of Santana. There is a wonderful walking route along the small promenade, beginning at the esplanade cafés at the eastern shingled beach leading to the swimming area popular in summer and the tiny "harbour". When you have reached the western beach bay, you will immediately see the *sugar mill,* which is one of the last still existing mills on the island and can be visited free of charge. You are welcome to taste the high-proof end products in the adjoining shop.

A good place to stop off is the rustic inn *A Pipa (Casas Próximas | mobile 9 68 52 74 00 | Budget–Moderate)*. The landlord Zé is well known among Madeirans for his particularly tasty fish dishes. If you would like to stay overnight in Porto da Cruz, a good recommendation situated right next to the sea is the family hotel *Vila Bela (12 rooms | Rua da Praia 23 | tel. 2 91 56 33 81 | www.vila-bela.com | Budget–Moderate)*.

QUEIMADAS (132 C5) (*LL3*)

From the car park of the *Rancho Madeirense* holiday village (on the road to Pico das Pedras) a shady path leads about 2 km/1.2 mi along a *levada* and through green laurel woodland to the *Queimadas forest lodge*. From Santana a narrow lane leads up to a former charcoal-burners' settlement. This is a picturesque spot at an altitude of 900 m/2953 ft in a clearing surrounded by rhododendrons and has an area with ponds and picnic tables. This is the starting point of the wonderful laurel forest hike along the *Levada do Caldeirão Verde* which offers stunning views of the coast and leads to the small green lake *Caldeirão Verde* that is fed by a small waterfall (around 4 hours there and back). Sure-footed hikers with a head for heights can continue hiking from the "Green Kettle") to the *Caldeirão do Inferno*, the "Kettle of Hell" (an additional 2 hours there and back).

SÃO JORGE (132 C2–3) (*LL2*)

The main attraction of the village (pop. 1500, 6 km/3.7 mi northwest of Santana) is the *Igreja de São Jorge*. With its gilded Baroque carvings and 18th-century tiled frieze, this parish church is regarded as the most beautiful and artistically valuable place of worship in the north of the island. Directly behind the church, a typical rectangular thatched house harbours a little restaurant, *Casa de Palha (Achada Grande | tel. 2 91 57 63 82 | Budget)*, where diners are served skilfully prepared regional dishes. Be sure to try the *consomé de camarão no pão*, a creamy shrimp soup in a bread bowl. From the church, a road leads to the *Ponta de São Jorge*, jutting into the sea with its lighthouse *(farol)*. From the former lookout for whale watching **INSIDER TIP** *Ponta Vigia* near the lighthouse you can enjoy the coastal views undisturbed.

The lookout point *Cabanas* on the road to Arco de São Jorge affords a dizzying vantage point. Farmers often sell tropical fruit here to tourists who come to take photos. Shortly before Arco de São Jorge, flower lovers should visit the *rose garden (Roseiral)* of the *Quinta do Arco (April–Nov. daily 11am–6pm | admission 5 euros | Sítio da Lagoa | tel.*

LOW BUDGET

The *camp site near Ribeira da Janela* has an area of 1.2 acres. The cost per person per night is 2.80 euros (up to 25 years of age: 1.70 euros). The price per tent ranges from 3 euros (up to 43 ft²) to 7 euros (over 269 ft²).

There are five *youth hostels (Centros de Juventude)* on the archipelago, one of them in Porto Moniz *(22 beds | tel. 2 91 85 39 15)*.

All hostels (Funchal, Calheta, Porto Moniz, Santana, Vila Baleira) are open to older guests. Those over the age of 30 pay an extra 3 euros above the normal price (6–9 euros).

2 91 57 02 50 | www.quintadoarco.com)
with over 1 700 different varieties. Just
a few metres away, the small *Museu do
Vinho e da Vinha (Tue–Sat 2-6pm | admis-
sion 2 euros)* is interesting for wine lovers.

CAPELINHA DO CALHAU
In 1692 a striking little chapel dedicat-
ed to St Vincent was built into the rock
that stands where the Ribeira de São

A – well-illuminated– journey to the interior of the volcano: the Grutas de São Vicente

SÃO VICENTE

(130–131 C–D 4–5) (ΰ G–H3) **The tiny
centre of the pretty little town São Vicente (pop. 3400) is so well concealed
behind a cliff that you have to look hard
not to miss it.**
While the coastal promenade and walkway through the greenery alongside the
river have generous dimensions, the
neat little houses in the old town are
squeezed into a few narrow alleyways
surrounding the parish church.

Vicente flows into the sea. Mosaics made
with pebbles from the beach adorn the
Baroque façade.

GRUTAS DE SÃO VICENTE ★●
How about going on a trip to the interior of the island? You will travel into
the geological past of Madeira on a
guided tour (Port./Engl.) through the
700 m/2297 ft long lava tunnel system. The easily accessible caves Grutas de São Vicente were created during a volcanic eruption 890,000 years
ago and offer a number of striking

features. In the adjoining *Centro do Vulcanismo (daily 10am–7pm | admission 8 euros | Sítio do Pé do Passo)*, you can learn more about volcanic phenomena in general and the origins of the island – and also travel into the interior of the earth with a lift!

IGREJA DE SÃO VICENTE

The sanctuary and side altars of this 18th-century church are decorated with the gilded carvings *(talha dourada)* typical of Portuguese Baroque. A beautiful azulejo frieze adorns the walls, and the painting on the ceiling of the nave shows St Vincent blessing the village that bears his name.

FOOD & DRINK

QUEBRA MAR ⚜

While you eat your hearty fish soup, the waves are breaking right next to you on the shingle beach… This inn really has the best location in the village and the finest view of the north coast. *Sítio do Calhau | tel. 2 91 84 23 38 | restaurante-quebramar.com | Budget–Moderate*

TABERNA DE SÃO VICENTE

Friendly and simple: this tasca offers native cooking and large portions and singing on Saturday evenings when it becomes transformed into a karaoke bar! *Closed Mon | ER 104 | tel. 2 91 84 64 51 | Moderate*

WHERE TO STAY

SOLAR DA BICA ⚜

The small family paradise is situated in the upper valley of São Vicente. The 13 rooms and one apartment all have a veranda where you can enjoy the view. You can relax in the heated pool, the sauna or in the pretty garden. *Sítio dos Lameiros | tel. 2 91 84 20 18 | www.solardabica.pt | Budget–Moderate*

WHERE TO GO

PONTA DELGADA (131 E3) *(*𝄞 J2*)*
Once a year, the otherwise tranquil village (pop. 1400, 7 km/4.4 mi east of *São Vicente*) experiences a mass invasion: on the first Sunday in September, pilgrims and islanders keen on festivities arrive to venerate the wooden figure of *Senhor Bom Jesusor* simply to amuse themselves at one of the largest church festivals on the island. The crucifix is said to have been washed up here in the 15th century in a chest. The church that was erected on the spot where it was found burned down almost completely in 1908, and the flames spread to the crucifix too. The charred remains of it were saved, and are kept in a glass case in the new church, which is decorated in the Baroque style.

If you take the ⚜ path that leads around the apse, you can enjoy a fine view towards the coast near São Jorge. The *Monte Mar Palace (111 rooms | tel. 2 91 86 00 30 | www.montemarpalace. com | Moderate)* hotel above the cliffs boasts a seawater pool, a health club, and courts for tennis and squash. A more intimate alternative to this luxury accommodation is situated 2 km/1.2 mi away among terraces of grapevines and vegetables in the village of *Boaventura.*In the cosy, rustic atmosphere of the *Solar da Boaventura (30 rooms | Serrão Boaventura | tel. 2 91 86 08 88 | www.solar-boaventura. com | Budget)*, a house dating from the 18th century with modern extensions and excellent cuisine, hikers will feel particularly comfortable and enjoy the fantastic restaurant *São Cristóvão*

(Sítio São Cristóvão | tel. 2 91 86 30 31 | Moderate) located on the green steep coast.

ROSÁRIO ☀ (131 D5) *(𝄙 G4)*

A bell tower stands alone on a hill 4 km/2.5 mi south of São Vicente. The local inhabitants had the tower built In the 1950s to honour the Virgin of Fátima. This meant that they now had their own Fátima chapel and no longer needed to visit the mainland on their pilgrimages. The ascent is well worth undertaking to have a panoramic view across the entire valley of São Vicente.

SEIXAL (130 A3) *(𝄙 E2)*

Seixal is 7.5 km/4.7 mi west of São Vicente. You can see the houses of this hamlet of around 650 residents already from afar, radiant on a rocky headland. Almost every house has its own garden with vines whose grapes are sold in the autumn to make wine. Both Seixal and the neighbouring Porto Moniz are ideal for swimming, although not many tourists venture this far. There is a seawater swimming pool and a black sandy beach below the plateau on which the village is situated.

The fish for the restaurant *Solmar (Sítio da Ponte | tel. 2 91 85 48 54 | www. residenciasolmar.com.pt | Budget–Moderate)* come straight from the sea to the table. You can also stay overnight in the restaurant's own guest house *(6 rooms | Budget)*. A good alternative is the *Casa das Videiras (4 rooms | Sítio da Serra d'Água | tel. 2 91 22 26 67 | www. casa-das-videiras.com | Budget)*, a country house almost like a museum on the slopes of the Serra de Água.

At the eastern end of Seixal, you can ascend the deep, green one-way valley *Chão da Ribeira* where the INSIDER TIP *Casa de Pasto Justiniano (tel. 2 91 85 45 59 | www.*

Lilies fringe the path to the Fátima Chapel of Rosário

casadepastojustiniano.com | Moderate) serves fresh trout and tasty beef skewers. If you really want to get away from it all, you can sleep in a luxurious tepee tent at the heart of nature – wonderful! This is offered by *Nature Inn (Chão da Ribeira | mobile 9 17 73 83 25 | www.nature innmadeira.com | Budget–Moderate)*.

THE EAST

The eastern part of Madeira displays an incredible diversity with a changing landscape, new valley and new view over the next bay every few kilometres.

Cool green hills are contrasted by barren desert-coloured earth and contemporary architecture is paired with the traditional locations of ancient crafts. Despite the great variety, the sea is never out of sight, frequently tempting you to go in for a swim.

Here in the gentle bays of the east were the first landing places for explorers, pirates and fleeing lovers: the places between Gaula and the Ponta de São Lourenço are more steeped in history than in other parts of the island. You are also highly likely to begin your journey in the east since this is the location of the modernised airport with its – now no longer feared – runway. The future of the island is most visible in this region: the container port at the former whale catching station Caniçal, the exclusive yacht harbour settlement Quinta do Lorde and the industrial areas bordering the highway leading to the west of the island. It is unfortunately true that progress is not always attractive, but there is no need to panic! If you wish to escape from the built-up coastal area, you only need to drive a few kilometres up the hills where you will still find the well-preserved original Madeira, including typical island venues for food and drink offering rustic meat skewers and potent *poncha*.

Plenty of history and contrasts – the east of the island is where the first explorers landed, and where projects for the future are emerging

CAMACHA

(139 E4) (*N7*) **Camacha nurtures its traditions. The craft of basketry is still very much alive in the highest-lying district of Madeira. And where would the football-crazy Portugal be now if a certain son from this village had not introduced this ball sport here?**

The year 1875 is proudly commemorated in a memorial in the main square. One of the sons of the wine merchant family Hinton had learned to play football while studying in England and subsequently wanted to tell his friends in Camacha about this game. This was how Madeirans became the first to learn to play football, a game no Portuguese could do without today.

The village with a population of 7500 is situated on a fertile mountain ridge almost 700 m/2297 ft above the sea. Apple trees are cultivated in the surrounding terraced fields which the fun-loving inhabitants have to thank for their annu-

The woven zoo at the Café Relógio is certainly a matter of taste

al apple festival – and the sparkling *cidra* (apple wine). There is plenty of folklore in this area: the local dance and music groups are said to be some of the most vivacious on the island. It could be that 'dancing to get warm' helps to overcome the frequently damp coolness at this altitude. While on the subject of dampness: some families still thank their entire livelihood to the craft of basketry: the *vimeiros* mostly sit in damp and cold cellars to work as the wicker stems are

more flexible in damp conditions. You can marvel at the products at the basketry market *Café Relógio*: some very useful (wonderful wicker furniture) and some totally impractical (delicately made dust catchers in the form of frogs). In the demonstration workshop in the basement, you can see the condition of the basket makers' hands after decades of weaving!

After your visit in the Café Relógio, it is well worth taking a look round the 'modern' Camacha nearby. When the village church on the main square became too small, the parish was provided with a new church in 1997. Its exceptional architecture is reminiscent of the Casino in Funchal designed by Oscar Niemeyer – the inhabitants of Camacha are therefore extremely proud of their unorthodox place of worship.

FOOD & DRINK

RESTAURANTE O CESTO

'The Basket' is a typical old-school family inn: with bar and café at the front and the dining area at the back. This is where you are most likely to meet the people of the village enjoying rustic Madeiran soups such as a warming wheat soup. The owner speaks good English and will help you choose from the menu. The soup is definitely to be recommended! *Rua Maria Ascenção 95 | tel. 2 91 92 20 68 | Budget*

SHOPPING

CAFÉ RELÓGIO

A cornucopia of basket products in all variations can be found on the two floors of the basket weaving centre which has sprung up around a now almost invisible clock tower from a former British summer residence: this explains its name

("Café Clock"). Although many products are somewhat kitschy, you will still find attractive and practical souvenirs. *Daily 9am–6pm | Largo Conselheiro Aires de Ornelas 12 | www.caferelogio.com*

WHERE TO STAY

CASAS VALLEPARAIZO
The nine beautifully restored manor houses are spread across a picturesque garden area in the Paradise valley of Camacha which certainly lives up to its name. The holiday homes accommodate between 2-6 guests. *Estrada Regional 102, Nr. 161 | tel. 2 91 92 21 74 | mobile 9 62 93 93 57 | www.valleparaizo. com | Moderate*

WHERE TO GO

PARQUE ECOLÓGICO DO FUNCHAL ⊛ (138–139 C–E 2–4) (*ℳ M6*)
Between Monte, the Pico do Arieiro, the Poiso Pass and Camacha, there is a protected area of around 1 000 hectares chiefly devoted to reforestation projects following forest fires. The *Centro de Recepção e Interpretação (Mon–Fri 9am–5pm | Estrada Regional 103, No. 259)* displays information charts on flora and fauna and offers workshops and environmental educational courses for school classes and other interested groups. Several hiking paths cross the nature reserve: information is available in the visitors' centre.

PASSO DO POISO (138 C2) (*ℳ M6*)
Roads from all four points of the compass meet at the top of the pass, which is located 10 km/6.2 mi northwest of Camacha at an elevation of 1400 m/4593 ft. From here you can drive up to the Pico do Arieiro, across to Santo da Serra, down to Funchal and also to Faial. What was once

a shepherd's shelter at the crossroads has recently been turned into the popular rustic restaurant *Casa de Abrigo do Poiso (8am–midnight | tel. 2 91 78 22 69 | Budget–Moderate)*, where the spicy bread soup called *açorda* and juicy beef skewers are served in front of a crackling open fire.

RIBEIRO FRIO (138 C1) (*ℳ M5*)
On the "cold stream", a few hairpin bends to the north of the Poiso Pass, 14 km/8.7 mi northwest of Camacha, the state forestry organisation has set up a trout farm and created a little botanical garden with camellias and laurel shrubs around the fish ponds, which are filled with water from the stream. Thanks to an ingenious system of sluices along the slope, the fish move from one pond to another as they increase in size. Finally you can admire enormous trout in a large round pool. Not far away fresh and smoked trout is served at the restaurant *Ribeiro Frio (9am–7pm | tel. 2 91 57 58 98 | Budget–Moderate)*.

Behind the restaurant is access to the ● ⚶ *Levada do Furado*, which surefooted walkers can follow for some 11 km/6.8 mi, with wonderful views of the north coast all the way, as far as the Portela Pass. If you prefer to take a short walk, look out on the road for

⭐ Museu da Baleia
The whaling museum in Caniçal tells the story of whales and how they were hunted from Madeira
→ p. 76

⭐ Ponta de São Lourenço
The eastern tip of Madeira – a wonderful treat for hikers → p. 77

MARCO POLO HIGHLIGHTS

a yellow sign marked „Balcões". From here it takes about 30 minutes to reach a ⬑⬏ lookout point.

MACHICO

(140 B3–4) (*M P5–6*) **Attractive squares and alleyways, a short but pretty coastal promenade and the light-coloured sandy beach that is Machico's pride and joy all provide an invitation to stroll around, relax and go for a swim. Madeira's oldest settlement has developed into an exciting small town (pop. 11,300) with a lively restaurant scene.**

The town is spread along the wide and fertile valley and up the steep mountain slopes. To experience the most vivid impression of the town, you should stroll along the Levada do Caniçal and take a look into the narrowest alleys: a new view across the Machico valley appears around every new corner. In 1419, the discoverers of the island first went ashore in this bay. They were, however, probably not the very first to reach the island; according to legend, a pair of English lovers, Anne Dorset and Robert Machyn, had previously been stranded here. It appears that the name of the settlement Machico was taken from his surname because the Portuguese explorers found a weather-beaten wooden cross engraved with this name. What would have been Madeira's fate if Anne had not died soon after the pair had been unintentionally stranded and had instead given birth to a few (English) children...

SIGHTSEEING

BANDA D'ALÉM

The historic fishermen's quarter lies on the east bank of the Ribeira da Machico. Where once ships' carpenters made wooden boats in a little shipyard, there is now a marina with a few pleasant cafés and restaurants. But Machico's greatest attraction is the INSIDER TIP light-coloured sandy beach which was created by deposits of sand brought from Africa and offers a perfect bathing site in the summer.

Playing dominoes is a serious business in Machico and not just for the players

CAPELA DOS MILAGRES

Largo dos Milagres, a square shaded by tall ficus trees, is the place where the first church on Madeira was built back in the year 1420. The "chapel of miracles" that stands there today dates from 1810. The previous building fell victim to disastrous floods, with the exception of the coat of arms on its gable and a doorway with a pointed arch. Fishermen miraculously salvaged the statue of Christ, which had been swept out to sea by the floods. A painting to the left of the altar depicts this event.

FORTS

In the 18th century the people of Machico tried to protect their easily accessible bay from pirate raids by constructing three forts. Two of these forts have survived: the *Forte de São João Baptista* to the east, which is not open to the public, and the triangular *Forte de Nossa Senhora do Amparo*. It is just a stone's throw from the latter to the newly developed promenade, between the new complex of the multipurpose *Forum Machico* and the mouth of the Machico river.

NOSSA SENHORA DA CONCEIÇÃO

The main parish church dates back to the 15th century. King Manuel I donated the side doorway with its three marble columns. The detailing on the main portal also still reflects the Manueline period: grotesque faces symbolise good and evil. As the interior of the church was thoroughly remodelled during the Baroque era, only the two side chapels hint at its original appearance. One of them displays the coat of arms of the Teixeira family. A statue of Tristão Vaz Teixeira, who ruled the eastern part of Madeira from Machico, stands on the square in front of the church.

Diagonally opposite is the *town hall*. It bears both of the town's coats of arms: the historic version, reportedly granted in 1499 by King Manuel I in the form of an armillary sphere, an astronomic instrument of that time, and the version chosen in the mid-20th century with an irrigation canal and two sugar-cane plants.

FOOD & DRINK

BAÍA BEACH CLUB

The 🌿 terrace directly on the coast is a perfect place to sit, particularly if you have a delicious ice-cream sundae in front of you! *Porto de Recreio | mobile 9 14 75 89 75 | Moderate*

PASTELARIA GALÃ

The inn is a pleasant combination of bar, confectioner's shop (with fantastic delicacies) and restaurant. Because of the reasonable prices and excellent food, you will meet a large number of islanders here. *Rua General António Teixeira de Aguiar 1/3 | tel. 2 91 96 57 20 | Budget–Moderate*

RESTAURANTE LILY'S 🌿

This fantastic restaurant situated above Machico is a gastronomic revelation! Lily will personally attend to your wellbeing and offers dishes including a delicious fish soup, beef in Madeira sauce and the 'catch of the day'. *Closed Mon | Estrada D. Manuel I 170 | Caramanchao | tel. 2 91 96 40 14 | www.restaurantelilys.com | Moderate*

WHERE TO STAY

DOM PEDRO BAÍA CLUB

Even though the hotel is somewhat outdated and is built in the form of a 'cube', you can spend a quiet holiday here directly on the coast. The rooms are clean and roomy and there is a large pool area and a hotel-run diving base. *218 rooms | Estrada de São Roque | tel. 2 91 96 95 00 | www.dompedrobaia hotel.com | Moderate*

RESIDENCIAL AMPARO

The rooms of this friendly guesthouse were designed by the star interior designer Nini Andrade. The guesthouse is located at the heart of Machico's historical quarter and only a few steps from the sea. The cuisine is excellent in the guesthouse's own restaurant. *12 rooms | Rua da Amargura | tel. 2 91 96 81 20 | www. amparohotel.com | Budget*

WHERE TO GO

CANIÇAL (140 C2) *(Q5)*

For a long time fishing, whaling and boat building put their stamp on Madeira's easternmost town (pop. 4000), 7 km/4.3 mi northeast of Machico. Today the large free-trade zone and the cargo port dominate the life of this rapidly growing community. For a reminder of Caniçal's past as a major whaling station visit the modern ★ *Museu da Baleia (Tue–Sun 10.30am–6pm | admission 10 euros | Rua Garcia Moniz 1 | www.ma deirawhalemuseum.org)*. This museum has information about the impressive sperm whales that were hunted and presents the history of whaling on Madeira, which continued until the 1980s, and the stages of the whaling business from manual harpooning from little rowing boats to the processing of the catch. For a snack, stop at *Muralha's Bar (tel. 2 91 96 14 68 | Budget)* opposite the new swimming pool, which has bags of character and mainly serves fish. It's one of the places where you can sometimes get INSIDER TIP *castanhetas*, small fish like anchovies. Some more bars and restaurants are strung out along the new harbour road as far as the shipyard or cargo terminal. further east, sailors prefer to drop anchor in the modern marine area *Quinta do Lorde (www.quintado lorde.pt)* where you will also find an exclusive swimming area, a smart restaurant and a cosy café.

In 1986 the sea near Caniçal was declared a ◉ *marine nature reserve*. This ensures that not only different whale species but also dolphins and the highly endangered monk seals can live undisturbed in these waters.

PICO DO FACHO ☼ (140 B–C3) *(P5)*

The bay of Machico is bordered on the east by the pointed 'beacon hill' which received its name during the time of pirate attacks when watchmen lit warning beacons on its peak. You can access this mountain via a small road beginning at the Caniçal Tunnel which leads to the hilltop at an altitude of 322 m/1056 ft (4.5 km/2.8 mi from the centre of Machico). From here you have a wonderful panorama not only over the bay of Machico and the airport, but also towards Caniçal and the Ponta de São Lourenço. At the weekend, the peak of this hill is a popular picnic area for local people.

PONTA DE SÃO LOURENÇO ★
(141 D–F2) (*Q–S5*)

The eastern tip of Madeira, 11 km/6.8 mi from Machico, is barren and windy. Clearing of the forest cover began here at an

hands of children, in the colours of ochre, rust-red, grey and greenish-black.
There is a picnic spot (no toilets) with a wonderful view of the sea and headland at Ponta do Rosto. The road leading to Ponta de São Lourenço ends at a car park (no toilets) for walkers above the *Baía de Abra*. The walk to the eastern tip of the island and back reveals you new scenic vistas at every twist and turn of the track.

Only a few metres of water separate the Ponta de São Lourenço from two islets, the Ilhéu de Agostinho and the Ilhéu de Fora. The latter is popularly known as

At Ponta de São Lourenço the coast drops almost vertically into the sea

early date, and later the land was used to pasture goats who immediately devoured any green shoots. As a result the landscape is now a scene of bare hills, which are carpeted in flowers in spring, and bizarrely shaped rocks that rise from the turquoise sea, as if piled up by the

Ilhéu do Farol, as Madeira's oldest lighthouse has occupied the summit since 1870. For the finest view of these off-shore islands and the lighthouse, you should go to the twin peaks of the 125 m/410 ft *Ponta do Furado*, the "pierced tip", as this hill is known thanks to holes that the sea has carved out of its rocks. The ascent is very steep, but spectacular views are the reward. You'll find an interesting visitor's centre in the Casa do Sardinha, home to the nature reserve's park rangers. The palm trees offer a nice shady spot for a picnic.

PORTELA (139 F1) (*m N5*)

This village, strung out along the road 9 km/5.6 mi northwest of Machico, marks the island's watershed. Its centre consists of a taxi rank, a bus stop and a lookout point with a rustic restaurant, the *aPortelaà vista (tel. 2 91 96 31 89 | Budget)*. From here the view across to the "eagle rock" Penha de Águia on the north coast is stunning. To the left, somewhat behind the flower stalls, is the start of a hiking path, which leads to Maroços in approximately 3 hours.

SANTO DA SERRA
(139–140 F2–A3) (*m O5*)

Long before Robert Trent Jones designed Madeira's first golf course at Santo da Serra (more precisely: at Santo António da Serra), many visitors came to the attractive, usually fresh and breezy hilly country 8.5 km/5.3 mi west of Machico in which this village (pop. 950) nestles.

Sugar magnates and other wealthy Madeirans built their summer homes here. Among them were the Blandy family, wine merchants who came to the island from England. Their estate, the Quinta do Santo da Serra near the church, is now public land, and the Madeirans love to come to its garden for a picnic. There is also a little zoo with ponies, deer and stags. At the rear of the garden, the a Miradouro dos Ingleses offers a panoramic view of the east of the island. From this place the Blandys once kept an eye on the ships approaching or passing by.

Snacks and meat skewers are on the menu in the rustic *A Nossa Aldeia restaurant (Sítio dos Casais Próximos | tel. 2 91 55 21 42 | Budget)*. For an overnight stay, the right address is the sky-blue *Porto Bay Serra Golf (21 rooms | Casais Próximos | tel. 2 91 55 05 00 | www.portobay. com | Moderate)*, stylish surroundings that can be enjoyed over INSIDER TIP afternoon tea.

SANTA CRUZ

(140 A–B 4–5) (*m O–P 6–7*) **Most tourists only see this small but pretty coastal town (pop. 7200) from the air**

FIRE, FIRE!

Every summer, everyone starts worrying: will there be fires again this year? The Madeirans are traumatised from the past few years in which fires broke out annually: in 2016, the fires even extended into the centre of Funchal. Is it because of climate change, arson or poor forestry? It is probably a combination of several factors which has led to

these now regular catastrophes. The island government has made attempts to reduce damage and reforesting with less problematic tree types than the highly inflammable eucalyptus and varieties of acacia. If there is suddenly really heavy rainfall during the winter, transforming the steep slopes to huge mudslides, all the work has been in vain.

a few seconds prior to landing at the neighbouring airport. Despite aircraft noise, it is well worth making a detour to visit the pleasant Santa Cruz.

You can stroll through the attractively paved streets to the atmospheric church square with the Igreja de São Salvador built in 1533 which still shows evidence of stonemasonry dating from the Manueline period. A promenade runs parallel to the sea and the shingle beach. While exploring, do not forget to pay a visit to the small INSIDERTIP *Market Hall*! At first sight, the building appears unpromising, but It is fascinating to watch the local inhabitants shopping there. Additionally, you can see agricultural and fishing scenes made of azulejo tiles by the Portuguese artist Outeiro Águeda.

FOOD & DRINK

TABERNA DO PETISCO

A rustic pub atmosphere, low prices, good poncha and delicious tapas – what more could you desire? Oh yes, you might also need a table... The message has got around the local inhabitants how good this tavern is! *Daily 6.30am–1am | Rua Cónego César de Oliveira 23 | tel. 2 91 64 35 25 | Budget*

ACTIVITIES & SPORTS

At the eastern end of the beach below a wall of black rock there is a pool, the *Praia das Palmeiras*. In *Ribeira da Boaventura* a *swimming complex* has been built with convenient access to the sea via a sheltered little bay between the area for water sports and the two swimming pools. A further attraction is the new *Aquapark* in Santa Cruz, which boasts pools, water chutes and all sorts of other fun.

Santa Cruz: fishing boat beneath a date palm

WHERE TO STAY

VILA GALÉ

This modern and comfortable hotel – although admittedly gigantic and frequently accommodating large groups – with its great location directly on the sea and only a few metres from the old town – owes its existence to the fact that the former football pitch was built over. The generously-proportioned pool area is amazing. *262 rooms | Rua São Fernando 5 | tel. 2 91 52 90 00 | www.vilagale. com | Expensive*

PORTO SANTO

Dourada, "the golden one", is what the locals call their island Porto Santo. **Almost 9 km/5.6 mi of golden fine-grained sand on the south coast live up to this name – and so does the caramel-coloured earth, which puts on a thin veil of green only in spring.**

Otherwise naked rock is the dominant feature of Madeira's dry little sister – which is proud of being the first island of the archipelago to have been discovered. Just a few thousand trees cling with their roots to several conical mountains – the first fruits of a forestation programme that began some time ago, after the revolution of 1974, and has now been adapted to the local conditions thanks to a local tree nursery and professional planting (by hand!).

Today it is almost inconceivable that forests of dragon trees once thrived, and later fields of corn swayed in the wind on the island, which is 11 km/6.8 mi long and 6 km/3.7 mi wide. Only a few years after a storm drove the Portuguese knights João Gonçalves Zarco and Tristão Vaz Teixeira to the coast of the previously undiscovered Porto Santo, the little island was being used as a supply station for seafarers undertaking long voyages. Christopher Columbus was one of the first of them when he landed on Madeira in 1478, though still in the role of a sugar merchant at that time. A little later, he married Felipa Moniz, the daughter of Bartolomeu Perestrelo, who was the first captain legate

The beauty of sand and rock – the charms of Madeira's island neighbour are miles of beach, crystal-clear ocean waters and lots of action

(a kind of governor) of Porto Santo at that time.

In the 16th century Spanish and Italian merchants discovered the riches that lay in the dragon-tree forests of Porto Santo: the resin of this palm-like plant was greatly coveted in Europe as a dye for textiles and lacquer. The merchants therefore bled the trunks of the dragon trees dry. This ruthless exploitation, but also forest clearance by fire and excessive pasturing, destroyed the island vegetation over a period of time. The soil dried out,

and fertile earth was washed into the Atlantic by the wind and rain. Much later the construction of a NATO air base swallowed up more agricultural land. Now the terraced fields on which fruit and vegetables were grown well into the 20th century largely lie fallow and the villages are in a state of decay.

Almost all of the 5500 inhabitants of Porto Santo live on the south coast now. Tourism has evolved into the main pillar of the economy. The visitors are for the most part Portuguese citizens from the

An idealised portrayal: Columbus in bronze

European mainland, and Madeirans too. In the peak season between July and September prices go through the roof: a hotel room costs twice as much in these months as in April or October. To compensate for this there is a lot going on – from a beach volleyball tournament to music and dance events. Outside the months when the Portuguese take their holidays, by contrast, the island goes back to sleep – even though it has a pleasant temperate climate almost all year round, and wonderful rock formations can be admired there at any time.

The tourism strategists are planning to change this situation, however, with the help of the broadly sweeping 18-hole golf course, which has been extended to the north by a further nine holes, and by improved marketing of the hydrotherapy treatment spa facilities and the sand, which is considered to have healing properties (e.g. for rheumatism). Additional hotels have been built, like the comfortable *Pestana Colombos Premium Club (185 rooms | tel. 2 91 14 40 50 | www.pestana. com | Expensive)*. Four restaurants and five bars cater to the all-inclusive guests at this five-star resort on the beach of Campo de Baixo. Like its luxurious affiliate, the *Pestana Porto Santo (275 rooms | tel. 2 91 14 40 00 | www.pestana.com | Expensive)* it is definitely moving more towards all-inclusive packages. Hotels with tropical gardens and elegant pool and spa facilities combined with the wonderful beach – no wonder that you will feel reminded of the Caribbean on Porto Santo.

VILA BALEIRA

(143 D3–4) (⌖ V–W11) **Do not be surprised if you feel you are in a village in the delightful main town. Vila Baleira**

with its population of 2600 is really not much bigger than a village, but is a highly attractive location!

This applies at least to the historic centre of Vila Baleira with its white houses, in whose shade sunburnt old men sit to play dominoes and a colourful mix of people meet for a cup of coffee.

About half of the island's residents have their homes in this miniature metropolis by the harbour, where there are at least a few banks and supermarkets. In summer the number of people crowding into this tranquil place is many times higher, especially on *Largo do Pelourinho*, in the pedestrian zone *Rua Zarco* with its cafés and bars and at the traditional-style stalls where grapes, melons and potatoes are on sale. The beach volleyball stadium at the harbour which was intended to pull crowds to new bars and clubs proved, however, to be an expensive misinvestment. The sums simply didn't add up as the young people preferred to play directly on the beach and spent their evenings celebrating in the beach cafés. The *Penedo de Sono* now stands abandoned just as the ambitiously (mis-) planned shopping centre Zarco west of the town. In contrast, the newly renovated promenade lined with palm trees was a resounding success: it is thronged with visitors strolling around and the modern *Market Hall* and the *Centro do Artesanato* made of glass and natural stone, providing a home for the tourist information office and handicraft shops in which craftsmen can be observed at work, are both popular destinations.

SIGHTSEEING

CASA DA CAMARA ANTIGA

The former town hall, flanked by two dragon trees, is a fine example of Portuguese Renaissance architecture. It was built in the 16th century, though several later alterations were made. The entrance, displaying the Portuguese coat of arms and the royal crown, is on the first floor, with two flights of steps leading up to it. Walk to the top of the steps to take a good look at the *Largo do Pelourinho*, which is shaded by palms and decoratively paved with stripes and a compass symbol in black and white.

CASA COLOMBO – MUSEU DO PORTO SANTO ★

The Columbus Museum collects material about seafaring and the history of Porto Santo, and above all anything connected with the life and the deeds of the famous explorer: ships' models, marine charts, engraved portraits. The collection occupies two buildings. The one at the rear is considered to have been the house where Columbus lived. He is said to have spent some time here in about 1480 as a sugar trader. The locals like to tell that Christopher Columbus looked out to sea here while living in his father-in-law's house and hatched the first plans for his later crossing of the Atlantic Ocean. The museum informs you not only about the story of Columbus and his voyages,

---

MARCO POLO HIGHLIGHTS

★ **Casa Colombo – Museu do Porto Santo**
It is a shrine to the navigator Christopher Columbus, who lived in this house for some time → p. 83

★ **Campo de Baixo**
A beach of fine sand runs all the way from the main town to the Ponta da Calheta, a distance of 9 km/5.6 mi → p. 85

but also about the age of the Spanish and Portuguese navigators in general. *Closed Mon | admission 2 euros | Travessa da Sacristia 2–4 | www.museucolombo-portosanto.com*

NOSSA SENHORA DA PIEDADE

An *azulejo* medallion shines as blue as the sea on the white façade of the parish church. This place of worship was founded in 1430 and attacked many times by pirates. Consequently, the Morgada chapel on the south side is the only original part that remains. The church owes its Baroque appearance to various architects of the 17th century and houses an altar painting by Max Römer, a German painter who visited Porto Santo several times in the 1940s. *Rua Cristóvão Colombo*

FOOD & DRINK

O FORNO

Visit this rustic grill restaurant if you would like to try top-class meat skewers on Porto Santo. *March–Oct. | Av. Henrique Vieira de Castro | tel. 2 91 98 40 35 | Moderate*

PANORAMA RESTAURANT & LOUNGE BAR ↘↙

The name says it all: there is a wonderful panoramic view over the southern side of the island, Vila Baleira and the beach and a cosy lounge atmosphere. And if that was not enough, the artfully prepared cuisine is also especially tasty. You should however always reserve a table as the window seats are very popular. *April–Dec., evenings only | Estrada Carlos Pestana Vasconcelos | Casinhas | tel. 9 66 78 96 80 | www.panorama-restaurante.pt | Moderate*

PÉ NA ÁGUA

Here you are sitting almost literally with one 'foot in the water' or at least in the sand! The beach restaurant primarily serves fresh fish, but you are also welcome to order a cool beer in the afternoon. In the summer, it is lively here until

Not meals in a basket – the whole restaurant is a basket: Pé na Água

late into the night with regular live music and DJ acts. *Sítio das Pedras Pretas | tel. 2 9198 3114 | www.facebook.com/penaagua | Moderate*

SHOPPING

CENTRO DE ARTESANATO

The shops in the craft centre sell miniature windmills, straw hats and various items made from sea shells. *Av. Doutor Manuel Gregório Pestana Jún.*

BEACHES

The golden-yellow sandy beach of ⭐ *Campo de Baixo* starts at the harbour and goes all the way to *Ponta da Calheta* (142 B5) (∅ U12). It is by far the most beautiful beach on the Madeiran archipelago, and is the reason why Porto Santo has evolved into a tourist destination for holidaymakers from Madeira and mainland Portugal. In summer it is crowded with sun-hungry and sand-loving tourists. To the west of Vila Baleira it gets broader, and is then supervised by lifeguards and equipped with toilets, showers (for a charge) and snack bars. To swim and sunbathe undisturbed, even in the peak season, go to the rocky INSIDER TIP *bay of Zimbralinho* (142 B5) (∅ U12) with its turquoise water. This beach can only be reached by walking from the little pass near Morenos.

ACTIVITIES & SPORTS

Some people might think that the only things to do on Porto Santo are to count the grains of sand, cool off in the water once in a while and perhaps play a little beach volleyball. A few others may recall that there is also an 18-hole golf course designed by the golf legend Severia-

Brilliant: a beach playground 9 km/5.6 mi long

no Ballesteros *Porto Santo Golfe (www.portosantogolfe.com)*. There is however much more to explore on the island, particularly in the summer when you can learn surfing, kite- and windsurfing or stand-up paddling: *On Water Academy (Cabeço da Ponta | mobile 9 64 83 85 35 | www.onwateracademy.com)*. Organised tours of the island are available including a jeep safari or explorations on foot at *Lazermar (mobile 9 63 50 14 88 | www.lazermar.com)*.

INSIDER TIP PORTO SANTO HORSE RIDING TOURS

Matias, Isa and their whole team including the horses will arrange wonderful horse-riding tours for everyone ranging from complete beginners to professional riders. *Portela, near the windmills | mobile 9 11 79 89 89*

CYCLING

Thanks to the cycle track built parallel to the beach, you can easily cycle around half the island. And if you hire a proper mountain bike, the hilly route round the rest of the island will also be no problem! Bicycles are available from *Auto Acessórios Colombo. Vila Baleira | Av. Vieira de Castro 64 | tel. 2 91 98 44 38 | www.aacolombo.com*

clude equipment, the tours are free of charge, but Matias would naturally welcome a tip.

HIKING

There are two signposted hiking routes: the ☆ "Vereda do Pico Branco e Terra Chã" (PR1) will lead you to the north-eastern tip of the island with great views (5.4 km/3.4 mi there and back) and the

The welcoming Vila Baleira in the evening: in summer, the village square is full of life

SNORKELING & DIVING

During the past few years, Porto Santo has developed into a paradise for scuba divers: numerous marine creatures can be observed in the clear and relatively warm water and wreck diving is an underwater highlight. Diving sessions, courses and trial courses are offered by *Rhea Dive (in the hotel Vila Baleira | mobile 9 39 33 37 77 | www.rheadive.com)* among others. If you wish to **INSIDER TIP** ▶ snorkel at special locations, Matias Teixeira will take you there: *Porto Santo Free Snorkeling Tour (mobile 9 11 79 89 89 | www.facebook.com/PortoSantoFree SnorkelingTour)*. Even though they in-

"Vereda do Castelo" (PR2), will take you on the 4.6 km/2.7 mi long track round the Pico do Facho, the highest peak on the island. From the ☆ Pico do Castelo, you have a great view over Vila Baleira and (sometimes) even as far as Madeira.

ENTERTAINMENT

In the summer, the beach cafés are transformed into great evening bars. The Caipirinha in the pirate bar *O Corsário Beach Bar (Rua Goulart Medeiros)* is especially delicious, but in the lounge bar *Bar do Henrique (April–Nov. daily 10.30am–2am | Praia do Ribeiro*

Cochino) the atmosphere certainly hots up on mild summer evenings.

CHALLENGER

You can let off steam while dancing to electro, hiphop and other dance music (late into the night) in this club all year round *Tue–Sat 1.30am–6 am (in the winter only on Sat) | Rua Estêvão Alencastre*

WINE BAR 3 V'S

The cosy wine bar serves Porto Santo wine from its own production, delicious sangria and tasty petiscos – the evenings can extend infinitely here. *June–Oct. 10pm–2am | Rua Gregó-rio Pestana 8 | tel. 917 85 67 98 | www.facebook.com/3vsportosanto*

WHERE TO STAY

CASA DO VELHO DRAGOEIRO

It is a shame that there are only three rooms in this friendly B & B! In good weather, breakfast is served on the roof terrace. The owner is a genuine artist, which is reflected in the ambience and cuisine of the adjoining INSIDER TIP restaurant which is considered the best on the island! *Rua Gregório Pestana 16a | tel. 2 91 63 44 13 | www.casadovelhodra goeiro.com | Moderate*

HOTEL PRAIA DOURADA

Centrally situated in Vila Baleira and only 200 m/656 ft from the "Golden Beach", this three-star hotel has all the amenities that the average guest requires, from air-conditioned rooms to a wonderful outdoor pool. *100 rooms | Rua Dom Estêvão de Alencastre | tel. 2 91 98 04 80 | www.portosantohotels.com | Moderate*

RESIDENCIAL CENTRAL

This guesthouse has a very central location. The Porto do Abrigo and the

beach are just a few minutes away. The rooms are simple and reasonably priced – something you don't often get on Porto Santo. *42 rooms | Rua Abel Magno Vasconcelos 1 | tel. 2 91 98 22 26 | residencial-Central.pt | Budget*

TORRE PRAIA

This comfortable, modern beach hotel close to the centre has a small pool, a large sun terrace and a tower bar. In the hotel restaurant *Salinas (Moderate)* you can enjoy a great meal (also open to non-residents) with the successful blend of national and international cuisine. *66 rooms | Rua Goulart Medeiros | tel. 2 91 98 04 50 | www.portosanto hotels.com | Expensive*

INFORMATION

POSTO DE TURISMO DO PORTO SANTO

Av. Doutor Manuel Gregório Pestana Júnior | in the Centro de Artesanato | tel. 2 91 98 52 44 | www.visitmadeira.pt

LOW BUDGET

The harbour of Porto Santo is a terminus not only for taxis and horse carriages, but also for *buses* (1.60 euro).

Several restaurants outside Vila Baleira offer a free *shuttleservice* for their guests.

The *Porto Santo Line* shipping company always has a special offer: e.g. a return ticket including an overnight stay that costs only 5–15 euros more than the price of the ticket only. *www.portosantoline.pt*

PORTO SANTO LINE
Ferries to and from Madeira can be booked online or through the hotels. *Info tel. 2 91 21 03 00 | www.portosantoline.pt*

CAMACHA (143 D2) (*ぱ V10*)
This village (pop. 450) 4 km/2.3 mi north of Vila Baleira is home to most of the island's vineyards. Most of the grapes that ripen here are destined for the table, but some are pressed to make a number of different wines, which have a high alcohol content. Near Camacha you can also stay in the quiet and charming *Quinta do Serrado (22 rooms | Sítio do Pedregal | tel. 2 91 98 02 70 | www.quintado serrado.com | Moderate)*. The estate has a small pool; in the restaurant delicious kid goat often features on the menu.

FONTE DA AREIA (142 C2) (*ぱ V 10*)
6 km/3.7 mi northwest of Vila Baleira fresh water springs from the ground with a backdrop of bizarrely shaped sandstone rock formations. With its pretty basin and lush green surroundings, the spring attracts locals and tourists who bring picnics. It used to be said that anyone who drank from the spring became 20 years younger. The water of the "sand spring" was originally thought to have healing properties, and was later used as a public washing place.

PONTA DA CALHETA (142 B5) (*ぱ U12*)
6 km/3.7 mi southwest of Vila Baleira, at the Ponta da Calheta, the end of Porto Santo is reached. However, directly off the southwestern tip of the island, looking almost close enough to touch, is the *Ilhéu de Baixo* with its strangely shaped limestone rocks. On some days a high jet of water spurts out of one of these rocks. The best place to enjoy this spectacle is the *Ponta da Calheta* restaurant *(Ponta da Calheta | tel. 2 91 98 43 80 | Moderate)*, where fish specialities are brought to the table and a free transfer picks up guests from Vila Baleira and takes them back.

SINKING SHIPS

As if divers on Porto Santo did not already have such favourable conditions: fairly warm, clean and turquoise water and a marine protection area surrounding the rock islands off the coastline – the island is certainly perfectly suited for diving... But, there are also two shipwrecks to explore! The Madeirense, once a passenger ship running for several decades from 1961 onwards between Lisbon and Funchal, was sunk in 2000. In the meantime, corals and shoals of fish have moved in to live in this artificial reef 30 m/98.4 ft beneath the sea. Since 2016, the ship has been joined by the corvette General Pereira D'Eça which served in the Portuguese Navy for 40 years. This method of "sinking ships" necessitates thorough preparation to ensure that the ship is sunk at the correct position and contains no hazardous material which could contaminate the sea so that the wreck is safe for divers to explore. Since this has been such a great success, Madeira is also planning to sink a disused marine vessel. Welcome to this wreck-divers' paradise!

Above Ponta da Calheta lies the ☀️ look-out point called *Pico das Flores*. There is an unimpeded view from here across the entire southern part of the island. On the left are the summits of Cabeço do Zimbralinho, Cabeço do Dragoal and *Pico de Ana Ferreira* (142 C4) *(ᗰ U12)*, on the northern flank of which a beautiful INSIDER TIP formation of basalt columns can be seen. On its eastern side is the *Adega das Levadas (Rua Morenos | tel. 2 91 98 25 57 | Budget–Moderate)*, a good old-fashioned place to eat meat on the skewer with home-made bread and drink strong *vinho do Porto Santo* produced by the owners themselves.

The INSIDER TIP *feast of São Pedro* on 29 June is an impressive occasion. The patron saint of fishermen is honoured with mass on the beach and a procession to his chapel at the foot of the Pico de Ana Ferreira.

PORTELA ☀️ (143 D–E3) *(ᗰ W11)*

A strong breeze blows across the island of Porto Santo on many days of the year. Many centuries ago the inhabitants took advantage of this by building windmills to grind grain, which was then still plentiful on the island. The date of construction of the first mill is a matter of dispute. It is reported that there were 30 *moinhos* on Porto Santo in the early 20th century. By now most of them have become dilapidated, but three old mills have been restored and placed on the Portela plateau.

QUINTA DAS PALMEIRAS
(142 C3) *(ᗰ U11)*

On the island, industrious hands have created a man-made oasis in the middle of the desert: in the little botanical garden 5 km/3.1 mi northwest of Vila Baleira, exotic birds flutter and twitter – flying free, in cages, and on perches. *Daily 10am–5pm | admission 3 euros | Sítio dos Linhares*

Elegant white calla lilies
in Quinta das Palmeiras

SERRA DE FORA AND
SERRA DE DENTRO

The ☀️ lookout point at *Portela* is on the way to the karst landscape of *Serra de Fora* (143 E3) *(ᗰ W11)*. On the edge of this sleepy village, 3 km/1.9 mi northeast of Vila Baleira, a circular stone threshing floor *(aira)* can be made out. It is a reminder of the age of the navigators, when Porto Santo supplied grain to Portuguese ships on their voyages to Africa. 2 km/1.2 mi to the north, *Serra de Dentro* (143 E2) *(ᗰ W10)* lies between the bare cones of the Pico Gandaia, Pico do Cabrito and Pico do Facho, the highest summit (517 m/1696 ft) on the island, from where beacon fires announced the approach of ships. This part of Porto Santo was once blessed with the most plentiful water supplies, but today nobody lives in the grey, partly decaying houses of basalt blocks any more.

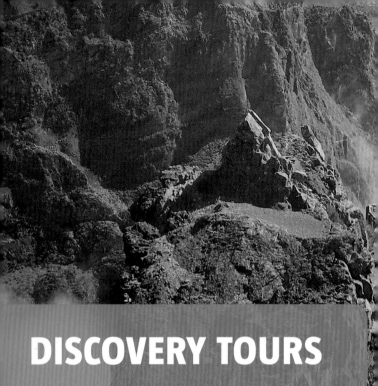

DISCOVERY TOURS

1 MADEIRA AT A GLANCE

START: **1** Funchal **END:** **1** Funchal	1 day Driving time (without stops) 6–7 hours
Distance:  approx. 200 km/124 mi	

COSTS: Car hire at least 30 euros/day, petrol approx. 50 euros, poncha 2 euros, lift 10 euros
WHAT TO PACK: swimming kit, hiking boots, drinking water

IMPORTANT TIPS: The mountain road leading from Paúl da Serra to the Encumeada Pass is sometimes closed in winter due to falling rocks or snowfall. If this road is closed, take ER209 from Paúl da Serra towards Canhas to return to the south coast. In general, be particularly careful when driving along Madeira's narrow coastal and mountain roads. It is often impossible to see oncoming traffic coming from a distance and good brakes are essential for the steep inclines.

Would you like to explore the places that are unique to this region? Then the Discovery Tours are just the thing for you – they include terrific tips for stops worth making, breathtaking places to visit, selected restaurants and fun activities. It's even easier with the Touring App: download the tour with map and route to your smartphone using the QR Code on pages 2/3 or from the website address in the footer below – and you'll never get lost again even when you're offline.

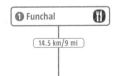

TOURING APP

→ p. 2/3

Is it possible to see all the highlights of Madeira on a single day? Yes, with the aid of this cleverly-planned "Perfect Route", you can climb from Funchal up to the stunning mountain and valley regions of the highlands, to the unspoilt north coast and along the high plateau in the west. You can return to Funchal through the coastal towns on the southern side of the island.

09:00am After breakfast in ❶ Funchal → p. 32, the island's sophisticated yet charming metropolis, head **towards the northwest, passing through Santo Antónioto** leave the bustling city behind you. Stop at the lookout

❶ Funchal	🍴

14.5 km/9 mi

Madeira (Port.)

② Eira do Serrado 🌄
5.5 km/3.4 mi

③ Curral das Freiras

15.5 mi/9.6 mi

④ Pico do Arieiro 🌄
11 km/6.8 mi

⑤ Ribeiro Frio 🚶 🌄
21.5 km/13.4 mi

⑥ Santana 🍴 🏛
12.5 km/7.8 mi

⑦ São Jorge 🚶
26 km/15.2 mi

⑧ São Vicente 🚶

point **② Eira do Serrado → p. 46** to enjoy the view of the Valley of the Nuns. Known locally as **③ Curral das Freiras → p. 46** and famous for its chestnuts, this valley is surrounded by spectacular mountains. Thanks to the modern tunnel, it is easy to take a quick detour to visit the village. A newly paved **mountain road, which begins at the upper tunnel entrance**, links the Valley of the Nuns with Madeira's third highest peak, the **④ Pico do Arieiro → p. 65**. After curving along the mountains while enjoying spectacular views, it is time to **head down towards the north coast**. Explore the lush forest of laurel trees in **⑤ Ribeiro Frio → p. 73** with its waters full of plump trout on a short hike to the lookout point **Balcões**.

12:00pm ⑥ Santana → p. 63 is famous for its colourful thatched houses as well as its exceptionally good home-style cooking. Why not try the wheat-based soup *sopa de trigo* for some local flavour? The winding **coastal road heading westward**, which is still not completely enclosed by tunnels, curves through idyllic villages worth visiting like **⑦ São Jorge → p. 66**, Arco de São Jorge and Ponta Delgada → p. 68. The local church hides behind the rocks in **⑧ São Vicente → p. 67** where you should definitely check out the small village centre. Have you ever seen a volcano from the inside? Head down into the inner depths of Madeira in the **Grutas de São Vicente** for a truly unique experience.

The tour continues **along the northern coastal road heading towards Porto Moniz**. Make sure to stop at the lookout point ⑨ **Véu da Noiva** to view the amazing waterfalls breaking through the rugged cliffs. Now you can see for yourself why modern tunnels have been built at certain points along this road – the old coastal route was simply too dangerous. A dip in the **saltwater pool** made of lava rock in ⑩ **Porto Moniz → p. 61** is an absolute must. The **Aquarium** in the old fortress is another highlight of this community.

It's time to get the hiking boots out of the car when you reach the plateau of ⑪ **Paúl da Serra → p. 55**. If the weather is fine, we recommend heading off on one of the trails leading around **Rabaçal → p. 55** into one of the island's most beautiful hiking areas. Once you're back in the car, the road leads straight ahead over the high moor before **winding down the mountain** to ⑫ **Encumeada Pass → p. 59**. With a bit of luck, you can see both the northern and southern coastlines from the road before heading **to the south coast** by way of ⑬ **Serra de Água → p. 58**. If you are not the one behind the wheel, you can enjoy a typical Madeira *poncha* – a cocktail made of lemon juice, sugar cane brandy and honey – at one of the local bars.

At the coast in ⑭ **Ribeira Brava → p. 57** stroll along the promenade and tour the **Ethnographic Museum** before taking off on the next adventure. A panoramic lift will take you down to the cove of ⑮ **Fajã dos Padres → p. 44**. Fruits and vegetables grow especially well in the special microclimate at the foot of these cliffs. You'll feel just like Robinson Crusoe as you explore the unpopulated pebble beach. Once you're back at the top of the cliffs, **head east and follow the signs to Cabo Girão**. After

8 km/5 mi

⑨ Véu da Noiva

10 km/6.2 mi

⑩ Porto Moniz

25 km/15.5 mi

⑪ Paúl da Serra

15.5 km/9.6 mi

⑫ Encumeada Pass

5.5 km/3.4 mi

⑬ Serra de Água

8 km/5 mi

⑭ Ribeira Brava

14 km/8.7 mi

⑮ Fajã dos Padres

The church square in Ribeira Brava

16 Cabo Girão	
6.5 km/4 mi	
17 Câmara de Lobos	
10.5 km/6.5 mi	
1 Funchal	

4 km/2.5 mi, you'll have reached the edge of **16** **Cabo Girão** → p. 44. From the top of one of the highest coastal cliffs in the world, the amazing view stretching over the sea as far as the bay of Funchal will simply take your breath away.

08:00pm You can catch your breath again in the fishing village of **17** **Câmara de Lobos** → p. 44 with its colourful harbour and picturesque houses dotted along the cliffs. After a stroll through the ‚house of the monk seal', as the town is called in Portuguese, you'll pass **through the hotel quarter on the way back to** **1** Funchal → p. 32 where it will be time for dinner followed by drinks in a local bar.

2 PICO DO ARIEIRO/PICO RUIVO – MADEIRA'S HIGHEST PEAKS

START: **1** Pico do Arieiro (car park) END: **7** Achada do Teixeira (car park)	5 hours Walking time (without stops) 4 hours
Distance: difficult ➡ 8.5 km/5.3 mi .ıll Height: 800 m/2625 ft	

COSTS: Taxi from Funchal to Pico do Arieiro/Achada do Teixeira to Funchal 120 euros (includes any wait)
WHAT TO PACK: hiking boots and maybe a walking stick, wind/weather gear, drinking water, picnic lunch, flashlight, binoculars

IMPORTANT TIPS: As there is no public transport to the starting point of the hike, you will need to order a car or taxi. To return to the hotel at the end of the hike, you will need to order a taxi to the car park at Achada do Teixeira in advance *(Taxi rank Santana: tel. 2 91 57 25 40)*.
During rough winters, parts of the trail may be inaccessible due to avalanches or falling rocks. Please contact the tourist office in advance to make sure there are no closures. In bad weather conditions (rain, strong winds or snowfall) the trail is impassable.

★ This hiking trail will lead you literally to the pinnacles of Madeira. You will become immersed in a largely unspoilt wilderness with rugged cliffs and barren mountain vegetation. The hike can, however, be quite tough at times. You have to surmount steep ascents and descents over high rock steps. The path is also very narrow and well-worn and you have to pass through five unlit tunnels through which water frequently flows. Surefootedness, a head for heights and a good physical condition are vital for this hike.

Set off as early as possible in the morning from Madeira's third highest mountain, the **❶ Pico do Arieiro → p. 65** for this difficult tour that is nonetheless wonderfully beautiful in good weather. Walk past the controversial NATO radar installation to the new **tourist centre** with its souvenir shop, café and WC where **a few steps lead up from the car park** to the summit of the Arieiro. The breathtaking mountain panorama will quickly erase any memory of the modern buildings below. **INSIDER TIP** At sunrise when the bizarre stone crags glow in the colours of mallows and lavender, or at sunset when the peaks are bathed in shades of copper, the view is truly magical. It is no less perfect when the mountain peaks emerge from the morning mist or white cushions of cloud enclose them.

Follow the red-yellow trail markers. At first, the trail is fairly wide and there are sometimes railings to help you along. After about 15 minutes, you will reach a rocky peak known as **❷ Ninho da Manta** (buzzard's nest) where you will find the first lookout point. This part of the trail is also easily accessible for less experienced hikers. In order to get to the second **❸ Miradouro** with its table made of tuff rock, you will have to **cross a small narrow ridge**. As a reward, you will be able to see the Pico Ruivo that the Pico das Torres (1851 m/6073 ft) has hidden up to now.

The route now makes a steep but secure lateral descent along the rock walls of the **Pico do Cidrão** (1798 m/5899 ft) **down countless steps and through a gap in the rocks to the foot of the ❹ Pico do Gato** (1780 m/5840 ft). Tree heath and gorse line the path before it is swallowed by the first tunnel. When the trail branches at the end of the tunnel, take **the easier route to the left,** where beautiful views and four more tunnels wait for you. **When both paths reunite,** the terrain becomes much more difficult. Following a mountain slide, a part of the path was resurfaced, but there is still a section of around 30 m/98.4 ft which is slightly narrower and rough and ready. Once this point has been passed, the only existing path lined with

❶ Pico do Arieiro

900 m/2953 ft

❷ Ninho da Manta

350 m/1148 ft

❸ Miradouro

650 m/2133 ft

❹ Pico do Gato

3 km/1.9 mi

High above the clouds: a hiker on the Paúl da Serra plateau

tree heathland ascends continually, first gently and then in hairpin bends. The path ascending from Achada do Teixeira meets this path on the right hand side and the **ascending path straight ahead** leads to the **⑤ Pico Ruivo Hut**. The hut is currently not open, but there is always the hope that the building will be let and re-opened after much necessary renovation as a mountain cabin. Until then, you have to bring your own picnic with you. At least the walls offer you a place for a midday rest.

All refreshed, it is time to tackle the summit. **Go up a few stone steps leading to the left. When the path forks, take the left-hand path** (the path to the right leads to the Encumeada Pass). In less than half an hour, you will be standing on top of the **⑥ Pico Ruivo → p. 65** (1862 m/6109 ft), Madeira's highest peak. In clear weather, you will be rewarded with a magnificent panoramic view of the Paúl da Serra plateau, the mountain peaks around the Curral das Freiras and Madeira's north coast. You might even be able to spot the island of Porto Santo and the Ponta de São Lourenço.

To hike back, **you will initially follow the same trail back to** the Pico Ruivo mountain hut. Shortly thereafter, take **the path that forks to the left in the direction of Achada do Teixeira**. This path with its many stone slabs

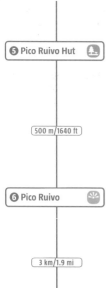

⑤ Pico Ruivo Hut

500 m / 1640 ft

⑥ Pico Ruivo

3 km / 1.9 mi

gently descends the mountain. When you cross the path heading to Ilha, ignore it and **continue straight ahead**. In less than an hour, you should reach the car park at the back of the mountain ⑦ **Achada do Teixeira**.

⑦ Achada do Teixeira

---

③ BOCA DO RISCO – PANORAMIC VIEW OF THE NORTH COAST

START: ❶ Caniçal Tunnel END: ❹ Porto da Cruz	**4 hours** Walking time (without stops) **3 hours**
Distance: medium difficulty 🚌 12 km/7.5 mi 📶 Height: 380 m/1247 ft	

COSTS: Bus ticket approx. 6 euros, swimming pool (only in summer) 2 euros
WHAT TO PACK: hiking boots and maybe a walking stick, wind/weather gear, sunscreen, drinking water, a snack, binoculars and perhaps swimming kit

IMPORTANT TIPS: Bus 113 from Funchal or Machico to the old Caniçal Tunnel (bus stop: Pico do Facho) runs 4 times on weekdays between 7am and 9am, 3 times on Saturday and 2 times on Sunday. Bus 53 for the return journey from Porta da Cruz to Machico or Funchal runs 4 times on weekdays after 1pm, at 3.50pm and 5.20pm on Saturdays and at 1.40pm on Sundays.
Do not attempt the hike up the narrow coastal path on the north side if you are not sure-footed or good with heights. In bad weather conditions (rain, strong winds or snowfall) the trail is impassable.

Few hiking routes on the island are as varied as this *levada* route leading from the eastern tip of Madeira to Porta da Cruz. You'll come across small clusters of houses, isolated pine forests, gorge-like gaps in the rocks and planted terraced plots along the way. The views of the rugged north coast from the trail will take your breath away.

Start from the little house on the left-hand side of the road at the western entrance of the old ❶ **Caniçal Tunnel** on the outskirts of **Machico** → p. 74. The **Levada do Caniçal** begins right in front of it. **At first you'll walk along a paved road, but before long it turns into a narrow path over the fields.** Enjoy the beautiful view of the valley of Machico and the Pico do Facho straight ahead before you enter the small forest. A wide-open view of terraced plots bearing bananas, wine grapes and vegetables awaits on the other side.

❶ Caniçal Tunnel

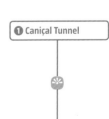

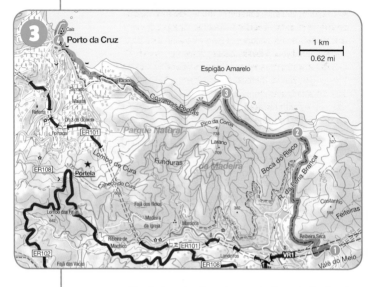

3 Cais
Porto da Cruz

1 km
0.62 mi

Espigão Amarelo

Larano
98
Serrapo
Maiata
Referta
Cruz da Guarda
ER101
Fenncal
Parque Natural
Covadas Pedras
Pico da Corôa
738
Larano
709
527

ER108
Lombo de Cura
Portela
Cabeço do Cura
Funduras
da Madeira
Boca do Risco
R. da Feira Branca

Lombo das Faias
642
Fajã dos Rolos
Madeira
da Igreja
Maroços
382
Castanho
358
Feiteiras

Ribeira de
Machico
ER101
Ribeira Seca

ER102
Fajã das Vacas
Landeiros
ER108
VR1
Vale do Meio

4.5 km/2.8 mi

❷ Boca do Risco

2.5 km/1.6 mi

❸ Ponta do Espigão
Amarelo

5 km/3.1 mi

After first passing through a gap in the rocks, the *levada* bends slightly to the right into a deep-cut little valley. **Follow the trail along the stream until you see two steps leading to a fork on the right** – take this path to Boca do Risco. The stone-studded trail gently ascends before dropping back down into a valley where it crosses through a pine forest and more terraced fields. After about 1.5 hours and a slight bend to the left, you will reach the rocky pass known as the ❷ **Boca do Risco**. From an elevation of about 450 m/1476 ft, the view stretches out over the eastern side of the rugged, largely unspoiled north coast.

A dense cover of tree heath and shrubs close in on the trail as it climbs on towards the west. Light often breaks through the jungle-like greenery where the vegetation is more sparse as the trail crosses more exposed terrain. Before long, the trail comes to a rock wall where it becomes steep and narrow with loose gravel. There is usually a rope hand rail provided for particularly difficult sections of the climb. If the rope is broken or missing you must be extremely careful and sure-footed. A knee-high mile marker identifies the headland known as ❸ **Ponta do Espigão Amarelo**. This lookout point offers a brilliant view of Penha de Águia (Eagle Rock) and neighbouring Porto da Cruz.

At this point, you have conquered more than half the trail and its most difficult sections. The landscape begins to change once again as slopes of eucalyptus and pine trees rise up around you. **A few stone steps take you down** to a deeply-cut water channel and through two other similar little gorges. Shortly thereafter you will see a dirt road. At a mostly steady elevation, it leads to a gap and to the left into a valley with terraced plots. **The trail still continues along a mountain ridge running** parallel to the coast, accompanied by a water channel. You will soon come across the first houses as you reach the tarmac road. **Follow the road steeply downhill for about 1 km/0.6 mi until right before a small hill. A concrete driveway with letterboxes branches off sharply to the right. On the left side of the driveway, steps lead down to a clearly visible** *levada* **path. Follow this path past fields of vegetables and cross over a dirt path. When you see a stable built into the rocks, turn left and head on towards the sea.**

The trail begins to descend steeply once again over a small ridge, through a dry (only in summer) stream bed and right across the cliff towards a group of houses. Head

Mountain climbing with an eagle's view – Penha de Águia

down the steps that you will find above the houses. Keep to the left as you continue over the hill until you reach a paved path. A stone wall marks the fork to the right that leads towards the coast. After you go around a stream bed with a collapsed bridge, the trail continues directly alongside the sea. Shortly thereafter you will come across the coastal path to ❹ **Porto da Cruz** → p. 65. It will bring you to the cafés on the seaside promenade, the saltwater swimming pool and the small harbour. Head up to the left to reach the church and the bus station.

RABAÇAL – A WILDERNESS OF MAGICAL WATERS

START: ❶ Rabaçal (trail car park)
END: ❶ Rabaçal (trail car park)

Distance: easy
🔄 11 km/6.8 mi 📶 Height: 320 m/1050 ft

5 hours
Walking time
(without stops)
4.5 hours

COSTS: Car hire at least 30 euros/day
WHAT TO PACK: hiking boots, wind/weather gear, sunscreen, drinking water, picnic lunch

IMPORTANT TIPS: There are usually many hikers on this trail, so it is well worth setting off early.
If you should reach the Rabaçal tunnel and be tempted to pass through it, be warned: you will get out at the southern part of Paúl da Serra and will eventually have to walk a long way back.

Almost all hikers on Madeira make their way to Rabaçal at some point. In the humid valley between the high plateau Paúl da Serra and the hilly ridge pointing towards the north coast between Pico da Fajã da Lenha and Fanal you will find several locations within a confined area which make you feel you are in the jungle. The *levadas* and streams are fringed with dense greenery and spring water plunges down the hillside. Water ripples and splashes between the ferns, trees, bushes and mosses.

Cascata do Risco and 25 Fontes are the two most beautiful and beloved attractions in Rabaçal. You can reach both by taking a small round trip of the area. Start off from the ❶ **Rabaçal** trail car park located on the road coming from Paúl da Serra. **From the car park, follow the paved road (cars are prohibited) for about 30 minutes downhill to the ❷ Rabaçal forester's house.** Alongside picnic tables

❹ Porto da Cruz

❶ Rabaçal
2 km/1.2 mi

❷ Rabaçal forester's house
350 m/1148 ft

and toilets, there is a small state-run hostel for hikers who have booked in advance. Signposts make it easy to determine which trails lead in which direction. **Take the wide, level path marked to ❸ Levada do Risco.** Shortly thereafter, where a fork in the road leads to the *levada* of the 25 springs, **stay on the trail going along the Levada do Risco for about another 15 minutes until a marked path branches off to the right.** It leads to the basin of the ❹ **Cascata do Risco** before ending at a ❺ **lookout point.** The veil of water cascading down the high rock wall at the first stop of this tour is truly amazing.

Retrace your steps and go back the way you came. There is no point in going underneath the waterfall and through the tunnel because the trail has been closed just a few meters further on for safety reasons. **Once you've reached the crossroads with the fork leading to the 25 springs, take a right.** Stone steps, hairpin bends and a second set of steps bring you to the ❻ **Levada das 25 Fontes**. **Follow the *levada* against the current.** Before long you will find a lookout point on the right from which you can see the continuing path of the levada and the valley below.

At the point where the levada disappears into the mountain, stone steps with wooden railings lead to a **bridge that will take you back up to the levada.** Just a little further on, you can **INSIDER TIP** gaze down into the Risco basin. **Follow the levada wall out over the cliff, which is only secured by tree heath, as far as the plateau where the path curves to the right down into the valley of the 25 springs.** From here, the trail goes straight on as it descends to the **Levada da Rocha Vermelha**. **Don't take this path, but follow the stream's current instead until you reach a second bridge where you bear to the right to follow the wider *levada*.** After a few more metres, the valley basin will open up to reveal the ❼ **25 Fontes**. In dry summer months, the water only seems to trickle over the rocks, if at all. During the rest of the year,

❸ Levada do Risco

900 m/2953 ft

❹ Cascata do Risco

100 m/328 ft

❺ Lookout point

1 km/0.6 mi

❻ Levada das 25 Fontes

1.5 km/0.9 mi

❼ 25 Fontes

however, you can expect to see water cascading down from the springs. Now you can enjoy your well-earned picnic lunch.

Idyllic location: the water flows into this *Lagoa das 25 Fontes* from 25 different sources

3 km/1.9 mi

❽ Levada do Risco

2 km/1.2 mi

❶ Rabaçal

Retrace your steps and go back the way you first came. This time, where the trail branches off to the forester's house, go straight on and follow the Levada das 25 Fontes further down to the valley. The path leads through a narrow rock gap, followed shortly thereafter by a set of steps made of red tuff rock. The steps wind up to the left to the **❽ Levada do Risco. There are more steps to climb after you cross the *levada* until you reach the courtyard in front of the WC facilities at Rabaçal house. Go past the house to get back on the paved road** that leads back to the trail car park in **❶ Rabaçal.**

5 THE SOUTHWEST – MADEIRA'S SUNNY SIDE

START: ① Ribeira Brava	**1/2 day**
END: ⑩ Porto Moniz	Driving time (without stops)
Distance: ➡ approx. 75 km/46.6 mi	2 hours

COSTS: Car hire at least 30 euros/day, cable car there and back from Achadas da Cruz to Faja 3 euros

CABLE CAR: Achadas da Cruz to Fajã, return ticket 3 euros

WHAT TO PACK: swimming kit, hiking boots, drinking water

IMPORTANT TIPS: The old coastal roads are often very narrow and run closely along the steep cliffs. In rainy winter weather, falling rocks may block the roads. If the road has been closed, you will need to follow the detour signs.

The best way to get to Ribeira Brava from Funchal is to take the motorway. A good coastal road runs from Porto Moniz over São Vicente to the Encumeada tunnel. It's just a quick drive from here back to the south coast.

The sunny south-west of Madeira Is normally omitted from most round trips although this part of the island is particularly unspoilt and has the best weather. The steep slopes are lined by seemingly endless banana terraces and the climate guarantees sweet fruits. In the small villages on the seashore, clocks appear to tick at a slower pace and the fish is freshly caught. This is also the ideal location to swim or surf in the Atlantic. You may even experience a free car shower – the coastal roads are full of surprises!

Start off in the morning from ① **Ribeira Brava** → p. 57, a bustling commercial town located at the mouth of its namesake river. After a short stroll through the market, a sweet treat in one of the **Pastelarias** on the harbour promenade and a visit to the baroque church of **São Bento**, it's time to **start heading west**. Unfortunately the first 3 km/1.9 mi of the coastal road are impassable, so you will have to **drive back towards the motorway for just a bit. At the roundabout leaving town, take the exit for the tunnel heading towards Ponta do Sol/Calheta (VR3).** You will pass through the banana plantations of Lugar de Baixo. Over the last few years this town has sadly become known for its poorly constructed marina. Although the sea has scraped away at much of the con-

① Ribeira Brava

5.5 km/3.4 mi

⑤ Madeira

Ponta do Tristão
ou da Fazenda

⑩ Porto Moniz

Achadas ⑨
da Cruz

Seixal

Ponta ⑧
do Pargo

São Vicente

Fajã da ⑦
Ovelha

1320 · *Parque* 1640

Paul ⑥ Paul da Serra

Paul d. M. ⑥
Jardim d. M. ⑤
Estreito da Calheta ④

Nat. *da*

Calheta

Madeira Ⓟ

Arco da Calheta ③

Ponta do Sol ②

①
Ribeira
Brava

6 km
3.73 mi

② Ponta do Sol
5 km/3.1 mi

③ Madalena do Mar
5 km/3.1 mi

④ Beach of Calheta
11.5 km/7.1 mi

⑤ Jardim do Mar
4.5 km/2.8 mi

⑥ Paúl do Mar
5.5 km/3.4 mi

crete, the half-finished ruins are still an eyesore. After passing through another tunnel, you will arrive in the pretty little town of **② Ponta do Sol → p. 59**. **At this point you will leave the motorway and take the old regional road ER101 that runs right along the sea. To do so, exit the roundabout in Ponta do Sol to the left in the direction of the church.** It is well worth taking a short break here to walk through the lovingly restored town centre.

The next section of the road is definitely the most spectacular on the island: You'll drive through old rock tunnels with the sea to the left and the high cliffs to the right – sometimes you'll even get a free car wash from one of the waterfalls cascading down the rocks. **③ Madalena do Mar → p. 54** lives mostly from the cultivation of bananas so you'll see banana plantations covering every square metre. Calheta is the next destination. **When the motorway (VR3) divides, take the old regional road (ER101),** which leads directly to the **④ beach of Calheta → p. 53**. Here's the perfect place for a swim. The golden sand was actually shipped in especially from Africa so that a beach could be made on the southwest coast. It is also worth touring the old INSIDER TIP **sugar cane mill**. Calheta is still one of the most important sugar cane growing regions on Madeira (although today most of the sugar is only used to make *Aguardente* for *Poncha*).

After Calheta, the regional road ER 222/223 winds through Estreito da Calheta, which sits at a slightly higher elevation, before heading back down to the sea. Surfers flock to **⑤ Jardim do Mar → p. 54** for the island's best, but also most challenging waves. The town has a real surfing vibe with its lounge-style cafés like **Joe's Bar** *(Vereda da Igreja | tel. 9 66 13 02 08)*. A long tunnel links Jardim do Mar with the fishing village of **⑥ Paúl do Mar → p. 54**. The **Xama** restaurant *(Estrada Regional 223, 4 | mobile 9 65 00 55 18 | Budget)* is a great place to stop for lunch – the fresh fish served at this snack bar is particularly tasty.

A steep serpentine road winds its way from the western **edge of town** up to ⑦ Fajã da Ovelha → p. 57. From here, the route departs from the coast to curve through many of the towns and villages located up on the plateaus before finally reaching Madeira's westernmost town, ⑧ Ponta do Pargo → p. 56. The lighthouse on the western point juts out impressively from the coast. You can learn more about the history of lighthouses on Madeira in the **Lighthouse Museum**. Enjoy the view of the sea from the cosy **tea room** at the lighthouse before getting back into the car to head along the ER101.

In ⑨ Achadas da Cruz → p. 56 a **cable car** connects the town with the fields on the fajã down at the coast. At the

| ⑦ Fajã da Ovelha |
| 11.5 km/7.1 mi |
| ⑧ Ponta do Pargo |
| 11 km/6.8 mi |
| ⑨ Achadas da Cruz |

Echium growing in front of the lighthouse at Ponta do Pargo

bottom, you'll really feel like you've reached the end of the world. It's particularly romantic to watch **INSIDER TIP** **the sunset** from the fajã, but don't forget that the last cable car going back up leaves at 8pm in summer and at 6pm in winter.

Shortly after you get **back on the main road** it will merge with the ER110 coming from Paúl da Serra. **The route heads straight on,** past Santa with its lovely lookout point, back down to ⑩ Porto Moniz → p. 61. This is the last stop of the tour. If you feel like it, you can take a refreshing dip in the local saltwater swimming pool or call it a day and enjoy a large plate of *lapas grelhadas* (grilled limpets) in one of the restaurants.

| 14.5 km/9 mi |
| ⑩ Porto Moniz |

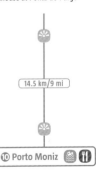

SPORTS & ACTIVITIES

Madeira is a multi-faceted paradise for hikers with its *levadas* and summit paths, but if you are looking for a bit more action, you will discover a wide range of available outdoor activities.

The 'pensioners' island' Madeira was long considered as an Eldorado for *levada* ramblers and golf players. And it is true that Madeira's two golf courses 🏌 *Santo da Serra (tel. 2 9155 0100 | www.santodaser ragolf.com)* and *Palheiro Golf (Rua do Bal ancal 29 | Funchal | tel. 2 9179 0120 | www. palheirogolf.com)* with 18 holes (green-fees from 65 euros) are both spectacular, above all for their amazing views, and visitors are always welcome there even if they would just like a cup of tea.

There are, however, a whole range of more radical sports: in the mountains you can go canyoning or undertake climbing and mountain bike tours, not to mention safaris in motorised quads or jeeps. Anyone who thinks 'hiking' is boring can instead go 'trekking' or on one of the now numerous ultra-trail competitions in which participants run for innumerable miles on paths crisscrossing through the mountains.

Water lovers will also find plenty to keep themselves occupied: activities range from swimming in the hotel pool, bathing at the seaside bathing complexes or on beaches with shingle or sand, surfing, stand-up paddling, sea kayaking and diving. And if you need some relaxation after so much activity? No problem, many hotels offer good spa and wellness areas!

From mountain biking to putting – all sorts of interesting activities complement the classic pastimes of walking and water sports

CANYONING

Advanced-level hiking: with a wetsuit, helmet and safety ropes participants descend through canyons and over waterfalls. This adventure gives you a real adrenalin rush – and is a whole lot of fun. Various operators organise canyoning, e.g. *Madeira Adventure Kingdom (mobile 9 68 10 18 70 | www.madeira-adventure-kingdom.com)* and *Madeira Outdoor (mobile 9 66 23 02 12 | www.madeiraoutdoor.com | from 60 euros per person)*.

DIVING

Exotic-looking species of fish abound in the often crystal-clear waters and delight divers as much as the bizarre underwater lava formations and caves. The diving stations are on the south and southeast coasts as well as on Porto Santo. The greatest diversity of sea life can be seen in the ◎ *Garajau marine national park*, which was established in 1986 to protect marine creatures. For information see e.g. *Manta Diving (in the Hotel Galoresort | Rua Robert Baden-Powell | Caniço de Baixo | tel. 2 91 93 55 88 | www. mantadiving.com); Madeira Divepoint (in the Hotel Carlton | Largo António Nobre | Funchal | tel. 2 91 23 95 79 | www. madeiradivepoint.com).*

HIKING

The best way to really get to know the landscape of Madeira is on foot – e.g. by doing a *levada* or mountain walk. Take care when planning a tour and bear in mind that the weather can change quickly, with fog and rain appearing or temperatures dropping suddenly. There is water in some tunnels all year round, and others are unlit. More and more trails are being equipped with waymarkers, fences and hand-ropes, so that some hikes which once presented the danger of a fall are now safe. As the start and finish of a hike may be far apart, it is often useful to agree a pickup with a taxi driver in order to get back to base.

Organised tours are offered by e.g. *Madeira Explorers (Centro Comercial Monumental Lido | Funchal | tel. 2 91 76 37 01 | mobile 9 69 52 80 22 | www.madeira-levada-walks.com)* or *Madeira Island Tours (Rampa Pico da Cruz 10 | Funchal | tel. 926 672 772 | www.madeira-island-tours.com).*

MOUNTAINBIKING

Steep climbs, breakneck descents, lonely mountain and forest tracks – what more could a cyclist want? You can hire bikes (mountain bikes and racing bikes) and book organised tours, for example via *Freeride (Loja B – Hotel Porto Mare | Rua Simplício Passos de Gouveia 21 | Funchal | freeridemadeira.com).*

SAILING & BOAT TRIPS

You can go on a boating excursion on a sailing yacht even if you do not have a sailing licence, either along the beach or to the Ilhas Desertas. Some trips include the opportunity to watch whales and dolphins, e. g. on board of ● *Bonita da Madeira (moors in Funchal-marina | tel. 2 91 76 22 18 | www.bonita-da-madeira.com)*: this two-masted ship – a 20 m/65.6 ft wooden caravel built in 1996 – can accommodate up to 50 passengers for whale- and dolphin-watching trips on Wednesdays and Sundays, for a INSIDER TIP trip to the Ilhas Desertas on Tuesdays, Thursdays and Saturdays, and for a tour of Madeira's loveliest bays on Fridays. "Sea Pleasure", "Sea the Best"and "Sea Nature" are the names of the catamarans run by *VMT Madeira (Marina do Funchal | tel. 2 91 22 49 00 | vm-tmadeira.com)* which sail daily on dolphin-watching trips (sometimes you might even see a sperm whale!) and on weekly trips to the Desertas islands every Saturday *(May to Sept.).* The Sunset Trip *(June–Sept. Wed, Fri and Sun)*, is a specially romantic tour to view the sunset while reclining and chilling out on the nets of the catamaran or even taking a short dip in the sea (trips from 35 euros).

STAND-UP-PADDLE

Beginners chiefly start off on the southwest coast as the sea is normally calmer here. If you are already up to a professional standard and would like to take to the waves on your SUP board, the organisers will find a suitable spot for you on the northern coast. Courses and equipment are offered by companies such as *Madeira SUP School (mobile 9 68 23 69 37 | www.madeira supschool.net)* and *Madeira Outdoor (mobile 9 66 23 02 12 | www.madeiraout door.com).* Sessions cost a minimum of 30 euros.

(Hotel Vila Bela | Rua da Praia 23 | Porto da Cruz | mobile 9 26 18 98 94 | www. madeiracalhausurfschool.com): instruc-

Indispensable if you want to enjoy the fantastic views on Madeira: sturdy shoes

SURFING

The waves off the Madeiran coast are a challenge for wavesurfers and windsurfing is only possible in individual locations such as the beach at Reis Magos in Caniço, instruction available from *www.albanoaktiv.com*. The coastal waters off Jardim do Mar, Paúl do Mar and east of São Vicente offer ideal conditions for experienced surfers. The best time of the year is between September and February. You can check the wave conditions at individual locations via *www.surf-forecast.com*. Anyone keen on learning how to surf can take lessons at the *Calhau Surf School*

tion normally takes place on the beach at Porto da Cruz where you can alternatively hire boards and wetsuits and go surfing independently.

WELLNESS

Several hotels have spa facilities offering saunas, steam baths, jacuzzis and massage. The spas are particularly good at the *Saccharum Hotel Resort & Spa (40 euros/day)* in Calheta (see p. 18), in *Vidamar (30 euros/half-day | www.vidamar resorts.com)* in Funchal and in the *Quinta Splendida (19 euros/day)* in Caniço (see p. 46). If you book a massage, admission is already included.

TRAVEL WITH KIDS

Only a few years ago, parents needed plenty of imagination to keep their kids happy when taking a holiday on Madeira. Nowadays there is a much bigger range of attractions for the younger generation.

The coasts may fall steeply into the Atlantic, and the sea may sometimes be rough, but man-made beach lagoons that slope gently into the water have now been created, for example in Calheta and Machico. And the lava pools at Porto Moniz are an exciting alternative to beaches. In general, parents need to keep a careful eye on their children when they are splashing around in the ocean, at bathing beaches or in lava pools. The surf and water currents can be quite strong.

FUNCHAL

In Funchal, families enjoy swimming in the open-air swimming pools Barreirinha, Lido and Ponta Gorda which offer easy entry into the sea. The latter two are situated on the coastal promenade in the hotel district.

The *Madeira Story Centre* (138 C6) *(ᗺ L8) (daily 9am–7pm | admission 5 euros, children 3 euros | Rua D. Carlos I 27 | www.madeirastorycentre.com)* is a fascinating museum displaying the history of the island in playful interactive form. Kids' eyes light up at the sight of the ● *Santa Maria de Colombo* (138 B–C6) *(ᗺ L8) (daily 10.30am and 3pm | trip lasts approx. 3 hours | 35 euros, children 17.50 euros | tel. 2 91 22 56 95 | www.santamariadecolombo.com)*. This replica of one of Columbus's ships anchors in the harbour; for trips to Cabo Girão and back the crew dress as pirates, and with a little luck leaping dolphins will escort the ship. Kids can discover the secrets of electricity at the INSIDER TIP *Museu da Electricidade* (138 C6) *(ᗺ L8) (Tue–Sat 10am–12.30pm and 2pm–6pm | admission 2.70 euros, children age 12–18 1.35 euros | Rua da Casa da Luz 2 | www.museucasadaluz.com)*, which was once Funchal's power station for district heating. They can even generate electricity themselves!

THE SOUTH

The yellow sandy beach in Calheta is a paradise for sand castle builders! The bathing cove is protected by two pier constructions. If you want to take kids on an expedition into Madeira's mountains, a stop on the way at the *Quinta Pe-*

Nature is an adventure – explore old ships, see colourful fish and discover secrets

dagógica dos Prazeres (128 C6) (*M C4*) (daily 9am–7pm, in summer until 9pm | admission to the garden free, zoo 1 euro (children up to 10 years old free admission) | Prazeres | www.prazeresdaquinta. com) is a chance to see ostriches and llamas. Many breeds of hens, pigs, turtles and rabbits can also be seen in the quinta garden.

THE NORTH

There's lots to discover and plenty of ways to work off energy on climbing frames and other playground equipment for kids in the Parque Temático da Madeira (133 D4) (*M M3*) (daily 10am–7pm, closed Mon in the off-season | admission 6 euros, children 4 euros | Fonte da Pedra | www.parquetematicoda madeira.pt) in Santana.
In the fort of Porto Moniz, the sharp teeth of the carnivorous tiger moray eel and the cleaner shrimp, which also work like toothbrushes, delight young

and old sea-lovers at the Aquário da Madeira (129 D1) (*M D1*) (daily 10am–6pm | admission 7 euros, children 4 euros | Rua Forte São João Batista).
An interesting excursion to the interior of the island: a guided tour in the Grutas de São Vicente (daily 10am–7pm | admission 8 euros, children 5–14 years, 6 euros | Sítio do Pé do Passo | São Vicente) first takes you through the lava tunnel caves and then by lift down to the visitors' centre to the centre of the earth. How do you get back to the surface? You will find out in the 3D cinema!

THE EAST

In Santa Cruz, (140 A5) (*M O7*) the INSIDER TIP Aquaparque (June–Nov. daily 10am–8pm | admission 5 euros, children 5–12 years, 2.50 euros) is a great attraction with features including five water slides and an artificial stream winding its way around the pools for young water rats to enjoy.

FESTIVALS & EVENTS

On Madeira, a *festa* is held in honour of everything: the wine harvest, the cherry harvest, the blossoms of spring. Religious festivals are marked by a mass and processions; after that things get more worldly with folklore, disco music, dancing and a hearty meal. As well as the traditional festivities, there is room in the calendar for events such as the Madeira Film Festival mid-April in Funchal.

FESTIVALS & EVENTS

FEBRUARY

Carnival: big parade from Rotunda do Porto to the centre of Funchal with samba dance groups and floats

APRIL/MAY

★ *Festa da Flor:* flower festival for the spring blossom in Funchal. The highlight is a procession through the streets with floats decorated with flowers

MAY

Fica na Cidade: this open-air music festival held in various locations across Funchal in the first half of May offers a great new excuse for residents to celebrate in the city (free of charge) every day over a period of two weeks. *www.ficanacidade.com*

JUNE

Festival do Atlântico: high-calibre concerts in Funchal, combined with an international firework competition and street music (all month, each Saturday: **INSIDER TIP** *firework concerts*)
Altares de São João: saint's day festival with an altar-building competition and lots to eat around Praça do Carmo in Funchal (*week of 24 June*)

JULY

Nos Summer Opening: well-known rock, hip hop, reggae and pop stars perform at the music festival in the Parque de Santa Catarina in Funchal. *www.nossummeropening.com*

AUGUST

Nossa Senhora do Monte: religious highlight of the year. On the day of the Assumption of the Virgin the people of Madeira honour the patron of their island with a pilgrimage to the lavishly decorated church of Monte

SEPTEMBER

Madeira Wine Festival: wine tasting and exhibitions on Avenida Arriaga and Praça do Povo in Funchal as well as in Estreito de Câmara de Lobos

Festa da Nossa Senhora da Piedade: procession of boats in Caniçal, at which a statue of the Virgin is conveyed by sea
Festa do Pêro: apple festival in Ponta do Pargo with a parade of tractors and the sale of farmers' products
Festival Colombo: over three days Porto Santo pays tribute to its most famous inhabitant with a medieval market, street performers and a historical parade. The climax is a re-enactment of Columbus' departure on the quay at Vila Baleira

OCTOBER/NOVEMBER/DECEMBER

INSIDER TIP *Festival da Natureza:* For an entire week, Madeira celebrates nature – its most valuable treasure. Various events and sporting activities are offered on land, on the water and in the air *(early Oct.)*
Festa do Senhor dos Milagres: night-time procession in honour of a miracle-working image of Jesus in Machico *(9 Oct)*
Chestnut Festival in Curral das Freiras with chestnut bread and liqueur, and folklore *(around 1 Nov)*
★ **New Year fireworks:** the end of the old year in Funchal begins in late November. The climax of the Festas do Fim do Ano is New Year's Eve, when the famous fireworks are set off in the bay

PUBLIC HOLIDAYS

1 Jan	*Ano Novo* (New Year's Day)
Shrove Tuesday	
	Carnival
Good Friday	
	Sexta-feira Santa
25 April	*Dia da Libertade* (Day of the Carnation Revolution 1974)
1 May	*Dia do Trabalhor* (Day of the Workers)
Corpus Christi	
	Corpo de Deus
10 June	*Dia de Portugal* (in honour of national poet Luís Vaz de Camões)
15 Aug	*Assunção* (Assumption Day)
5 Oct	*Implantação da República* (Foundation of the Republic 1910)
1 Nov	*Todos os Santos* (All Saints' Day)
1 Dec	*Restauração da Independência* (end of the personal-union with Spain in 1640)
8 Dec	*Imaculada Conceição* (Conception Day)
25 Dec	*Natal* (Christmas)

LINKS, BLOGS, APPS & MORE

LINKS & BLOGS

cultura.madeira-edu.pt Madeira Cultura provides information on events, festivals and museums

short.travel/mdr6 Glide over the hills of Madeira down to the beach – test this with the "flycam" of the head of the Paragliding Center in Arco da Calheta

Tripomatic Madeira the detailed map also functions without internet connection, meaning that you will never get lost on Madeira and Porto Santo

www.madeiratourism.com This is the official tourism website of Madeira, with pages in English. It gives a good overview of what to do and where to stay

www.madeiraarchipelago.com An independent database with photos, films and a variety of information about the island. Madeira is presented not only as a holiday paradise but also as the home of the photographers, most of them locals

www.madeira-web.com More information for your holiday, including weather, walks and live pictures from various webcams

www.madeira-island.com This site is useful for shopping, museums and details of the festivals celebrated on the island

blog.windbirds.pt English-language blog of a travel operator in Funchal specialised in sustainable nature tourism (e.g. bird watching, whale watching). Also deals with up-to-date environmental topics

madeiraislanddirect.com/blo Full English-language blog about current events. News, information and lots of topics are presented concisely and illustrated with matching photos or films. Sponsored by a real-estate company

www.madeirablog.eu Private blog with lots of amusing photos and helpful information

www.facebook.com/SecretMadeira This facebook community posts beautiful pictures and info about Madeira's secret and not so secret spots.

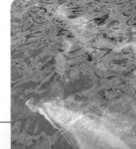

Regardless of whether you are still researching your trip or are already on Madeira: these adresses will provide you with more information, videos and networks to make your holiday even more enjoyable

VIDEOS

www.netmadeira.com/webcams-madeira The most pressing question on Madeira is: what's the weather like? The webcams are a godsend for walkers who are planning a hiking tour on the other side of the island

www.vimeo.com/13538576 Some good photos, and above all fantastic films of flying over the hills of Madeira taken using the "flycam" of the Paragliding Centre in Arco da Calheta

www.youtube.com/watch?v=PGKP8EsP2Nk A slide show of historic photographs. If you make a direct comparison of the scene today with these 100-year-old pictures, in some places it seems as if time has stood still

www.youtube.com/watch?v=oETGAkOtSIU Even if you are not a diver, you can get a magical view of the world of fish, monk seals, octopuses and rays of the coast of Madeira by watching the film "Madeira Aquatica" taken by the underwater photographer Gonçalo Gomes

www.youtube.com/watch?v=TKDh8mX_apk Enjoying Madeira in 1967: A British couple has recorded their trip to sunny Madeira on 8 mm film. Watch Funchal, market scenes, mountain roads and the locals with a nostalgic tint (in two parts and in full colour).

www.youtube.com/watch?v=C3NvgXDlw2A In this short clip you get a little foretaste of Madeira's fantastic lookout points and most dangerous hiking paths

APPS

madeira-street-map Apple provides this detailed street and road map of the island and the capital Funchal to download for your iPhone

Walkme Levadas Practical hiking app developed by Madeiran software engineers: descriptions, photos, maps for Android and iPhone

Madeira Island Activities All kinds of information about outdoor activities like canyoning, *levada* walks, jeep safaris, whale watching; for Android

Madeira is sun 1.0 All beaches and swimming sites on Madeira for iPhone and iPad

Porto Santo Line Timetables and fares of the ships between Madeira and Porto Santo, as well as special cruises, sights and accommodation on Madeira's neighbour island

TRAVEL TIPS

ACCOMMODATION

There are currently about 28,000 beds for visitors to Madeira, mostly in Funchal and Caniço, and the majority are four- or five-star hotels (graded by Portuguese standards). Add to this apartment hotels ranging from basic to luxurious, *estalagens* (simple hotels), albergarias, guesthouses (pensão, residencial) and rural accommodation organised by the *turismo de habitação (TH) or turismo rural (TR)*. Some of these were once residences of the wealthy (quintas) – though hotels also like to use this coveted name. There are also a few hostels and guesthouses: favourable prices (chiefly in multi-bed rooms) and a young clientele.

RESPONSIBLE TRAVEL

It doesn't take a lot to be environmentally friendly whilst travelling. Don't just think about your carbon footprint whilst travelling to and from your holiday destination *(www. atmosfair.de; www.myclimate. org)* – e.g. by planning your route environmentally responsibly *(www.routerank.com)* – but also about how you can protect nature and culture abroad. As a tourist it is especially important to respect nature, look out for local products, cycle instead of driving, save water and much more. If you would like to find out more about eco-tourism please visit: *www.ecotourism.org*

ARRIVAL

🛫 Package holidays with a flight and accommodation are the simplest and generally also the cheapest way to go to Madeira. A charter flight from western Europe in summer without hotel costs 300–400 euros. The prices are slightly cheaper for TAP Portugal's scheduled flights, which go several times daily – but you have to change in Lisbon. In summer TAP also flies several times a week from Lisbon direct to Porto Santo. Otherwise you can get there from Madeira up to five times daily with Aero Vip flights (flying time approx. 20 minutes).

Madeira's airport (tel. 2 91 52 07 00) is located in Santa Catarina near Santa Cruz, some 20 km/12.4 mi from the centre of Funchal. Please note that despite the extension of the runway, difficult cross-wind conditions can make it impossible to land there. The best option is then to land on Porto Santo and take the ferry to Madeira, but frequently the plane will fly back to Lisbon and attempt a new landing the next day.

Once you have landed on Madeira and wish to travel to Funchal by bus, the Aerobus *(5 euros or 8 euros return)* stops in front of the arrival hall and will take you to the hotel district.

🚢 Cruise ships often put in at Funchal. The *Lobo Marinho ferry (approx. 2 hours | return ticket from 46.95 euros at off-peak times | tel. 2 91 21 03 00 | www.portosantoline.pt)* crosses daily from Funchal to Madeira's neighbouring island Porto Santo.

From arrival to weather

Your holiday from start to finish: the most important addresses and information for your trip to Madeira

CAMPING

Camping on Madeira outside official camping sites is only permitted with a special permit issued by the *Forestry Department IP-RAM (tel. 2 91 74 00 60 | ifcn. madeira.gov.pt)*. You will find a list of the natural campsites on the web site. Madeira's camping site is near Ribeira da Janela and the camping ground on Porto Santo is situated near the main town of Vila Baleira.

CAR HIRE

National and international car hire firms have offices at the airports, in the capitals of Madeira and Porto Santo and in Caniço de Baixo. Local operators tempt visitors with special offers, but it is certainly worth comparing their prices with the offers available when booking at home. Drivers of hire cars must be at least 21 years old. A car costs between 25 and 70 euros per day, with unlimited mileage.

CLIMATE

Madeira enjoys a mild climate all year round. Even in January and February it is exceptional for the daytime temperature on the south coast to fall below 15°C/59°F. The warmest months are July, August and September, when the thermometer can show more than 25°C/77°F on the south coast. Go prepared for rain showers, especially in winter and spring. The weather on Madeira can be extremely changeable, and differ from one place to another at any one time. The weather forecasts pinned to hotel notice boards *(e.g. from www.madei-ra-weather.info)* should only be seen as a general guide. Webcams *(e.g. www. madeirawebcams.com)* may be more helpful for planning your day. When the trade winds blow from the northeast, it is often cloudy in the mountains and on the north coast, but stable. A southeast wind *(leste)* from the Sahara means warm and sunny weather for most of the island. West winds cause changeable and rainy weather, as they carry alternating fronts of warm and cold air.

BUDGETING

Poncha	1.75–2.65 £/2.25–3.35 $	
	for a cocktail	
Bica	0.60 £/0.80 $	
	for an espresso	
Lapas	5.30–7 £/6.70–9 $	
	for a portion of limpets	
Petrol	1.23 £/1.57 $	
	for 1 l of unleaded	
Pool	1.75–3.50 £/2.25–4.50 $	
	per day at sea-water pools	
Souvenir	16–22 £/20–28 $	
	for a bottle of Madeira wine (aged for 10 years)	

CONSULATES

– *British honorary consulate | Mon, Tue, Thu, Fri 10am–12.30pm | Rua da Alfandega 10, 3C | Funchal | tel. 2 91 21 28 60 | e-mail: Britcon.Funchal@Net Madeira.com*
– *U.S. citizens should contact the embassy in Lisbon, www.portugal.usembassy.gov*

CUSTOMS

Within the European Union goods for personal use can be imported and exported duty-free. However note that some limits should not be exceeded, e.g. 800 cigarettes, 10 l/2.6 gal of spirits per person (over the age of 17). Visitors from other countries must observe the following limits, except for items for personal use. Duty free are: max. 50 ml/1.7 oz perfume, 200 cigarettes, 50 cigars, 250 g/8.8 oz tobacco, 1l/34 oz of spirits (over 22 % vol.), 2 l/68 oz of spirits (under 22 % vol.), 5 litres of any wine.

DRIVING

The speed limit on Madeira in towns is 50 km/h/30 mph, on country roads 90 km/h/55 mph and on the *via rápida*, Madeira's fast highway, 100 km/h/62 mph. The legal limit of blood-alcohol is 0.5 g/L and the use of seat belts is obligatory. In case of a breakdown drivers leaving the vehicle must wear a high-vis jacket. The main roads on Madeira and Porto Santo are surfaced with asphalt and are generally in good condition; many of them now run through tunnels. Exercise extreme caution when driving on mountain roads in heavy rain. Stones and debris often roll down the slopes onto the road. Drive carefully in fog in the highlands as cows on the road are often quite difficult to see from a distance. Parking spaces in the centre of Funchal are scarce and cost money.

ELECTRICITY

The two-pin sockets in Portugal and on Madeira are the same as those in continental Europe, so visitors from Britain and North America should take an adapter. The power supply is 220 volts AC.

EMERGENCY SERVICES

– *Emergency/ambulance: tel. 112*
– *SANAS sea rescue: tel. 2 91 23 01 12*
– *Mountain rescue (Protecção Civil): tel. 2 91 70 01 12*

HEALTH

Since the end of 2012, cases of dengue fever have been reported on Madeira. The illness is spread by mosquitoes. Symptoms include fever, rash and aching joints. To prevent mosquito bites, wear long, light-coloured clothing and use insect repellent. Many hotels can call a hotel doctor in an emergency. A medical consultation should be paid for immediately. EU citizens can recoup the costs at home by producing an invoice.

It is recommended to take out a holiday health insurance policy, as some costs for medicine and treatment have to be borne by the patient, and in some cases return transport to the home country may be necessary. The EHIC (European Health Insurance Card) entitles EU citizens to treatment in state hospitals and health centres. You can find a list of appropriate contact addresses at *www.sesaram.pt*.

The state-run Hospital *Dr. Nélio Mendonça (Av. Luís de Camões | tel. 2 91 70 56 00)* is close to the hotel quarter in Funchal. The small private *Clinica da Sé (Rua das Murças 42 | tel. 2 91 20 76 76)*, where English is spoken, provides specialist help from consultants round the clock. English-speaking dentists are also available here. All towns on the island have a health clinic *(centro de saúde)*. The address on Porto Santo is Unidade de *Saúde Dr. Francisco Rodrigues Jardim (Rua Dr. José Diamantino Lima | tel. 2 91 98 00 60)*.

There are enough pharmacies, at least in the towns *(farmácias, postos de medicamentos)*, and one of them is always open; the up-to-date schedule of opening times is on display on the door of every pharmacy.

IMMIGRATION

EU citizens need only an ID card or passport to travel to Madeira. Children under the age of 16 must be registered on a parent's passport or carry a child's passport. A valid passport is required for entry into Portugal (Non-EU); all children must travel with their own passports.

INFORMATION

POSTO DE TURISMO
www.visitmadeira.pt
– Tourist information in Funchal: *Av. Arriaga 16 | tel. 2 91 21 19 02*
– Tourist information at the airport: *arrivals hall | tel. 2 91 52 49 33*
– Tourist information in Porto Santo: *Av. Dr. Manuel Gregório Pestana Junior | tel. 2 91 98 52 44*
www.visitmadeira.pt

LANGUAGE

The people of Madeira speak Portuguese with their own dialect, which the mainland Portuguese recognise at once. Visitors to the island can get by very well speaking English. In hotels, restaurants and agencies the staff have often been well trained at the school of tourism to look after foreign visitors and may be fluent in more than one foreign language. Spanish is understood quite well on Madeira, but speaking Spanish to the locals is not the way to make yourself popular. Portuguese is spoken worldwide by approx. 210 million people, and anyone who would like to learn it on Madeira can book an individual language course, e.g. at the *Academia*

de Línguas da Madeira (ALM) (www.alm-madeira.com).

MEDIA

TV channels in English are available in many hotels. International newspapers are on sale at kiosks, often a day after publication, and the English-speaking magazine "Madeira Life" has lots of information, including bus timetables and events listings.

MONEY & PRICES

As in the rest of Portugal, the currency in circulation on Madeira is the euro. Cash machines (ATMs, *multibancos*)

CURRENCY CONVERTER

£	€	€	£
1	1.15	1	0.88
3	3.45	3	2.64
5	5.75	5	4.40
13	14.95	13	11.44
40	46	40	35.20
75	86.25	75	66
120	138	120	105.60
250	287.50	250	220
500	575	500	440

$	€	€	$
1	0.90	1	1.10
3	2.70	3	3.30
5	4.50	5	5.50
13	11.70	13	14.30
40	36	40	44
75	67.50	75	82.50
120	108	120	132
250	225	250	275
500	450	500	550

For current exchange rates see www.xe.com

can be found almost everywhere. The amount that can be withdrawn is limited to two times 200 euros daily. Payment by credit card or EC cheque card is accepted in larger hotels, restaurants and shops. Price levels are not much different from those in other EU countries. Basic foodstuffs such as bread are cheap, but products such as cosmetics and toiletries tend to be more expensive. The cost of living is lower outside the main tourist areas.

OPENING HOURS

Tourist offices, small shops and public institutions are normally open Mon–Fri 9am–12.30pm and 2.30–6pm, Sat 9am–1pm. Museums are often closed Mon. Banks open Mon–Fri 9am–3pm. Supermarkets and shopping centres are open daily as a rule until 10pm without a midday break.

Unless otherwise shown, the restaurants described in this guide are open daily noon–3pm and from 6pm (usually until approx. 11pm). Evening shopping is possible in shopping centres *(e.g. Madeira Shopping and Forum Madeira)* until 11pm and at the weekend even until midnight.

PHONE, MOBILE PHONE & WIFI

Country codes: UK 0044, Ireland 00353, USA and Canada 001. For calls to Madeira/Porto Santo 00 351.

European mobile phones work everywhere on Madeira and Porto Santo via the Portuguese networks (e.g. Vodafone and MEO). Since the dropping of roaming charges within Europe you can use your mobile on your domestic rates.

Most hotels offer free WiFi, at least in the lobby. WiFi is also available in some public places in Funchal and in almost all cafés.

POST

A red and white sign with a horse rider and the letters CTT identifies post offices. Their usual hours are Mon–Fri 9am–6pm. The main post office in Funchal *(Av. Zarco)* opens Mon–Fri 8.30am–7pm and Sat 9am–1pm. Stamps *(selos)* are also on sale in licensed bars, newsagents and kiosks. Postcards and letters up to 20 g within Europe need a stamp for 0.75 euros.

PUBLIC TRANSPORT

Almost any place on Madeira and the great majority of sights can be reached by bus. *See the back flap of this book for a map of the routes.*

There is a small electric bus route in the centre of Funchal *(Linha Eco)*. Bustickets can normally be purchased from the driver: single tickets cost 1.95 euros. You can however buy a "giro" card for 1.35 euros (plus a single surcharge of 0.50 for the ticket itself which has to be topped up at the ticket machine before boarding the bus). Multi-day tickets are also available (e.g. 21,85 euros for 7 days) for all lines within the city.

Madeira has no unified bus network but instead a number of bus operators who are responsible for different regions. In the Funchal area the bus company is *Horários do Funchal (www.horariosdo funchal.pt, with bus timetable for the Funchal region)*, EACL (www.eacl.pt) links the island's capital to Caniço, Rodoeste has the routes to the west of *Madeira (www. rodoeste.pt)* and *SAM (www.sam.pt)* the east. There is a kind of central bus station on the edge of the old quarter of Funchal: most buses depart between the cable-car terminus and Praça da Autonomia. Others stop along Avenida do Mar, as do many private hotel shuttle buses and the *airport bus (aerobus)*, which takes about 40 minutes from the airport to the hotel zone (5 euros).

TAXIS

Taxis have a meter for journeys in Funchal and a copy of the tariff for reference. The minimum fare is 2.50 euros (6am–10pm on weekdays). To call a taxi in Funchal dial *tel. 2 91 76 44 76*, or ask the hotel reception. For tours of the island, the price should be 50–100 euros. Trips to and from the airport cost 20–30 euros, depending on the distance. Overland journeys are charged according to a list of fixed prices, even though the meter is not switched on.

TIME

Madeira is in the GMT zone. The clocks are put forward one hour from late March to late October, so visitors from the UK do not need to reset their watches.

TIPPING

In restaurants the amount on the bill is usually rounded up or 5–10 per cent of the sum are added as a tip. Simply leave your tip on the plate on which the bill is brought. Taxi drivers, chambermaids, porters, tour guides and shoe cleaners are also pleased by a bit of extra earnings.

WATER

The tap water is safe to drink but tastes slightly chlorinated and has often been chemically treated. There is no reason not to use it for cleaning your teeth, but it is advisable to buy drinking water in a supermarket, e.g. as a five-litre canister.

WEATHER IN FUNCHAL

	Jan	Feb	March	April	May	June	July	Aug	Sept	Oct	Nov	Dec
Daytime temperatures in °C/°F	14/57	14/57	16/61	18/64	21/70	25/77	28/82	28/82	26/79	22/72	18/64	14/57
Nighttime temperatures in °C/°F	7/45	7/45	9/48	11/52	13/55	17/63	20/68	20/68	19/66	15/59	11/52	9/48
☀ Sunshine hours/day	5	5	6	8	10	10	12	10	8	6	5	4
☂ Precipitation days/month	9	8	8	7	5	3	1	3	6	11	9	12
≋ Water temperatures in °C/°F	14/57	13/55	14/57	14/57	17/63	20/68	23/73	25/77	23/73	21/70	18/64	15/59

USEFUL PHRASES PORTUGUESE

PRONUNCIATION

To help you say the Portuguese words we have added a simple pronunciation guide in square brackets and an apostrophe ' before the syllable that is stressed. Note the following sounds shown in the pronunciation guide:
"zh" like the "s" in "pleasure", "ng" indicates a nasal sound at the end of a word (i.e. not with distinct consonants as in English) , e.g. "não" is shown as "nowng", "ee" as in "fee", "ai" as in "aisle", "oo" as in "zoo"

IN BRIEF

Yes/No/Maybe	sim [seeng]/não [nowng]/talvez [tal'vesh]
Please	se faz favor [se fash fa'vor]
Thank you	obrigado (m)/obrigada (f) [obri'gadoo/obri'gada]
Sorry/ Excuse me, please	Desculpa! [dish'kulpa]/Desculpe! [dish'kulp]
May I...?/ Pardon?	Posso...? ['possoo]/ Como? ['komoo]
I would like to...	Queria ... [ke'ria]
Have you got...?	Tem...? [teng]
How much is...	Quanto custa...? ['kwantoo 'kooshta]
good/bad/broken/ doesn't work	bem [beng]/mal [mal]/estragado [ishtra'gadoo]/ não funciona [nowng fung'siona]
too much/much/little	demais [de'maish]/muito ['mooitoo]/pouco ['pokoo]
all/nothing	tudo ['toodoo]/nada ['nada]
Help!/Attention!/Caution!	Socorro! [soo'korroo]/Atenção! [atten'sowng]
ambulance	ambulância [amboo'langsia]
police/fire brigade	polícia [pu'lisia]/bombeiros [bom'beyroosh]
prohibition/forbidden	interdição [interdi'sowng]/proibido [prooi'bidoo]
danger/dangerous	perigo [pe'rigoo]/perigoso [peri'gosoo]

GREETINGS, FAREWELL

Good morning!/after- noon!/evening!/night!	Bom dia! [bong 'dia]/Bom dia! [bong 'dia]/ Boa tarde! ['boa 'tard]/Boa noite! ['boa 'noyt]
Hello!/Goodbye!	Olá! [o'la]/Adeus! [a'dy-oosh]
See you	Cião! [chowng]
My name is...	Chamo-me... ['shamoo-me]
What's your name?	Como se chama? ['komoo se 'shama] Como te chamas? ['komoo te 'shamas]
I'm from...	Sou de... [so de]

Falas português?

"Do you speak Portuguese?" This guide will help you to say the basic words and phrases in Portuguese.

Monday/Tuesday	segunda-feira [se'goonda 'feyra]/terça-feira ['tersa 'feyra]
Wednesday/Thursday	quarta-feira ['kwarta 'feyra]/quinta-feira ['kinta 'feyra]
Friday/Saturday	sexta-feira ['seshta 'feyra]/sábado ['sabadoo]
Sunday	domingo [doo'mingoo]
today/tomorrow/	hoje ['ozhe]/amanhã [amman'ya]/
yesterday	ontem ['onteng]
hour/minute	hora ['ora]/minuto [mi'nootoo]
day/night/week	dia [dia]/noite [noyt]/semana [se'mana]
month/year	mês [meysh]/ano ['anoo]
What time is it?	Que horas são? [ke 'orash sowng]
It's three o'clock	São três horas. [sowng tresh 'orash]
It's half past three	São três e meia. [sowng tresh i 'meya]

TRAVEL

open/closed	aberto [a'bertoo]/fechado [fe'shadoo]
entrance	entrada [en'trada]
exit	saída [sa'ida]
departure/arrival	partida [par'tida]/chegada [she'gada]
toilets/restrooms/	sanitários [sanni'tariush]/
ladies/gentlemen	senhoras [sen'yorash]/senhores [sen'joresh]
(no) drinking water	água (não) potável ['agwa (nowng) po'tavel]
Where is...?/Where are...?	Onde é...? ['onde e]/Onde são...? ['onde sowng]
left/right	à esquerda [a ish'kerda]/à direita [a dee'reyta]
straight ahead/back	em frente [eng 'frente]/para atrás ['para'trash]
bus	autocarro [auto'karroo]
stop	paragem [pa'razheng]
parking lot	estacionamento [eshtassiona'mentoo]
street map/map	mapa ['mappa]/mapa da cidade ['mappa da see'dad]
train station/	estação ferroviária [eshta'sowng ferrovi'aria]/
harbour/airport	porto ['portoo]/aeroporto [a-eyro'portoo]
schedule/ticket	horário [o'rariyu]/bilhete [bil'yet]
single/return	só ida [so 'ida]/ida e volta ['ida i 'vollta]
train/platform	comboio [kom'boyoo]/linha ['linya]
I would like to rent...	Gostaria de alugar... [goshta'ria de alloo'gar]
a car/a bicycle/	um carro [oong 'karroo]/uma bicicleta [ooma
a boat	bissi'kletta]/um barco [oong 'barkoo]
petrol/gas station/	bomba de gasolina ['bomba de gaso'lina]/
petrol/gas / diesel	petróleo [pe'troleo]/gasóleo [ga'soleo]
breakdown/repair shop	avaria [ava'ria]/garagem [ga'razheng]

FOOD & DRINK

Could you please book a table for tonight for four?	Se faz favor, pode reservar-nos para hoje à noite uma mesa para quatro pessoas. [se fash fa'vor, 'pode reser'varnoosh 'para 'oshe ah noit ooma 'mesa 'para 'kwatroo pe'ssoash]
The menu, please	A ementa, se faz favor. [a i'menta, se fash fa'vor]
bottle/glass	garrafa [gar'raffa]/copo ['koppoo]
salt/pepper/sugar	sal [sall]/pimenta [pi'menta]/açúcar [a'ssookar]
vinegar/oil	vinagre [vi'nagre]/azeite [a'zeite]
milk/cream/lemon	leite ['leyte]/natas ['natash]/limão [li'mowng]
with/without ice/sparkling	com [kong]/sem [seng] gelo ['zheloo]/gás [gash]
vegetarian/allergy	vegetariano/-a [vezhetari'anoo/-a]/alergia [aller'zhia]
May I have the bill, please?	A conta, se faz favor. [a 'konta, se fash fa'vor]

SHOPPING

Where can I find...?	Quero ... ['keroo]/Procuro ... [pro'kooroo]
pharmacy/chemist	farmácia [far'massia]/drogaria [droga'ria]
baker/market	padaria [pada'ria]/mercado [mer'kadoo]
shopping centre	centro comercial ['sentroo kommer'ssial]
100 grammes/1 kilo	cem gramas [seng 'grammash]/um quilo [oong 'kiloo]
expensive/cheap/price	caro ['karoo]/barato [ba'ratoo]/preço ['pressoo]
more/less	mais [maish]/menos ['menoosh]

ACCOMMODATION

I have booked a room	Reservei um quarto. [rezer'vey oong 'kwartoo]
Do you have any ... left?	Ainda tem ...? [a'inda teng]
single room	um quarto individual [oong 'kwartoo individu'al]
double room	um quarto de casal [oong 'kwartoo de ka'sal]
breakfast/	pequeno-almoço [pe'kaynoo al'mossoo]/
half board/	meia pensão ['meya pen'sowng]/
full board (American plan)	pensão completa [pen'sowng kom'pleta]
shower/sit-down bath	ducha [doosha]/banho ['banyoo]
balcony/terrace	varanda [va'randa]/terraço [ter'rassoo]
key/room card	chave ['chav-e]/cartão [kar'towng]
luggage/suitcase	bagagem [ba'gazheng]/mala ['mala]/saco ['sakoo]

BANKS, MONEY & CREDIT CARDS

bank/ATM	banco ['bankoo]/multibanco ['multibankoo]
pin code	código pessoal ['kodigoo pessoo'al]
cash/	em dinheiro [eng din'yeyroo]/
credit card	com cartão de crédito [kong kar'towng de 'kreditoo]
note/coin	nota ['nota]/moeda [mo'ayda]

HEALTH

doctor/dentist/ paediatrician	médico ['medikoo]/dentista [den'tishta]/ pediatra [pedi'atra]
hospital/ emergency clinic	hospital [oshpi'tal]/ urgências [oor'zhensiash]
fever/pain	febre ['feybre]/dores ['doresh]
diarrhoea/nausea	diarreia [diar'reya]/enjoo [eng'zho]
sunburn	queimadura [keyma'doora]
inflamed/injured	inflamado [infla'madoo]/ferido [fe'ridoo]
plaster/bandage	penso ['pengshoo]/ligadura [liga'doora]
tablet	comprimido [kompri'midoo]

POST, TELECOMMUNICATIONS & MEDIA

stamp/letter/postcard	selo ['seloo]/carta ['karta]/postal [posh'tal]
I'm looking for a prepaid card for my mobile	Procuro um cartão SIM para o meu telemóvel. [pro'kooroo oong kar'towng sim 'para oo meyoo tele'movel]
Where can I find internet access?	Onde há acesso à internet? ['onde a a'ssessoo a 'internet]
computer/battery/ rechargeable battery	computador [kompoota'dor]/pilha ['pilya]/ bateria [bate'ria]
internet connection	ligação à internet [liga'sowng a 'internet]

LEISURE, SPORTS & BEACH

beach/sunshade/ lounger	praia ['praya]/guarda-sol [gwarda 'sol]/ espreguiçadeira [eshpregissa'deyra]
low tide/high tide/ current	maré baixa [ma're 'baisha]/maré alta [ma're alta]/ corrente [kor'rente]

NUMBERS

0	zero ['zeroo]	20	vinte [veengt]
1	um, uma ['oong, 'ooma]	21	vinte e um ['veengt e 'oong]
2	dois, duas ['doysh, 'dooash]	30	trinta ['treengta]
3	três [tresh]	40	quarenta [kwa'renta]
4	quatro ['kwatroo]	50	cinquenta [seeng'kwengta]
5	cinco ['seengkoo]	100	cem ['seng]
6	seis ['seysh]	200	duzentos [doo'zentoosh]
7	sete ['set]	1000	mil ['meel]
8	oito ['oytoo]	2000	dois mil ['doysh meel]
9	nove ['nov]	10.000	dez mil ['desh meel]
10	dez ['desh]	½	um meio [oong 'meyoo]
11	onze ['ongs]	¼	um quarto [oong 'kwartoo]

ROAD ATLAS

The green line indicates the Discovery Tour "Madeira at a glance"
The blue line indicates the other Discovery Tours

All tours are also marked on the pull-out map

Photo: The village of Boaventura in the north of Madeira

Exploring Madeira

The map on the back cover shows how
the area has been sub-divided

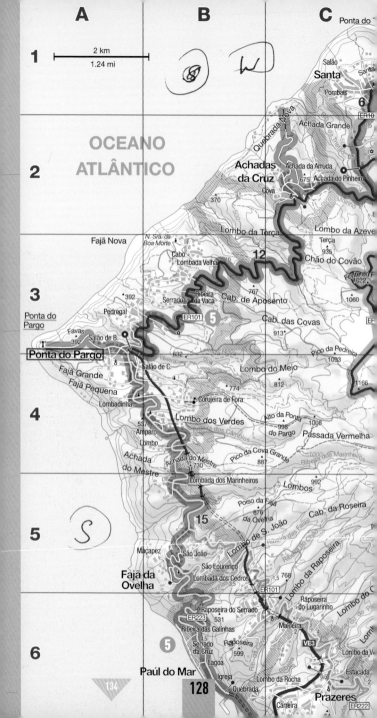

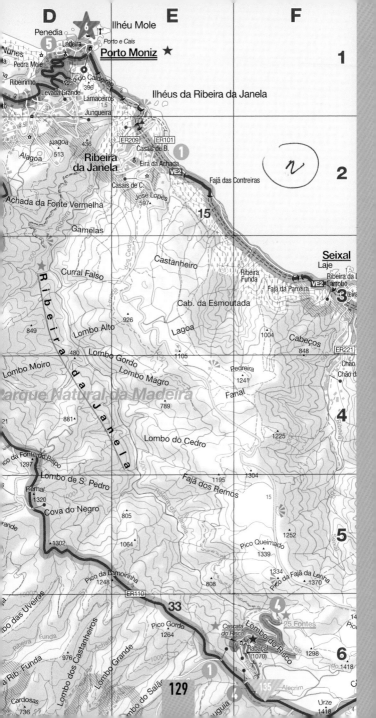

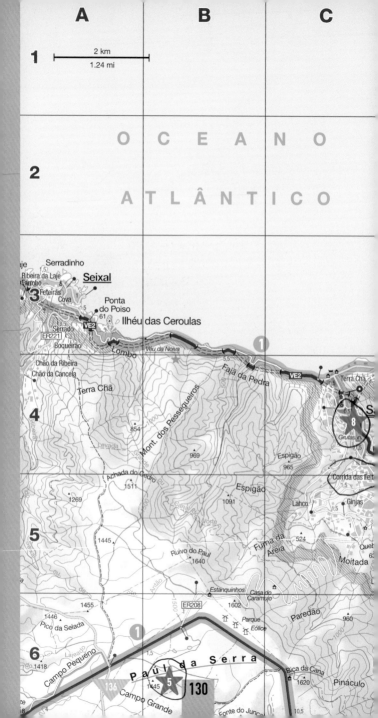

A   B   C

1

2 km
1.24 mi

O C E A N O

2

A T L Â N T I C O

Serradinho
Ribeira da Laje
Farrobo
Seixal
Feteiras
Cova
Ponta
do Poiso
3
61
Ilhéu das Ceroulas
Serrado
VE2
ER221
Boqueirão
Lombo
Véu da Noiva
Faja da Pedra
VE2
Terra Chã
Chão da Ribeira
Chão da Cancela
Terra Chã
S.
8
Grutas
854
4
Mont. dos Pessegueiros
969
Espigão
965
Corrida das Feit
Achada do Cedro
1511
Espigão
1091
Lahco
Ginjas
1269
Fuma da
Areia
524
5
1445
Ruivo do Paul
1640
Moitada
Queb
Estanquinhos
Casa do
Caramujo
1602
Paredão
960
1446
1455
ER208
Parque
Eólice
Pico da Selada
Bica da Cana
1418
Campo Pequeno
6
Paul d a S e r r a
136
1445
5
130
Pináculo
1620
Campo Grande
Fonte do Junca
10,5

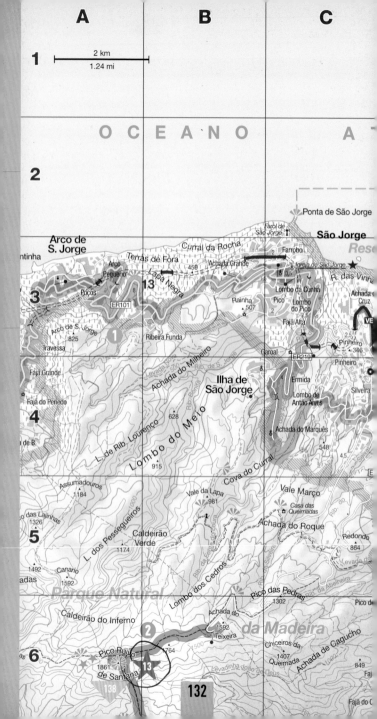

A B C

1

2 km
1.24 mi

O C E A N O   A

2

Ponta de São Jorge

Farol de
São Jorge   **São Jorge**

Arco de
S. Jorge   Curral da Rocha   Rese

ntinha   Terras de Fora   Farrobo

Arco   450   Achada Grande   Igreja do São Jorge ★   R. das Vinha
Pequeno   Lapa Negra

3   Poços   **13**   8   0.5   Lombo da Cunha   Achada
ER101   Rainha   Pico   Lombo   Cruz   VE
                507   do Pico
Arco de S. Jorge   Fajã Alta
825   Ribeira Funda   Pinheiro   346
Travessa   Garoal   ER219   Pinheiro

Fajã Grande   Achada do Milheiro   **Ilha de
São Jorge**   Ermida   Silveira

Fajã do Penedo   L. de Rib. Lourenço   Lombo de
Antão Alves

4   628
                Achada do Marquês
de B.   Lombo do Meio   548
        915   Cova do Curral   4.5   E

Assumadouros   Vale Março
1184   Vale da Lapa
o das Lajinhas   981   Casa das   Rib. do
1326   Queimadas
L. dos Pessegueiros   Achada do Roque
5   Caldeirão   Redondo
        Verde   864
        1174
1492   Canario   Levadinha
        1592   Lombo dos Cedros   Pico das Pedras   Pico d
ados   1302

Parque Natural   da Madeira

Caldeirão do Inferno   **2**   Achada do
        1592   Teixeira   Chiceiros da   849
6   Pico Ruivo   1764   1407   Queimada   Achada de Cagucho
        1861   **13**   Levadinha do São
de Santana   Deus   Fajã
138

132

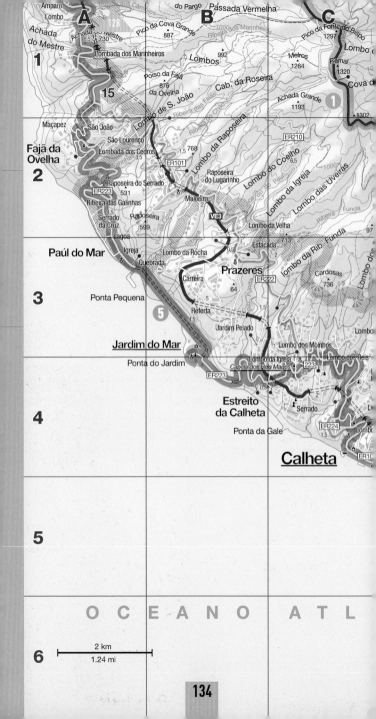

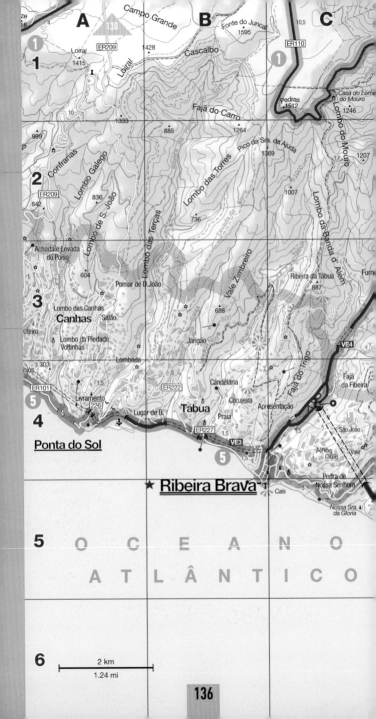

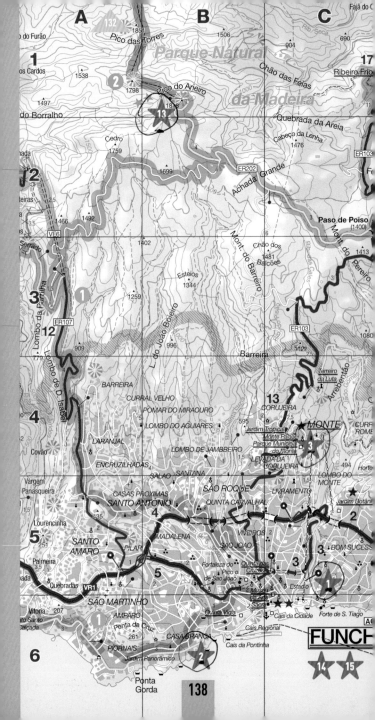

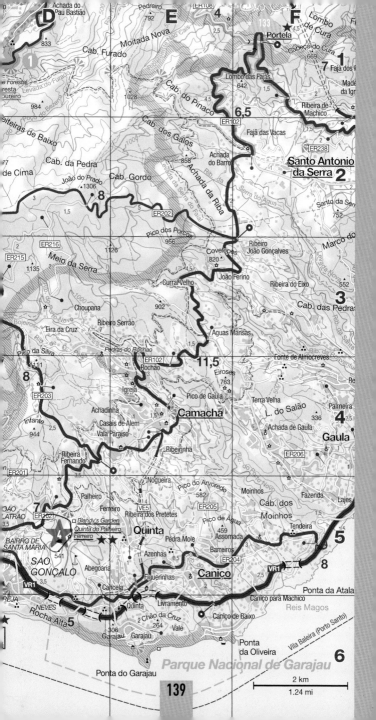

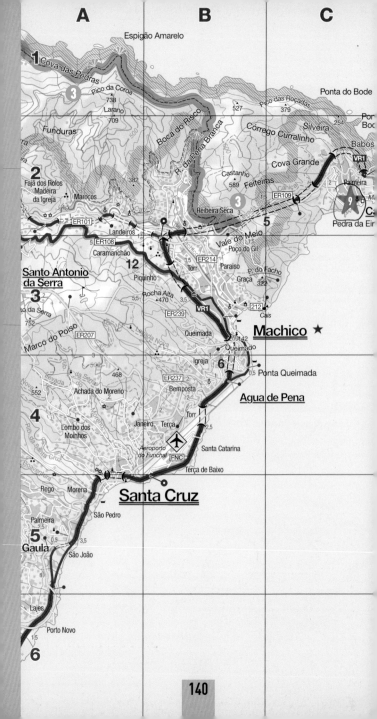

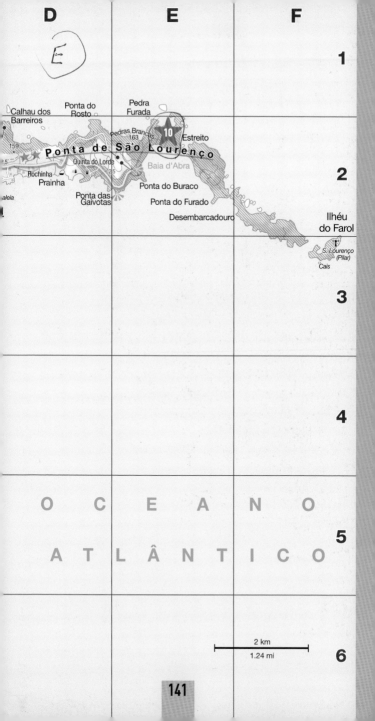

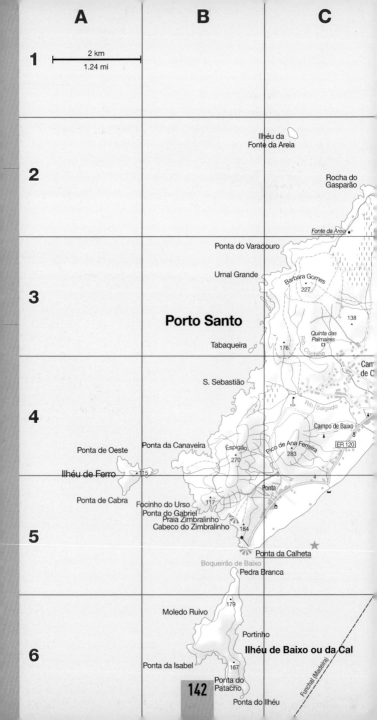

Porto Santo

	A	B	C

1 — 2 km / 1.24 mi

2
Ilhéu da Fonte da Areia
Rocha do Gasparão
Fonte da Areia

3
Ponta do Varadouro
Urnal Grande
Barbara Gomes 227
138
Porto Santo
Quinta das Palmaires
Tabaqueira
176
Rib. Cochino
Cam de C

4
S. Sebastião
Rib. Salgado
Campo de Baixo
ER 120
Ponta de Oeste
Ponta da Canaveira
Espigão 270
Pico de Ana Ferreira 283
Ilhéu de Ferro 115
4
Ponta de Cabra
Ponta

5
Focinho do Urso
Ponta do Gabriel
Praia Zimbralinho 117
Cabeço do Zimbralinho 184
Ponta da Calheta
Boqueirão de Baixo
Pedra Branca

6
Moledo Ruivo 179
Portinho
Ilhéu de Baixo ou da Cal
Ponta da Isabel 167
Ponta do Patacho
142
Ponta do Ilhéu
Funchal (Madeira)

	D	E	F

F

Ilhéu da Fora

Baixo do Meio

1

Baixa dos Barbeiros

Focinho da Forte

Furnas das Amasiadas

Ilhéu das Cenouras

2

Rib. do Pedregal

120

4,5

Rib. das Ferreiras

1,5

Pico Juliana
440

Pico das Urzes
450

Serra de Dentro

Serra de Dentro

Camacha

ER 120

Pico do Facho
517

Pico do Castelo
437

ER 120

Pico do Concelho
324

Serra de Fora

Ponta dos Ferreiros

3

3

3

Dragool

Capela de
N.ª Sra. da
Graça

275

1,5

ER 260

Rib. do Galhal

ER 120

Casinhas
163

Penedo

Pico do Macarico
285

1,5

Ponta
da Galé

Boqueirão de Cima

Saloës

11

Barroca

2

Portela

Mus de Cristóvão ★

Porto
de Abrigo

Ilhéu de Cima
119

Vila Baleira
(Porto Santo)

1,5

4

O C E A N O

5

A T L Â N T I C O

6

KEY TO ROAD ATLAS

Autobahn · Gebührenpflichtige Anschlussstelle · Gebührenstelle · Anschlussstelle mit Nummer · Rasthaus mit Übernachtung · Raststätte · Kleinraststätte · Tankstelle · Parkplatz mit und ohne WC		Motorway · Toll junction · Toll station · Junction with number · Motel · Restaurant · Snackbar · Filling-station · Parking place with and without WC
Autobahn in Bau und geplant mit Datum der voraussichtlichen Verkehrsübergabe	Datum Date	Motorway under construction and projected with expected date of opening
Zweibahnige Straße (4-spurig)		Dual carriageway (4 lanes)
Fernverkehrsstraße · Straßennummern	14 E45	Trunk road · Road numbers
Wichtige Hauptstraße		Important main road
Hauptstraße · Tunnel · Brücke		Main road · Tunnel · Bridge
Nebenstraßen		Minor roads
Fahrweg · Fußweg		Track · Footpath
Wanderweg (Auswahl)		Tourist footpath (selection)
Eisenbahn mit Fernverkehr		Main line railway
Zahnradbahn, Standseilbahn		Rack-railway, funicular
Kabinenschwebebahn · Sessellift		Aerial cableway · Chair-lift
Autofähre · Personenfähre		Car ferry · Passenger ferry
Schifffahrtslinie		Shipping route
Naturschutzgebiet · Sperrgebiet		Nature reserve · Prohibited area
Nationalpark · Naturpark · Wald		National park · natural park · Forest
Straße für Kfz. gesperrt	X X X X X	Road closed to motor vehicles
Straße mit Gebühr		Toll road
Straße mit Wintersperre	XII-II	Road closed in winter
Straße für Wohnanhänger gesperrt bzw. nicht empfehlenswert		Road closed or not recommended for caravans
Touristenstraße · Pass	Weinstraße 1510	Tourist route · Pass
Schöner Ausblick · Rundblick · Landschaftlich bes. schöne Strecke		Scenic view · Panoramic view · Route with beautiful scenery
Heilbad · Schwimmbad		Spa · Swimming pool
Jugendherberge · Campingplatz		Youth hostel · Camping site
Golfplatz · Sprungschanze		Golf-course · Ski jump
Kirche im Ort, freistehend · Kapelle		Church · Chapel
Kloster · Klosterruine		Monastery · Monastery ruin
Synagoge · Moschee		Synagogue · Mosque
Schloss, Burg · Schloss-, Burgruine		Palace, castle · Ruin
Turm · Funk-, Fernsehturm		Tower · Radio-, TV-tower
Leuchtturm · Kraftwerk		Lighthouse · Power station
Wasserfall · Schleuse		Waterfall · Lock
Bauwerk · Marktplatz, Areal		Important building · Market place, area
Ausgrabungs- u. Ruinenstätte · Bergwerk		Arch. excavation, ruins · Mine
Dolmen · Menhir · Nuraghen		Dolmen · Menhir · Nuraghe
Hünen-, Hügelgrab · Soldatenfriedhof		Cairn · Military cemetery
Hotel, Gasthaus, Berghütte · Höhle		Hotel, inn, refuge · Cave

Kultur
		Culture
Malerisches Ortsbild · Ortshöhe	WIEN (171)	Picturesque town · Elevation
Eine Reise wert	★★ MILANO	Worth a journey
Lohnt einen Umweg	★ TEMPLIN	Worth a detour
Sehenswert	Andermatt	Worth seeing

Landschaft
		Landscape
Eine Reise wert	★★ Las Cañadas	Worth a journey
Lohnt einen Umweg	★ Texel	Worth a detour
Sehenswert	Dikti	Worth seeing

MARCO POLO Erlebnistour 1		**MARCO POLO Discovery Tour 1**
MARCO POLO Erlebnistouren		**MARCO POLO Discovery Tours**
MARCO POLO Highlight	⭐	**MARCO POLO Highlight**

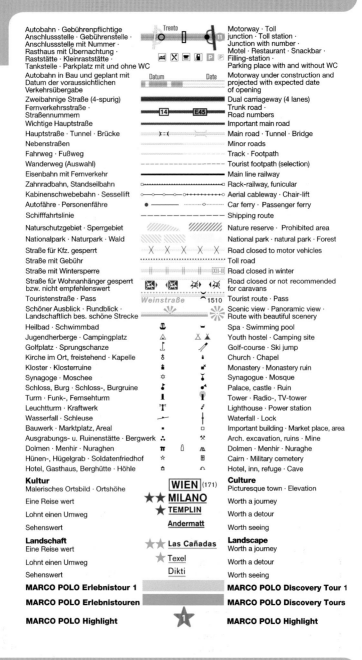

MARCO POLO TRAVEL GUIDES

The travel guides with **Insider Tips**

INDEX

This index lists all places, museums and destinations mentioned in this guide. Page numbers in bold type refer to the main entry.

WRITE TO US

e-mail: info@marcopologuides.co.uk
Did you have a great holiday?
Is there something on your mind?
Whatever it is, let us know!
Whether you want to praise, alert us
to errors or give us a personal tip –
MARCO POLO would be pleased to
hear from you.
We do everything we can to provide the
very latest information for your trip.

Nevertheless, despite all of our authors'
thorough research, errors can creep in.
MARCO POLO does not accept any
liability for this. Please contact us by
e-mail or post.
MARCO POLO Travel Publishing Ltd
Pinewood, Chineham Business Park
Crockford Lane, Chineham
Basingstoke, Hampshire RG24 8AL
United Kingdom

PICTURE CREDITS
Cover photograph: View of the "Eagle Rock" and Porto da Cruz (Schapowalow: G. Gräfenhain)
Photos: G. Amberg (49, 113); Design Center Nini Andrade Silva: Nick Bayntun (18 centre); DuMont Bildarchiv: Leue (9, 10, 62, 114 top, 114 bottom), Schwarzbach (111); Getty Images/EyeEm: R. Seskaitis (19 top); Getty Images/Gallo Images: D. Delimont (47); Getty Images/hemis.fr: F. Guiziou (2); Getty Images/RooM (19 bottom); R. Hackenberg (11, 43, 99); huber-images: Gräfenhain (12/13, 32/33, 45, 70/71), Schmid (112/113); Laif/Hemis: J. Frumm (52); Laif/robertharding: H.-P. Merten (23); Look: H. Leue (7); Look/age fotostock (115); Lúcia Sousa: Renato Nunes (18 bottom); mauritius images: Coll (flap left, 4 top, 64), M. Siepmann (28 right); mauritius images/age fotostock: K. O`Hara (18 top); mauritius images/Alamy (3, 14, 38, 93, 96); mauritius images/Alamy/ffoto (25); mauritius images/imagebroker: C. Handl (105), K. Kreder (102); mautitius images/Alamy: K. Sriskandan (29); Schapowalow: G. Gräfenhain (1 top); Schapowalow/SIME: O. Fantuz (80/81); T. Stankiewicz (8, 28 left, 30, 30/31, 69, 82, 84, 86, 89, 109, 110/111, 112); vario images/Imagebroker (5, 6, 22, 36); vario images/Westend61 (106/107); H. Wagner (flap right, 17, 20/21, 72, 90/91); T. P. Widmann (50/51, 60/61, 77); E. Wrba (4 bottom, 26/27, 31, 34, 40/41, 54, 56, 57, 59, 67, 74, 79, 85, 110, 126/127)

3rd edition – fully revised and updated 2019
Worldwide Distribution: Marco Polo Travel Publishing Ltd, Pinewood, Chineham Business Park,
Crockford Lane, Basingstoke, Hampshire RG24 8AL, United Kingdom. Email: sales@marcopolouk.com
© MAIRDUMONT GmbH & Co. KG, Ostfildern
Chief editor: Marion Zorn; author: Rita Henss; co-author: Sara Lier; editor: Arnd M. Schuppius
Programme supervision: Lucas Forst-Gill, Susanne Heimburger, Johanna Jiranek, Nikolai Michaelis, Kristin Wittemann;
Picture editors: Gabriele Forst, Veronika Plajer; What's hot: Sara Lier; wunder media, Munich
Cartography street atlas and pull-out map: © MAIRDUMONT, Ostfildern
Cover design, p. 1, pull-out map cover: Karl Anders – Büro für Visual Stories, Hamburg; design inside:
milchhof:atelier, Berlin; design p. 2/ 3, Discovery Tours: Susan Chaaban Dipl.-Des. (FH)
Translated from German by John Sykes, Jennifer Walcoff Neuheiser and Lindsay Chalmers-Gerbracht
Editorial office: SAW Communications, Redaktionsbüro Dr. Sabine A. Werner, Mainz: Julia Gilcher, Cosima Talhouni,
Dr. Sabine A. Werner; prepress: SAW Communications, Mainz, in cooperation with alles mit Medien, Mainz
Phrase book in cooperation with Ernst Klett Sprachen GmbH, Stuttgart,
Editorial by PONS Wörterbücher

DOS & DON'TS ☞

In Portuguese the polite phrase for "don't" is por favor, não!

TOPLESS TOURISTS

Like other Portuguese and southern Europeans, for Madeirans it is important to be correctly clothed. Except on the beach, for men to walk around bare-chested is absolute taboo, and many residents of both towns and villages also react with displeasure when women are scantily dressed. For women to go topless is only acceptable around a hotel pool, if anywhere at all; in public pools and on the beach this really causes offence.

SAYING "GRACIAS"

Most Portuguese can understand Spanish very well and know that "Gracias" is easy to say for many tourists. But they are all the more pleased when visitors to the island make the effort to say "thank you" in their own language: "Obrigado!" (if the speaker is a man) or "Obrigada!" (if a woman). Although the relations between Spain and Portugal are more relaxed than they often were in the past, the Portuguese don't like to be treated or spoken to as if they were Spanish.

HIGH HEELS

Madeira is not the right place for high heels. Even in the capital, steep slopes and cobblestones make strolling around a little less smooth than it is in other cities. Trainers are more suitable than sandals or fashionable but unpractical footwear. If you go hiking in the mountains, make sure to wear proper hiking boots that protect your ankles. The trails are often narrow and exposed to vertiginous drops. They are seldom maintained or fenced, and often slippery, which means real danger.

UNDERESTIMATING DISTANCES

Measured in miles or kilometres, the distances from A to B on Madeira seem modest. However, on almost any journey, there are ravines and mountains in the way. The number of tunnels is increasing all the time, but in many places the journey still takes you over narrow, steep and winding roads. Fog, road blocks, rocks on the road (Careful, this is often the case, especially after heavy rain!) or slow-moving construction vehicles are further obstacles. Allow plenty of time when planning your tour.

CAREFUL WITH FIRE

Although Madeira is blessed with plentiful rainfall, in summer the vegetation can dry out to a surprising extent. A lighted cigarette carelessly thrown away or a badly tended barbecue can then cause a catastrophic fire. Especially in the sparsely populated west of the island, large-scale fires break out almost every year, and strong winds fan the flames.

ARRANGE URGENT APPOINTMENTS AFTER YOUR HOLIDAY

It is remotely possible – even in the height of summer – to become stranded on Madeira because all flights have been cancelled. The complex crosswinds sometimes prevent planes from landing at the airport. If this happens, your holiday will be extended by one day – paid for by the relevant airline.

To Harriet with love from Uncle David

Ladybird books are widely available, but in case of difficulty may be ordered by post or telephone from:
Ladybird Books – Cash Sales Department Littlegate Road Paignton Devon TQ3 3BE
Telephone 01803 554761

A catalogue record for this book is available from the British Library

Published by Ladybird Books Ltd Loughborough Leicestershire UK
Ladybird Books Ltd is a subsidiary of the Penguin Group of companies
© David Pace MCMXCVI
The author/artist has asserted his moral rights
LADYBIRD and the device of a Ladybird are trademarks of Ladybird Books Ltd

Edward
goes exploring

David Pace

Edward loved animals...

and more than anything else in the world he
wanted to be the first to discover a *new* animal.

So one day...

Edward set out into the wild to see what
he could find.

He hadn't gone very far when he heard a
SQUEAKING and a RUSTLING in the big green bush…

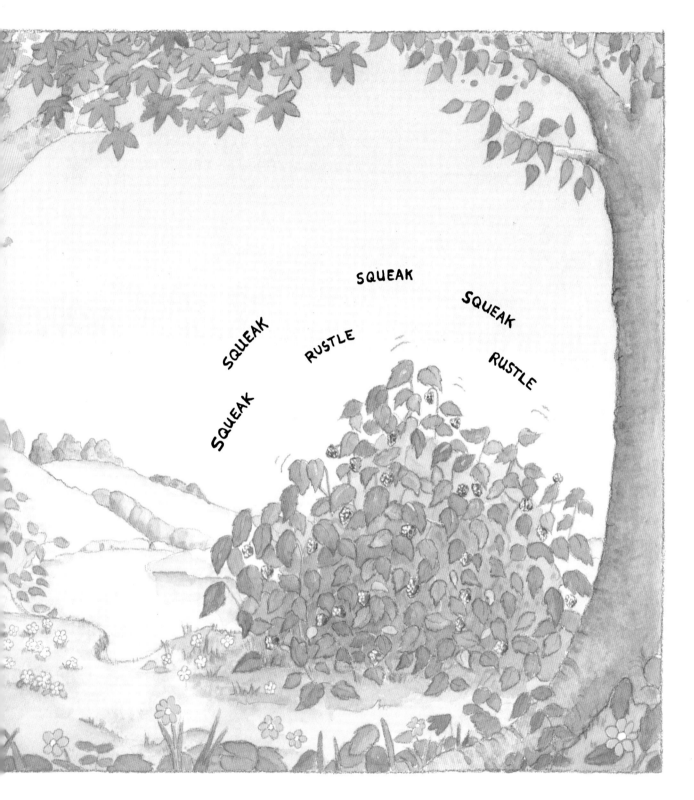

"Ah-haaa!" said Edward. "What's this?
I have discovered some Weenynibbles."

"SQUEEAK! SQUEEAK! We aren't Weenynibbles, we're mice!" squeaked the mice.

So Edward wrote a note in his book: mice

A little further on Edward heard a CROAK,
CROAK, CROAKING from down by the pond.

"Ah-haaa!" said Edward. "What's this?
I have discovered some Croakyjumpers."

"CROAK, CROAK! We aren't Croakyjumpers, we're frogs!" croaked the frogs.

So Edward wrote a note in his book: frogs

Next Edward heard a HISS, HISS, HISSING,
high up in the branches of an old apple tree.

"Ah-haaa!" said Edward. "What's this?
I have discovered a Slitheryslip."

"Hisssssssssssss, I'm not a Slitheryslip,
I'm a snake!" hissed the snake.

So Edward wrote a note in his book:

QUACK

QUACK

QUACK

Then Edward heard a QUACK, QUACK, QUACKING from down among the reeds.

"Ah-haaa!" said Edward. "What's this? I have discovered some Puddlequackers."

"QUAAACK, QUAAACK! We aren't Puddlequackers, we're ducks!" quacked the ducks.

So Edward wrote a note in his book:

A little further on Edward heard a MEWING
and a MIAOWING from behind a tree.

"Ah-haaa!" said Edward. "What's this?
I have discovered a Tiggamog."

"MIAOOOOOW! I'm not a Tiggamog, I'm a cat!"
miaowed the cat.

So Edward wrote a note in his book: cat

Then Edward heard a WOOF, WOOF, WOOFING
from behind a wall.

"Ah-haaa!" said Edward. "What's this?
I have discovered a Waggywoof."

"WOOF, WOOF! I'm not a Waggywoof,
I'm a dog!" barked the dog.

So Edward wrote a note in his book:

Then Edward heard a very, very, very soft
CHOMP, CHOMP, CHOMPING.

"Ah-haaa!" whispered Edward. "What's this?
I have discovered a Leafchomper!"

"CHOMP, CHOMP! I'm not a Leafchomper, I'm a caterpillar,"
said the caterpillar in a small voice.

So Edward wrote a note in his book:

caterpillar

CHOMP CHOMP

CHOMP CHOMP CHOMP

Suddenly Edward heard...

A SQUEAKING, a RUSTLING and a CROAK, CROAK, CROAKING. A HISS, HISS, HISSING and a QUACK, QUACK, QUACKING. A MEWING, a MIAOWING and a WOOF, WOOF, WOOFING and a very, very, very soft CHOMP CHOMP CHOMPING.

And... the strangest sound of all.

"Ah-haaa!" said Edward. "What's this?
I have discovered a Splosherwasher!

"I'm not a Splosherwasher! I'm a Mum!"
said Edward's mum. "And I have discovered
an Edward who needs a bath!"

Then Mum wrote a note in Edward's book:

Bath!

Picture Ladybird

Books for reading aloud with 2–6 year olds

The exciting *Picture Ladybird* series includes a wide range
of animal stories, funny rhymes, and real life adventures that are
perfect to read aloud and share at storytime or bedtime.

A whole library of beautiful books for you to collect

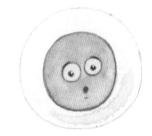

RHYMING STORIES

Easy to follow and great for joining in!

Jasper's Jungle Journey, Val Biro
Shoo Fly, Shoo! Brian Moses
Ten Tall Giraffes, Brian Moses
In Comes the Tide, Valerie King
Toot! Learns to Fly,
Geraldine Taylor & Jill Harker
Who Am I? Judith Nicholls
Fly Eagle, Fly! Jan Pollard

IMAGINATIVE TALES

Mysterious and magical, or just a little shivery

The Star that Fell, Karen Hayles
Wishing Moon, Lesley Harker
Don't Worry William, Christine Morton
This Way Little Badger, Phil McMylor
The Giant Walks, Judith Nicholls
Kelly and the Mermaid, Karen King

FUNNY STORIES

Make storytime good fun!

Benedict Goes to the Beach, Chris Demarest
Bella and Gertie, Geraldine Taylor
Edward Goes Exploring, David Pace
Telephone Ted, Joan Stimson
Top Shelf Ted, Joan Stimson
Helpful Henry, Shen Roddie
What's Wrong with Bertie? Tony Bradman
Bears Can't Fly, Val Biro
Finnigan's Flap, Joan Stimson

REAL LIFE ADVENTURE

Situations to explore and discover

Joe and the Farm Goose,
Geraldine Taylor & Jill Harker
Going to Playgroup,
Geraldine Taylor & Jill Harker
The Great Rabbit Race, Geraldine Taylor
Pushchair Polly, Tony Bradman

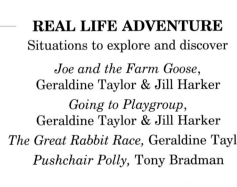